G. F. Popham Byth

The holy week and the forty days

Being a continuous narrative in the words of the Evangelists Vol. I

G. F. Popham Byth

The holy week and the forty days
Being a continuous narrative in the words of the Evangelists Vol. I

ISBN/EAN: 9783741194900

Manufactured in Europe, USA, Canada, Australia, Japa

Cover: Foto ©Andreas Hilbeck / pixelio.de

Manufactured and distributed by brebook publishing software
(www.brebook.com)

G. F. Popham Byth

The holy week and the forty days

THE HOLY WEEK

AND

THE FORTY DAYS.

THE HOLY WEEK

AND

THE FORTY DAYS:

BEING

A CONTINUOUS NARRATIVE IN THE WORDS OF THE EVANGELISTS.

CONSTRUCTED FROM THE FOUR GOSPELS.

WITH

𝕬 Commentary and Appendices

BY THE REV.

G. F. POPHAM BLYTH, M.A.,

SENIOR CHAPLAIN, H.M. INDIAN (BENGAL) SERVICE;
CHAPLAIN TO THE EARL OF KIMBERLEY.

IN TWO VOLUMES.—VOL. I.

London:

W. SKEFFINGTON & SON, 163, PICCADILLY.

1879.

LONDON:
PRINTED BY WILLIAM CLOWES AND SONS,
STAMFORD STREET AND CHARING CROSS.

INTRODUCTION.

THE result of a study of the period of our Lord's ministry included in this work, will probably, in any case, produce the impression which it has left upon the mind of the author—that he has essayed a far more difficult and important task than he had previously conceived. The anticipations of ancient Scripture, and the voice of prophecy, find their realization within this period. And not only so: there is contained within it the epitome of the Gospel itself, and its climax.

At this most eventful crisis our Lord employs no new methods of instruction; He affords no new evidence of His claim; He brings forward nothing hitherto kept in reserve; He makes no fuller revelation of His mission. But there is evident the drawing together and concentration of all means which He has employed, during the course of His public ministry upon earth. Whatever modes of instruction, or of evidence, have, during the course of our Lord's ministry, been made familiar to the multitudes of Judea, of Galilee, of the regions round about Jordan, who were now congregated to the great national festival, at the holy city, these alone are employed now; but with intensity of earnestness, with distinct authority, and with power. There is brought forward now, as throughout His three years' proclamation of His mission from the Father, our Lord's direct oral doctrine, His teaching by parable, His declaration of Scripture, His application of type, His illustration of prophecy. And there is repeated, plainly and decisively, the concurrent testimony in favour of His claims, of miraculous signs and wonders, of the fulfilment of prophecy, and of the voice of God Himself from heaven. What is remarkable in His present teaching, rather than any novelty, is the careful pointing, recasting, and direct application of former parables and discourses; and the impressive assertion of authority, as a Teacher sent from God—a position always assumed by Christ, but now with manifest Divinity.

To the chosen disciples alone, there is a further unfolding of our Lord's claims, of the manner of the kingdom, and of their own particular calling; there is a deeper manifestation of love and mercy towards them, than they had been able to receive during the previous years of their companionship with Him. For the support of their faith in the hour of trial, and for their comfort under the pressure of shame, our Lord gives them the minute prediction of various events of His Passion, and of their individual failure, verified within the few succeeding hours. And to them is spoken that remarkable prophecy, in which, whilst using the forms and imagery common to the great prophets of old, our Lord speaks as one who knew personally the deep counsels of heaven, and as "the Lord God of the holy prophets" alone could speak.

II. This period further embraces the accomplishment of the act of salvation, to which our Lord's whole life and teaching had reference, and for which His claims were promulgated and enforced. What was absolutely necessary for the redemption of man, and for his reception into heavenly places, was the death of Christ in his stead, His resurrection from the dead, as the first-born of many brethren, and His ascension into heaven (1 Cor. xv. 1–4). The Church of Christ was not, however, founded upon the declaration of the crucifixion, but on that of the resurrection, as it was established in the world immediately after the ascension of Christ, and took, as the proclamation of the Gospel, "Jesus and the resurrection." Those who believed and accepted that truth, were members of the Church of Christ; thus, belief in the historical fact of the resurrection lies at the foundation of our faith.

We may leave, therefore, as of secondary importance, any disquisitions upon the probability of this doctrine, analogies from nature, its suitableness to the aspirations and destiny of man, and so forth; let *the fact* be admitted, and individually accepted, and the principal point is gained (Rom. x. 9, 10). Thus we have, in the Gospels, a most simple and inartificial narration of the several instances of our Lord's appearing, treated as naturally as possible, and stated by witnesses as straightforward and unimaginative, as any similar number of men could well be; and their simple statement of the fact, without deduction, application, or theory founded upon it, is the more striking and suggestive of its simple necessity, as we consider the infinite importance of the truth thus made known to us.

III. As this view of the importance of the historical fact takes its prominent ground, it supersedes, to a certain extent, the spiritual and doctrinal application of the

Scripture, as a *primary* object in these notes ; and brings forward that of the literal explanation, exact meaning, and practical bearing of the text.

"The Scripture writers deal not with doctrines, but with occurrences. The revelation given to us may, as Butler observes, be considered wholly historical" (Rawlinson, "Hist. Illust. of O. T."). The principle of interpretation based upon this view is a sound one. Though we may not neglect the spiritual interpretation of Scripture, by any means, yet that of many commentators of modern date, whose aim, to state it broadly, appears to be the extraction of something about our Lord from every verse in the Bible, is scarcely one which would throw much light on Holy Scripture; and is certainly one little in consonance with the present spirit of the age, which clings to facts, and loves to find, in the experience of scholarship, science, and travel, incidental corroboration of such facts. Perhaps human aid towards the establishment of a saving faith (its foundation being of God) can be most effectively given in the advancement of Scriptural knowledge; much is effected when any light is thrown upon Scripture history, antiquities, localities, and especially when lucid explanation and illustration are given of the literal meaning of the text.

The adoption of this as a primary principle of interpretation, necessitates our dependence (and the reliance is a safe one) upon the Holy Spirit Himself, rather than on any human assistance, for the unveiling of the inner spiritual mysteries of the truth of God's word, and its personal application to the requirements of the individual soul. It is His special office and mission "to take of the things of Christ" (of which the Evangelists have told us in plain record), "and show them unto us " spiritually. He will impress their vital truth upon every mind which is sincere and teachable; under His guidance, even "the wayfaring man, though a fool" (as to the world's wisdom), "may not err therein." And certainly every scholar who studies the historical truth, and the exact meaning of the text of God's word, in order to believe with the heart, or to strengthen his faith, "shall be taught of God;" such a reader will not fall into the danger of believing with the head, and not with the heart. Meanwhile the whole light of modern discovery, science, criticism, and every kind of knowledge, may be profitably brought to bear upon the interpretation, and illustration, of the text.

A general principle is here enunciated, and that in very general terms. The spiritual understanding of Holy Scripture is that which must save the soul; other knowledge, however excellent, may not be necessary to salvation, but it may be most conducive to the spread of Divine truth, and may be a means owned and blessed by the effectual operation of God's grace.

We may, therefore, safely pray and hope for the illumination of the Spirit, when we do the best we can to put into circulation, knowledge, so essentially grounded on the truth of God. For mankind cannot afford to be ignorant of anything connected with the study of Scripture, which God may be pleased to open to human intellect, and to place within our reach. We may feel sure that, to the prayerful and reverent mind, God's Spirit will unfold those mysteries of His word which must be spiritually discerned, and which are His especial province. The pious thoughts of devout minds may be greatly instrumental in helping us to such an understanding, may be one means of His access to our hearts; but as to the spiritual knowledge of Scripture, we must be " all taught of God."

> " God is His own interpreter,
> And He will make it plain."

IV. It remains to state the mode in which the author has dealt with the authorities referred to in the preparation of this work. A list of the authors read in connection with the subject is subjoined. Direct quotations are named; but, very frequently, the sense of several writers together is expressed in language which, of course, can be attributed to none of them, and is therefore only generally acknowledged. All passages from original languages have been given in translation, and, where possible, in the words of any known translation, such as Whiston's " Josephus," or the " Library of the Fathers." The words of Scripture, where a more literal translation has been necessary, have been given in English, the object of the author being to be readily intelligible to the ordinary English reader; and the reference to original languages, and to early writers, is sufficiently easy to the scholar. It is his hope also, should this work be received with approval, to render it available for use in one of the vernacular languages, of the people amongst whom his present duties lie. For these reasons minute and multiplied references to books not generally accessible, seem objectionable. The author has here the pleasant duty of acknowledging the assistance he has received from his brother, the Rev. F. C. Blyth, vicar of Quatford, in revising these pages for the press; and the point which has been given to some of the notes from the stores of his wide reading.

The text is given first by itself, as it cannot be questioned that the clearest view of the transactions of these important days, will be gained by a simple perusal of the narrative in the words of the sacred writers. The marginal references show, as far as possible, the point of divergence, from the words of one Evangelist to another. The text is repeated with the notes, for the sake of convenience and clearness.

The Appendix contains information of various kinds, which may be valuable in connection with the object of this work, but which would only encumber the notes.

V. Occasionally, in the course of the notes, and in several instances in the appendices, the author has availed himself of illustrations of his subject afforded by Indian experience. He trusts that the approval of the reader will justify him in doing so; for there is certainly much that is common to the Eastern world, from whatever portion of it the illustration may be brought, which may help the Western mind to understand many passages of Scripture. Both the Jew and the Hindu have, for instance, borrowed much from the Persian; it is not, therefore, unusual to find, in Indian life, many an incident illustrative of Jewish life. India is a portion of the empire of which any Englishman may be justly proud; and, proud as the citizen of Rome may have been of his birthright, in a far truer and higher sense may our countrymen value themselves on the just and faithful administration of their Indian empire. One of the most conscientious and religious-minded of our Viceroys, after eighteen months' residence, said to the author, "I have not yet met the Englishman in India from whom I have not been able to gain some useful information, and to learn something." He may himself add that, after a long sojourn in that land, he has not known the official, high or low, to whom the charge of venality, corruption, or intentional injustice in any degree attached. If all were as religious-minded as they are honest and zealous, if they all worked as earnestly for the interests of God, as they do for those of the people they govern, nothing more could be desired from the administrators and agents of Government in India. The Englishman in India may justly feel proud of his fellow-countrymen; and if as apt illustrations might have been borrowed from the customs of other Eastern countries, surely no apology is needed from the author, for having given preference occasionally to those from a land which interests him so deeply, and in which his life's work lies.

VI. The author may not, however, put forth his work altogether without an " apology." He feels how in-adequate is its execution to the magnitude of the subject; and he is aware at how great disadvantage such a study is prosecuted in India, partly through want of ready access to many standard sources of information, and partly through the difficulties resulting from the climate, and the constant demand upon his time of the occupa-tions which form the special duty of his life. Years have therefore passed in the preparation of these pages.

But no humblest effort can be vain which is sustained in the cause of Christ; and he will have sufficient cause for thankfulness, and for congratulation, if the result of a study which has proved most pleasurable and advan-tageous to himself, shall, in any degree, prove so to others through his means.

LIST OF AUTHORS.

Ælfric : Homilies.
Alford, Dean : Greek Testament.
——————— How to Study the New Testament.
Andrewes, Bishop : Sermons.
Apostolic Fathers, the.
Aquinas, S. Thomas : Catena Aurea.
Augustine, S. : Sermons, etc.
Barrow, I. : Works.
Bede, the Venerable : Works.
Bengel : Gnomon.
Benham : On S. Matthew's Gospel.
Besser : On S. John's Gospel.
Beveridge, Bishop : Works.
Bloomfield : Greek Testament.
Blunt, Professor J. J. : On the Study of the Early Fathers.
Brown, Bishop H. : On the Thirty-Nine Articles.
Burgon, Dean : Plain Commentary on the Gospels.
Chrysostom, S. : Homilies.
Clarke : On the Four Evangelists.
Commentary on the New Testament.   S.P.C.K.
Cornelius à Lapide : Commentaries.
Cranmer, Archbishop : On the Sacrament of the Lord's Supper.
D'Oyley and Mant : New Testament.
Ebrard : The Gospel History.
Ellicott, Bishop : Historical Sketches on the Life of our Lord.
——————— New Testament for English Readers.
Elsley : Annotation on the Gospels.
Fairbairn, Patrick : The Typology of Scripture.

Farrar, Dr. F. W.: Life of Christ.
Ford, J.: On the Gospels.
Forster: The Gospel Narrative.
Fuller: Harmony of the Gospels.
Geikie: Life and Words of Christ.
Goodwin, Bishop H.: Gospels of SS. Matthew, Mark, and Luke.
Greswell: Harmony of the Gospels.
————— Dissertation on the Harmony of the Gospels.
Hall, Bishop: Works.
Hammond: New Testament.
Hanna: The Last Day of our Lord's Passion.
——— The Forty Days after our Lord's Resurrection.
Hengstenberg: On S. John's Gospel.
Hook, Dean: Church Dictionary.
Hooker: Works.
Jones and Churton, Archdeacons: Illustrated New Testament.
Josephus: Works.
Keble, Rev. John: Works.
Lange: The Life of Christ.
Latimer, Bishop H.: Sermons and Remains.
Lightfoot: Works.
Lisco: On the Parables.
Littledale: Essentials of New Testament Study.
Liddon, Dr. H. P.: Divinity of our Lord and Saviour Jesus Christ.
    Bampton Lectures, 1866.
Maldonatus: On the Four Evangelists.
Milman, Dean: History of the Jews.
————— History of Christianity.
Moberly, Bishop: Sayings of the Great Forty Days.
Nicholl: Help to Reading the Bible.
Norris: Key to the Narrative of the Four Gospels.
Olshausen: On the Gospels.
Ostervald: Arguments.
Paley: Evidences of Christianity.
Palestine, Exploration of.
Paragraph Bible, Notes and Harmony.
Parkhurst: Lexicon on the New Testament.
Pearson, Bishop: On the Creed.

Pound: The Gospel in Unity.
Pusey: On the Real Presence.
Rosenmüller: Scholia on the New Testament.
Sadler: Church Doctrine Bible Truth.
Schleusner: Lexicon on the Greek Testament.
Smith: Dictionary of the Bible.
Speaker's Commentary.
Stanley, Dean: Sinai and Palestine.
Stier: Words of the Lord Jesus.
Taylor, Bishop Jeremy: Works.
Tholuck: On S. John's Gospel.
Tittmann: On S. John's Gospel.
Townsend, Canon: New Testament.
Trapp: On the Four Gospels.
Trench, Archbishop: On the Miracles.
——————————————— On the Gospels.
——————————————— Studies in the Gospels.
Valpy: Greek Testament, with Latin Notes.
Warren: Underground Jerusalem.
Wilson and Warren: Recovery of Jerusalem.
Webster and Wilkinson: Greek Testament.
Westcott: The Gospel of the Resurrection.
Whitby: On the New Testament.
Williams, I.: Devotional Commentary on the Gospel Narrative.
Wilson, Bishop: On the Holy Communion.
Wordsworth, Bishop Christopher: Greek Testament.
——————————————————————— Theophilus Anglicanus.

INDEX AND HARMONY OF SECTIONS.

I. The Holy Week.

Page of Notes.	Section.	Heading of Sections.	S. Matt.	S. Mark.	S. Luke.	S. John.	Locality.
		Palm Sunday.					
Vol. I. 125	I.	Christ's entry into Jerusalem as the King	xxi. 1-11	xi. 1-11	xix. 29-44	xii. 12-19	Bethany. Jerusalem.
		Monday.					
142	II.	The barren fig tree	xxi. 18, 19	xi. 12-14	. . . . . .	. . . . . .	Road from Bethany.
145	III.	The cleansing of the Temple	xxi. 12, 13	xi. 15-19	xix. 45, 46	. . . . . .	The Temple.
		Tuesday.					
153	IV.	The withered fig tree.' Lessons of faith and forgiveness	xxi. 19-22	xi. 20-26	. . . . . .	. . . . . .	Road from Bethany.
155	V.	Christ asserts His authority. The Baptism of John	xxi. 23-27	xi. 27-33	xx. 1-8	. . . . . .	The Temple.
158	VI.	Parable of the two sons	xxi. 28-32	. . . . . .	. . . . . .	. . . . . .	,,
162	VII.	,, the wicked husbandmen	xxi. 33-46	xii. 1-12	xx. 9-19	. . . . . .	,,
173	VIII.	,, the marriage of the King's Son	xxii. 1-14	. . . . . .	. . . . . .	. . . . . .	,,
183	IX.	Questions of Pharisees and Herodians. Tribute to Cæsar	xxii. 15-22	xii. 13-17	xx. 20-26	. . . . . .	,,
189	X.	,, Sadducees. The Resurrection	xxii. 23-33	xii. 18-27	xx. 27-39	. . . . . .	,,
195	XI.	,, Lawyer. First and great Commandment	xxii. 34-40	xii. 28-34	. . . . . .	. . . . . .	,,
199	XII.	Jesus questions the Pharisees concerning the Christ	xxii. 41-46	xii. 34-37	xx. 40-44	. . . . . .	,,
202	XIII.	Christ reproves the Scribes and Pharisees	xxiii. 1-12	xii. 38-40	xx. 45-47	. . . . . .	,,
207	XIV.	The eight woes	xxiii. 13-39	. . . . . .	. . . . . .	. . . . . .	,,
220	XV.	The widow's mite	. . . . . .	xii. 41-44	xxi. 1-4	. . . . . .	,,
222	XVI.	Greeks desire to see Christ. He foretells His death	. . . . . .	. . . . . .	. . . . . .	xii. 20-36	,,

II. The Forty Days.

Easter Day.

161	I.	The Resurrection					The Holy Sepulchre and the road to Jerusalem.
161	....	The women set out to the Sepulchre	xxviii. 1	xvi. 1	xxiv. 1	xx. 1	,, ,,
162	....	Descent of the Angel. The earthquake. Terror (and departure?) of the Guard	xxviii. 2–4				,, ,,
164	....	The arrival of the women		xvi. 2–4	xxiv, 1, 2	xx. 1	,, ,,
165	....	Mary Magdalene runs back to tell Peter and John				xx. 1, 2	,, ,,
166	....	The women enter the Sepulchre, and see the Angel	xxviii. 5–7	xvi. 5–7	xxiv. 4–7		,, ,,
166	....	The women leave the Sepulchre on their return to the City	xxviii. 8	xvi. 8.	xxiv. 8, 9		,, ,,
170	....	By another road Peter and John set out for the Sepulchre; Mary Magdalene following them			xxiv. 12	xx. 3, 4, 11	,, ,,
170	....	Peter and John at the Sepulchre			xxiv. 12	xx. 5–10	,, ,,
173	....	Mary Magdalene remains at the Sepulchre. First appearance of Christ—to Mary Magdalene		xvi. 9		xx. 11–17	,, ,,
179	....	Second appearance of Christ—to the women on their way to the City	xxviii. 9, 10				,, ,,
180	....	The women (Mary Magdalene with them) bring their tidings to the Apostles		xvi. 10, 11	xxiv. 9–11	xx. 18.	Jerusalem.
181	II.	Report of the Guard	xxviii. 11–15				,,
		Christ is "seen of Cephas" (1 Cor. xv. 5)					
184	III.	Christ appears to the disciples that went to Emmaus		xvi. 12–13	xxiv. 13–35		Emmaus, and the road from Jerusalem.
194	IV.	Christ appears to the Apostles. Thomas absent		xvi. 14	xxiv. 36–43	xx. 19–23	Jerusalem.
201	....	Incredulity of Thomas				xx. 24, 25	,,

Second Lord's Day.

203	V.	Christ appears to the Apostles. Thomas present				xx. 26–31	,,

Page of Notes.	Section.	Heading of Sections.	S. Matt.	S. Mark.	S. Luke.	S. John.	Locality.
		During the Forty Days.					
207	VI.	Christ appears to seven disciples at the Sea of Tiberias				xxi. 1 24	Galilee.
219	VII.	Christ appears to the Apostles; and to "above five hundred brethren at once" (1 Cor. xv. 6)	xxviii. 16-20	xvi. 15–18			"
		Christ is "seen of James" (1 Cor. xv. 7)					
		Holy Thursday.					
227	VIII.	The Ascension, in the presence of "all the Apostles" (1 Cor. xv. 7)		xvi. 19, 20	xxiv. 50–52 [Acts i. 9-12]		Mount of Olives, near Bethany.
227	....	The farewell charge			xxiv. 44–49 [Acts i. 4–8]		Road to Bethany.
232	....	The Ascension		xvi. 19, 20	xxiv. 50–52 [Acts i. 9-12]		
233	....	The message of angels			[Acts i. 10, 11]		
235	....	Christ's return into heaven		xvi. 19	xxiv. 51	[Dan. vii. 13, 14]	
236	....	The Apostles return to Jerusalem: they commence their mission		xvi. 20	xxiv. 52, 53 [Acts i. 12]		Jerusalem.

THE HOLY WEEK

AND

THE FORTY DAYS.

I. The Holy Week.

Palm Sunday.

I. CHRIST'S ENTRY INTO JERUSALEM AS THE KING.

S. Matt. xxi. 1-11; S. Mark xi. 1-11; S. Luke xix. 29-44;
S. John xii. 12-19.

WHEN they drew nigh unto Jerusalem, and were *Matt. 21. 1.*
come to Bethphage, unto the mount of Olives,
then sent Jesus two of His disciples, saying unto
them, Go into the village over against you; and as *Mark 11. 2.*
soon as ye be entered into it, ye shall find an ass
tied, and a colt with her, whereon yet never man
sat; loose him, and bring *him* unto Me. And if *Luke 19. 31.*
any man ask you, Why do ye loose *him*? say ye,
The Lord hath need of him; and straightway he
will send him hither. And they went their way, *Mark 11. 4.*
and found the colt tied by the door without in a
place where two ways met; and they loose him.
And as they were loosing the colt, the owners *Luke 19. 33.*
thereof said unto them, Why loose ye the colt?

VOL. I.   B

and they said, The Lord hath need of him : and
they let them go. And they brought him to Jesus,
and cast their garments upon the colt, and they set
Jesus thereon. And as He went, they spread their
Matt. 21. 4. clothes in the way. All this was done, that it
might be fulfilled which was spoken by the prophet,
Isa. 62. 11. saying, **Tell ye the daughter of Zion, Behold, thy**
Zech. 9. 9. **King cometh unto thee, meek, and sitting upon**
John 12. 16. **an ass, and a colt the foal of an ass.** These things
understood not His disciples at the first : but when
Jesus was glorified, then remembered they that
these things were written of Him, and *that* they
had done these things unto Him.

Luke 19. 37. And when He was come nigh, even now at the
descent of the mount of Olives, the whole multitude of the disciples began to rejoice and praise
God with a loud voice for all the mighty works
Ps.118.25,26. that they had seen ; saying, Blessed *be* the King
that cometh in the name of the Lord, peace in
Luke 2. 4. heaven, and glory in the highest. And some of
the Pharisees from among the multitude said unto
Him, Master, rebuke Thy disciples. And He answered and said unto them, I tell you that, if these
Hab. 2. 11. should hold their peace, the stones would immediately cry out.

John 12. 12. Much people that were come to the feast, when
they heard that Jesus was coming to Jerusalem,
took branches of palm trees, and went forth to meet
John 12. 17. Him. The people therefore that was with Him
when He called Lazarus out of his grave, and
raised him from the dead, bare record. For this
cause the people also met Him, for that they heard
that He had done this miracle.

Matt. 21. 8. And a very great multitude spread their garments
in the way ; others cut down branches from the
trees, and strawed *them* in the way. And the
multitudes that went before, and that followed,
cried, saying, **Hosanna** to the Son of David :

Blessed *is* **He that cometh in the Name of the** Ps.118.25,26.
Lord: Hosanna in the highest; Blessed *is* the King John 12. 13.
of Israel that cometh in the name of the Lord.
Blessed *be* the kingdom of our father David, that Mark 11. 10.
cometh in the name of the Lord : Hosanna in the
highest.

The Pharisees therefore said among themselves, John 12. 19.
Perceive ye how ye prevail nothing ? behold, the
world is gone after Him.

And when He was come near, He beheld the city,
and wept over it, saying, If thou hadst known, even
thou, at least in this thy day, the things *which*
belong unto thy peace ! but now they are hid from
thine eyes. For the days shall come upon thee,
that thine enemies shall cast a trench about thee, Dan. 9. 26.
and compass thee round, and keep thee in on every Luke 21. 23, 24.
side, and shall lay thee even with the ground, and
thy children within thee ; and they shall not leave
in thee one stone upon another ; because thou
knewest not the time of thy visitation.

And when He was come into Jerusalem, all the Matt. 21. 10.
city was moved, saying, Who is this ? And the
multitude said, This is Jesus the prophet of Nazareth of Galilee.

And Jesus entered into Jerusalem, and into the
temple : and when He had looked round about
upon all things, and now the eventide was come,
He went out unto Bethany with the twelve.

Monday in Holy Week.

II. *THE BARREN FIG TREE.*

S. Matt. xxi. 18, 19 ; S. Mark xi. 12-14.

Now in the morning, as He returned into the city Matt. 21. 18.
from Bethany, He was hungry : and seeing a fig Mark 11. 12.
tree afar off having leaves, He came, if haply He

might find anything thereon : and when He came to it, He found nothing but leaves ; for the time of figs was not *yet*. And Jesus answered and said unto it, No man eat fruit of thee hereafter for ever. And His disciples heard it.

III. *THE CLEANSING OF THE TEMPLE.*

S. Matt. xxi. 12, 13 ; S. Mark xi. 15-19 ; S. Luke xix. 45, 46.

Mark 11. 15.   And they come to Jerusalem : and Jesus went into the temple of God, and began to cast out them that sold and bought in the temple, and overthrew the tables of the moneychangers, and the seats of them that sold doves ; and would not suffer that any man should carry *any* vessel through the temple. And He taught, saying unto them, Is it
Isa. 56. 7. not written, **My house shall be called of all nations**
Jer. 7. 11. **the house of prayer ?** but ye have made it **A den of thieves.** And the scribes and chief priests heard *it*, and sought how they might destroy Him : for they feared Him, because all the people was as-
Luke 19. 48. tonished at His doctrine : and could not find what they might do : for all the people were very attentive to hear Him.

Matt. 21. 14.   And the blind and the lame came to Him in the temple ; and He healed them. And when the chief priests and scribes saw the wonderful things that He did, and the children crying in the temple, and saying, Hosanna to the Son of David ; they were sore displeased, and said unto Him, Hearest thou what these say ? And Jesus saith unto them,
Ps. 8. 2. Yea ; have ye never read, **Out of the mouth of babes and sucklings thou hast perfected praise ?** And He left them, and when even was come He went out of the city into Bethany ; and He lodged there.

Tuesday in Holy Week.

IV. *THE WITHERED FIG TREE: LESSONS OF FAITH AND FORGIVENESS.*

S. Matt. xxi. 19–22 ; S. Mark xi. 20–26.

And in the morning, as they passed by, they saw Mark 11. 20. the fig tree dried up from the roots. And Peter calling to remembrance saith unto Him, Master, behold, the fig tree which Thou cursedst is withered away. And Jesus answering saith unto them, Have faith in God. For verily I say unto you, That whosoever shall say unto this mountain, Be thou removed, and be thou cast into the sea ; and shall not doubt in his heart, but shall believe that those things which he saith shall come to pass ; he shall have whatsoever he saith. Therefore I say unto you, What things soever ye desire, when ye pray, believe that ye receive *them*, and ye shall have *them*. And when ye stand praying, forgive, if ye have ought against any : that your Father also which is in heaven may forgive you your trespasses. But if ye do not forgive, neither will your Father which is in heaven forgive your trespasses.

V. *CHRIST ASSERTS HIS AUTHORITY. THE BAPTISM OF JOHN.*

S. Matt. xxi. 23–27 ; S. Mark xi. 27–33 ; S. Luke xx. 1–8.

And they come again to Jerusalem : and when Mark 11. 27. He was come into the temple, the chief priests, Matt. 21. 23. and the scribes, and the elders of the people came unto Him, as He was teaching, and said, By what authority doest Thou these things? and who gave Thee this authority? And Jesus answered and said unto them, I will also ask you one thing, which if ye tell me, I in like wise will tell you by what

Mark 11. 30. authority I do these things. The baptism of John,
whence was it? from heaven, or of men? Answer
Matt. 21. 25. Me. And they reasoned with themselves, saying,
If we shall say, From heaven; He will say unto
us, Why did ye not then believe Him? But if we
Luke 20. 6. shall say, Of men; we fear the people; all the
Matt. 21. 27. people will stone us: for all hold John as a prophet. And they answered Jesus, and said, We cannot tell. And He said unto them, Neither tell I
you by what authority I do these things.

VI. *THE PARABLE OF THE TWO SONS.*

S. Matt. xxi. 28–32.

Matt. 21. 28. But what think ye? A *certain* man had two sons;
and he came to the first, and said, Son, go work
to-day in my vineyard. He answered and said,
I will not: but afterward he repented, and went.
And he came to the second, and said likewise.
And he answered and said, I *go*, sir; and went not.
Whether of them twain did the will of *his* father?
They say unto him, The first. Jesus saith unto
Luke 7.29,30. them, Verily I say unto you, That the publicans and
the harlots go into the kingdom of God before you.
For John came unto you in the way of righteous-
ness, and ye believed him not; but the publicans
and harlots believed him: and ye, when ye had
seen *it*, repented not afterward, that ye might
believe him.

VII. *THE PARABLE OF THE WICKED HUSBANDMEN.*

S. Matt. xxi. 33–46; S. Mark xii. 1–12; S. Luke xx. 9–19.

Matt. 21. 33. Hear another parable: There was a certain
Isa. 5. 1, 2. householder, which planted a vineyard, and hedged
it round about, and digged a winepress in it, and

built a tower, and let it out to husbandmen, and
went into a far country for a long time: and when
the time of the fruit drew near, he sent his servants
to the husbandmen, that they might receive of the
fruits of the vineyard.　And the husbandmen took
his servants, and beat one, and killed another, and
stoned another.　Again, he sent other servants
more than the first; and they did unto them likewise.

Then said the lord of the vineyard, What shall　Luke 20. 13.
I do?　Having yet therefore one son, his well-　Mark 12.
beloved, he sent him also last unto them, saying,
They will reverence my son.　But when the husbandmen saw the son, they said among themselves,
This is the heir; come, let us kill him, and let
us seize on his inheritance.　And they caught
him, and cast *him* out of the vineyard, and slew
him.　When the lord therefore of the vineyard
cometh, what will he do unto those husbandmen?
They say unto him, He will miserably destroy those
wicked men, and will let out *his* vineyard to other
husbandmen, which shall render him the fruits in
their seasons.　And when they heard *it*, they said,　Luke 20. 16.
God forbid.　And He beheld them and said, What
then is this that is written, **The stone which the**　Ps. 118. 22.
builders rejected, the same is become the head of
the corner: this is the Lord's doing, and it is mar-
vellous in our eyes?　Whosoever shall fall upon　Isa. 8. 14, 15.
that stone shall be broken; but on whomsoever it
shall fall, it will grind him to powder.　Therefore　Matt. 21. 43.
I say unto you, The kingdom of God shall be taken
from you, and given to a nation bringing forth the
fruits thereof.

And when the chief priests and Pharisees had
heard His parables, they perceived that He spake
of them.　But when they sought to lay hands on
Him, they feared the multitude, because they took
Him for a prophet.　And they left Him, and went　Mark 12. 12.
their way.

VIII. *THE PARABLE OF THE MARRIAGE OF THE KING'S SON.*

S. Matt. xxii. 1–14.

Matt. 22. 1.   And Jesus answered and spake unto them again by parables, and said,

The kingdom of heaven is like unto a certain king, which made a marriage for his son, and sent forth his servants to call them that were bidden to the wedding: and they would not come. Again, he sent forth other servants, saying, Tell them which are bidden, Behold, I have prepared my dinner: my oxen and *my* fatlings *are* killed, and all things *are* ready: come unto the marriage. But they made light of *it*, and went their ways, one to his farm, another to his merchandise: and the remnant took his servants, and entreated *them* spitefully, and slew *them*. But when the king heard *thereof*, he was wroth: and he sent forth his armies, and destroyed those murderers, and burned up their city. Then said he to his servants, The wedding is ready, but they which were bidden were not worthy. Go ye therefore into the highways, and as many as ye shall find, bid to the marriage. So those servants went out into the highways, and gathered together all as many as they found, both bad and good: and the wedding was furnished with guests.

And when the king came in to see the guests, he saw there a man which had not on a wedding garment: and he saith unto him, Friend, how camest thou in hither not having on a wedding garment? And he was speechless. Then said the king to the servants, Bind him hand and foot, and take him away, and cast *him* into outer darkness: there shall be weeping and gnashing of teeth.

For many are called, but few *are* chosen.

IX. *QUESTION OF THE PHARISEES AND HERODIANS CONCERNING TRIBUTE TO CÆSAR.*

S. Matt. xxii. 15-22; S. Mark xii. 13-17; S. Luke xx. 20-26.

Then went the Pharisees, and took counsel how Matt. 22 15. they might entangle Him in *His* talk. And they sent out unto Him their disciples with the Herodians, spies which should feign themselves just Luke 20. 20. men, that they might take hold of His words, that so they might deliver Him unto the power and authority of the governor. And when they were Mark 12. 14. come, they say unto Him, Master, we know that thou art true, and carest for no man: for thou regardest not the person of men, but teachest the way of God in truth. Tell us, therefore, what Matt. 22. 17. thinkest thou? Is it lawful for us to give tribute unto Cæsar, or not? Shall we give, or shall we Mark 12. 15. not give? But Jesus perceived their wickedness, Matt. 22. 18. and said, Why tempt ye Me, *ye* hypocrites? Shew Me the tribute money. And they brought unto Him a penny. And He saith unto them, Whose *is* this image and superscription? They say unto Him, Cæsar's. Then saith He unto them, Render therefore unto Cæsar the things which are Cæsar's; and unto God the things that are God's. And Luke 20. 26. they could not take hold of His words before the people: and they marvelled at His answer, and held their peace; and left him, and went their way. Matt. 22. 22.

X. *QUESTION OF THE SADDUCEES CONCERNING THE RESURRECTION.*

S. Matt. xxii. 23-33; S. Mark xii. 18-27; S. Luke xx. 27-39.

The same day came unto Him the Sadducees, Matt. 22. 25. which say that there is no resurrection, and asked Him, saying, Master, Moses wrote unto us, If a man Deut. 25. 5.

die, having no children, his brother shall marry his wife, and raise up seed unto his brother. Now there were with us seven brethren : and the first, when he had married a wife, deceased, and, having no issue, left his wife unto his brother : likewise the second also, and the third, unto the seventh :

Luke 20. 31. and they left no children, and died. Last of all

Mark 13. 23. the woman died also. In the resurrection, therefore, when they shall rise, whose wife shall she

Matt. 22. 29. be of them ? for the seven had her to wife. Jesus answered and said unto them, Ye do err, not know-

Luke 20. 34. ing the Scriptures, nor the power of God. The children of this world marry, and are given in marriage : but they which shall be accounted worthy to obtain that world, and the resurrection from the dead, neither marry nor are given in marriage : neither can they die any more : for they are equal unto the angels ; and are the children of God, being the children of the resurrection. Now that the dead are raised, even Moses shewed

Ex. 3. 6. at the bush, when he calleth the Lord **The God of Abraham, and the God of Isaac, and The God of Jacob.** For He is not a God of the dead, but of

Mark 12. 27. the living ; for all live unto Him : ye therefore do

Matt. 22. 33. greatly err. And when the multitude heard *this*,

Luke 20. 39. they were astonished at His doctrine. Then certain of the scribes answering said, Master, Thou hast well said.

XI. *QUESTION OF THE LAWYER CON-CERNING THE FIRST AND GREAT COM-MANDMENT.*

S. Matt. xxii. 34-40 ; S. Mark xii. 28-34.

Matt. 22. 34. But when the Pharisees had heard that He had put the Sadducees to silence, they were gathered together. Then one of them, *which was* a lawyer,

Mark 12. 28. having heard them reasoning together, and perceiving that He had answered them well, asked *Him a question* tempting Him, and saying, Master, which is the great commandment in the law? And Jesus answered him, The first of all the commandments is, **Hear, O Israel; the Lord our God is one Lord: and thou shalt love the Lord thy God with all thy heart, and with all thy soul, and with all thy mind, and with all thy strength.** This is the first and great commandment. And the second *is* like unto it, **Thou shalt love thy neighbour as thyself.** There is none other commandment greater than these. On these two commandments hang all the law and the prophets. And the scribe said unto Him, Well, Master, Thou hast said the truth: for there is one God; and there is none other but He: and to love Him with all the heart, and with all the understanding, and with all the soul, and with all the strength, and to love *his* neighbour as himself, is more than all whole burnt offerings and sacrifices. And when Jesus saw that he answered discreetly, He said unto him, Thou art not far from the kingdom of God.

Matt. 22. 35.

Mark 12. 29.

Deut. 6. 4.

Matt. 22. 38.

Lev. 19. 18.

Mark 12. 31.

Matt. 22. 40.

Mark 12. 32.

XII. *JESUS QUESTIONS THE PHARISEES CONCERNING THE CHRIST.*

S. Matt. xxii. 41-46; S. Mark xii. 34-37; S. Luke xx. 40-44.

While the Pharisees were gathered together, Jesus asked them, saying, What think ye of Christ? Whose son is He? They say unto Him, *The son* of David. He saith unto them, How then doth David in spirit call Him Lord, saying, The **Lord said unto my Lord, Sit Thou on My right hand, till I make Thine enemies Thy footstool.** If David then call him Lord, how is He his son?

Matt. 22. 41.

Ps. 110. 1.

And no man was able to answer Him a word, neither durst any *man* from that day forth ask Him any more *questions*.

Mark 12. 37. And the common people heard Him gladly.

XIII. *CHRIST REPROVES THE SCRIBES AND PHARISEES.*

S. Matt. xxiii. 1-12 ; S. Mark xii. 38-40 ; S. Luke xx. 45-47.

Luke 20. 45.
Matt. 23. 1. Then in the audience of all the people spake Jesus to the multitude, and to His disciples, saying, The scribes and the Pharisees sit in Moses'seat : all therefore whatsoever they bid you observe, *that* observe and do; but do not ye after their works : for they say and do not. Beware of the scribes, for they bind heavy burdens, and grievous to be borne, and lay *them* on men's shoulders ; but they *themselves* will not move them with one of their fingers. But all their works they do for to be seen of men : they desire to walk in long robes, they make broad their phy-lacteries, and enlarge the borders of their gar-ments, and love the uppermost rooms at feasts, and the chief seats in the synagogues, and greet-ings in the markets, and to be called of men, Rabbi, Rabbi. But be not ye called Rabbi : for one is your Master, *even* Christ, and all ye are brethren. And call no man your father upon the earth : for one is your Father, which is in heaven. Neither be ye called masters : for one is your Master, *even* Christ. But he that is greatest among you shall be your servant. And whoso-ever shall exalt himself shall be abased, and he that shall humble himself shall be exalted.

XIV. *THE EIGHT WOES.*

S. Matt. xxiii. 13-39.

But woe unto you, scribes and Pharisees, hypo- Matt. 23. 13. crites! for ye shut up the kingdom of heaven against men: for ye neither go in *yourselves,* neither suffer ye them that are entering to go in.

Woe unto you, scribes and Pharisees, hypocrites! for ye devour widows' houses, and for a pretence make long prayer: therefore ye shall receive the greater damnation.

Woe unto you, scribes and Pharisees, hypocrites! for ye compass sea and land to make one proselyte, and when he is made, ye make him twofold more the child of hell than yourselves.

Woe unto you, *ye* blind guides, which say, Whosoever shall swear by the temple, it is nothing; but whosoever shall swear by the gold of the temple, he is a debtor! *Ye* fools and blind: for whether is greater, the gold, or the temple that sanctifieth the gold? And, Whosoever shall swear by the altar, it is nothing; but whosoever sweareth by the gift that is upon it, he is guilty. *Ye* fools and blind: for whether *is* greater, the gift, or the altar that sanctifieth the gift? Whoso therefore shall swear by the altar, sweareth by it, and by all things thereon. And whoso shall swear by the temple, sweareth by it, and by Him that dwelleth therein. And he that shall swear by heaven, sweareth by the throne of God, and by Him that sitteth thereon.

Woe unto you, scribes and Pharisees, hypocrites! for ye pay tithe of mint and anise and cummin, and have omitted the weightier *matters* of the law, judgment, mercy, and faith: these ought ye to have done, and not to leave the other undone. *Ye* blind guides, which strain at a gnat, and swallow a camel.

Woe unto you, scribes and Pharisees, hypocrites ! for ye make clean the outside of the cup and platter, but within they are full of extortion and excess. *Thou* blind Pharisee, cleanse first that *which is* within the cup and platter, that the outside of them may be clean also.

Woe unto you, scribes and Pharisees, hypocrites ! for ye are like unto whited sepulchres, which indeed appear beautiful outward, but are within full of dead *men's* bones, and of all uncleanness. Even so ye also outwardly appear righteous unto men, but within ye are full of hypocrisy and iniquity.

Woe unto you, scribes and Pharisees, hypocrites ! because ye build the tombs of the prophets, and garnish the sepulchres of the righteous, and say, If we had been in the days of our fathers, we would not have been partakers with them in the blood of the prophets. Wherefore ye be witnesses unto yourselves, that ye are the children of them which killed the prophets. Fill ye up then the measure of your fathers. *Ye* serpents, *ye* generation of vipers, how can ye escape the damnation of hell ?

Wherefore, behold, I send unto you prophets, and wise men, and scribes : and *some* of them ye shall kill and crucify ; and *some* of them shall ye scourge in your synagogues, and persecute *them* from city to city : that upon you may come all the righteous blood shed upon the earth, from the blood of righteous Abel unto the blood of Zacharias son of Barachias, whom ye slew between the temple and the altar. Verily I say unto you, All these things shall come upon this generation.

O Jerusalem, Jerusalem, *thou* that killest the prophets, and stonest them which are sent unto thee, how often would I have gathered thy children together, even as a hen gathereth her chickens under *her* wings, and ye would not ! Behold, your house is left unto you desolate. For I say unto you, Ye shall not see Me henceforth, till ye shall say, **Blessed** *is* **he that cometh in the name of** Ps. 118. 26. **the Lord.**

XV. *THE WIDOW'S MITE.*

S. Mark xii. 41–44 ; S. Luke xxi. 1–4.

And Jesus sat over against the treasury, and Mark 12. 41. beheld how the people cast money into the treasury : and many that were rich cast in much. And there came a certain poor widow, and she threw in two mites which make a farthing. And He called *unto Him* His disciples, and saith unto them, Verily I say unto you, That this poor widow hath cast more in, than all they which have cast into the treasury : for all these have of their abundance cast in unto Luke 21. 4. the offerings of God ; but she of her penury did cast in all that she had, *even* all her living.

XVI. *GREEKS DESIRE TO SEE CHRIST.*
HE FORETELLS HIS DEATH.

S. John xii. 20–36.

And there were certain Greeks among them that John 12. 20. came up to worship at the feast : the same came therefore to Philip, which was of Bethsaida of Galilee, and desired him, saying, Sir, we would see Jesus. Philip cometh and telleth Andrew : and again Andrew and Philip tell Jesus. And Jesus answered them, saying, The hour is come, that the Son of man should be glorified. Verily, verily, I say unto you, Except a corn of wheat fall into the ground and die, it abideth alone : but if it die, it bringeth forth much fruit. He that loveth his life shall lose it ; and he that hateth his life in this

world shall keep it unto life eternal. If any man
serve Me, let him follow Me; and where I am,
there shall also My servant be: if any man serve
Me, him will *My* Father honour. Now is My soul
troubled; and what shall I say? Father, save Me
from this hour; but for this cause came I unto
this hour. Father, glorify Thy name. Then came
there a voice from heaven, *saying*, I have both
glorified *it*, and will glorify *it* again. The people,
therefore, that stood by, and heard *it*, said that it
thundered: others said, An angel spake to Him.
Jesus answered and said, This voice came not
because of Me, but for your sakes. Now is the
judgment of this world: now shall the prince of
this world be cast out. And I, if I be lifted up
from the earth, will draw all *men* unto Me. This
He said, signifying what death He should die.

The people answered Him, We have heard out
of the law that Christ abideth for ever: and how
sayest Thou, The Son of man must be lifted up?
who is this Son of man? Then Jesus said unto
them, Yet a little while is the light with you. Walk
while ye have the light, lest darkness come upon
you: for he that walketh in darkness knoweth not
whither he goeth. While ye have the light, believe
in the light, that ye may be the children of light.

These things spake Jesus, and did hide Himself
from them.

XVII.   *THE DISBELIEF OF THE JEWS;*
AND THE DOCTRINE OF CHRIST WHICH
THEY REJECTED.

S. John xii. 37–50.

John 12. 37.   But though He had done so many miracles
before them, yet they believed not on Him: that
the saying of Esaias the prophet might be fulfilled,

Isa. 53. 1.   which he spake, **Lord, who hath believed our re-**

port? and to whom hath the arm of the Lord been revealed? Therefore they could not believe, because that Esaias said again, **He hath blinded their eyes, and hardened their heart; that they should not see with** *their* **eyes, nor understand with** *their* **heart, and be converted, and I should heal them.** These things said Esaias, when he saw His glory, and spake of Him. Isa. 6. 9, 10.

These things said Esaias, when he saw His glory, and spake of Him. Isa. 6. 1.

Nevertheless among the chief rulers also many believed on Him; but because of the Pharisees they did not confess *Him*, lest they should be put out of the synagogue: for they loved the praise of men more than the praise of God.

The Doctrine.

Jesus cried and said, He that believeth on Me, believeth not on Me, but on Him that sent Me. And he that seeth Me seeth Him that sent Me. I am come a light into the world, that whosoever believeth on Me should not abide in darkness. And if any man hear My words, and believe not, I judge him not: for I came not to judge the world, but to save the world. He that rejected Me, and receiveth not My words, hath one that judgeth him: the word that I have spoken, the same shall judge him at the last day. For I have not spoken of Myself; but the Father which sent Me, He gave Me a commandment, what I should say, and what I should speak. And I know that His commandment is life everlasting: whatsover I speak therefore, even as the Father said unto Me, so I speak.

XVIII.   *CHRIST'S GREAT PROPHECY OF THE DESTRUCTION OF THE JEWISH CHURCH AND·NATION; AND OF HIS OWN COMING.*

S. Matt. xxiv. ; S. Mark xiii. ; S. Luke xxi. 5–38.

Matt. 24. 1.   And Jesus went out, and departed from the
Mark 13. 1.   temple.   And as He went out of the temple, one
of His disciples saith unto Him, Master, see what
manner of stones, and what buildings *are here !*
And Jesus answering said unto him, Seest thou
these great buildings? there shall not be left one
stone upon another, that shall not be thrown down.

And as He sat upon the mount of Olives over
against the temple, Peter and James and John
and Andrew asked Him privately, Tell us, when
shall these things be? and what *shall be* the sign
Matt. 24. 3.   when all these things shall be fulfilled? what shall
be the sign of Thy coming, and of the end of the
world?

· And Jesus answered and said unto them, Take
heed that no man deceive you.   For many shall
Luke 21. 8.   come in My name, saying, I am Christ ; and the
Matt. 24. 5.   time draweth near ; and shall deceive many : go
ye not therefore after them.   And ye shall hear
of wars and rumours of wars : see that ye be not
Luke 21. 9.   troubled : for these things must first come to pass ;
but the end *is* not by and by.   Then said He
unto them, Nation shall rise against nation, and
kingdom against kingdom : and great earthquakes
shall be in divers places, and famines, and pestilences ; and fearful sights and great signs shall
Matt. 24. 8.   there be from heaven.   All these are the beginning
of sorrows.

Luke 21. 12.   But take heed to yourselves : before all these,
Mark 13. 9.   they shall lay their hands on you, and persecute
you, and shall kill you : they shall deliver you

up to councils; and in the synagogues ye shall be beaten; and ye shall be brought before rulers and kings for my sake for a testimony against them. And it shall turn to you for a testimony; Luke 21. 13. and ye shall be hated of all nations for my name's sake. But when they shall lead *you*, and deliver Mark 13. 11. you up, take no thought beforehand what ye shall speak, neither do ye premeditate; but whatever shall be given you in that hour, that speak ye: for it is not ye that speak, but the Holy Ghost: for I will give you a mouth and wisdom which all Luke 21. 15. your adversaries shall not be able to gainsay nor resist. And then shall many be offended, and shall Matt. 24. 10. betray one another, and shall hate one another. Now the brother shall betray the brother to death, and the father the son; and children shall rise up against *their* parents, and shall cause them to be put to death. And ye shall be hated of all Luke 21. 17. *men* for my name's sake. But there shall not an hair of your head perish. In your patience possess ye your souls. And many false prophets shall Matt. 24. 11. rise, and shall deceive many. And because iniquity shall abound, the love of many shall wax cold. But he that shall endure to the end, the same shall be saved. And this gospel of the kingdom shall be preached in all the world for a witness unto all nations; and then shall the end come.

And when ye shall see Jerusalem compassed Luke 21. 20. with armies, then know that the desolation thereof is nigh. When ye therefore shall see the abomina- Matt. 24. 15. tion of desolation, spoken of by Daniel the prophet, Dan. 9. 27; stand in the holy place, (whoso readeth let him 12. 11. understand); then let them which be in Judea flee to the mountains; and let them which are Luke 21. 21. in the midst of it depart out; and let not them which are in the countries enter thereinto: let Matt. 24. 17. him which is on the housetop not come down to take anything out of his house; neither let him

which is in the field return back to take his
clothes.   For these be the days of vengeance, that
all things which are written may be fulfilled.
But woe unto them that are with child, and to
them that give suck, in those days ! for there shall
be great distress in the land, and wrath upon this
people.   And they shall fall by the edge of the
sword, and shall be led away captive into all
nations: and Jerusalem shall be trodden down of
the Gentiles until the times of the Gentiles be
fulfilled.   But pray ye that your flight be not in
the winter, neither on the sabbath day.   For *in*
those days shall be affliction, such as was not from
the beginning of the creation which God created
unto this time, neither shall be.   And except that
the Lord had shortened those days, no flesh should
be saved: but for the elect's sake, whom He hath
chosen, He hath shortened the days.   And then
if any man shall say unto you, Lo, here *is* Christ;
or, lo, *He is* there; believe *him* not: for false
Christs and false prophets shall rise, and shall
shew signs and wonders, to seduce, if *it were* possible, even the elect.   But take ye heed: behold,
I have foretold you all things.   Wherefore if they
shall say unto you, Behold, He is in the desert;
go not forth : behold, *He is* in the secret chambers;
believe *it* not.   For as the lightning cometh out
of the east, and shineth even unto the west; so
shall also the coming of the Son of man be.   For
wheresoever the carcase is, there will the eagles
be gathered together.

Immediately after the tribulation of those days
there shall be signs in the sun, and in the moon,
and in the stars, the sun shall be darkened, and
the moon shall not give her light, and the stars
shall fall from heaven ; and upon the earth distress
of nations with perplexity; the sea and the waves
roaring ; men's hearts failing them for fear, and

for looking after those things which are coming
on the earth: for the powers of heaven shall be
shaken: and then shall appear the sign of the Matt. 24. 30.
Son of man in heaven: and then shall all the
tribes of the earth mourn, and they shall see the
Son of man coming in the clouds of heaven with
power and great glory. And when these things Luke 21. 28.
begin to come to pass, then look up, and lift up
your heads; for your redemption draweth nigh.
And He shall send His angels with a great sound
of a trumpet, and they shall gather together His
elect from the four winds, from one end of heaven
to the other.

Now learn a parable of the fig tree; when his Matt. 24. 32.
branch is yet tender, and putteth forth leaves, ye
know that summer is nigh; so likewise ye, when
ye shall see all these things, know that it is near,
even at the doors. Verily I say unto you, This
generation shall not pass, till all these things be
fulfilled. Heaven and earth shall pass away, but
My words shall not pass away.

But of that day and *that* hour knoweth no man, Mark 13. 32.
no, not the angels which are in heaven, neither the
Son, but the Father. But as the days of Noe *were,* Matt. 24. 37.
so shall also the coming of the Son of man be.
For as in the days that were before the flood
they were eating and drinking, marrying and
giving in marriage, until the day that Noe entered
into the ark, and knew not until the flood came,
and took them all away; so shall also the coming
of the Son of man be. Then shall two be in the
field; the one shall be taken, and the other left.
Two *women shall be* grinding at the mill; the one
shall be taken, and the other left.

Watch therefore: for ye know not what hour your
Lord doth come. But know this, that if the goodman of the house had known in what watch the
thief would come, he would have watched, and

would not have suffered his house to be broken up. Therefore be ye also ready : for in such an hour as ye think not the Son of man cometh. Who then is a faithful and wise servant, whom his lord hath made ruler over his household, to give them meat in due season ? Blessed is that servant, whom his lord when he cometh shall find so doing. Verily I say unto you, That he will make him ruler over all his goods. But and if that evil servant shall say in his heart, My lord delayeth his coming; and shall begin to smite his fellow-servants, and to eat and drink with the drunken ; the lord of that servant shall come in a day when he looketh not for *him*, and in an hour that he is not aware of, and shall cut him asunder, and appoint him his portion with the hypocrites ; there shall be weeping and gnashing of teeth.

Mark 13. 33.   Take ye heed, watch and pray : for ye know not when the time is. *For the Son of man is* as a man taking a far journey, who left his house, and gave authority to his servants, and to every man his work; and commanded the porter to watch. Watch ye therefore : for ye know not when the master of the house cometh, at even, or at midnight, or at cockcrowing, or in the morning : lest coming suddenly he find you sleeping. And what I say unto you I say unto all, Watch.

Luke 21. 34.   And take heed to yourselves, lest at any time your hearts be overcharged with surfeiting, and drunkenness, and cares of this life, and *so* that day come upon you unawares. For as a snare shall it come on all them that dwell on the face of the whole earth. Watch ye therefore, and pray always, that ye may be accounted worthy to escape all these things that shall come to pass, and to stand before the Son of man.

XIX. *PARABLE OF THE TEN VIRGINS.*

S. Matt. xxv. 1–13.

Then shall the kingdom of heaven be likened Matt. 25. 1.
unto ten virgins, which took their lamps, and went
forth to meet the bridegroom. And five of them
were wise, and five *were* foolish. They that *were*
foolish took their lamps, and took no oil with
them: but the wise took oil in their vessels with
their lamps. While the bridegroom tarried, they
all slumbered and slept.

And at midnight there was a cry made, Behold,
the bridegroom cometh; go ye out to meet him.
Then all those virgins arose, and trimmed their
lamps. And the foolish said unto the wise, Give
us of your oil; for our lamps are gone out. But
the wise answered, saying, *Not so*, lest there be
not enough for us and you: but go ye rather to
them that sell, and buy for yourselves. And while
they went to buy, the bridegroom came; and they
that were ready went in with him to the marriage:
and the door was shut. Afterward came also the
other virgins, saying, Lord, Lord, open to us. But
he answered and said, Verily I say unto you, I
know you not.

Watch therefore, for ye know neither the day nor
the hour wherein the Son of man cometh.

XX. *PARABLE OF THE TALENTS.*

S. Matt. xxv. 14–30.

For *the kingdom of heaven is* as a man travelling Matt. 25. 14.
into a far country, *who* called his own servants, and
delivered unto them his goods. And unto one he
gave five talents, to another two, and to another
one; to every man according to his several ability;

and straightway took his journey. Then he that had received the five talents went and traded with the same, and made *them* other five talents. And likewise he that *had received* two, he also gained other two. But he that had received one went and digged in the earth, and hid his lord's money.

After a long time the lord of those servants cometh, and reckoneth with them. And so he that had received five talents came and brought other five talents, saying, Lord, thou deliveredst unto me five talents: behold, I have gained beside them five talents more. His lord said unto him, Well done, *thou* good and faithful servant: thou hast been faithful over a few things, I will make thee ruler over many things: enter thou into the joy of thy lord. He also that had received two talents came and said, Lord, thou deliveredst unto me two talents: behold, I have gained two other talents beside them. His lord said unto him, Well done, good and faithful servant: thou hast been faithful over a few things, I will make thee ruler over many things: enter thou into the joy of thy lord. Then he which had received the one talent came, and said, Lord, I knew thee that thou art an hard man, reaping where thou hast not sown, and gathering where thou hast not strawed: and I was afraid, and went and hid thy talent in the earth: lo, *there* thou hast *that is* thine. His lord answered and said unto him, *Thou* wicked and slothful servant, thou knewest that I reap where I sowed not, and gather where I have not strawed: thou oughtest therefore to have put my money to the exchangers, and *then* at my coming I should have received mine own with usury. Take therefore the talent from him, and give *it* unto him which hath ten talents. For unto every one that hath shall be given, and he shall have abundance: but from him that hath not shall be taken away even that which he hath.

And cast ye the unprofitable servant into outer darkness: there shall be weeping and gnashing of teeth.

XXI. *THE LAST JUDGMENT.*

S. Matt. xxv. 31-46.

When the Son of man shall come in His glory, Matt. 25. 31. and all the holy angels with Him, then shall He sit upon the throne of His glory: and before Him shall be gathered all nations: and He shall separate them one from another, as a shepherd divideth *his* sheep from the goats: and He shall set the sheep on His right hand, but the goats on the left.

Then shall the King say unto them on His right hand, Come, ye blessed of My Father, inherit the kingdom prepared for you from the foundation of the world: for I was an hungered, and ye gave Me meat: I was thirsty, and ye gave Me drink: I was a stranger, and ye took Me in: naked, and ye clothed Me: I was sick, and ye visited Me: I was in prison, and ye came unto Me. Then shall the righteous answer Him, saying, Lord, when saw we Thee an hungered, and fed *Thee?* or thirsty, and gave *Thee* drink? When saw we Thee a stranger, and took *Thee* in? or naked, and clothed *Thee?* Or when saw we Thee sick, or in prison, and came unto Thee? And the King shall answer and say unto them, Verily I say unto you, Inasmuch as ye have done *it* unto one of the least of these My brethren, ye have done *it* unto Me. Then shall He say also unto them on the left hand, Depart from Me, ye cursed, into everlasting fire, prepared for the devil and his angels; for I was an hungered, and ye gave Me no meat: I was thirsty, and ye gave Me no drink: I was a stranger, and ye took Me not in: naked, and ye clothed Me not:

sick, and in prison, and ye visited Me not. Then shall they also answer Him, saying, Lord, when saw we Thee an hungered, or athirst, or a stranger, or naked, or sick, or in prison, and did not minister unto Thee? Then shall He answer them, saying, Verily I say unto you, Inasmuch as ye did *it* not to one of the least of these, ye did *it* not to Me.

And these shall go away into everlasting punishment: but the righteous into life eternal.

Luke 21. 37. And in the daytime He was teaching in the temple: and at night He went out and abode in the mount that is called the mount of Olives. And all the people came early in the morning to Him in the temple, for to hear Him.

Wednesday in Holy Week.

XXII. *CHRIST DECLARES HIS BETRAYAL. THE RULERS CONSPIRE AGAINST HIM. SATAN PREPARES JUDAS TO BETRAY HIM.*

S. Matt. xxvi. 1–5, 14–16; S. Mark xiv. 1, 2, 10–11; S. Luke xxii. 1–6.

Matt. 26. 1. And it came to pass, when Jesus had finished all these sayings, He said unto His disciples, Ye know that after two days is *the feast of* the passover, and the Son of man is betrayed to be crucified.

Then assembled together the chief priests, and the scribes, and the elders of the people, unto the palace of the high priest, who was called Caiaphas, and consulted that they might take Jesus by subtilty, and kill *Him.* But they said, Not on the feast *day,* lest there be an uproar among the

Luke 22. 2. people: for they feared the people.

Then entered Satan into Judas surnamed Iscariot,

being of the number of the twelve. And he went his way, and communed with the chief priests and captains how he might betray Him unto them; and said *unto them*, What will ye give me, and I will deliver Him unto you? And when they heard *it*, they were glad, and promised to give him money. And they covenanted with him for thirty pieces of silver. And he promised, and from that time he sought opportunity to betray Him unto them in the absence of the multitude.

Matt. 26. 15.
Mark 14. 11.
Matt. 26. 15.
Luke 22. 6.
Matt. 26. 16.
Luke 22. 6.

Thursday in Holy Week.

XXIII. *THE APOSTLES PREPARE THE PASSOVER.*

S. Matt. xxvi. 17–19; Mark xiv. 12–16; S. Luke xxii. 7–13.

Then came the day of unleavened bread, when the passover must be killed. And He sent Peter and John, saying, Go and prepare us the passover, that we may eat. And they said unto Him, Where wilt Thou that we prepare? And He said unto them, Behold, when ye are entered into the city, there shall a man meet you, bearing a pitcher of water; follow him into the house where he entereth in. And ye shall say unto the goodman of the house, The Master saith unto thee, My time is at hand; I will keep the passover at thy house with My disciples; where is the guestchamber? And he will shew you a large upper room furnished *and* prepared: there make ready for us.

Luke 22. 7.

Matt. 26. 18.

Mark 14. 14.

And His disciples went forth, and came into the city, and found as He had said unto them: and they made ready the passover.

XXIV. *CHRIST'S LAST PASSOVER.*

S. Matt. xxvi. 20–29 ; S. Mark xiv. 17–25 ; S. Luke xxii. 14–30 ;
S. John xiii., xiv.

(a.) *The Supper.*

S. Matt. xxvi. 20 ; S. Mark xiv. 17 ; S. Luke xxii. 14–18.

Mark 14. 17.   And in the evening He cometh with the twelve.
Luke 22. 14. And when the hour was come He sat down, and
the twelve apostles with Him.

And He said unto them, With desire I have desired to eat this passover with you before I suffer :
for I say unto you, I will not any more eat thereof,
until it shall be fulfilled in the kingdom of God.
And He took the cup, and gave thanks, and said,
Take this, and divide *it* among yourselves : for I say
unto you, I will not drink of the fruit of the vine
until the kingdom of God shall come.

(b.) *The Strife for Precedence.*

S. Luke xxii. 24–30.

Luke 22. 24.   And there was also a strife among them, which
of them should be accounted the greatest.   And
He said unto them, The kings of the Gentiles exercise lordship over them ; and they that exercise
lordship upon them are called benefactors.   But
ye *shall* not *be* so : but he that is greatest among
you, let him be as the younger ; and he that is
chief, as he that doth serve.   For whether *is* greater,
he that sitteth at meat, or he that serveth ? *is*
not he that sitteth at meat ? but I am among you
as he that serveth.   Ye are they which have continued with Me in My temptations.   And I appoint
unto you a kingdom, as my Father hath appointed
unto Me ; that ye may eat and drink at My table
in My kingdom, and sit on thrones judging the
twelve tribes of Israel.

(e.) *Christ washes the Disciples' Feet.*

S. John xiii. 1–20.

Now before the feast of the passover, when Jesus knew that His hour was come that He should depart out of this world unto the Father, having loved His own which were in the world, He loved them unto the end.

John 13. 1.

And supper being ended [*Gk. being prepared*], the devil having now put into the heart of Judas Iscariot, Simon's *son*, to betray him; Jesus knowing that the Father had given all things into His hands, and that He was come from God, and went to God; He riseth from supper, and laid aside his garments; and took a towel, and girded Himself. After that He poureth water into a basin, and began to wash the disciples' feet, and to wipe *them* with the towel wherewith He was girded. Then cometh He to Simon Peter: and Peter saith unto Him, Lord, dost Thou wash my feet? Jesus answered and said unto him, What I do thou knowest not now, but thou shalt know hereafter. Peter saith unto Him, Thou shalt never wash my feet. Jesus answered him, If I wash thee not, thou hast no part with Me. Simon Peter saith unto Him, Lord, not my feet only, but also *my* hands and *my* head. Jesus saith to him, He that is washed needeth not save to wash *his* feet, but is clean every whit: and ye are clean, but not all. For He knew who should betray Him; therefore said He, Ye are not all clean.

So after He had washed their feet, and had taken His garments, and was set down again, He said unto them, Know ye what I have done to you? Ye call Me Master and Lord: and ye say well; for *so* I am. If I then, *your* Lord and Master, have washed your feet; ye also ought to wash one another's feet. For I have given you an example, that ye should do as I have done to you. Verily, verily, I say unto you, The servant is not greater than his lord; neither is he that is sent greater than He that sent him. If ye know these things, happy are ye if ye do them. I speak not of you all: I know whom I have chosen: but that the scripture may be fulfilled, **He that eateth bread with Me hath lifted up his heel against Me.** Now I tell you before it come, that, when it is come to pass, ye may believe that I am *He*. Verily, verily, I say unto you, He that receiveth whomsoever I send receiveth Me; and he that receiveth Me receiveth Him that sent Me.

Ps. 41. 9. (margin reference)

(d.) *Christ foreshows His Betrayal.*

S. Matt. xxvi. 21–25; S. Mark xiv. 18–21; S. Luke xxii. 21–23; S. John xiii. 21–38.

When Jesus had thus said, He was troubled in spirit, and testified, and said, Verily, verily, I say unto you, that one of you which eateth with Me shall betray Me. Then the disciples looked one on another, doubting of whom He spake. And they began to be sorrowful, and to say unto Him one by one, Lord, *Is* it I? and another *said*, Is it I? And He answered and said unto them, *It is* one of the twelve, that dippeth with Me in the dish. The Son of man indeed goeth, as it is written of Him: but woe to that man by whom the Son of man is betrayed! good were it for that man if he had never been born. Then Judas, which betrayed Him, answered and said, Master, is it I? He said unto him, Thou hast said. And they began to enquire among themselves, which of them it was that should do this thing.

Now there was leaning on Jesus' bosom one of His disciples whom Jesus loved. Simon Peter therefore beckoned to him, that he should ask who it should be of whom He spake. He then lying on Jesus' breast saith unto Him, Lord, who is it? Jesus answered, He it is to whom I shall give a sop, when I have dipped *it*. And when He had dipped the sop, He gave *it* to Judas Iscariot, *the son* of Simon. And after the sop Satan entered into him. Then said Jesus unto him, That thou doest, do quickly. Now no man at the table knew for what intent He spake this unto him. For some *of them* thought, because Judas had the bag, that Jesus had said unto him, Buy *those things* that we have need of against the feast; or, that he should give something to the poor. He then having received the sop went immediately out: and it was night.

Therefore, when he was gone out, Jesus said, Now is the Son of man glorified, and God is glorified in Him. If God be glorified in Him, God shall also glorify Him in Himself, and shall straightway glorify Him. Little children, yet a little while I am with you. Ye shall seek Me: and as I said unto the Jews, Whither I go, ye cannot come; so now I say to you. A new commandment I give unto you, That ye love one another; as I have loved you, that ye also love one another. By this shall all *men* know that ye are My disciples, if ye have love one to another.

Simon Peter said unto Him, Lord, whither goest thou? Jesus answered him, Whither I go, Thou canst not follow Me now; but thou shalt follow Me afterwards. Peter said unto Him, Lord, why cannot I follow Thee now? I will lay down my life for Thy sake. Jesus answered him, Wilt thou lay down thy life for My sake? Verily, verily, I say unto thee, The cock shall not crow, till thou hast denied Me thrice.

(*c.*) *The Institution of the Lord's Supper.*

S. Matt. xxvi. 26–29 ; S. Mark xiv. 22–25 ; S. Luke xviii.
19, 20 ; [1 Cor. xi. 24–25.]

Matt. 26. 26.   And as they were eating, Jesus took bread, and gave thanks, and blessed *it*, and brake *it*, and gave
Luke 22. 19.   *it* to the disciples, and said, Take, eat ; this is My Body which is given for you : this do in remem-
Matt. 26. 27.   brance of Me.   And He took the cup after supper, and gave thanks, and gave it to them, saying, Drink ye all of it : for this is My Blood of the new testament, which is shed for many for the re- mission of sins.

But I say unto you, I will not drink henceforth of this fruit of the vine, until that day when I drink it new with you in My Father's kingdom.

XXV.   *THE FAREWELL DISCOURSES.*

St. John xiv.–xvi.

(*a.*) *Christ consoles His Disciples.   Faith and Prayer.*

S. John xiv. 1–14.

John 14. 1.   Let not your heart be troubled : ye believe in God, believe also in Me.   In My Father's house are many mansions : if *it were* not *so*, I would have told you.   I go to prepare a place for you. And if I go and prepare a place for you, I will come again, and receive you unto Myself : that where I am, *there* ye may be also.   And whither I go ye know, and the way ye know.   Thomas saith unto Him, Lord, we know not whither Thou goest ; and how can we know the way ?   Jesus saith unto him, I am the way, the truth, and the life : no man cometh unto the Father, but by Me.   If ye had known Me, ye should have known My Father also : and from henceforth ye know Him, and have seen Him. Philip saith unto Him, Lord, show us the Father, and it sufficeth us. Jesus saith unto him, Have I been so long time with you, and yet hast thou not known Me, Philip? he that hath seen Me hath seen the Father: and how sayest thou *then*, Shew us the Father? Believest thou not that I am in the Father, and the Father in Me? the words that I speak unto you I speak not of Myself: but the Father that dwelleth in Me, He doeth the works. Believe Me that I *am* in the Father, and the Father in Me: or else believe Me for the very works' sake. Verily, verily, I say unto you, He that believeth on Me, the works that I do shall he do also; and greater works than these shall he do; because I go unto My Father. And whatsoever ye shall ask in My name, that will I do, that the Father may be glorified in the Son. If ye shall ask anything in My name, I will do *it*.

(*b.*) *The Promise of the Comforter.*

S. John xiv. 15-31.

If ye love Me, keep My commandments. And I will pray the Father, and He shall give you another Comforter, that He may abide with you for ever; *even* the Spirit of truth; whom the world cannot receive, because it seeth Him not, neither knoweth Him : but ye know Him; for He dwelleth with you, and shall be in you.

I will not leave you comfortless : I will come to you. Yet a little while, and the world seeth Me no more; but ye see Me: because I live, ye shall live also. At that day ye shall know that I *am* in My Father, and ye in Me, and I in you. He that hath My commandments, and keepeth them, he it is that loveth Me: and he that loveth Me shall be loved of My Father, and I will love him, and will manifest myself to him. Judas saith unto Him, not Iscariot, Lord, how is it that Thou wilt manifest thyself unto us, and not unto the world ? Jesus answered and said unto him, If a man love Me, he will keep My words : and My Father will love him, and We will come unto him, and make Our abode with him. He that loveth Me not keepeth not My sayings : and the word which ye hear is not Mine, but the Father's which sent Me.

These things have I spoken unto you, being *yet* present with you. But the Comforter, *which is* the Holy Ghost, Whom the Father will send in My name, He shall teach you all things, and bring all things to your remembrance, whatsoever I have said unto you. Peace I leave with you, My peace I give unto you : not as the world giveth, give I unto you. Let not your heart be troubled, neither let it be afraid. Ye have heard how I said unto you, I go away, and come *again* unto you. If ye loved Me, ye would rejoice, because I said, I go unto the Father : for My Father is greater than I. And now I have told you before it come to pass, that, when it is come to pass, ye might believe. Hereafter I will not talk much with you : for the prince of this world cometh, and hath nothing in Me. But that the world may know that I love the Father ; and as the Father gave Me commandment, even so I do.

Arise, let us go hence.

(c.) *The True Vine.*

S. John xv. 1–17.

John 15. 1.   I am the true vine, and My Father is the husbandman. Every branch in Me that beareth not fruit He taketh away: and every *branch* that beareth fruit, He purgeth it, that it may bring forth more fruit. Now ye are clean through the word which

I have spoken unto you. Abide in Me, and I in you. As the branch cannot bear fruit of itself, except it abide in the vine; no more can ye, except ye abide in Me. I am the vine, ye *are* the branches: he that abideth in Me, and I in him, the same bringeth forth much fruit; for without Me ye can do nothing. If a man abide not in Me, he is cast forth as a branch, and is withered; and *men* gather them, and cast *them* into the fire, and they are burned. If ye abide in Me, and My words abide in you, ye shall ask what ye will, and it shall be done unto you. Herein is My Father glorified, that ye bear much fruit; so shall ye be My disciples. As the Father hath loved Me, so have I loved you: continue ye in My love. If ye keep My commandments, ye shall abide in My love; even as I have kept My Father's commandments, and abide in His love.

These things have I spoken unto you, that My joy might remain in you, and *that* your joy might be full. This is My commandment, That ye love one another, as I have loved you. Greater love hath no man than this, that a man lay down his life for his friends. Ye are My friends, if ye do whatsoever I command you. Henceforth I call you not servants; for the servant knoweth not what his lord doeth: but I have called you friends; for all things that I have heard of My Father I have made known unto you. Ye have not chosen Me, but I have chosen you, and ordained you, that ye should go and bring forth fruit, and *that* your fruit should remain: that whatsoever ye shall ask of the Father in My name, He may give it you. These things I command you, that ye love one another.

(*d.*) *Persecution by the World. Perpetuity of the Witness of Christ.*

S. John xv. 18–xvi. 4.

John 15. 18. If the world hate you, ye know that it hated Me before *it hated* you. If ye were of the world, the world would love his own : but because ye are not of the world, but I have chosen you out of the world, therefore the world hateth you. Remember

John 13. 16. the word that I said unto you, The servant is not greater that his lord. If they have persecuted Me, they will also persecute you : if they have kept My saying, they will keep yours also. But all these things will they do unto you for My name's sake, because they know not Him that sent Me. If I had not come and spoken unto them, they had not had sin : but now have they no cloke for their sin. He that hateth Me hateth My Father also. If I had not done among them the works which none other man did, they had not had sin : but now they have both seen and hated both Me and My Father. But *this cometh to pass*, that the word might be fulfilled that is written in their law,

Ps. 35. 19; **They hated Me without a cause.** But when the
69. 4. Comforter is come, Whom I will send unto you from the Father, *even* the Spirit of truth, Which proceedeth from the Father, He shall testify of Me : and ye also shall bear witness, because ye have been with Me from the beginning.

These things have I spoken unto you, that ye should not be offended. They shall put you out of the synagogues : yea, the time cometh, that whosoever killeth you will think that he doeth God service. And these things will they do unto you, because they have not known the Father nor Me. But these things have I told you, that when the time shall come, ye may remember that

I told you of them. And these things I said not
unto you at the beginning, because I was with you.

*(e). The Departure of Christ. The Advent of the Spirit
of Truth.*

S. John xvi. 5-33.

But now I go My way to Him that sent Me; and none of you asketh Me, Whither goest Thou?
But because I have said these things unto you,
sorrow hath filled your heart. Nevertheless, I
tell you the truth; It is expedient for you that
I go away: for if I go not away, the Comforter
will not come unto you; but if I depart, I will
send Him unto you. And when He is come, He
will reprove the world of sin, and of righteousness,
and of judgment: of sin, because they believe not
on Me; of righteousness, because I go to My
Father, and ye see Me no more; of judgment,
because the prince of this world is judged.

I have yet many things to say unto you, but ye
cannot bear them now. Howbeit when He, the
Spirit of truth, is come, He will guide you into all
truth: for He shall not speak of Himself; but
whatsoever He shall hear, *that* shall He speak:
and He will shew you things to come. He shall
glorify Me: for He shall receive of Mine, and
shall shew *it* unto you. All things that the Father
hath are Mine: therefore said I, that He shall take
of Mine, and shall shew *it* unto you.

A little while, and ye shall not see Me: and
again, a little while, and ye shall see Me, because
I go to the Father. Then said *some* of His disciples
among themselves, What is this that He saith unto
us, A little while, and ye shall not see Me: and
again, a little while, and ye shall see Me: and,
Because I go to the Father? They said therefore,
What is this that He saith, A little while? We

cannot tell what He saith. Now Jesus knew that they were desirous to ask Him, and said unto them, Do ye enquire among yourselves of that I said, A little while, and ye shall not see Me: and again, a little while, and ye shall see Me? Verily, verily, I say unto you, That ye shall weep and lament, but the world shall rejoice: and ye shall be sorrowful, but your sorrow shall be turned into joy. A woman when she is in travail hath sorrow, because her hour is come: but as soon as she is delivered of the child, she remembereth no more the anguish, for joy that a man is born into the world. And ye now therefore have sorrow: but I will see you again, and your heart shall rejoice, and your joy no man taketh from you.

And in that day ye shall ask Me nothing. Verily, verily, I say unto you, Whatsoever ye shall ask the Father in My name, He will give *it* you. Hitherto have ye asked nothing in My name: ask, and ye shall receive, that your joy may be full.

These things have I spoken unto you in proverbs: but the time cometh, when I shall no more speak unto you in proverbs, but I shall shew you plainly of the Father. At that day ye shall ask in My name: and I say not unto you, that I will pray the Father for you: for the Father Himself loveth you, because ye have loved Me, and have believed that I came out from God. I came forth from the Father, and am come into the world: again, I leave the world, and go to the Father.

His disciples said unto Him, Lo, now speakest thou plainly, and speakest no proverb. Now are we sure that Thou knowest all things, and needest not that any man should ask Thee: by this we believe that Thou camest forth from God.

Jesus answered them, Do ye now believe? Behold, the hour cometh, yea, is now come, that ye shall be scattered, every man to his own, and shall leave Me alone : and yet I am not alone, because the Father is with Me. These things have I spoken unto you, that in Me ye might have peace. In the world ye shall have tribulation : but be of good cheer ; I have overcome the world.

XXVI. *THE PRAYER OF CHRIST.*

S. John xvii.

These words spake Jesus, and lifted up His eyes to John 17. 1. heaven, and said, Father the hour is come ; glorify Thy Son, that Thy Son may also glorify Thee : as Thou hast given Him power over all flesh, that He should give eternal life to as many as Thou hast given Him. And this is life eternal, that they might know Thee the only true God, and Jesus Christ whom Thou hast sent. I have glorified Thee on the earth : I have finished the work which Thou gavest Me to do. And now, O Father, glorify thou Me with Thine own Self with the glory which I had with Thee before the world was.

I have manifested Thy name unto the men which Thou gavest Me out of the world : Thine they were, and Thou gavest them Me ; and they have kept Thy word. Now they have known that all things whatsoever Thou hast given Me are of Thee. For I have given them the words which Thou gavest Me ; and they have received *them*, and have known surely that I came out from Thee, and they have believed that Thou didst send Me. I pray for them : I pray not for the world, but for them which Thou hast given Me ; for they are Thine. And all Mine are Thine, and Thine are Mine ; and I am glorified in them. And now I am no more in the world, but these are in the world, and I come to Thee. Holy Father, keep through Thine own Name those whom Thou hast given Me, that they may be one, as we *are*. While I was with them in the world, I kept them in Thy Name: those that Thou gavest Me have I kept, and none of them is lost, but the son of perdition; that the scripture might be fulfilled. And now I come to Thee; and these things speak I in the world, that they might have My joy fulfilled in themselves. I have given them Thy word; and the world hath hated them, because they are not of the world, even as I am not of the world. I pray not that Thou shouldest take them out of the world, but that Thou shouldest keep them from the evil. They are not of the world, even as I am not of the world. Sanctify them through Thy truth: Thy word is truth. As Thou hast sent Me into the world, even so have I also sent them into the world. And for their sakes I sanctify Myself, that they also might be sanctified through the truth.

Neither pray I for these alone, but for them also which shall believe on Me through their word; that they all may be one; as Thou, Father, *art* in Me, and I in Thee, that they also may be one in us: that the world may believe that Thou hast sent Me. And the glory which Thou gavest Me I have given them; that they may be one, even as we are one: I in them, and Thou in Me, that they may be made perfect in one; and that the world may know that Thou hast sent Me, and hast loved them, as Thou hast loved Me.

Father, I will that they also, whom Thou hast given Me, be with Me where I am; that they may behold My glory, which Thou hast given Me: for Thou lovedst Me before the foundation of the world. O righteous Father, the world hath not known Thee: but I have known Thee, and these have known that Thou hast sent Me. And I have declared unto them Thy name, and will declare *it:* that the love wherewith Thou hast loved Me may be in them, and I in them.

XXVII. *THE WALK TO GETHSEMANE: PETER WARNED.*

S. Matt. xxvi. 30–35 ; S. Mark xiv. 26–31 ; S. Luke xxii. 39, 31–38 ; S. John xviii. 1.

When Jesus had spoken these words, and when they had sung an hymn, they went out over the brook Cedron, into the mount of Olives. Then saith Jesus unto them, All ye shall be offended because of Me this night : for it is written, **I will smite the shepherd, and the sheep of the flock shall be scattered abroad.** But after I am risen again, I will go before you into Galilee. Peter answered and said unto Him, Though all shall be offended because of Thee, *yet* will I never be offended. And the Lord said, Simon, Simon, behold, Satan hath desired *to have* you, that he may sift *you* as wheat : but I have prayed for thee, that thy faith fail not : and when thou art converted, strengthen thy brethren. And he said unto Him, Lord, I am ready to go with Thee, both into prison, and to death. And He said, I tell thee, Peter, that this day, *even* in this night, before the cock crow twice, thou shalt thrice deny that thou knowest Me. But he spake the more vehemently, If I should die with Thee, I will not deny Thee in any wise. Likewise also said all the disciples.

And He said unto them, When I sent you without purse, and scrip, and shoes, lacked ye any thing ? And they said, Nothing. Then said He unto them, But now, he that hath a purse, let him take *it*, and likewise *his* scrip : and he that hath no sword, let him sell his garment, and buy one. For I say unto you, that this that is written must yet be accomplished in Me, **And He was reckoned among the transgressors** : for the things concerning Me have an end. And they said, Lord, behold, here *are* two swords. And He said unto them, It is enough.

XXVIII *GETHSEMANE. THE AGONY.*

S. Matt. xxvi. 36–46 ; S. Mark xiv. 32–42 ; S. Luke xxii. 40–46 ;
S. John xviii. 1, 2.

Matt. 26. 36. Then cometh Jesus with them unto a place called
John 18. 1. Gethsemane, where was a garden, into the which He entered, and His disciples. And Judas also, which betrayed Him, knew the place : for Jesus
Matt. 26. 36. ofttimes resorted thither with His disciples. And He saith unto the disciples, Sit ye here, while I go
Luke 22. 40. and pray yonder. Pray that ye enter not into temptation.

Mark 14. 33. And He taketh with him Peter, and James, and John, and began to be sore amazed, and to be very heavy ; and saith unto them, My soul is exceeding sorrowful unto death : tarry ye here, and watch
Luke 22. 41. with Me. And He was withdrawn from them about a stone's cast, and kneeled down, and fell on His
Mark 14. 36. face, and prayed, saying, Abba, Father, all things are possible unto Thee ; take away this cup from Me : nevertheless not what I will, but what Thou
Luke 22. 43. wilt. . And there appeared an angel unto Him from heaven, strengthening Him. And being in an agony He prayed more earnestly : and His sweat was as it were great drops of blood falling down to the ground.

And when He rose up from prayer, and was come to the disciples, He found them sleeping for
Mark 14. 37. sorrow, and said unto Peter, Simon, sleepest thou ? couldest not thou watch one hour ? Watch ye and pray, lest ye enter into temptation. The spirit truly *is* ready, but the flesh *is* weak.

Matt. 26. 42. He went away again the second time, and prayed, saying, O my Father, if this cup may not pass away from Me, except I drink it, Thy will be done.

Mark 14. 40. And He came and found them asleep again : for their eyes were heavy, neither wist they what to answer Him.

And He left them, and went away again, and Matt. 26. 44.
prayed the third time, saying the same words.

Then cometh He to His disciples, and saith unto
them, Sleep on now, and take *your* rest : it is Mark 14. 41.
enough, the hour is come ; behold, the Son of man
is betrayed into the hands of sinners. Rise up, let
us go ; lo, he that betrayeth Me is at hand.

XXIX. *THE BETRAYAL AND APPREHEN-SION OF CHRIST.*

S. Matt. xxvi. 47–56 ; S. Mark xiv. 43–52 ; S. Luke xxii. 47–53 ;
S. John xviii. 3–12.

And immediately, while He yet spake, cometh Mark 14. 43.
Judas, one of the twelve, and with him a great
multitude, and officers with lanterns and torches John 18. 3.
and weapons, from the chief priests, and the Mark 14. 43.
Pharisees, and the scribes and elders.

Jesus therefore, knowing all things that should John 18. 4.
come upon Him, went forth, and said unto them,
Whom seek ye ? They answered Him, Jesus of
Nazareth. Jesus saith unto them, I am *He*.
And Judas also, which betrayed Him, stood with
them. As soon, then, as He had said unto them,
I am *He*, they went backward, and fell to the
ground. Then asked He them again, Whom seek
ye ? And they said, Jesus of Nazareth. Jesus
answered, I have told you that I am *He*: if ye seek
Me, let these go their way ; that the saying might
be fulfilled which He spake, Of them which Thou John 17. 12.
gavest Me have I lost none.

And he that betrayed Him had given them a Mark 41. 44.
token, saying, Whomsoever I shall kiss, that same
is He : take Him, hold Him fast, and lead Him
away safely. And forthwith he came to Jesus, and Matt. 2.6 49.
said, Hail, Master ; and kissed Him. And Jesus

said unto him, Friend, wherefore art thou come ?
Luke 22. 48. Judas, betrayest thou the Son of man with a kiss ?
Matt. 26. 50. Then came they, and laid hands on Jesus, and
Luke 22. 49. took Him. When they that were about Him saw what would follow, they said unto Him, Lord, shall
John 18. 10. we smite with the sword ? Then Simon Peter having a sword drew it, and smote the high priest's servant, and cut off his right ear. The servant's
Luke 22. 51. name was Malchus. And Jesus answered and said, Suffer ye thus far. And He touched his ear, and
John 18. 11. healed him. Then said Jesus unto Peter, Put up thy sword into the sheath : for all they that take the sword shall perish with the sword : the cup
Matt. 26. 53. which My Father hath given Me, shall I not drink it ? Thinkest thou that I cannot now pray to My Father, and He shall presently give Me more than twelve legions of angels ? But how then shall the scriptures be fulfilled, that thus it must be ?
Luke 22. 52. Then Jesus said unto the chief priests, and captains of the temple, and the elders, which were come to him, Be ye come out, as against a thief, with swords and staves ? When I was daily with you teaching in the temple, ye stretched forth no hands against Me : but this is your hour, and the
Matt. 26. 56. power of darkness. All this was done, that the scriptures of the prophets might be fulfilled.
John 18. 12. Then the band and the captains and officers of the Jews took Jesus, and bound Him.
Matt. 26. 56. Then all the disciples forsook Him, and fled.
Mark 14. 51. And there followed Him a certain young man, having a linen cloth cast about *his* naked *body* ; and the young men laid hold of him : and he left the linen cloth, and fled from them naked.

XXX. *JUDICIAL PROCEEDINGS AGAINST CHRIST.*

S. Matt. xxvi. 57–75 ; S. Mark xiv. 53–72 ; S. Luke xxii. 54–62 ;
S. John xviii. 13–27.

(*a.*) *Christ before Annas.*

S. John xviii. 13, 14.

And they that had laid hold on Jesus led *Him* Matt. 26. 57.
away to Annas first ; for he was father-in-law to John 18. 13.
Caiaphas, which was the high priest that same
year. Now Caiaphas was he which gave counsel
to the Jews, that it was expedient that one man
should die for the people.

(*b.*) *Christ before Caiaphas* (*preliminary*).

S. Matt. xxvi. 57 ; S. Mark xiv. 53 ; S. Luke xxiv. 54 ; S. John
xviii. 19–24.

Now Annas had sent Him bound unto Caiaphas John 18. 24.
the high priest. Then took they Him, and led Luke 22. 54.
Him, and brought Him into the high priest's
house : and with him were assembled all the chief Mark 14. 53.
priests and the elders and the scribes.
And Simon Peter followed Jesus afar off, even John 18. 15.
into the palace of the high priest ; and *so did* Mark 14. 54.
John 18. 15.
another disciple : that disciple was known unto the
high priest, and went in with Jesus into the palace
of the high priest. But Peter stood at the door
without. Then went out that other disciple, which
was known unto the high priest, and spake unto
her that kept the door, and brought in Peter.
And he went in, and sat with the servants, to Matt. 26. 58.
see the end.

Peter's first Denial.

S. Matt. xxvi. 58–70 ; S. Mark xiv. 54, 66–68 ; S. Luke xxii. 54–57 ;
S. John xviii. 15–18.

John 18. 18.   And the servants and officers stood there, who had made a fire of coals ; for it was cold : and they warmed themselves : and Peter stood with them, and warmed himself.

Mark 14. 66.   And as Peter was beneath in the palace, there
John 18. 17. cometh one of the maids of the high priest, the
Mark 14. 67. damsel that kept the door, and when she saw Peter warming himself, she looked earnestly upon him
Luke 22. 56. as he sat by the fire, and said, This man was
Mark 14. 67. also with Him : thou also wast with Jesus of
Matt. 26. 70. Nazareth. But he denied before them all, saying,
Mark 14. 68. Woman, I know Him not : I know not, neither understand I what thou sayest. And he went out into the porch ; and the cock crew.

John 18. 19.   The high priest then asked Jesus of His disciples, and of His doctrine. Jesus answered him, I spake openly to the world ; I ever taught in the synagogue, and in the temple, whither the Jews always resort ; and in secret have I said nothing. Why askest thou Me ? ask them which heard Me, what I have said unto them ; behold, they know what I said.

And when He had thus spoken, one of the officers which stood by struck Jesus with the palm of his hand, saying, Answerest Thou the high priest so ? Jesus answered him, If I have spoken evil, bear witness of the evil : but if well, why smitest thou Me ?

Good Friday.

(c.) *Christ before the Sanhedrim.*

S. Matt. xxvi. 59–68 ; S. Mark xiv. 53–65 ; S. Luke xxii. 66–71.

And as soon as it was day, the elders of the Luke 22. 66.
people and the chief priests and the scribes came
together, and led Him into their council, saying,
Art Thou the Christ? tell us. And He said unto
them, If I tell you, ye will not believe : and if I
also ask *you*, ye will not answer Me, nor let *Me* go.

And all the council sought false witness against Matt. 26. 59.
Jesus to put Him to death; and found none. For Mark 14. 55.
many bare false witness against Him, but their
witness agreed not together. At the last came two Matt. 26. 60.
false witnesses, and said, This *fellow* said, I am able
to destroy the temple of God, and to build it in
three days. But neither so did their witness agree Mark 14. 59.
together. And the high priest stood up in the
midst, and asked Jesus, saying, Answerest Thou
nothing? what *is it which* these witness against
Thee? But He held His peace, and answered
nothing. And the high priest answered and said Matt. 26. 63.
unto Him, I adjure Thee by the living God, that
Thou tell us whether Thou be the Christ, the Son of
God. Jesus saith unto him, Thou hast said: nevertheless I say unto you, Hereafter shall ye see the
Son of man sitting on the right hand of power, and
coming in the clouds of heaven. Then said they Luke 22. 70.
all, Art Thou then the Son of God? And He
said unto them, Ye say that I am.

Then the high priest rent his clothes, saying, He Matt. 26. 65
hath spoken blasphemy : what farther need have
we of witnesses? behold, now ye have heard His
blasphemy. What think ye? And they all con- Mark 14. 64.
demned Him to be guilty of death.

· And the men that held Jesus mocked Him, and Luke 22. 63.

Mark 14. 65.
Matt. 26. 67.
Luke 22. 65. smote Him. And some began to spit in His face. And others, when they had blindfolded Him, struck Him on the face with the palms of their hands, and asked Him, saying, Prophesy unto us, Thou

Luke 22. 65. Christ, Who is he that smote Thee? And many other things blasphemously spake they against Him.

Peter's second Denial.

S. Matt. xxvi. 71, 72 ; S. Mark xiv. 69, 70 ; S. Luke xxii. 58 ;
S. John xviii. 25.

John 18. 25.
Luke 22. 58.
Mark 14. 69. And Peter stood and warmed himself. And after a little while a maid saw him again, and began to say to them that stood by, This is *one* of them.

Matt. 26. 71. And he denied it again. And when he was gone out into the porch, another maid saw him, and said unto them that were there, This *fellow* was

Luke 22. 58. also with Jesus of Nazareth. And another saw him, and said, Thou art also of them. And Peter

John 18. 25. said, Man, I am not. They said therefore unto him, Art not thou also *one* of His disciples?

Matt. 26. 72. And again he denied with an oath, I do not know the man.

Peter's third Denial.

S. Matt. xxvi. 73-75 ; S. Mark xiv. 70-72 ; S. Luke xxii. 59-62 ;
S. John xviii. 26, 27.

Luke 22. 59. And about the space of one hour after, another confidently affirmed, saying, Of a truth this *fellow* also was with Him: for he is a Galilean. And

John 18. 26. Peter said, Man, I know not what thou sayest. One of the servants of the high priest, being *his* kinsman whose ear Peter cut off, saith, Did I not see thee in

Mark 14. 70. the garden with Him? And they that stood by said

Matt. 26. 73. again to Peter, Surely thou art one of them ; for thy speech bewrayeth thee. Then began he to curse

and to swear, *saying*, I know not this man of whom Mark 14. 71.
ye speak.

And immediately, while he yet spake, the second Luke 22. 60.
time the cock crew. And the Lord turned, and
looked upon Peter. And Peter remembered the
word of the Lord, how He had said unto him,
Before the cock crow twice, thou shalt deny Me Mark 14. 72.
thrice. And he went out, and when he thought Matt. 26. 75.
thereon, he wept bitterly.

Christ is led away to Pilate.

S. Matt. xxvii. 1, 2 ; S. Mark xv. 1 ; S. Luke xxiii. 1 ; S. John
xviii. 28.

And straightway in the morning the chief priests Mark 15. 1.
held a consultation with the elders and scribes
and the whole council against Jesus to put Him Matt. 27. 1.
to death : and when they had bound Him, the Luke 23. 1.
whole multitude of them arose and led Him away, Matt. 27. 2.
and delivered Him to Pontius Pilate the governor.

Judas hangs himself.

S. Matt. xxvii. 3–10 ; [Acts i. 18, 19].

Then Judas, which had betrayed Him, when he Matt. 27. 3.
saw that He was condemned, repented himself,
and brought again the thirty pieces of silver to the
chief priests and elders, saying, I have sinned, in
that I have betrayed the innocent blood. And
they said, What *is that* to us? see thou *to that.*
And he cast down the pieces of silver in the temple,
and departed, and went and hanged himself.

And the chief priests took the silver pieces, and
said, It is not lawful for to put them into the
treasury, because it is the price of blood. And
they took counsel, and bought with them the

potter's field, to bury strangers in. Wherefore that
field was called, The field of blood, unto this day.
Then was fulfilled that which was spoken by Jeremy
Zech. 11. 12. the prophet, saying, **And they took the thirty**
13.   **pieces of silver, the price of Him that was valued,**
whom they of the children of Israel did value;
and gave them for the potter's field, as the Lord
appointed me.

(d.) *Christ before Pilate.*

S. Matt. xxvii. 11–14 ; S. Mark xv. 2–5 ; S. Luke xxiii. 2–7 ;
S. John xviii. 28–38.

John 18. 28.   Then led they Jesus from Caiaphas, unto the
hall of judgment: and it was early; and they
themselves went not into the judgment hall, lest
they should be defiled, but that they might eat the
passover.

Pilate then went out unto them, and said, What
accusation bring ye against this man? They
answered and said unto him, If He were not a
malefactor, we would not have delivered Him up
unto thee. Then said Pilate unto them, Take ye
Him, and judge Him according to your law. The
Jews therefore said unto him, It is not lawful for
us to put any man to death : that the saying of
Jesus might be fulfilled, which He spake, signify-
Matt. 20. 19. ing what death He should die.

Luke 23. 2.   And they began to accuse Him, saying, We found
this *fellow* perverting the nation, and forbidding to
give tribute to Cæsar, saying that He Himself is
Christ a king.

John 18. 33.   Then Pilate entered into the judgment hall
Matt. 27. 11. again, and called Jesus : and Jesus stood before
the governor : and the governor asked Him, saying,
John 18. 34. Art Thou the King of the Jews? Jesus answered
him, Sayest thou this thing of thyself, or did others
tell it thee of Me? Pilate answered, Am I a Jew?

Thine own nation and the chief priests have delivered Thee unto me: what hast Thou done?
Jesus answered, My kingdom is not of this world:
if My kingdom were of this world, then would My
servants fight, that I should not be delivered to the
Jews: but now is My kingdom not from hence.
Pilate therefore said unto Him, Art Thou a king
then? Jesus answered, Thou sayest that I am a
king. To this end was I born, and for this cause
came I into the world, that I should bear witness
unto the truth. Every one that is of the truth
heareth My voice. Pilate saith unto Him, What is
truth?

And when he had said this, he went out again
unto the Jews, and saith unto them, I find in Him
no fault *at all*.

And the chief priests accused Him of many Mark 15. 3.
things: but He answered nothing. And Pilate
asked Him again, saying, Answerest Thou nothing? behold how many things they witness
against Thee. But Jesus yet answered nothing;
so that Pilate marvelled. And they were the Luke 23. 5.
more fierce, saying, He stirreth up the people,
teaching throughout all Jewry, beginning from
Galilee to this place. When Pilate heard of
Galilee, he asked whether the man were a Galilæan. And as soon as he knew that He belonged
unto Herod's jurisdiction, he sent Him to Herod,
who himself also was at Jerusalem at that time.

(e.) *Christ before Herod.*

S. Luke xxiii. 8-12.

And when Herod saw Jesus, he was exceeding Luke 23. 8.
glad: for he was desirous to see Him of a long
season, because he had heard many things of Him;
and he hoped to have seen some miracle done by
Him. Then he questioned with Him in many words;

but He answered him nothing. And the chief priests and scribes stood and vehemently accused Him. And Herod with his men of war set Him at nought, and mocked *Him*, and arrayed Him in a gorgeous robe, and sent Him again to Pilate.

And the same day Pilate and Herod were made friends together : for before they were at enmity between themselves.

(*f.*) *Christ again before Pilate.*

S. Matt. xxvii. 15–32 ; S. Mark xv. 6–21 ; S. Luke xxiii. 13–25 ; S. John xviii. 39–xix. 16.

Luke 23. 13.   And Pilate, when he had called together the chief priests and the rulers and the people, said unto them, Ye have brought this man unto me, as one that perverteth the people : and, behold, I, having examined *Him* before you, have found no fault in this man touching those things whereof ye accuse Him : no, nor yet Herod : for I sent you to him ; and, lo, nothing worthy of death is done unto Him. I will therefore chastise Him, and release *Him*.

Matt. 27. 15.   Now at that feast the governor was wont to release unto the people one prisoner, whomsover they desired.   And they had then a notable prisoner Mark 15. 7. called Barabbas, *which lay* bound with them that had made insurrection with him, who had committed murder in the insurrection. And the multitude crying aloud began to desire *him to do* as he had ever done unto them.   But Pilate answered Matt. 27. 17. them, saying, Whom will ye that I release unto you ? Mark 15. 10. Barabbas, or Jesus which is called Christ ? For he knew that the chief priests had delivered Him for envy.

Matt. 27. 19.   When he was set down on the judgment seat, his wife sent unto him, saying, Have thou nothing to do with that just man : for I have suffered many things this day in a dream because of Him.

But the chief priests and elders persuaded the multitude that they should ask Barabbas, and destroy Jesus. The governor answered and said unto them, Whether of the twain will ye that I release unto you? They said, Barabbas. And Pilate, Mark 15. 12. willing to release Jesus, answered and said unto them, What will ye then that I shall do *unto Him* whom ye call the King of the Jews? And they cried out again, Crucify Him. And he said unto Luke 23. 22. them the third time, Why, what evil hath He done? I have found no cause of death in Him : I will therefore chastise Him, and let *Him* go. And they were instant with loud voices, requiring that He might be crucified. And the voices of them and of the chief priests prevailed.

When Pilate saw that he could prevail nothing, Matt. 27. 24. but *that* rather a tumult was made, he took water, and washed *his* hands before the multitude, saying, I am innocent of the blood of this just person : see ye to it. Then answered all the people, and said, His blood *be* on us, and on our children.

And *so* Pilate, willing to content the people, gave Mark 15. 15. sentence that it should be as they required. And Luke 23. 24. he released unto them him that for sedition and murder was cast into prison, whom they had desired ; but he delivered Jesus, when he had scourged Mark 15. 15. *Him*, to their will, to be crucified.

Then the soldiers of the governor took Jesus into Matt. 27. 27. the common hall, called Prætorium ; and gathered unto Him the whole band *of soldiers.* And they stripped Him, and put on Him a purple robe. And when they had platted a crown of thorns, they put *it* upon His head, and a reed in His right hand : and they bowed the knee before Him, and mocked Him, saying, Hail, King of the Jews ! And they spit upon Him, and took the reed, and smote Him on the head.

Pilate therefore went forth again, and saith unto John 19. 4.

them, Behold, I bring Him forth to you, that ye may know that I find no fault in Him. Then came Jesus forth, wearing the crown of thorns, and the purple robe. And *Pilate* saith unto them, Behold the man !

When the chief priests therefore and officers saw Him, they cried out, Crucify *Him*, crucify *Him*. Pilate saith unto them, Take ye Him, and crucify *Him :* for I find no fault in Him. The Jews answered him, We have a law, and by our law He ought to die, because He made Himself the Son of God.

When Pilate therefore heard that saying, he was the more afraid ; and went again into the judgment hall, and saith unto Jesus, Whence art Thou ? But Jesus gave him no answer. Then saith Pilate unto Him, Speakest Thou not unto me ? knowest Thou not that I have power to crucify Thee, and have power to release Thee ? Jesus answered, Thou couldest have no power *at all* against Me, except it were given thee from above : therefore he that delivered Me unto thee hath the greater sin. And from thenceforth Pilate sought to release Him : but the Jews cried out, saying, If thou let this man go, thou art not Cæsar's friend : whosoever maketh himself a king speaketh against Cæsar.

When Pilate therefore heard that saying, he brought Jesus forth, and sat down in the judgment seat in a place that is called the Pavement, but in the Hebrew, Gabbatha. And it was the preparation of the passover, and about the sixth hour : and he saith unto the Jews, Behold your King ! But they cried out, Away with *Him*, away with *Him*, crucify Him. Pilate saith unto them, Shall I crucify your King ? The chief priests answered, We have no king but Cæsar.

Then delivered he Him therefore to be crucified.

Mark 15 20. And when they had mocked Him, they took off

the purple robe from Him, and put his own clothes on Him, and led Him out to crucify Him.

Christ bearing the Cross.

S. Matt. xxvii. 32 ; S. Mark xv. 21 ; S. Luke xxiii. 26–32 ;
S. John xix. 17.

And as they came out, they found a man of Matt. 27. 32.
Cyrene, Simon by name, the father of Alexander Mark 15. 21.
and Rufus, coming out of the country, and on him
they laid the cross, that he might bear it after Luke 23. 26.
Jesus. And there followed Him a great company
of people, and of women, which also bewailed and
lamented Him.

But Jesus turning unto them said, Daughters of
Jerusalem, weep not for Me, but weep for yourselves, and for your children. For, behold, the days
are coming, in the which they shall say, Blessed *are*
the barren, and the wombs that never bare, and
the paps which never gave suck. **Then shall they** Hos. 10. 8.
**begin to say to the mountains, Fall on us; and to
the hills, Cover us.** For if they do these things in
a green tree, what shall be done in the dry ?

And there were also two other, malefactors, led
with Him to be put to death.

XXXI. *THE CRUCIFIXION.*

S. Matt. xxvii. 33–44 ; S. Mark xv. 22–32 ; S. Luke xxiii. 33–43 ;
S. John xix. 17–27.

And when they were come to the place, which is Luke 23. 33.
called Calvary, that is to say, being interpreted,
the place of a skull, which is called in the Hebrew John 19. 17.
Golgotha, they gave Him to drink wine mingled Mark 15. 23.
with myrrh : and when He had tasted *thereof*, He Matt. 27. 34.
would not drink. And there they crucified Him, Luke 23. 33.
and the malefactors, one on the right hand, and

John 19. 18. the other on the left, on either side one, and Jesus
Mark 15. 28. in the midst. And the scripture was fulfilled,
Isa. 53. 12. which saith, **And He was numbered with the transgressors.**

Luke 23. 34. Then said Jesus, 𝔉𝔞𝔱𝔥𝔢𝔯, 𝔣𝔬𝔯𝔤𝔦𝔟𝔢 𝔱𝔥𝔢𝔪, 𝔣𝔬𝔯 𝔱𝔥𝔢𝔢 𝔨𝔫𝔬𝔴 𝔫𝔬𝔱 𝔴𝔥𝔞𝔱 𝔱𝔥𝔢𝔢 𝔡𝔬.

John 19. 19. And Pilate wrote a title, and put it over His head on the cross. And the writing was, JESUS OF NAZARETH THE KING OF THE JEWS. This title then read many of the Jews: for the place where Jesus was crucified was nigh to the city: and it was written in Hebrew, *and* Greek, *and* Latin. Then said the chief priests of the Jews to Pilate, Write not, The King of the Jews; but that He said, I am King of the Jews. Pilate answered, What I have written, I have written.

Then the soldiers, when they had crucified Jesus, took His garments, and made four parts, to every soldier a part; and also *His* coat: now the coat was without seam, woven from the top throughout. They said therefore among themselves, Let us not rend it, but cast lots for it whose it shall be: that
Ps. 22. 18. the scripture might be fulfilled, which saith, **They parted My raiment among them, and for My vesture they did cast lots.** These things therefore
Matt. 27. 36. the soldiers did. And sitting down they watched Him there.

Luke 23. 35. And the people stood beholding. And they that
Matt. 27. 39. passed by reviled Him, wagging their heads, and saying, Ah, Thou that destroyest the temple, and buildest it in three days, save Thyself. If Thou be the Son of God, come down from the cross. Likewise also the chief priests mocking *Him*, with the scribes and elders, said, He saved others; Himself
Luke 23. 35. He cannot save. Let Him save Himself, if He be
Matt. 27. 42. Christ, the chosen of God. If He be the King of Israel, let Him now come down from the cross, and
Ps. 22. 8. we will believe Him. **He trusted in God; let Him**

deliver Him now, if He will have Him : for He said, I am the Son of God.

And the soldiers also mocked Him, coming to Him, and offering Him vinegar, and saying, If Thou be the King of the Jews, save Thyself. Luke 23. 36.

The Penitent Malefactor.

S. Luke xxiii. 39–43.

And one of the malefactors which were hanged railed on Him, saying, If Thou be the Christ, save Thyself and us. But the other answering rebuked him, saying, Dost not thou fear God, seeing thou art in the same condemnation ? And we indeed justly ; for we receive the due reward of our deeds : but this man hath done nothing amiss. And he said unto Jesus, Lord, remember me when Thou comest into Thy kingdom. And Jesus said unto him, 𝔙𝔢𝔯𝔦𝔩𝔶 𝔌 𝔰𝔞𝔶 𝔲𝔫𝔱𝔬 𝔱𝔥𝔢𝔢, 𝔗𝔬-𝔡𝔞𝔶 𝔰𝔥𝔞𝔩𝔱 𝔱𝔥𝔬𝔲 𝔟𝔢 𝔴𝔦𝔱𝔥 𝔐𝔢 𝔦𝔫 𝔭𝔞𝔯𝔞𝔡𝔦𝔰𝔢. Luke 23. 39.

Christ commends His Mother to S. John.

S. John xix. 25–27.

Now there stood by the cross of Jesus His mother, and His mother's sister, Mary the *wife* of Cleophas, and Mary Magdalene. When Jesus therefore saw His mother, and the disciple standing by, whom He loved, He saith unto His mother, 𝔚oman, 𝔟𝔢𝔥𝔬𝔩𝔡 𝔱𝔥𝔶 𝔰𝔬𝔫 ! Then saith He to the disciple, 𝔅𝔢𝔥𝔬𝔩𝔡 𝔱𝔥𝔶 𝔪𝔬𝔱𝔥𝔢𝔯 ! And from that hour that disciple took her unto his own *home*. John 9. 25.

Christ dieth.

S. Matt. xxvii. 45–53 ; S. Mark xv. 33–38 ; S. Luke xxiii. 44–46 ;
S. John xix. 28–30.

Matt. 27. 45. Now from the sixth hour there was darkness over all the land unto the ninth hour. And about the ninth hour Jesus cried with a loud voice, saying,

Ps. 22. 1. Eli, Eli, lama sabachthani ! that is to say, **My God, my God, why hast Thou forsaken Me ?** Some of them that stood there, when they heard *that*, said, This *man* calleth for Elias.

John 19. 28. After this, Jesus knowing that all things were now accomplished, that the scripture might be fulfilled, saith, **I thirst.** Now there was set a vessel full

Matt. 27. 48. of vinegar : and straightway one of them ran, and took a spunge, and filled *it* with vinegar, and put it on a reed, and gave Him to drink. The rest said, Let be, let us see whether Elias will come to save Him.

John 19. 30. When Jesus therefore had received the vinegar, He
Luke 23. 46. said, **It is finished.** And when He had cried again with a loud voice, He said, **Father, into Thy hands**
John 19. 30. **I commend My spirit:** and having said thus, He
Matt. 27. 50. bowed His head, and yielded up the ghost.

Luke 23. 45.
Matt. 27. 51. And the sun was darkened ; and, behold, the veil of the temple was rent in twain from the top to the bottom ; and the earth did quake, and the rocks rent ; and the graves were opened ; and many bodies of the saints which slept arose, and came out of the graves after His resurrection, and went into the holy city, and appeared unto many.

Impressions of the Crucifixion.

S. Matt. xxvii. 54–56 ; S. Mark xv. 39–41 ; S. Luke xxiii. 47–49.

Matt. 27. 54. Now when the centurion, and they that were with him, watching Jesus, saw the earthquake, and

those things that were done, and that He so cried Mark 25 39.
out, and gave up the ghost, they feared greatly; Matt. 27. 54.
and he glorified God, saying, Certainly this was a Luke 23. 47.
righteous man: truly this man was the Son of God. Mark 15. 39.

And all the people that came together to that Luke 23. 48.
sight, beholding the things which were done, smote
their breasts and returned.

And all His acquaintance, and many women Matt. 27. 55
were there beholding afar off, which followed Jesus
from Galilee, ministering unto Him : among which
was Mary Magdalene, and Mary the mother of Mark 15. 40.
James the less and of Joses, and Salome the Matt. 27 56.
mother of Zebedee's children; and many other Mark 15. 41.
women which came up with Him unto Jerusalem.

His Side is pierced.

S. John xix. 31–37.

The Jews therefore, because it was the prepa- John 19. 31.
ration, that the bodies should not remain upon the
cross on the sabbath day, (for that sabbath day
was an high day,) besought Pilate that their legs
might be broken, and *that* they might be taken
away. Then came the soldiers, and brake the legs
of the first, and of the other which was crucified
with Him. But when they came to Jesus, and
saw that He was dead already, they brake not His
legs : but one of the soldiers with a spear pierced
His side, and forthwith came there out blood and
water. And he that saw *it* bare record, and his
record is true : and he knoweth that he saith true,
that ye might believe. For these things were
done, that the scripture should be fulfilled, **A bone** Ex. 12. 46.
of Him shall not be broken. And another scrip-
ture saith, **They shall look on Him whom they** Zech. 12. 10.
pierced.

𝔈aster 𝔈be.

XXXII. *CHRIST IS BURIED.*

S. Matt. xxvii. 57–61 ; S. Mark xv. 42–47 ; S. Luke xxiii. 50–56 ;
S. John xix. 38–42.

Mark 15. 42. And now when the even was come, because it was the preparation, that is, the day before the
Matt. 27. 57. sabbath, there came a rich man of Arimathæa,
Isa. 53. 9.
Mark 15. 43. named Joseph, an honourable counsellor, which also waited for the kingdom of God, who also him-
John 19. 38. self was Jesus' disciple, but secretly for fear of the
Luke 23. 50. Jews : *and he was* a good man, and a just: (the same had not consented to the counsel and deed
Mark 15. 43. of them ;) this *man* went in boldly unto Pilate, and craved the body of Jesus. And Pilate marvelled if He were already dead ; and calling *unto him* the centurion, he asked him whether He had been any while dead. And when he knew it of the centurion, he gave the body to Joseph.

John 19. 39. And there came also Nicodemus, which at the first came to Jesus by night, and brought a mixture of myrrh and aloes, about an hundred pound *weight*. Then took they the body of Jesus down, and wound it in linen clothes with spices, as the manner of the Jews is to bury.

Now in the place where He was crucified there was a garden ; and in the garden a new sepulchre,
Mark 15. 46. which was hewn out of a rock, wherein was never
Luke 23. 53.
John 19. 42. man yet laid. There laid they Jesus therefore because of the Jews' preparation *day ;* for the
Matt. 27. 60. sepulchre was nigh at hand ; and rolled a great stone to the door of the sepulchre, and departed.

Luke 23. 55. And the women also, which came with Him from
Mark 15. 47. Galilee, Mary Magdalene, and Mary the mother of
Luke 23. 55. Joses, followed after, and beheld the sepulchre, and how His body was laid. And they returned

and prepared spices and ointments; and rested the sabbath day according to the commandment.

His Sepulchre is sealed and watched.

S. Matt. xxvii. 62-66.

Now the next day, that followed the day of the preparation, the chief priests and Pharisees came together unto Pilate, saying, Sir, we remember that that deceiver said, while He was yet alive, After three days I will rise again. Command therefore that the sepulchre be made sure until the third day, lest His disciples come by night, and steal Him away, and say unto the people, He is risen from the dead: so the last error shall be worse than the first. Pilate said unto them, Ye have a watch: go your way, make *it* as sure as ye can.

So they went, and made the sepulchre sure, sealing the stone, and setting a watch.

Matt. 27. 62.

II. **The forty Days.**

Easter Day.

I. *THE RESURRECTION.*

The Women set out to the Sepulchre.

S. Matt. xxviii. 1 ; S. Mark xvi. 1 ; S. Luke xxiv. 1 ; S. John xx. 1.

Matt. 28. 1. In the end of the sabbath, when it was yet dark, as it began to dawn towards the first *day* of the
Mark 16. 1. week, came Mary Magdalene, and Mary the *mother* of James, and Salome, and certain others with
Luke 24. 1. them to see the sepulchre; bringing the spices
Mark 16. 1. which they had prepared, that they might come and anoint Him.

Descent of the Angel. The Earthquake. Terror (and Departure ?) of the Guard.

S. Matt. xxviii. 2-4.

Matt. 28. 2. And, behold, there was a great earthquake; for the angel of the Lord descended from heaven, and came and rolled back the stone from the door, and sat upon it. His countenance was like lightning, and his raiment white as snow: and for fear of him the keepers did shake, and became as dead *men.*

The Arrival of the Women.

S. Mark xvi. 2-4 ; S. Luke xxiv. 1, 2 ; S. John xx. 1.

And very early in the morning, the first *day* of Mark 16. 2.
the week, they [*the women*] came unto the sepulchre at the rising of the sun. And they said
among themselves, Who shall roll us away the
stone from the door of the sepulchre? And when
they looked, they saw that the stone was rolled
away : for it was very great.

Mary Magdalene runs back to tell Peter and John.

S. John xx. 1, 2.

Mary Magdalene seeth the stone taken away John 20. 1.
from the sepulchre. Then she runneth, and cometh
to Simon Peter, and to the other disciple, whom
Jesus loved.

The Women enter the Sepulchre, and see the Angel. They return.

S. Matt. xxviii. 5-8 ; S. Mark xvi. 5-8 ; S. Luke xxiv. 4-9.

And they [*the other women*] entered into the Luke 24. 3.
sepulchre, and found not the body of the Lord
Jesus. And it came to pass, as they were much
perplexed thereabout, behold, they saw a young man Mark 16. 5.
sitting on the right side, clothed in a long white
garment; and they were affrighted. And as they Luke 24. 5.
were afraid, and bowed down *their* faces to the
earth, the angel answered and said unto the women, Matt. 28. 5.
Fear not ye : for I know that ye seek Jesus of
Nazareth, which was crucified. Why seek ye the Luke 24. 5.
living among the dead? He is not here : for He is Matt. 28. 6.
risen, as He said. Come, see the place where the

Lord lay. And go quickly, and tell His disciples and Peter that He is risen from the dead; and, behold, He goeth before you into Galilee; there shall ye see Him: lo, I have told you. Remember how He spake unto you when He was yet in Galilee, saying, The Son of man must be delivered into the hands of sinful men, and be crucified, and the third day rise again.

And they remembered His words, and they went out quickly, and fled from the sepulchre with fear and great joy; for they trembled and were amazed: neither said they any thing to any *man;* for they were afraid: and did run to bring His disciples word.

By another Road, Peter and John arrive at the Sepulchre :
Mary Magdalene following them.

S. Luke xxiv. 12 ; S. John xx. 1–11.

Mary Magdalene cometh to Simon Peter, and to the disciple whom Jesus loved, and saith unto them, They have taken away the Lord out of the sepulchre, and we know not where they have laid Him.

Peter therefore went forth, and that other disciple, and came to the sepulchre. So they ran both together: and the other disciple did outrun Peter, and came first to the sepulchre. And he stooping down, *and looking in,* saw the linen clothes lying; yet went he not in. Then cometh Simon Peter following him, and went into the sepulchre, and seeth the linen clothes lie, and the napkin, that was about His head, not lying with the linen clothes, but wrapped together in a place by itself. And *he* departed, wondering in himself at that which was come to pass.

Then went in also that other disciple, which came first to the sepulchre, and he saw, and believed. For as yet they knew not the scripture, that He must rise again from the dead. Then the disciples went away again unto their own home.

Mary Magdalene remains at the Sepulchre: Christ appears first to her.

S. Mark xvi. 9–11 ; S. John xx. 11–18.

But Mary stood at the sepulchre weeping: and John 20. 11. as she wept, she stooped down, *and looked* into the sepulchre, and seeth two angels in white sitting, the one at the head, and the other at the feet, where the body of Jesus had lain. And they say unto her, Woman, why weepest thou? She saith unto them, Because they have taken away my Lord, and I know not where they have laid Him.

And when she had thus said, she turned herself back, and saw Jesus standing, and knew not that it was Jesus. Jesus saith unto her, Woman, why weepest thou? whom seekest thou? She, supposing Him to be the gardener, saith unto Him, Sir, if Thou have borne Him hence, tell me where Thou hast laid Him, and I will take Him away. Jesus saith unto her, Mary. She turned herself, and saith unto Him, Rabboni ; which is to say, Master. Jesus saith unto her, Touch Me not ; for I am not yet ascended to My Father : but go to My brethren, and say unto them, I ascend unto My Father, and your Father ; and *to* My God, and your God.

Mary Magdalene came and told the disciples, as Mark 16. 10. they mourned and wept, that she had seen the John 20. 18. Lord, and *that* He had spoken these things unto her. And they, when they had heard that He was Mark 16. 11. alive, and had been seen of her, believed not.

Christ appears to the other Women on their way to the City.

S. Matt. xxviii. 9, 10.

Matt. 28. 9.   And as they [*the other women*] went to tell His disciples, behold, Jesus met them, saying, All hail. And they came and held Him by the feet, and worshipped Him. Then said Jesus unto them, Be not afraid : go tell My brethren that they go into Galilee, and there shall they see Me.

The Women (Mary Magdalene included) bring their Tidings to the Apostles.

S. Matt. xxviii. 8 ; S. Mark xvi. 10, 11 ; S. Luke xxiv. 9–11 ; S. John xx. 18.

Luke 24. 9.   And [*they*] returned from the sepulchre, and told all these things unto the eleven, and to all the rest.

It was Mary Magdalene, and Joanna, and Mary *the mother* of James, and other *women that were* with them, which told these things unto the apostles. And their words seemed to them as idle tales, and they believed them not.

II.   *REPORT OF THE GUARD.*

S. Matt. xxviii. 11–15.

Matt. 28. 11.   Now when they were going, behold, some of the watch came into the city, and shewed unto the chief priests all the things that were done. And when they were assembled with the elders, and had taken counsel, they gave large money unto the soldiers, saying, Say ye, His disciples came by night, and stole Him *away* while we slept. And if this come to the governor's ears, we will persuade him, and secure you.

So they took the money, and did as they were

taught: and this saying is commonly reported among the Jews until this day.

III. *CHRIST APPEARS TO THE DISCIPLES THAT WENT TO EMMAUS.*

S. Mark xvi. 12, 13; S. Luke xxiv. 13-35.

After that He appeared in another form unto two of them, as they walked, and went into the country that same day to a village called Emmaus, which was from Jerusalem *about* threescore furlongs. Mark 16. 12 Luke 24. 13.

And they talked together of all these things which had happened. And it came to pass, that, while they communed *together* and reasoned, Jesus Himself drew near, and went with them. But their eyes were holden that they should not know Him.

And He said unto them, What manner of communications *are* these that ye have one to another, as ye walk, and are sad? And the one of them, whose name was Cleopas, answering said unto Him, Art thou only a stranger in Jerusalem, and hast not heard the things which are come to pass there in these days? And He said unto them, What things? And they said unto Him, Concerning Jesus of Nazareth, which was a prophet mighty in deed and word before God and all the people: and how the chief priests and our rulers delivered Him to be condemned to death, and have crucified Him. But we trusted that it had been He which should have redeemed Israel: and beside all this, to-day is the third day since these things were done. Yea, and certain women also of our company made us astonished, which were early at the sepulchre; and when they found not His body, they came, saying, that they had also seen a vision of angels, which said that He was alive. And certain of them which were with us went to the sepulchre, and found *it* even so as the women had said: but Him they saw not.

Then said He unto them, O fools, and slow of heart to believe all that the prophets have spoken: ought not Christ to have suffered these things, and to enter into His glory? And beginning at Moses and all the prophets, He expounded to them in all the scriptures the things concerning Himself.

And they drew nigh unto the village, whither they went: and He made as though He would have gone further. But they constrained Him, saying, Abide with us: for it is toward evening, and the day is far spent. And He went in to tarry with them. And it came to pass, as He sat at meat with them, He took bread, and blessed *it*, and brake, and gave to them. And their eyes were opened, and they knew Him; and He vanished out of their sight. And they said one to another, Did not our heart burn within us, while He talked with us by the way, and while He opened to us the scriptures?

And they rose up the same hour, and returned to Jerusalem, and found the eleven gathered together, and them that were with them, saying, The Lord is risen indeed, and hath appeared to Simon. And they told what things *were done* in the way, and how He was known of them in breaking of bread.

Mark 26. 1.   Neither believed they them.

IV.   *CHRIST APPEARS TO THE APOSTLES. THOMAS ABSENT.*

S. Mark xvi. 14 ; S. Luke xxiv. 36–43 ; S. John xx. 19–23.

Luke 24. 36.   And as they thus spake, the same day at evening,
John 20. 19.   being the first *day* of the week, when the doors were shut, when the disciples were assembled for

fear of the Jews, came Jesus and stood in the midst, as they sat at meat; and saith unto them, Peace *be* unto you.

But they were terrified and affrighted, and sup- Luke 24. 37. posed that they had seen a spirit. And He said unto them, Why are ye troubled? and why do thoughts arise in your hearts? Behold My hands and My feet, that it is I Myself: handle Me, and see; for a spirit hath not flesh and bones, as ye see Me have. And when He had thus spoken, He shewed them *His* hands, and *His* feet, and His John 20. 20. side. And while they yet believed not for joy, and Luke 24. 41. wondered, He said unto them, Have ye here any meat? And they gave Him a piece of a broiled fish, and of a honeycomb. And He took *it*, and did eat before them. Then were the disciples glad, when John 20. 20. they saw the Lord. And [*He*] upbraided them Mark 16. 14. with their unbelief and hardness of heart, because they believed not them which had seen Him after He was risen.

Then saith Jesus to them again, Peace *be* unto John 20. 21. you: as *My* Father hath sent Me, even so send I you. And when He had said this, He breathed on *them*, and saith unto them, Receive ye the Holy Ghost: whose soever sins ye remit, they are re-mitted unto them; *and* whose soever *sins* ye retain, they are retained.

Incredulity of Thomas.

S. John xx. 24-25.

But Thomas, one of the twelve, called Didymus, John 20. 24. was not with them when Jesus came. The other disciples therefore said unto him, We have seen the Lord. But he said unto them, Except I shall see in His hands the print of the nails, and put my finger into the print of the nails, and thrust my hand into His side, I will not believe.

𝕿𝖍𝖊 𝕾𝖊𝖈𝖔𝖓𝖉 𝕷𝖔𝖗𝖉'𝖘 𝕯𝖆𝖞.

V. *CHRIST APPEARS TO THE APOSTLES. THOMAS PRESENT.*

S. John xx. 26–31.

John 20. 26. And after eight days again His disciples were within, and Thomas with them : *then* came Jesus, the doors being shut, and stood in the midst, and said, Peace *be* unto you. Then saith He to Thomas, Reach hither thy finger, and behold My hands ; and reach hither thy hand, and thrust *it* into My side : and be not faithless, but believing. And Thomas answered and said unto Him, My Lord and my God. Jesus saith unto him, Thomas, because thou hast seen Me, thou hast believed : blessed *are* they that have not seen, and *yet* have believed.

And many other signs truly did Jesus in the presence of His disciples, which are not written in this book : but these are written, that ye might believe that Jesus is the Christ, the Son of God ; and that believing ye might have life through His name.

𝕯𝖚𝖗𝖎𝖓𝖌 𝖙𝖍𝖊 𝖋𝖔𝖗𝖙𝖞 𝕯𝖆𝖞𝖘.

VI. *CHRIST APPEARS TO SEVEN DIS- CIPLES AT THE SEA OF TIBERIAS.*

S. John xxi. 1–24.

John 21. 1. After these things Jesus shewed Himself to the disciples at the sea of Tiberias ; and on this wise shewed He *Himself*.

There were together Simon Peter, and Thomas called Didymus, and Nathanael of Cana in Galilee, and the *sons* of Zebedee, and two other of His disciples. Simon Peter saith unto them, I go a fishing. They say unto him, We also go with thee. They went forth, and entered into a ship immediately; and that night they caught nothing. But when morning was now come, Jesus stood on the shore: but the disciples knew not that it was Jesus. Then Jesus saith unto them, Children, have ye any meat? They answered Him, No. And He saith unto them, Cast the net on the right side of the ship, and ye shall find. They cast therefore, and now they were not able to draw it for the multitude of fishes. Therefore that disciple whom Jesus loved saith unto Peter, It is the Lord. Now when Simon Peter heard that it was the Lord, he girt *his* fisher's coat *unto him*, (for he was naked,) and did cast himself into the sea. And the other disciples came in a little ship; (for they were not far from land, but as it were two hundred cubits,) dragging the net with fishes. As soon then as they were come to land, they saw a fire of coals there, and fish laid thereon, and bread. Jesus saith unto them, Bring of the fish which ye have now caught. Simon Peter went up, and drew the net to land full of great fishes, an hundred and fifty and three: and for all there were so many, yet was not the net broken. Jesus saith unto them, Come *and* dine. And none of the disciples durst ask Him, Who art Thou? knowing that it was the Lord. Jesus then cometh, and taketh bread, and giveth them, and fish likewise. This is now the third time that Jesus shewed Himself to His disciples, after that He was risen from the dead.

So when they had dined, Jesus saith to Simon Peter, Simon, *son* of Jonas, lovest thou Me more than these? He saith unto Him, Yea, Lord; Thou knowest that I love Thee. He saith unto him, Feed My lambs. He saith to him again the second time, Simon, *son* of Jonas, lovest thou Me? He saith unto Him, Yea, Lord; Thou knowest that I love Thee. He saith unto him, Feed My sheep. He saith unto him the third time, Simon, *son* of Jonas, lovest thou Me? Peter was grieved because He said unto him the third time, Lovest thou Me? And he said unto Him, Lord, Thou knowest all things, Thou knowest that I love Thee. Jesus saith unto him, Feed My sheep. Verily, verily, I say unto thee, When thou wast young, thou girdest thyself, and walkedst whither thou wouldest: but when thou shalt be old, thou shalt stretch forth thy hands, and another shall gird thee, and carry *thee* whither thou wouldest not. This spake He, signifying by what death he should glorify God. And when He had spoken this, He saith unto him, Follow Me.

Then Peter, turning about, seeth the disciple whom Jesus loved following; which also leaned on His breast at supper, and said, Lord, which is he that betrayeth Thee? Peter seeing him saith to Jesus, Lord, and what *shall* this man *do?* Jesus saith unto him, If I will that he tarry till I come, what *is that* to thee? follow thou Me. Then went this saying abroad among the brethren, that that disciple should not die: yet Jesus said not unto him, He shall not die; but, If I will that he tarry till I come, what *is that* to thee?

This is the disciple which testifieth of these things, and wrote these things: and we know that his testimony is true.

VII. *CHRIST APPEARS TO THE APOSTLES, AND TO "ABOVE FIVE HUNDRED BRETHREN AT ONCE."*

S. Matt. xxviii. 16–20; S. Mark xvi. 15–18; [1 Cor. xv. 6.]

Matt. 28. 16.   Then the eleven disciples went away into Galilee, into a mountain where Jesus had appointed them.

And when they saw Him, they worshipped Him : but some doubted. And Jesus came and spake unto them, saying, All power is given unto Me in heaven and in earth. Go ye therefore into all the world, and teach all nations, baptizing them in the name of the Father, and of the Son, and of the Holy Ghost : teaching them to observe all things whatsoever I have commanded you. He that believeth and is baptized shall be saved ; but he that believeth not shall be damned. And these signs shall follow them that believe ; In My Name shall they cast out devils ; they shall speak with new tongues ; they shall take up serpents ; and if they drink any deadly thing, it shall not hurt them ; they shall lay hands on the sick, and they shall recover. And, lo, I am with you alway, *even* unto the end of the world. Amen.

Mark 16. 15.

Matt. 28. 19.

Mark. 16. 16.

Matt. 28. 20.

𝔥𝔬𝔩𝔶 𝔗𝔥𝔲𝔯𝔰𝔡𝔞𝔶.

VIII. *THE ASCENSION, IN THE PRESENCE "OF ALL THE APOSTLES."*

S. Mark xvi. 19, 20 ; S. Luke xxiv. 44–53 ; [Acts i. 3–12 ; 1 Cor. xv. 7.]

The Farewell Charge.

S. Luke xxiv. 44–49 ; [Acts i. 4–8.]

And being assembled together with them, He said unto them, These *are* the words which I spake unto you, while I was yet with you, that all things must be fulfilled, which were written in the law of Moses, and *in* the prophets, and *in* the psalms, concerning Me. Then opened He their understanding, that they might understand the scriptures, and said unto them, Thus it is written, and thus it behoved Christ to suffer, and to rise from the dead

Acts 1. 4.

Luke 24. 44.

the third day : and that repentance and remission of sins should be preached in His name among all nations, beginning at Jerusalem. And ye are witnesses of these things. And, behold, I send the promise of My Father upon you : but tarry ye in the city of Jerusalem, until ye be endued with

Acts. 1. 5. power from on high. For John truly baptized with water ; but ye shall be baptized with the Holy Ghost not many days hence.

When they therefore were come together, they asked of Him, saying, Lord, wilt Thou at this time restore again the kingdom to Israel ? And He said unto them, It is not for you to know the times or the seasons, which the Father hath put in His own power. But ye shall receive power, after that the Holy Ghost is come upon you : and ye shall be witnesses unto Me both in Jerusalem, and in all Judæa, and in Samaria, and unto the uttermost part of the earth.

The Ascension.

S. Mark xvi. 19–20 ; S. Luke 50–52 ; [Acts i. 9–12.]

Mark 16. 19 So then after the Lord had spoken unto them,

Luke 24. 50. He led them out as far as to Bethany, and He lifted up His hands, and blessed them. And it came to pass, while He blessed them, while they beheld, He

Mark 16. 19. was parted from them, and carried up into heaven,

Acts 1. 9. and sat on the right hand of God ; and a cloud received Him out of their sight.

The Message of Angels.

[Acts i. 10, 11.]

Acts 1. 10. And while they looked stedfastly toward heaven as He went up, behold, two men stood by them in white apparel ; which also said, Ye men of Galilee,

why stand ye gazing up into heaven? This same
Jesus, which is taken up from you into heaven,
shall so come in like manner as ye have seen Him
go into heaven.

Christ's Return into Heaven.

S. Mark xvi. 19 ; S. Luke xxiv. 51 ; [Dan. vii. 13, 14.]

So then He was received up into heaven. *Mark 16. 19.*

And, behold, *one* like the Son of man came with *Dan. 7. 13.*
the clouds of heaven, and came to the Ancient of
days, and they brought Him near before Him. And
there was given Him dominion, and glory, and a
kingdom, that all people, nations, and languages,
should serve Him: His dominion *is* an everlasting
dominion, which shall not pass away, and His
kingdom *that* which shall not be destroyed.

And [*He*] sat on the right hand of God. *Mark 16. 19.*

The Apostles return to Jerusalem : they commence their Mission.

S. Mark xvi. 20 ; S. Luke xxiv. 52, 53 ; [Acts I. 12.]

And they worshipped Him, and returned to Jeru- *Luke 24. 52.*
salem with great joy, from the mount called Olivet, *Acts 1. 12.*
which is from Jerusalem a sabbath day's journey;
and were continually in the temple, praising and *Luke 24. 53.*
blessing God.

And they went forth, and preached everywhere, *Mark 16. 20.*
the Lord working with *them*, and confirming the
word with signs following. Amen.

PART I.

The Holy Week.

THE events which mark the last week of our Lord's life form a distinct era in His earthly ministry, and also in the history of man's redemption. No special attention which can be given to the subject, which may make this week stand forth in its proper relief from the rest of the Gospel history, can be labour thrown away. In the calm flow of Evangelic record we pass without remark into the midst of the scenes of this week; but a careful examination, and study of the harmony of the four Gospels, will show us that, whilst our attention is not specially called to it, it is really to this period, as to a climax, that the whole history tends.

There is perhaps this amongst other reasons why no special notice is called to this era. Our Lord Himself can scarcely be said to have made now any special effort, or to have laboured for man's redemption now more devotedly, or more successfully than before. In the midst of the general excitement which characterizes the actions of men (whether impelled by the powers of darkness, as were His enemies, or absorbed in their own sorrows, as were His friends), He is now, as ever, watchful of every opportunity of doing His Father's will; ready to seize, and turn to account, any passing occasion in the interests of His mission. He is never, for one instant, at a loss what to speak, or to do, amidst the varying complications of events. Whilst the results of His whole ministry were being gathered, as it were, into a focus within this brief space, we see that He holds the reins of all events in His hands, as one who was now fulfilling the last duties entrusted to Him, in the full consciousness that all was coming to pass exactly as foreseen, and provided for, in the councils of the Eternal Trinity, before ever the world was.

But, whilst no special attention is called to the prominence of this week, in the narrative of the Gospels, we see how carefully Christ Himself makes preparation for it. The steps of His progress towards Jerusalem are detailed in App. I.; and without regard to these we cannot gain a clear view of the position this week occupies in the history of our redemption: it merely appears invested with the natural interest of the last scenes of the Saviour's ministry. But as we carefully regard these steps of His progress, we see that, after such declaration as might best show His full consciousness of all that was before Him, and His acquiescence in it; and as might most effectively prepare, so far as their preconceptions would allow it, the minds of His followers for what must be, He resolutely advanced towards Jerusalem. There was apparent in His mien at times a remarkable gravity, and purpose; indeed, His bearing arrested the attention of the disciples, and impressed them, more than His distinct announcement that He was going up to die at Jerusalem (S. Mark x. 32).

There are two points, or principles, which should be regarded in our Lord's public life at this period. They may be distinctly traced, not only in the transactions of the Holy Week itself, but in all that tends towards them. These are (1) His observance of the exact line between the slightest courting of danger, or of precipitation of the course of events, and the slightest avoidance of them; and (2) His employing only modes of teaching used generally by Him throughout His ministry, and parables containing an outline common to others spoken before by Him. In a word, He makes no special ministerial effort of any kind; He merely resets truths formerly delivered, with an infinite earnestness, and adaptation to the opportunity of the moment, but not with any manifestation of power unemployed before. These points are carefully regarded in the notes as they present themselves for remark. The first places our Lord in contrast with most even of His noblest martyrs; for neither by word, nor deed, by assertion of His claims, nor by taunt, did He prompt, or influence, the action of His enemies against Him, nor give leading to their malevolence, nor exasperate their passions. He was as far from thus forcing their will, as when He foresaw the whole scene in the councils of Eternity; but at each precise moment for His own action He advanced, as resolutely and as calmly, as when He came down from heaven upon His errand of mercy and love. The second point shows us the perfection of all that had been done before; that nothing had been left undone which gave room for the trial of special means, or for the manifestation of special power. "What more could have been done in His vineyard, that He had not done in it?" Our Lord, indeed, evidently sympathizes with the natural feeling common to mankind generally, that a dying effort must be a concentrated and solemn effort; but He is not like ourselves in feeling the necessity of making a special effort, in trying to do then what might have been done better before, and so repairing omissions, or negligences, or mistakes of the past. The fact that He had perfectly done what He was commissioned to do, throughout the course of His public ministry, must help us to understand why we find no new and special effort now; and His resetting and applying parables, and modes of teaching and of action, of which we have previous instances, shows that there can be none, even the gravest occasions, to which these are not applicable.

We see, too, the great value of His example in the

early days of His ministry amongst men. In the quiet tenor of His daily walk and work, there was nothing, more or less, than God required as the perfection of devotion to His will; nor anything which, when the days of pressure and of supreme action arrived, required to be dropped, or supplemented, in the finishing of the work which God gave into His hands. The inference is obvious, that they best serve God who serve Him in the quieter hours of life, and they are most fitted to encounter the pressure of an extreme crisis; and that such seasons are not really occasions for the putting forth of new strength, husbanded before, but for the trial of strength already perfected and matured by use, as God's ordinary service has developed it.

With regard to our Lord's personal bearing at this season of trial, we see much of Divine majesty and power, and of a love beyond that of man's endurance; yet at no time during His career upon earth is His humanity more patent. The Son of God, and the Son of man, One in an inseparable nature, is revealed to us now with a distinctness never before manifest.

Beyond the study of the steps before mentioned, we need not go far for an introduction to the mysteries of this week. The scene opens at Bethany, where He had lately, though in fact some weeks before, raised Lazarus from the dead—an act of Divine power with which all Jerusalem was ringing. To this quiet village He returned by the road from Jericho; and it was soon known in the city that He had arrived there the evening before the sabbath, and would enter Jerusalem when the day of rest was passed. Many of the Jews came out to see Him, and to see Lazarus also; some of the rulers were amongst them, with the intention of watching for any pretext He might give them for compassing His death. They were there watching Lazarus also, whose death, as a troublesome witness for Christ, was also decreed. We see here, and again in the armed force set to watch the Saviour's tomb, evidence of the persuasion of the rulers, that, though once raised from the dead, the subjects of Almighty power in resurrection might forthwith be put to death again.

On that evening, or perhaps on that after the close of the sabbath, occurred a memorable event, to which SS. Matthew and Mark give a place in their record of the Holy Week, by retrospection; probably because it introduced the betrayal of our Lord, which is the first act of the Passion. There was a great feast of welcome made for Him in the house of Simon, once " the leper," to which He had brought so much rejoicing. There sat amongst the guests Lazarus, whom He had brought back to earth from the rest of the dead; Martha, his sister, served. As they reclined at supper, Mary came in behind them with a costly box of very precious ointment; which she broke, and poured it upon His head as He sat at meat. His feet also she anointed with the spikenard, and wiped them with her hair. The house was presently filled with the exquisite perfume of the costly unguent, as the world has ever since been (says an early writer) with the excellence of her charity.

This scene was observed by perhaps more than one of our Lord's followers with a secret repugnance; by one, certainly, with a terrible repulsion. If any objected to the interruption, or to the unusual exhibition of tenderness, or familiarity, Judas, on his part, coveted the value of the gift thus, to his mind, thrown away; and he expressed his objection bitterly, though plausibly, saying how very much better its value had been laid out, in the service of the poor. Our Lord points out the extraordinary faith of Mary, and the unique interest of the present occasion; whilst, for the charity of the liberal minded, there were for ever His poor waiting on the almoners of mercy. Mary, alone of all who loved Him, now accepted His declaration that He must die. We miss her presence, indeed, amongst those who went into Jerusalem with Him, and there ministered to Him; but here she performs her act of singular faith and devotion, anticipating (so He declared who read it in her heart) scenes in which she did not, perhaps, bear a personal part.

Our Lord's acceptance is the glorious award, that, side by side with the narrative of His Passion and death, and with the proclamation of His Gospel, should go down, through all ages and into all lands, the record of this act, for a memorial of her who first accepted the truth that the Christ should suffer.

His reproof to Judas, decidedly though gently expressed, sunk down into his heart, prompting not repentance and concealment, but hardening him for action; and he left Bethany before Christ, under the leading of the evil spirit, to betray Him to His death for a paltry portion of that larger value, which he had considered wasted upon the anointing of his Lord. He, too, now accepted the truth that Christ should suffer; but what a difference there was in the effect of the revelation upon his mind, and upon that of Mary of Bethany. She had done what she could to honour Him; he went out to secure what he could by selling His life to His enemies; and Judas well knew where and how to find those whose secret plans were already familiar to him.

Palm Sunday.

I.* When the sacred rest of the sabbath was past, and towards the cool of the evening of the next day, Jesus continued His progress towards Jerusalem. He set forth in the midst of a company already numerous; multitudes of His friends and disciples, besides the Apostles, were around Him, and many of those who had come from Jerusalem on hostile errands crowded His footsteps. All apparently expected some unusual manifestation from Him on the present occasion. For the moment it seemed as if their impression would be realized; for, as

* The sections here numbered refer to those of the Harmony, Text, and Notes of Part I.

they were upon the road, upon the confines of the neigh-
bouring districts of Bethany and Bethphage, He sent two
of His disciples forward to the latter village, telling them,
in the exercise of prophetic vision, that they there should
find, under circumstances which He exactly described,
the ass's colt on which, as Zechariah had foreshown, He
should ride upon His entry into Jerusalem. Upon it
they placed garments in honour, and some overspread
the way with branches of palms; and they brought Him
forward in triumph, hailing Him as "the Son of David,"
"the King that cometh in the Name of the Lord." The
multitude around, against the envious remonstrances of
the rulers, took up the cry of the disciples; and so they
advanced towards the holy city. As they approached,
they met a considerable multitude, who had come forth
to meet them; and these turned round and preceded the
procession from Bethany, raising the same acclamations.

As they turned the corner of Olivet, and the glorious
city burst upon their view, they halted for a short space.
The Saviour stayed to weep over the city, towards which
He was being conducted royally. He knew well what
awaited Him there, and the worth of the greetings with
which the mountain side now resounded; and He thought
of the multitudes filling up therein the measure of their
iniquity, and refusing the day of their visitation of grace;
and, alas! this blindness and obstinacy was destined to
be the ruin of their city, and the destruction of their
national life.

As He entered the city, the multitudes therein thronged
forward, asking, "Who is this?" And many a voice from
Galilee, for the present proud of their Prophet, replied,
"This is Jesus the Prophet of Nazareth of Galilee!"

It seems strange that presently all this concourse
should melt away. Few followed Christ to the Temple;
few waited His coming back again into the city; none,
so far as we know, desired He would eat bread with them.
His Apostles went with Him into the House of God, and
saw Him look round upon the signs of irreverence, and

appliances of the ungodly traffic which profaned the sanctuary. These He noted with indignation and sorrow. But the day of worship and of business was over in the Temple; and He returned, apparently unnoticed, and unattended, to Bethany with the twelve.

Monday.

II. The next morning our Lord returned to Jerusalem; and as He walked by the way, "He was hungry." This statement of the Evangelist attracts attention; it at once speaks to us of our Lord's human nature asserting itself, as it does prominently and frequently at this period, and it suggests also that, as is afterwards told us, He had passed much of the night upon the Mount of Olives in prayer and meditation. This sense of hunger is prompted by the sight of a fig tree in the distance, having a profusion of leaves, which, though premature and unseasonable, argued that the fruit was already ripe. Our Lord approached it, and found none; and then He doomed the tree to perish—that never again should any seek fruit thereon, and be deceived in the expectation. The disciples took note of an apparent impatience so unusual; but nothing was said by them, as they walked on towards Jerusalem.

III. When our Lord entered the Temple, it was already crowded with Jewish worshippers and with strangers. The court of the Gentiles was become a common thoroughfare for all passers; it was also full of buyers and sellers of sacrifices. The Temple resounded with the lowing of oxen, the call of the doves offered for sale, and the chaffering of the traffickers. The ring of the coins upon the money-changers' table was a sound utterly foreign to the House of God; and as our Lord looked upon the scene, He saw those who had purchased the prescribed victims for sacrifice, or who went into the inner court to offer the shekel of the sanctuary in the treasury, enter with sullen and angry faces, still vexed with the unjust advantage which had been taken of their necessities. There was no devotion and holy awe upon their countenances; evidently many of them "abhorred the offering of the Lord." And there stood round a group of Gentiles, scornful and contemptuous, as they noted the ungodly transactions which degraded the worship of God in the court to which they were admitted; and drawing strange conclusions as to what might be the profanations of the inner penetralia.

As our Lord looked upon this wickedness corrupting the religion of the land at its very fountain head, the zeal of God's House even consumed Him; and with an authority more than that of man, and with an irresistible power, He drove them all forth, cleansed the Temple of its pollutions, and declared that God's House should be "for all nations the House of Prayer."

Word was soon brought to the rulers, who were probably sitting in their council chamber, Gazith, close at hand, within the Temple; and they took council how they might destroy Him, before proceeding to action. As they were deliberating, the Temple, cleansed of the "thieves" who had profaned it, became full of blind and lame suppliants for Christ's mercy. They knew well that their time had come, and the place was appropriate for their claims; and Christ willingly healed them. The children too crowded around Him, recognizing their place prepared for them in God's House, and readily discerning that the gestures of His wrath against evil-doers were changed into a gracious welcome to their innocence; and their cries, repeating the acclamations of which they had heard the day before, broke the silence which had fallen upon the Temple of God. They hailed Him as "the Son of David." Some of the chief priests and scribes, who were watching Him, could not bear that the voices of children should thus hail Him unreproved, and asked, "Hearest Thou what these say!" "I hear it, and accept it," He replies. "Have ye never read, Out of the mouths of babes and sucklings Thou hast perfected praise " (or " founded strength," as the Hebrew words mean)?—" in the presence of God's enemies," the original passage (Ps. viii. 2), declares; the omission of the words being left purposely to the consciences of His audience.

He presently left the Temple, and the city, and retired again to Bethany.

Tuesday.

IV. The morning dawns upon a day most eventful and remarkable : as it advances we see the climax of the struggle between our Lord and the powers of darkness in opposition to Him; and with it closes the witness of His public ministry.

He leaves Bethany early with the disciples; and as they passed along the road, they noticed the fig tree, but yesterday flourishing in its strength, dried upwards from the very roots. In exceeding awe they call His attention to the evidence, now first seen, of His power in destruction. The prominent lesson is evidently that of the doom of hypocrisy, of a fruitless profession; but He answers some thought of admiration mixing in their mind, and liable to bring forth dangerous error if unchecked, and bids them doubt not that, at their own word, such devastation might follow, nay, that the very mountains should be removed before them : but the answer to prayer must have its true success in the forgivingness and charity which prompted it, not in the anger which might draw forth a hasty and angry curse ; and before such a spirit of mercy the mountains of prejudice and error should be cast down, which opposed the progress of the Gospel in the hearts of men, and in the world. He, the Judge of all the earth, might show the vengeance reserved alone to God ; His ministers and Apostles must offer prayer without wrath or doubting, and their forgivingness of injuries and their firm faith would establish His cause.

V. When He reached the Temple, there met Him a

deputation from the Sanhedrim, which approached Him with outward courtesy, and demanded formally, in the presence of the people, His authority for the act of yesterday. It was right and necessary that they should ask it. But, knowing their motive to be evil, He replies with a challenge: " Resolve the questions depending upon John's baptism, and his witness to me ; and I will declare the authority upon which I have thus proceeded in taking action within the House of God ! " They hesitated. If they owned the Divine mission of John, they acknowledged that of Christ ; if they denied it, they had reason to dread the popular displeasure, for the people generally acknowledged John as a true prophet. They said therefore, " We cannot tell ; " and, freely and naturally, our Lord held them unfit to hear plainly stated, what all knew must follow, that He had acted with Divine authority in His Father's House.

VI. But He will not dismiss them with a simple refusal of reply. He would draw them on, if not yet utterly reprobate, to the same confession of sin, and to the same place of forgiveness, which had rejoiced the hearts of many of those who had heard John preach. The parable of the two sons, which He now addressed to them, shows how the son which had refused God's will (as these men of evil living had openly done), on the call to repentance, received the baptism of John ; whilst the elder son, in spite of every profession of devotion, avoided the path of obedience. These professors of religion, so loud in their assertions of sanctity and devotion, would that they would take heart of grace and follow John's hearers, whom they had seen treading the path of repentance and faith, and enter the gate through which they had passed into the favour of heaven !

VII. "Hear another parable," He adds ; noting that His words are thrown away, but willing still to warn them of the destruction inevitable upon their obduracy. He then spoke the parable of the vineyard ; in which He gathered the imagery and warnings of Isaiah's prophecy of Israel, and points out how a long succession of God's messengers had come forward, and had ever been repulsed by the authorized guardians of His Church on earth ; and that, even now, they were taking counsel how to destroy the Son, the heir of all, who had been sent last to recall them to their allegiance. The interest of the parable carries them away; and as He asks, "What will the lord of the vineyard do to those wicked husbandmen who had slain the son?" some say, "He will miserably destroy them"—passing sentence, half unwittingly, against themselves ; whilst others, more closely seeing the application, and conscience stricken, say, "God forbid!" To these He answers, in words spoken before of such evil master-builders in the Church of God: "The stone which the builders rejected, the same is become the Head of the corner;" and He adds, Whosoever shall fall, in the pride of His own system of religion, upon this stone shall be broken ; though it may be his errors may be repaired, and his life and hope amended: but for all on whom it shall fall in the power of judgment, there must be irreparable and eternal ruin. He then gives the plain application of the parable of the vineyard, "The kingdom of God shall be taken from you, and given to a nation bringing forth the fruits thereof."

The rulers were filled with unmixed fury, and would there and then have arrested Him, as they had already in council decreed should be done. Their fear of the people, as the expression of God's restraining power, alone withheld them from immediate action. So they turned away towards the council chamber, and left Him for a season.

VIII. One other parable, that of the marriage of the king's son, Christ now addressed to those who stood around. In the Notes is traced its sequence upon, and connection with, the two preceding parables. In it He calls the members of His visible Church to the feast of the Gospel, already long promised, and to which they had been previously invited. The time was come, all was ready, and the guests are now called in. They refused, on various pretexts, to come ; and they scorned and slew His messengers. Upon this He sent forth His armies, and destroyed their political and religious existence. And He widened the invitation to all outside the former limits of His bidding, and gathered the Gentiles to the Gospel. The scene now changes to the great gathering for judgment. The king comes in to see the guests, and one is found who, in his profanity and audacity, had dared to come under other than the terms of invitation ; he is an *individual* in the parable, to show that every such offender will be discerned, and doomed ; and then the angel-ministers of the king hurry such an offender to his deserved execution. If God spared not those first bidden, upon their simple refusal to come, He would not pardon the wilful sin of any who dared to come but nominally within His Church, and there to do despite to the spirit of His grace.

IX. The rulers had retired to arrange a plan of procedure ; and now there advances towards our Lord a deputation, of venerable aspect, outwardly observant of reverence and courtesy towards Him. These were Pharisees and Herodians. They came forward to ask Him, as an acknowledged teacher, fearless and incorruptible, to solve one of the great questions of the day, the most interesting to the excitable people now present, from all parts of the country, in Jerusalem. Is the continuance of tribute to Rome lawful, or not lawful, to the chosen people of God ? They concluded He must say either that it was lawful,—in which case, as they thought, He would own Himself before the people no true Messiah; or that it was unlawful,—in which case He would utter treason against Rome. He did neither ; He made them, as in their application of the parable of the vineyard, give judgment in their own cause. He called for a coin of the current standard, and asked whose likeness it bore, and with whose titles it was superscribed. They owned it Cæsar's ; and the maxim of their own schools was to the

effect that, where a king's coin was current, he was the
sovereign entitled to custom and tribute. He adds a
stern monition that they should render to Cæsar his
acknowledged tributary dues ; and not withhold from
God, upon any plea of expediency or political exigency,
those devotions of primary service which were His paramount right.

They wondered at His wisdom, and they could not
answer it before the people ; but yet, a few days later,
they condemned Him in the Sanhedrim, and alleged to
the people that He had pronounced for Cæsar ; whilst
before the Roman judge they dared to declare that He
had counselled to withhold the tribute from Cæsar,
advancing claims to a royalty of His own.

X. Whilst He remained in the Temple, another deputation came forward with another question : the Sadducees came to ask Him to clear away certain difficulties
with regard to the cardinal doctrine of His religion—the
resurrection of the dead. Their object was not the less
malevolent than that of the Pharisees, because it was
simply intended to involve Him in the dilemma of an
absurdity in doctrine, whilst the Pharisees had asked
a question which placed His liberty and life at stake.
They quoted the law of Moses, known now as the
" levirate law," by which, when a man died childless, his
brother married the widow. They allege the case where
seven brothers in succession married the same wife, who
survived them all ; and they ask Christ (leaving the
imaginations of the hearers to picture grotesque scenes of
dissension in the kingdom of the resurrection), " Whose
wife shall she be of the seven ? " Unfortunately for
their reputation, our Lord is not placed in this supposed
dilemma ; and, to their confusion, He makes evident their
ignorance, both to themselves and to their audience.
They had argued in ignorance of the laws of eternal life :
they had assumed marriage as an estate of the kingdom
of the resurrection ; there was there no such estate at all,
so at once their ingenious difficulty fell to pieces. And

then He points out that, in their doubts of the resurrection, they throw discredit upon the original covenant declaration of God to their forefathers, who had revealed His name to the sons of Israel as the God of Abraham, Isaac, and Jacob; thus declaring them alive as to their spirits, and foreshadowing their resurrection from such an imperfection of being, to a fuller and eternal life.

The multitude were astonished at the power and originality of His doctrine; and even of the scribes there were some unprejudiced enough to accord Him the title and homage of a teacher, owning, " Master, Thou hast answered well ! "

XI. One more question is proposed to Him ; and apparently by one who, though a Pharisee and an official scribe (a *lawyer* also, as he was designated for his skill and learning in the law), came forward with some sincere desire to receive from Christ the solution of a religious difficulty. The theological schools were divided on the question as to which is the great commandment in the law ; what was the decision of Him who had spoke before so wisely ? Christ declared no one word of God more or less binding than another, but He put together the spirit of all laws of God, and classed them, as commands referring to God, and commands referring to man. The former were greater, as their object was superior ; but the second was closely related in importance. All the law, and all that the prophets had written, were but comments on the supreme law of love to God, in the first place, and a love to man, equal to the love of self, in the second. " Thou hast said the truth," admits the candid questioner ; and our Lord, reading what sincerity was in His heart, and how fair hope there was with regard to his salvation, did he but advance in the same path, speaks of him words that seem to accompany salvation : " Thou art not far from the kingdom of God."

XII. Whilst these Pharisees, amongst whom the scribe stood, were gathered around Him, Christ asked them a momentous question. We may suppose it prompted by the opening offered, like a gleam of hope, by the better feeling of the candid scribe. " What think *ye* of Christ? whose son is He ? " They give at once the obvious reply, " The son of David." The first step is gained. He does not proceed to point to what every one knew, His own lineal claims, but endeavours to lead them on to admit that higher claim of His, as the Son of God ; He asks how King David, in the Spirit and in God's Name, called his son his Lord, bidding Him sit upon God's right hand until His enemies were made His footstool. For as David was God's vicegerent upon earth, his son, if his Lord, must be his God also. The stroke reached their heart, but it was hardened against any confession unto salvation. The common people, however, heard Him gladly; and it is painful to read of these willing listeners, how they suffered themselves to be misled from the right way.

XIII., XIV. All trials now had failed : our Lord could neither convince, nor win, those whom He would fain gather to Himself; and who, though He must die, need not have been the agents of His death. He must now, however, for the sake of the people, who were attentive still to hear Him, keep no longer terms with the hypo-crites and counsellors of evil. He then, after cautioning His own followers against such a standard for them-selves, delivered the remarkable series of denunciation known as " the eight woes," in which He exposed and branded the selfishness, pretence, and hypocrisy of the leaders of the nation, specifying those sins particularly which distinguished them as teachers of a corrupted religion ; and He closes with the most pathetic lamenta-tion (because of the intensest and truest feeling) ever uttered over sinners. He gathers them under the figure of their holy city Jerusalem, and mourns over the loss of His travail for them, and for their refusal of His love and grace, and for the desolation now inevitable. And yet His words are not of final exclusion. She shall be desolate until she shall say, " Blessed is He that cometh in the name of the Lord;" she shall therefore yet arise to confess Him.

XV. As our Lord ceases now to speak publicly, He sits down to rest in the court of the women. It was an hour when gifts were being brought into the treasury; little did the givers think that He who sat there resting, was He to whom their gifts were offered. He marked how many gave nobly, and willingly. Some came in, perhaps vexed with the extortion which had robbed them, in their exchange of provincial for the sacred money. Amongst them came a poor widow. She had two of the smallest of current coins, and He knew that she had nothing else; she put both into the treasury, and went away. His peace doubtless went with her, and His blessing that maketh to prosper; but He spoke not to her. To the disciples He declared hers the noblest gift offered there, for it was her all. Thus we learn that God expects that he that has little shall " gladly give even of that little," and that the offering of the poor is accepted as graciously as are the richest gifts ; and also that God regards not only what is *given*, but what is still *left* after the gift is made ; judging not only the amount of our offering, but its proportion to our means.

XVI. As He sat there resting, word is brought to Him that certain Greeks in the court of the Gentiles desire to converse with Him. It is possible that these men had witnessed His public entry into Jerusalem, His cleansing of the Temple, the pollutions of their court especially, and heard with gladness His declaration that the Gospel should be extended to the Gentile world. An interesting tradition (see App. VII.) makes some of them at least members of an embassy from Abgarus, King of Edessa. Their arrival at this season was a striking and memorable event ; they came as representatives of the Gentile world, to claim their portion in Christ. Our Lord places a very high significance on this their visit, and takes occasion to declare how widely effective for good will be the consequence of His death to the Gentiles. He appeals solemnly to heaven, to the Father, to attest the mighty significance of His death ; and the voice of the Eternal God speaks from heaven in answer to the appeal. He then goes on to declare His death the " crisis " of the world, the date of the fall of the power of evil. It seemed a difficulty to the people that Christ should die, who, as they supposed, should " abide for ever " ; and they make this objection as an interruption of His address to the Greeks who came to Him. One word of warning gave He in reply, that but a little while, and the light would be withdrawn from them, and then they must stumble and fall in the darkness of those whose light is gone out. He then withdrew Himself from those who so little appreciated His presence amongst them.

XVII. S. John concludes this portion of His narrative with a statement of explanation concerning the apparent failure of Christ's mission in Israel, through the disbelief of the Jews ; and their verification of Esaias' prophecy of them. He states, however, that there were many of the rulers who really believed, but did not now dare to confess Him. Some of them may have been graced with a bolder spirit when the test of His crucifixion and resurrection was laid upon them. The passage concludes with Christ's emphatic declaration of His doctrine, and the authority upon which He delivered it. The word He spoke was that which God had committed to Him, and upon that word, accepted or rejected, would proceed the judgment of the last day; the award of eternal life was His commission from the Father; the decision of death, which neither He nor the Father desired to pronounce upon man, was the decision of that word now spoken.

He then left the Temple for the last time; there was nothing more to do in the House of God ; His work was finished, and His public ministry ended.

XVIII. As they went forth they looked back upon the Temple, beautiful for situation, and decked with the glory of the declining day, and one of the disciples called our Lord's attention to the magnificence of the buildings and

the magnitude of the stones of its construction. It is
evident that the remark was connected in his mind with
the words of doom which our Lord had lately spoken of
it. He now confirms the prophecy of its utter destruction, for of these stones of beauty and wondrous size, not
one should stand upon another in the day of its down-
fall.

As they went up the ascent of Olivet towards Bethany,
He sat looking down upon the Temple; and four of the
Apostles come together and ask Him when shall be the
end of the Jewish Temple, the date of His advent, which
they connect with it, and the end of that dispensation?
His reply is that grave and solemn prophecy in which
He unfolds the future of His Church to the end of time,
foretelling also the nearer end of the Jewish Church,
and the troubles which must precede it; troubles of the
infant Church, and the deeper distresses of those who
had no anchor of their soul, in their faith in the dawning
day. The two events are wrapped together in the mist
of prophecy; but we can in a great degree follow our
Lord's declarations, for so much as has been fulfilled
in the destruction of the Jewish Church and nation, is
clear to us. The troubles, also, which should surround
the infant Church of Christ, are matters of history. To
use the striking figure, which compares the successive
developments of prophecy, to the ranges of mountain
scenery which rise one behind another to the eye of the
traveller, as he surmounts each in turn, until there lies
the untrodden range of eternal snow: so have we passed
beyond more than one of the eras spoken of by our
Lord, and there remains before us, in nearer view, the
grand end of all things, beyond which is the kingdom of
the invisible world. It seems as if many of the signs
of the Lord's coming to destroy the Jewish dispensation
may be repeated as warnings of the supreme end; and
there certainly runs through the whole prophecy a common thread of admonition, applicable to both events—
the exhortation to *watch*, lest the Lord should come

unawares upon a Church, and upon individuals, unprepared for His advent.

XIX. This exhortation is, towards the close of the Great Prophecy, expanded into two of our Lord's most interesting and most solemn parables. The first, that of the wise and foolish virgins, describes the advent of our Lord, which comes upon all as a surprise. But the wise are in a state of readiness to meet the Bridegroom. The unwise are not so; and, though conscious of the truth, and outwardly professors of it, they have preparations to make, which, in the hurry of the end, cannot be made, and they are shut out from the presence of their Lord. The parable, in fact, repeats the lesson before noticed as so strikingly that of our Lord's own life—that, to be prepared for the final crisis, men must make the best use of the day of ordinary work; the neglect of the opportunities of life cannot be repaired in the excitement and hurry of its close.

XX. The second parable carries us a step further, and presents a different aspect of the subject. The great King has come to reckon with his servants for their fulfilment of the trust of life. He rewards those who have made the most of their opportunities of service; the one (an *individual* instance, like that of the man without a wedding garment, as being representative of every such case) who had buried his Lord's gifts, and used them not, is consigned to the doom he has merited; and even were he not borne away to punishment, his wilful misconception of his Lord's character shows him unworthy to share His eternal joy. We are left to conclude, from the punishment of those who simply leave undone the duties of life, the destiny of those who spend their time and talents in the direct service of evil.

XXI. There is a third and last scene, in which our Lord passes out of the figures of parable, and describes in plain terms the award of the Day of Judgment. Separation has been made between the righteous and the wicked; and they stand severally to receive judgment. The terms of the sentence affect all with surprise; it does not proceed upon the intrinsic excellence or wickedness of the actions of life. Our Lord represents Himself as having received charity, mercy, and love from the good servants, in various exigencies of distress. They have no consciousness of having seen their Lord under these circumstances; but He declares that in the person of the least of His suffering servants, they have succoured, and ministered to Himself. The wicked are condemned, because in the offices of their life they never ministered to Him, in the person of His brethren. Nothing spoken by our Lord shows so clearly, and with such infinite comprehensiveness, the intimate "union that is betwixt Christ and His Church," and the supreme sacredness of the duties and offices of daily life. Dean Goulburn's idea of a "*tetralogy*" of these parables of judgment, is very striking, and will repay the reference to it. (See "Personal Religion," pp. 352, 353.)

The close of this extraordinary discourse seems to have brought our Lord to Bethany, where He spent the evening. One of the Evangelists, in his summary of the week's incidents, says that "at night He went out, and abode in the mount that is called the Mount of Olives," in the exercise (so we gather elsewhere) of intercession and prayer.

Wednesday.

XXII. This day seems to have been spent by our Lord and His disciples in retirement. Three things only are recorded which have reference to the progress of events.

Our Lord declared to His disciples that, on the third day from that on which He spoke, the day of the Passover, He should be crucified; and that He was already betrayed to His death. Probably, whilst He was speaking to the disciples, the rulers were holding their council,

of which we are informed, in the palace of Caiaphas,
and "consulting how they might put Him to death."
They were saying, that it must not be at this feast,
because of the effect upon the people of His teaching,
during the earlier days of the week; and therefore a
popular interference was to be dreaded; when an unexpected opportunity offered. Judas, with whom they had
already had dealings, entered amongst them; and offered
to betray Christ into their hands, in the privacy of His
retirement, when popular interference was impossible.
Satan, doubtless, who now influenced him, brought him
thus opportunely forward, to give the assistance which
was necessary to the execution of the designs of the
rulers, who were willing to be the agents of his malice.

It seems most probable that our Lord's declaration to
the disciples, was coincident in time with the decision
formed by the rulers in concert with Judas; and that He
declares what was as open, to His sight and hearing, as
if He were then present in their council chamber.

Thursday.

XXIII. Our Lord remained still in His retirement at
Bethany, until the evening of this day, "the day of preparation." With regard to the difficulties concerning
the date of this day, and other matters of dispute connected with it, and with the observance of the Passover
festival by our Lord and His disciples, and by the Jews,
very ample discussion has been entered into in the notes;
and it may therefore suffice here, to state only the order
of the facts and events of the day.

Sufficiently early in the day to give time for all preparations to be made, our Lord sent two of His disciples
into Jerusalem, to arrange for His celebration with them
of the Passover. He gives directions with an extraordinary minuteness, which, in their exact fulfilment,
left no room for doubt or question; and all was done as
He commanded. The word of "the Master" was suffi-

cient to justify any departure from prescribed customs, and seasons, which might seem strange and unusual. And, with the precaution of this preparation being made in the house of a friend, and in the privacy of the twilight hour, He came into Jerusalem with the twelve Apostles; amongst whom Judas had now again presented himself, with the hideous consciousness of accomplished treachery upon his mind. It was the last occasion on which the twelve stood together in association.

XXIV. (*a.*) As they were about to sit down to the table, Jesus spoke to them with deep solemnity: earnestly had He desired to eat this Last Supper with them upon the eve of His death, for never again would He sit down with them in like manner upon this earth.

(*b.*) And now there appears to have arisen a singular dissension amongst them. What were the grounds of it we can hardly conjecture. Whether it arose from anxiety to be nearest to Him at this last festival; or whether they thought that it was the last, in the sense of being an inauguration of the kingdom which they desired, and that they must now claim the precedence hereafter to be taken; or for what other reason, or combination of reasons, we cannot distinctly say. Strange it seems that such a strife of vain pride should arise, at such a moment, amongst men burdened with sorrowful apprehensions. Our Lord points out to them that, whilst the lords and rulers of the Gentiles insist on their precedence, and authority, the lords over His heritage, and the spiritual rulers of His kingdom, must not so strive; for the greatest ruler in the kingdom of heaven, should be he who had been most successful in ministration to others. Supreme as He was, He had yet lived amongst them as one that served them in all things, spiritual and temporal. But such eminence in the humility of service, was the true road to the distinctions they coveted; there awaited them, if faithful, apostolic thrones of paramount precedence over the twelve tribes of the house of Israel. Our Lord does not now, as once before, say "*twelve* thrones;"

and one of them was conscious already, that he should never sit amongst the throned Apostles in heaven.

(*c*.) There follows a careful and specific statement, of our Lord's consciousness of all things which were about to happen, of His full knowledge of the sovereignty which rested upon Himself, and of His departure to heaven now at hand; yet, being thus, He proceeded to take upon Himself the office of service, which there was neither host, nor servant present to take, and which the Apostles, in their pride, each strove to avoid. Before them all He made preparation, and took upon Him the form of a servant; and began to perform the ordinary service before eating, namely, washing their feet. When He came to Peter (perhaps others before him had submitted in silence; amongst them, it may be, Judas), the zealous Apostle's warm affection took alarm. Christ, his Lord, should never wash his *feet*. Our Lord bids him submit, and wait awhile for explanation; but Peter again withdraws himself, declaring such service shall never be rendered to him. Christ now declares that if He washes him not, he has lost part with Himself. Peter now runs to the opposite excess; he will be washed, not his feet only, but hands and head. Jesus corrects him : he that is once bathed, needs only to wash the soil of travel from his feet, and is clean; thus, they were all clean, but one, who had repudiated, and lost the efficacy of his original washing. Whether now, or afterwards, they knew that He represented the perpetual efficacy of the laver of baptismal washing, and the necessity that from Himself must also come that remission and cleansing of daily sin, with which they should be clean. The present lesson, however, which He inculcated from this act, was the necessity of humility; and, for their encouragement, He adds in direct words, what He had already revealed to the four, on the Mount of Olives, if not to them all, that he that received the Apostle minister received *Christ*, and ministered to Him; nay, more, received the Father that sent Him. Whether in the services of Christian duty, or with regard to the message of salvation, this is the rule of His kingdom. (See App. VI. 13.)

(*d.*) And now a wave of irrepressible sadness, as it were, rolls across our Lord's mind; whether set in motion by some angry response in the mind of Judas, to the warning that his throne was in jeopardy, if not already lost, or how, who shall say? He suddenly breaks off, with the abrupt announcement, "But, behold, the hand of him that betrayeth Me is with Me on the table!" And then He declares, "One of *you*, one that eateth with Me, bound by the sacred covenant of salt, shall betray Me." Horror-stricken, and sorrowing, all ask, in an agony of apprehension, yet conscious that no such intention defiled them, "Lord, is it I?" and Judas also dares to ask, "*Master*, is it I?" And then He declares to them the necessity that He must die, as it was written; but since, though eternally foreseen, it was not a decree of God that one of themselves *must* commit that unpardonable treachery, and, further, the crowning sin of doing his best to destroy the Life and Redemption of the world, it had been indeed "better for that man if he had never been born."

Peter beckoned to John, who leant upon his Lord in close and familiar position, to ask privately who was the traitor; it seems likely that, if he could know this, his hand which presently smote Malchus, would be raised to stop the mouth of the traitor. Our Lord told John, but he did not now communicate with Peter; and then He gave the sop (the token spoken of to John) to Judas; and then Satan entered into possession of him, as he refused the last appeal of his Lord. Jesus, intolerant of the intrusion of the tempter, and of the presence of the now abandoned traitor, bade him go forth and do his work quickly. He went out from amongst them, and the disciples let him go, thinking no evil of him, nor supposing his business to be anything but the execution of some ordinary errand. Thus silently, and thus unnoticed, may often pass the day of grace from one abandoned by Christ, as he lives and acts amongst many who themselves also greatly need His forgiveness and mercy, but who happily have not spurned it.

The departure of Judas removes the pressure of present distress from the Saviour's mind; and "when he was gone out," our Lord declares the glory of victory which was before Him: but a little while, and He would be gone away from them; and therefore now He gives them a last command, new in its pureness, unselfishness, and comprehensiveness, that they shall love one another as He had loved them. This should be the evidence to the world that they had been with Him.

Peter, ardent and self-trusting, professes himself ready to follow Jesus at once, and to the death. Our Lord sadly warns him that, within a few hours, before the night had passed, he would, with threefold deliberation, deny that he ever knew Christ personally.

(*e.*) And now they resume the meal so broken and interrupted; "and as they were eating," our Lord takes the bread, and then again the cup, of the feast before them, and institutes a memorial Supper, to be observed until the world's end, for His sake. Yet not memorial merely, nor a simple celebration of past events; the breaking of the bread, and the drinking of the cup, should be a Sacrament of the Real Presence of the lifegiving Saviour's Body, broken for the life of the world, and of His Blood that cleanseth from all sin. Whatever of solemnity in His institution of this Sacrament, and of interest in the occasion of its being so ordained, and of blessing promised, could combine to give this act unprecedented force and obligation, all were united in His command: "Do this in remembrance of Me."

XXV. (*a.–e.*) And now follow the farewell discourses of our Lord to His disciples, in which He consoles them for His departure, and inculcates the duties of faith and of prayer, and the vital necessity of all in unity with Himself, as the centre of success and of life. He promises the presence of the Comforter, the Holy Spirit of truth, proceeding from Himself and from the Father, whose mission it should be to remain with His Church in the world until the end of time. He speaks of the persecution that awaited them, as they took up the witness which He gave into their hands; but yet there shall be present with them His peace which passeth knowledge, which the world cannot conceive of, but which is inexhaustible in the spirit of the believer; and there should be with them the cheering assurance of His victory, and of their own through Him. Every sentence in these discourses, the main heads of which are here most briefly referred to, is full of interest and of the most important and saving truth. They are carefully treated of in the notes; but so only show how deep is the instruction which lies in them, beyond all that man's wisdom can unfold or grasp. They were delivered in the Supper-room, partly whilst our Lord still reclined amongst His disciples at the table, and partly after He had risen from this last meal, before going forth to die.

XXVI. Having thus spoken, He kneels down, and, with gesture, and in terms, which engrave themselves on the minds of the disciples, He offers that great high-priestly prayer of intercession, in which He desires (as One of right to will), first for Himself as the Messiah, then specially for the Apostles, and lastly for all believers to the end of time, the strength and protection of the Almighty God, in all things necessary to the accomplishment of their several missions upon earth. If His opponents were once compelled to own, " Never man spake like this man," His faithful servants must, one and all, own that none other could breathe prayer like this; and may take heart and comfort, in all the exigencies of life, that such an Advocate " still liveth to make intercession for us," until in His strength " unto the God of Gods appeareth every one of us in Zion," where He is.

XXVII. We now resume the thread of historic narrative. The celebration of the Last Supper concluded with a hymn of praise, no doubt the "greater Hallel;" and then they set out, lighted by the beauty of the rising moon, towards the Mount of Olives. As they walk, our Lord repeats the warning concerning His Passion, and foretells that this same night they shall be scattered from Him, as sheep that have no shepherd; but He would rise again, and, as a shepherd, go before them into Galilee. Again Peter repeats his rash protest that, though all should fail Him, yet never, to the death, would he; and once more our Lord forewarns him of his threefold denial that he had ever known Him. And He adds that Satan had demanded that he might sift them as wheat; but that He had prayed specially for Peter, and upon his restoration it should be his peculiar grace to strengthen the faith of those who had fallen less utterly than himself. Thus is given, to those raised from the depth of a fall, the special commission to go and raise the fallen. Our Lord then tells them that though, when they were sent forth as His heralds for the first time, they went without money, and without provision—for His bounty went with them, and sustained them—yet now, when He was gone, and they went forth in His name to preach the Gospel, they would have need of all possible means of self-support, and even of self-defence, in the prosecution of their work. They misunderstand Him to speak of present means of defence, and say there are with them "two swords." "It is enough," He rejoins; for He must leave them to understand His meaning afterwards.

XXVIII. So speaking to them, they come to the garden, or olive-yard, of Gethsemane, a favourite resort of His; for there, amongst the trees that grew thickly around, He found privacy for prayer, even within sound of the busy hum of the great city. Judas too knew the place, and even now he was getting a band of men to apprehend Christ. Leaving the majority of the disciples near the road, He took Peter, James, and John

apart into a more retired spot; and, desiring them to pray with Him, went a little further, and entered into His agony. Whilst they continued to watch, they saw Him kneel down, bend forward, and then fall upon His face in the earnestness of His prayer; and they could see, in the pale moonlight, the gleam of the great drops of the sweat of blood, which gathered and fell from His brow. It is strange that they could sleep under such circumstances, and again His especial desire for their sympathy in prayer; but it is the natural tendency of great sorrow to benumb the senses, into a deep and tranquil slumber. Thrice did our Lord pray for strength to do His Father's will; and there appeared to Him (they knew it from Himself afterwards, for they saw not) an angel of God, ministering strength to Him sufficient to meet the physical strain of the necessity that was upon Him; else had human nature failed in the extremity of His anguish. He had twice roused them to watch and pray, if not with Him, at least against their own peril; but the third time, when His agony was past, He found them sleeping, and He now roused them to meet the armed force, which was already within the olive-yard, and. upon them. Well might Peter now know his own weakness, when he, who had professed himself ready to dare all for Christ, could not, on trial, watch one hour.

XXIX. As He bade them rise, Judas stepped forward, from the gloom and shades of the garden, and behind him were men with lanterns, torches, and weapons. Every precaution had been taken that, neither by force, nor under cover of the shady groves of the garden, should escape be possible to Christ. "Knowing all things that should come upon Him" (once more repeats the Evangelist), our Lord advanced to meet them, announcing Himself as He whom they sought. And, as He answers, His word is once again with power, for all fall prostrate before Him; and thus they learn that their weapons and lanterns must prove useless against Him at His will. Judas, ranked amongst them, to the sorrow

and indignation of his fellow-disciples, now experiences
the power of Christ, and falls with them. But nothing
harms them, and, as they rise again, Christ yields
Himself to them; and then Judas advances, and gives
the preconcerted token of betrayal, "the kiss of Judas,"
before which the officers have no orders to take Him who
declares Himself to be their object of search. As they
advance to seize Him, Peter's courage in the face of
actual danger arms him in his Lord's defence; and with
his sword he wounds the high priest's servant, who was
prominent amongst those surrounding our Lord. Christ
rebukes his mistimed zeal, and heals the man, destined
(if tradition be true) to rank amongst our Lord's disciples
hereafter, and not amongst His foes. Even at this
moment He had provided for the freedom of the Apostles,
who take advantage of the confusion of the moment, and,
one and all, abandon Him.

One of the Apostles, John, turned quickly, and followed
close enough to be an eye-witness of all that transpired;
and there came out after them a young man, who followed
so near them that he appears to have been mistaken for
a disciple, and was in imminent danger of apprehension.
This, tradition asserts, was Mark, afterwards the Evangelist of Christ.

XXX. (*a.*) Our Lord's captors led Him quickly away,
and brought Him first to Annas; of right, though not
actually, the high priest. Though critics are divided
upon the question, it seems most probable that no formal
examination of Christ took place here; but the assent of
Annas was certainly given to the proceedings against
Him, for He was taken forward, bound by the direct
order of Annas, for examination before Caiaphas.

(*b.*) Early as was the hour, and short the notice, there
were gathered round the chair of Caiaphas many of the
chief priests and rulers; and, as it was not yet time to
bring Him before the Sanhedrim, the interval was spent
in examination by Caiaphas, by whom it was hoped that
Christ would make some admission which could be used
against Him.

John had followed, and had entered into the palace of the high priest, where he was known. At his word to the porteress, Peter also was admitted; for he too had recovered himself, and had followed those who took Christ. This kindness brought him speedily into temptation, and trouble; for, as he warmed himself in the courtyard amongst the guard, standing within the light of the fire, the maid, who had admitted him with some suspicion, now looks earnestly at him, and recognizes him as a disciple of Christ. She challenges him as such, and at once he denies that he at all understood what she was asserting. The cock crew, but Peter noticed it not; he was in terrible anxiety to escape observation, and withdrew himself into the porch, into the shadow.

Meanwhile the examination of Christ was commenced in the palace above. The high priest questioned Him as to the number, and strength of His followers, and as to His doctrine; evidently he desired to found a charge, of a confederacy, especially amongst men in the suspected districts of Galilee, which might be producible before the Romans. Our Lord appealed to the people; He had ever taught in public, and the witnesses to what He said were then, in thousands, in Jerusalem. As He spoke, one of the officers of the high priest, to cover his lord's failure, struck Christ with the open palm of his hand, saying, "Answerest thou the high priest so?" Our Lord pointed out that, if He had answered contrary to the laws of witness, and without due respect, it shall be stated against Him; as it was, such an outrage on a bound and defenceless prisoner, was an insult upon the forms of justice.

Good Friday.

(c.) Evidently there was nothing to hope from such an informal procedure; and, as now the day was dawning, and the great council had been assembled, (illegally early as it was,) our Lord was led into the presence of the supreme tribunal. His case was already prejudged; but some form and semblance of order must be maintained, and the perjured witnesses were ready, when called upon to give their false evidence.

"Art thou the Christ?" was their first question; but it was one which they, not He, should long ago have decided. If I assert it, He replies, you will not admit My claim, or examine it; and if I question you upon points connected with My claim, you will not reply; nor will you release Me, whether My claims are established, or remanded for future investigation. It was evident to them that He knew their intention, and it was useless for them further to question Him. The false witnesses were called; they did their best, but not even such judges as these could found a sentence upon their contradictory lies. At length came forward the two required of the law, who agreed that Christ had, years before, threatened to destroy the Temple, and asserted that He could rebuild it in three days. He had said that (as was soon to be fulfilled) *they* should destroy the temple of His body, which He would raise up again in three days. What He meant was fairly understood by the rulers, so we gather from their statement when asking a guard over His sepulchre from Pilate. But even if He had spoken against the Temple, it was no capital offence, much less when coupled with the word of restoration. And even now their evidence, intended to rouse the assembly to frenzy against Him, became confused and contradictory, whilst He calmly faced them without a word of reply. The high priest, in rising wrath, from his tribunal strode forward, and commanded Him to reply; but not a word did our Lord utter. He left them to make the best of their own failure and confusion. And then the high priest ventured his last chance; he solemnly, in the name of God, as the lawful representative of the Divine authority, adjured Christ to say whether He is the Christ, the Son of God. And now our Lord at once breaks that silence at which men marvelled, and speaks words which

He had spared to utter before, for they were words of
judgment: "Thou hast said;—I am. And further, from
henceforth ye shall see the spiritual kingdom of the Son
of man, whom ye refused, established with power, and
hereafter ye shall see the *Son of man* sitting enthroned
in glory, and coming to judgment in the clouds of
heaven." "Art thou the Son of God?" they all ask with
an instant excitement; for our Lord's words gave unmis-
takeable reference to Daniel's prophecy of the enthrone-
ment and dominion of the *Son of man*, as the Son of God,
at God's right hand. "I am," He replies. Enough was
spoken for the purpose of the high priest. He casts aside
all fear and regard to the future; he rends his clothes,
and with every gesture of utter horror, well assumed and
apparently sincere, now declares further evidence useless, that Christ had spoken blasphemy. He collected
their votes, and they all condemned Him guilty of death.

Never was there such a scene as this in any earthly
court; never such a prisoner stood before such judges;
never so utter a prostitution of justice and truth crushed
innocence and goodness. And what followed was worthy
of the initiative of the court. In the very presence of
the venerable assembly, taking their example from the
rulers, those who held Christ began to heap every possible indignity upon Him, striking Him, spitting upon
Him, blindfolding Him, and then challenging the spirit
of His prophecy again to awake, and name the wretch
that buffeted Him. The most degraded court would have
been rendered infamous by such foul insult of a helpless
prisoner in bonds.

As this was passing, Peter is again challenged by the
maid-servant in the court below, and she expresses her
suspicion of him to the bystanders. Peter denies the
charge of discipleship; but a companion of hers (who was
busy about the porch where Peter had taken refuge at
first, and from which he had again emerged towards the
firelight), at once taking up the assertion, declares also
her own conviction that he was a disciple of Christ.

Peter turned to her and asseverated his denial. Several persons standing round said, "Art thou certainly not one of His disciples?" And Peter made his denial with an oath. Thus, for the second time, did he publicly deny his Lord.

About an hour later, and probably whilst Jesus was being mocked and insulted by the guard, Peter is again challenged. A man who had noticed his rough Galilæan accent, points it out as a suspicious circumstance; and then the bystanders turn upon him, and declare it is sufficient evidence of discipleship. Whether they do this with intent to apprehend him, or seeing merely the vexation it causes him, is not apparent; at least, they take no steps beyond asserting that he is a disciple. Peter takes oath, and utters imprecations; he declares he knows nothing of his Lord. As he speaks, again the cock crew; and in an instant the Saviour's words flash upon his memory, and an overpouring shame subdues him. He looks upward, and meets the eye of Christ, now being led forth from before the judges; and what he reads there (sorrow but not vengeance), fills him with self-accusation and with penitence; and he rushes forth from the porch, and weeps bitterly for his fall.

It was now morning, though still early; and, as speedily as possible, the whole council held a short and formal sitting, in which they passed sentence of death against Christ. And then, as they must gain the sanction of the Roman governor to His execution, they bound Him with a convict's bonds, with chains probably, and led Him away to Pontius Pilate; the whole court following.

Judas too had witnessed the sentence, or had at least seen Him led away as a sentenced criminal; and remorse smote him; alas! not such repentance as Peter's, but a hopeless despair of himself seized him; Satan, still in possession of his soul, hurried him away in gloomy despair. He ran to the Temple, where some of the priests, with whom he had bargained, were now preparing for the solemn services, and sacrifices of the day. He said abruptly, " I have sinned, I have betrayed innocent blood ! "   Good men, seeing the despair of the wretch, might have uttered words of pity or concern ; but these were " of their father the devil," and spoke at his suggestion, and drove Judas away, declaring his sin and remorse no interest of their's.   He threw down the blood-money before them, on the Temple court ; and, with no further thought of Christ, or prayer for mercy, went and accomplished his own ruin.   He went and hanged himself. In his last act he spurned mercy and forgiveness, and held close to his despair.

Whilst he is dying (and terrible circumstances lent horror to his death), a strange and contemptible consultation takes place in the Temple.   The chief priests will not throw away the silver pieces, but they scruple to put them into the treasury.   Jerusalem is full of strangers, and their dead must be buried ; and so they buy the plot of ground on which Judas died, and set it apart as an appropriate cemetery for the interment of " sinners of the Gentiles."   Thus, Judas is said to have " purchased a field with the reward of his iniquity."

(*d.*) The scene again changes to the palace of the governor.   Our Lord and His accusers have arrived there, and are clamouring for Pilate.   It is still too early for the legal sitting of Pilate's court ; but their impatience will have no delay.   They will not deign to enter Pilate's house, in the pride of their self-righteousness ; it would be defilement to them, which would render them unclean before the Passover. So he must fain come forth to them ; and he does so, sensitive of the insult. They bring forward Christ, for order of execution upon their own sentence ; but Pilate, already enraged, will not tolerate this additional insolence, and demands the accusation upon which Christ is to be tried.   " If He were not a malefactor, should we have brought Him hither ? " is their haughty reply.   Pilate desires them to take away their malefactor, and deal with Him according to their

own law.   This will not answer their purpose; and so they
drop their insolent bearing, and say that they may not
lawfully put any man to death.   We may imagine the
scorn with which Pilate heard them thus confess their perversion of justice, and intention of murder in the name
of law.   Then they lay an accusation different, totally,
from that under which they themselves had tried Christ;
utterly baseless, and absurd, even within the knowledge
of the Roman judge.   "We *found* this fellow guilty of
sedition, and exhorting to refuse tribute to Rome, and
advancing claims to a royalty of His own."

This was a charge which Pilate must take notice of;
though he perceived their malice, and knew the reputation of their prisoner; and felt the insolence of their
supposing himself ignorant of there being such treason
in agitation, unknown to the governor of the land.

Pilate called Jesus into the court into which they
refused to enter; and our Lord read in his mind, not
only indignation against the Jewish rulers, but some
awe and interest in Himself; and therefore (willing to
lead him to better things, through those hidden impulses
of good), when Pilate asked, "Art Thou the King of the
Jews?" He answered strangely, "Desirest thou to know
the truth for thyself; or askest thou merely in echo of
the rulers' words?"   Christ probed the depth of Pilate's
heart, but his pride instantly rises; Christ's words also
imply that if Pilate drops a charge urged merely in such
transparent malevolence, the accusation is *ipso facto*
not sustained by the authority of Rome.   But he turns
off from our Lord's meaning, and demands, Is *he* a Jew,
to argue the intricacies of Jewish claims?   What has
Christ *done* to substantiate such a charge? for an accusation such as this must be based upon facts.   Christ
waives this question; Pilate knew well that He had
done nothing; but He replies to the former question
concerning His royalty, and explains that, though a
King, His kingdom was evidently not one of earthly
rivalry against Cæsar; for were it such, His servants would

have fought, and there would have been armed resistance against His capture by the rulers. The fact of
there being no resistance disproved the charge of sedition. Pilate perceived that He claimed a kingdom, and
asked with some interest, but also with much scorn,
"Art *Thou* a king? Thou, a prisoner, without support,
and disowned by the nation—art *Thou* a king?" Our
Lord replies, "I am a king; I came into this world to
be a king, and to bear authoritative witness to the truth
of God. Every one who is of the truth recognizes the
claims of My sovereignty; such as do so are the subjects
of My kingdom." This was the "good confession"
which, S. Paul says, our Lord "witnessed before Pontius Pilate." What was said was sufficient for Pilate;
he stifled whatever interest his heart owned in such
questions. He was a man of education and philosophic
thought; he had heard such sentiments advanced by
the masters of the schools of Greek and Roman philo-
sophy. What could the meaning be, of such a Jewish
prisoner, abandoned by all, even His own disciples?
Could He give superior information to that which every
philosopher professed to give, but with which none could
satisfy the mind? "What is *truth?*" asks Pilate, with
contemptuous scorn; and then he went forth to the
rulers, and said, "My *finding* is, that there is no fault in
Him; no ground for the trial on this charge."

And then follows a strange scene of passion and excitement : voice after voice loudly clamours in accusation ; all kinds of charges are advanced, but not a word
is substantiated. Pilate is struck, no less with the malice
of His accusers, than with the dignity, and evident
innocence, of the prisoner ; and he is again conscious of
an impression, that before him stands One who is no
ordinary *man*. At last the words "from Galilee," spoken
by some excited clamourer, catch his ear ; and he seizes
cleverly the chance, of getting rid of the embarrassment
of refusing to detain the prisoner, against whom men
of so much influence and position pressed condemnation ;

and, at the same time, of paying a compliment, convenient to himself, to Herod, with whom he had quarrelled upon some violence offered to his Galilæan subjects ; and so he orders Christ to be taken to Herod for hearing.

(*e.*) Herod received the courtesy with expressions of gratification. He had not the slightest regard for the Jewish excitement against Christ, but he had a strong wish to see our Lord, with whom he had never come into personal contact ; for he scarcely doubted that He would make a friend of him, in this hour of need, by the performance, at his request, of some striking deed of wonder. Herod therefore asked Him many questions, as the chief priests stood around vehemently accusing Him ; but to questions born of idle curiosity, and of the insolence of vanity in power, which offered no point worthy the Saviour's regard, He answered not a word. Herod, therefore, having amused himself, and his men of war, with mocking Christ as an aspirant to royalty, arrayed him in a gorgeous robe of patent derision, and sent Him back to Pilate ; returning Pilate's hollow compliment in kind, when it was convenient to get rid of the case. A very unworthy friendship was cemented between Herod and Pilate on this occasion, in place of their former dissension.

(*f.*) Pilate now assembled the Jews formally, and gave an official declaration of the innocence of Christ ; pointing out how their own native prince had ridiculed the idea, of attaching any consequence to their accusation of conspiracy against Rome. He did not, however, dare to release Christ untouched, but sentenced Him to be scourged—for what ?

Pilate was, however, anxious to release Him, and he readily caught at the custom of releasing a prisoner, to the popular demand, in honour of the feast, and in memory of the release of Israel from the prison of Egypt. He thought that, at least, the popular voice would be raised in favour of Jesus ; but this circumstance only served to bring into a striking and awful prominence, the utter degeneracy of the nation. There was then in prison an adventurer of note, who was under sentence for the actual offence of which the rulers had falsely accused our Lord; he had raised insurrection against Rome, and had taken opportunity, in the aid of his deluded adherents, to commit horrible excesses of robbery and murder. He was a pretended Messiah, a false Christ, and he bore the suggestive name of Jesus Barabbas (*son of the Father*); in all respects he was a hideous caricature of the true Christ. There seems a moment's hesitation, during which the rulers are busy with their advice; and at that juncture a message comes to Pilate from his wife, warning him earnestly against allowing Jesus to be injured, for she had had a most significant dream concerning Him. Pilate felt the influence of superstition, supported as it was by the mystery which surrounded Christ. He now repeats his question as to who shall be released—Barabbas, or Jesus which is called Christ? "Release Barabbas, and crucify Jesus Christ," is the popular decision. The governor remonstrates against such an unprecedented exhibition of rancour and wickedness; and as a chance of rousing, if not sympathy, at least pride in a national dignity, asks, "What shall I do to Him whom ye call the King of the Jews?" They shriek forth the frenzied demand, "Crucify Him." Once more Pilate points to His innocence, and weakly renews his proposal to gratify them by the sight of the scourging of their victim; but all, rulers and people, insist upon His crucifixion—and prevail.

But yet Pilate makes one further appeal. He washes his hands, before them all, of the blood of the prisoner, whom they resolved to murder in the name of law; but their awful and ready answer, "His blood be upon us and our children," convinces him that they were exasperated nearly to the point of insurrection, and that they cared nothing for his opinions, and despised him for his vacillation; and so he crowns all phases of his weakness and irresolution past by giving sentence that it should be, not as justice or even expediency required, but simply as they willed.

Then the soldiers of the governor gratified the Jews by an exhibition of their ingenuity in derision. They exceeded the mockery of Herod's men of war. They not only clad Him in a miserable caricature of a royal robe, but they crowned Him with a circlet of thorns, putting a reed into His hand as a sceptre; then they bowed the knee before Him, crying, "Hail, King of the Jews;" and, wearied at last of their play, snatched from the grasp of His manacled hand His mock sceptre, and struck Him with it on the head.

Then Pilate brought Him forth again, not without some hope that the compassion of those He had so often blessed with mercy, would at last awake in his favour. Once more he declared Him innocent. "Behold the man!" he says, pointing at Him, who (though He stood in mock royal robes, and crowned with thorns, bleeding with the laceration with which the blows had driven these into His forehead), was yet "*the man*," the representative man of a ransomed race, redeemed by His death and suffering to a new and glorious heritage.

"Crucify Him!" they howl in reply. "Take ye Him and crucify Him; I find no fault in Him!" The rulers would not rest with this permission; they would have a form of law observed, and they saw they could obtain it from the weakness of the governor. "We have a law," they urge, "which dooms Him to die, for He has assumed to Himself the title of the Son of God."

Pilate was now alarmed in earnest; it was not rarely fabled, in the mythology of his own education, that the gods had visited earth in human form; and his superstition inclined him to fear, that one so divinely patient, and so wise, was indeed the Son of God. He therefore called Him once more apart into the judgment hall, and asked with awe, "Whence art thou?" Christ gave no reply; it was superstition, not anxiety for the truth, that demanded answer. Again the Roman's pride awoke: "*To me* speakest Thou not? knowest Thou not that I have power to crucify Thee, and have power to release Thee?" "Thy power is permitted thee from above; those therefore who know more, and make use of this thy power, have the greater sin." Thus did Christ, the prisoner sentenced to die, apportion, as the Judge of heart and conscience, the relative degrees of sin in those who were rejecting Him; and Pilate's conscience felt the sovereignty of his award; and now in earnest he laboured to release Him. But it was too late; the Jews at once recognized the purpose which awoke in him, and they played their last stroke. "If thou let this man go, thou art not 'Cæsar's friend;' whosoever maketh himself a king speaketh against Cæsar;" and the Cæsar of the day was one most prompt to act upon the bare assertion of such a charge. And so Pilate easily passes to the opposite extreme; he sits down formally on the official seat of Roman judgment, upon the Pavement, and after the vain appeal, "Shall I crucify your King?" delivered Him finally to be crucified.

They are prompt to lead Him forth, lest there should be reversion of the sentence; and, as now, weakened by weariness, sleeplessness, agony, and the laceration of the scourge, He cannot carry His cross as quickly as they desire, they place the weight of it upon Simon of Cyrene, afterwards one who took up the cross, and followed Christ as a true disciple. This man, chancing, in God's providence, to pass, was pressed for the present service.

Christ had met no pity from men, but a company of women followed, and bewailed Him. Jesus turned towards them, and bade them not weep for Him, but for the miseries which this day's wickedness would entail, which many of them would live to see; and He so warns them, in order that they may believe His word, and escape the troubles which were impending over the ungodly. Mere compassion He did not desire, but He would fain reward their expression of sympathy with the offer of salvation.

On either side of Him two malefactors, probably followers of Barabbas, laboured under the burden of their crosses : they were to die with Him.

XXXI. At last they reach Calvary ; and there was offered to Him (perhaps by the kindly ministration of countrywomen, for there were some whose compassion generally supplied this last act of mercy) an opiate to dull the sensibility of pain. He simply tasted it, but would not drink ; for He would shrink from no agony of death which could befall any son of man. And then they drove the nails into His hands and feet, and erected His cross between those of the two other who were crucified with Him ; thus was He "numbered with the transgressors."

As they erected the cross, He prayed for all who wronged Him in this officiousness of ignorance : " 𝕱𝖆𝖙𝖍𝖊𝖗, 𝖋𝖔𝖗𝖌𝖎𝖇𝖊 𝖙𝖍𝖊𝖒, 𝖋𝖔𝖗 𝖙𝖍𝖊𝖞 𝖐𝖓𝖔𝖜 𝖓𝖔𝖙 𝖜𝖍𝖆𝖙 𝖙𝖍𝖊𝖞 𝖉𝖔."

When He thus hung upon the cross, a title was put over His head, which Pilate ordered, " This is the King of the Jews ! " Pilate wrote it in scorn of those who had rejected Christ : perhaps in this way he gratified his own thought, that such a man was worthy to reign ; for at least He was the worthiest of the Jews.

Many that passed (for the place of crucifixion was close to the thoroughfare of the busy city) read it, and some of them with pity, and perhaps with secret approval of its real truth ; and therefore the malicious rulers would prevent the slightest expression, or glance of favour, and they went and desired Pilate to alter it to a sentence of pretension—" He *said*, I am King of the Jews." But Pilate had now gone as far as even he would go, in compliance with their desires.

Below the cross sat four soldiers on duty, to watch at the cross ; these men, in painful contrast with His anguish, cast dice for their perquisite of the garments of the crucified. Long ages before, this careless act of indifference had been foreshown by the prophet ; and all now noticed its wantonness.

There was a great crowd around ; many were passing,

and repassing. It was necessary that those who had brought Him to die should, by ridicule, if possible, prevent any growth of sympathy for Him ; any passer-by might be one who had been healed by Him, and reaction in His favour might set in. So they bitterly mocked Him, bidding Him who could destroy the Temple, and rebuild it in three days, look at it, as it towered in majestic stability above Him, and think of saving Himself. Others owned He had saved other men, but jeeringly declared He had no power to save Himself ; if He would now come down from the cross, they promised to own Him as the Christ. And then others laughed about His trust in God, to whom He had so constantly referred His every action : " He said, I am the Son of God ; then let God now deliver Him, if He will acknowledge Him ! " The soldiers entered into the spirit of their mockery, and offered Him their sour wine, as some royal draught, and bade the King of the Jews save Himself.

Even the malefactors turned in their agony, and derided Him. Perhaps both at first did so ; but one of them, at least, was prompt to see what none other saw, the true royalty of Him who bore such scorn and reproach so patiently ; and, to his eternal happiness, grace was given him, to discern now, what he had hazarded his life to find, and had been disappointed of—the true Messiah. " Lord, remember me when Thou comest in Thy kingdom," is his prayer. Our Lord replies (and that with a power which had lost no attribute, notwithstanding all that was befallen Him), " To-day shalt thou be with Me in paradise." Not in the future, will He cast a compassionate thought towards His fellow-sufferer, when He is seated on the throne of glory ; but to-day, he shall enter with Him, in the triumph of His victory, into the paradise of the good. It was the most astonishing act of faith, by which any had yet acknowledged His cause.

The weary moments of agony pass ; and again the Saviour's attention is called, and exercised in mercy.

Near His cross stood Mary His mother, weeping, but not
with the tears of unbelief. None nearer of relationship
to her stood by, than the beloved disciple, whose faith
was now revived; to his care, and to his ministration in
the spiritual truth of His gospel, He now commits her,
for her life on earth. "Woman," He says, with respect
and tenderness, as He glances towards S. John, "behold
thy son;" and to John, "Behold thy mother." And
John led her at once from the scene of death, which
Christ desired to spare her, to his home; and took her,
as Christ's bequest, to his own heart also.

And now, for three hours, darkness fell upon the scene
of crucifixion, and doubtless silence upon the mocking
tongues of His enemies; if man recognized no Saviour
in Him, the powers of Nature knew the Creator, and were
ashamed to look upon His dying struggle. It may be
that in the gloom, also, the powers of darkness pressed
around Him, for it was "their hour." At the end of the
third hour, the Saviour's voice (strong in the power of
life, which none could take but at His will) cried to the
Father, "My God, My God, why hast Thou forsaken
Me?" He was bearing the sins of the world, and the
displeasure of God against sin was manifest to His
spirit; He perceived the horror of spiritual death.
Worst of all that mocked, was the voice that, at such a
moment, could miserably play upon His words of
anguish; it was a Jewish voice, for none but a Jew
could have made reference to Elias. He spoke again,
"I thirst;" and the expression of His humanity touched
one of the Roman soldiers with an answering pity, who
ran to bring Him a vessel of the soldiers' wine. It is this
man's distinction to have done the last act of mercy to
the dying Christ. Those around would have prevented
the act; and either they interrupt, or he himself
(perhaps covering his act with the repetition of their
words—it is not plain which) says, "Let be; let us see
if Elias will come and save Him." Whether the Jew
spoke of Elijah, or of John who had been put to death,

whom Christ had declared the Elias prophesied of, there is an equal mockery in the spirit of the remark. The vinegar was given Him, and it cooled the fever of His tongue. Not one thing now remained to be done to satisfy God's justice, and to accomplish His will; and our Lord declared, "*It is finished,*" the whole work of His salvation. And then at once, with a loud voice, in which there was no accent of death, He committed His soul to God, "*Father, into Thy hands I commend My Spirit,*" and in His own power "yielded up the ghost."

"The sun was darkened in the heaven thereof" when the Saviour died; but His death was the act of universal redemption. Salvation was the gift of God to the wide world; "the kingdom of heaven was opened to all believers." And not without outward sign. For the great veil of the Temple, sixty feet in length, and a foot in thickness, was rent, as if by Heaven's hand, from the top downwards to the ground; and thus was for ever rent in twain the veil of separation, between the Jew and the Gentile, and also the way was opened into the holiest heaven, by the blood of Christ. The earth too was convulsed, and the graves opened; and after Christ Himself had risen, many who had died before Him in His faith, arose from their graves, and entered into Jerusalem, and were recognized there as His witnesses. More about them we know not.

There was one other act of confession made, and (no doubt tradition asserts with truth) of salvation wrought, at the foot of the cross. The centurion, who had marked all that occurred, with a wondering mind, when he heard Christ command death, with the clear tones of one who was Lord of life, declared that He truly was a righteous man; nay, that He was indeed the Son of God.

And now shame and remorse fell upon those, who had come in numbers to see "the sight" of His death; they smote their breasts in self-reproach and gloom, and returned to their homes.

The Evangelist notices the sympathizing presence, at a short distance, of many of His acquaintance, and prominently of many women, who came from Galilee, and he names specially three of them—Mary Magdalene, Mary the mother of James and Joses, and Salome, mother of S. John. Our Lord's mother, then, had not remained; though John himself had returned, and was amongst the eye-witnesses.

It would seem that some of the Jewish rulers had left the scene of crucifixion, before Christ died; they had gone to Pilate, to beg him to hasten the end, by breaking the legs of the crucified. He complied, and sent soldiers to do this work. They came, and first gave the final stroke to the malefactors, who were still alive; passing by Christ, no doubt upon the representation of the centurion and guard at the cross. They all saw that He was dead. But yet the order given them, to make sure of death, must be carried out; and so one of them, ran his spear (not in wantonness, but for certainty against any trance, or feint of death) into the heart of Christ, and thence came out blood and water. The beloved disciple, who records it, saw the spiritual significance of the fact; the soldier saw the evidence of death, and this his evidence has been accepted, as affording positive certainty of the act of death, to all who would demand proof. In this, and in the fact that no bone of Him was broken, were fulfilled minute predictions, amongst the many prophecies which rested on His Passion, and death.

XXXII. But others had also gone to Pilate, and upon a holier errand. Two of the rulers, Joseph of Arimathæa, and Nicodemus, were now gathered to the side of Christ, by the constancy of His witness in death. They had before been His true disciples secretly, but now they came forward and owned Him publicly. Joseph went to Pilate and begged His body; and when Pilate had had official testimony, from the centurion, to the fact of death, he willingly complied with his request. And he, and Nicodemus, took down the body, reverently and lovingly, from the cross ; and they wound up with it, in costly and fine linen, abundant spices which they had prepared, as if for the royal burial of one of David's line ; intending, after the sabbath, to complete the last offices, which they must discharge hurriedly now.

Close to the place of crucifixion was a garden belonging to Joseph, in which he had, for his own sepulture, made ready a tomb, hewn out of the living rock. None had ever lain there—a fact not only appropriate to the burying of Christ, but in itself an assurance that none but Christ Himself rose from that place of burial.

There these pious, and now resolute friends, laid the dead Christ ; and they rolled close the great stone of entrance, to seal the sepulchre, and departed.

Their act of burial was witnessed by some of the women, who had come in from Galilee ; amongst them those already specified by name. It is likely they knew not fully that Joseph and Nicodemus had thus, as their act argued, of intention professed themselves His disciples ; but they remained till these had gone, taking careful note of the sepulchre, in which they had seen how the body was laid. And then they also went into Jerusalem, to make such hurried preparations as time allowed, for the sabbath was just upon them. And so "they" rested the sabbath day, according to the commandment, which, in their faith, they would not break, for what seemed even an act of necessity and piety ; and truly there was reward laid up for their devotion ; for the scrupulous performance of duty, and of God's command, is near to the perfect and acceptable service, which the angels do Him in heaven.

There was yet one thing to do, and there were those who hesitated not to break the sabbath to do it. The rulers came once more to Pilate, and said, in terms which showed how fully they had understood the words which they had misused against Christ, "We remember how that this deceiver said, while He was yet alive, After three days I will rise again." They desired him therefore to make the sepulchre sure, so that neither could He come forth, nor yet His disciples open it, and steal the body, and declare Him risen. They would also have a guard; that if He did rise again, as their consciences feared, He might encounter the swords of the soldiers, as He returned to earth. Pilate gives the order that a guard (of sixty men, if of the usual strength) should be told off from the body of soldiers, already placed at the disposal of the Sanhedrim, for the exigencies of this festival; and that all precaution should be adopted to satisfy their fears.

They therefore placed their official seal upon the stone, and they planted the guard at the entrance.

It was a vain precaution; vain from their point of view, but affording a proof, which they did not intend to furnish, of the integrity of the sepulchre; and destined to give official evidence of the resurrection, which they desired to deny.

So lay the body of Christ in rest, whilst His soul was in paradise; yet neither severed from His Divinity by the act of death. He had been numbered with the transgressors; He had borne the sins of the world; His death had been with the wicked, by the rich had been His burial. Believing hands had laid His body in the grave, and to His enemies was given the custody of His sepulchre. And the last sabbath day of the old dispensation brought rest upon the world.

Palm Sunday.

I. *CHRIST'S ENTRY INTO JERUSALEM AS THE KING.*

S. Matt. xxi. 1–11 ; S. Mark xi. 1–11 ; S. Luke xix. 29–44 ;
S. John xii. 12–19.

When they drew nigh unto Jerusalem, and were

1. The events of the Holy Week form the most interesting portion
of our Lord's life on earth. Whether we regard His teaching, direct
or by parable ; His miracles ; His example, we find all summed up,
reset, and put before us with a greater force and application than
earlier in His ministry. Our Lord's plans of action have a special
reference to this week. (See xviii. 96, xx. 2, xxiv. *b.* 3, 8, 13 ; II.
vi. 5.) The Evangelists are most careful to show how, from the time
when "He stedfastly set His face to go to Jerusalem," all things
tend, and work together, towards the great consummation of His
ministry. The fact is distinctly and carefully impressed upon us, that
no fortuitous concurrence of circumstances brought about this end ;
but that our Lord's will and purpose, in exact harmony with the
declarations of prophecy, were directly engaged in the simple fulfilment of what God had foreordained. All agencies combining, either
through ignorance or malice, to effect the purposes of God, acted their
part unwittingly ; but the Son of man went straight forward in the
execution of God's will, voluntarily accomplishing, and acquiescing in,
all that was required of Him.

From the narrative of the Gospels it appears that all the disciples
(Matt. xx. 20, 21 ; Luke xix. 37, 38), and the Jews generally (Luke
xvii. 20, xix. 11), were prepared to expect some special and authoritative manifestation of our Lord's mission, about this time. The events
connected with the raising of Lazarus had produced a profound impression on the public mind, and strengthened this expectation.

All the Evangelists record this progress to Jerusalem with marked
particularity, and the previous tenor of their Gospels seems intended
to lead our minds to share the general feeling of the occasion, and to
mark our Lord's entry into Jerusalem as one of the main incidents
in His mission, and as introductory to the most important and solemn
portion of His life. (App. L) It did not occur on the evening of
the sabbath ; for on the sabbath day, until after six o'clock, when it
would be too late, the journey could not be undertaken. Christ must
therefore have rested at Bethany, where the supper and anointing
took place, for the sabbath day ; and towards evening of the next

come to Bethphage, unto the mount of Olives, then sent

day, the first day of the week, He set out to Jerusalem. Bishop Jeremy Taylor notices, that our Lord had only two days of triumph in His life: that of His Transfiguration, and this of His entry into Jerusalem.

2. *they drew nigh.*—This was the day when the Paschal lamb was to be selected and set apart (Exod. xii. 3), and so, S. Chysostom notes, Christ is brought into God's chosen city, where alone the Passover could be killed (Deut. xvi. 2, 5, 6), and where it was ordained, and in the offering of Isaac prefigured, that He should be provided a sacrifice for the world's sin (Gen. xxii. 14). The eye of God, and of His holy angels, thus beheld each Jewish household within the city, setting solemnly apart their typical lamb of sacrifice; and beheld also "the Lamb of God that taketh away the sins of the world," of whom all these were types, going voluntarily forward to offer Himself without spot to God. S. John (xii. 12) mentions that "the next day," after the anointing, they went up to Jerusalem, thus marking the day as that of the legal selection of the victim: the fact is surely more than a coincidence.

3. *Jerusalem.*—This was our Lord's seventh recorded visit to "the city of the great king." He had been brought in His infancy to be presented to the Lord (Luke ii. 22); in His childhood, when He was twelve years of age, He went up with His parents to keep the Passover (Luke ii. 42); He kept the Passover there in the first year of His ministry (John ii. 23); He went up to the city, to "a feast of the Jews," probably the Passover, in the second year of His ministry (John v. 1); He went again at the Feast of Tabernacles, in the last year of His ministry, about six months before this triumphal visit (John vii. 10); and again, three months later, at the Feast of the Dedication (John x. 22, 23). Besides these visits, he was brought there by Satan in His temptation (Luke iv. 9). Each of these occasions is marked by its separate incidents of importance and interest. No doubt our Lord visited Jerusalem, as did all the Jews, at the great festivals, before His ministry began, though there is no special mention of His having done so.

4. *Bethphage.*—Lit. "the house of figs:" a suburb, or village of the priests, on the eastern slope of the Mount of Olives, between Bethany and the city. It was remarkable for the numerous fig-trees which grew about it; these were bare of leaves at this season of the year, with perhaps the sole exception of the tree so conspicuous from afar (Matt. xxi. 19). No trace of the village has as yet been identified as marking its exact site. S. Mark and S. Luke here read "Bethphage and Bethany;" but they are omitting what specially occurred at Bethany, with the apparent intention of recording uninterruptedly the journey up to Jerusalem at this feast, and its results to our Lord, from the time when He first "stedfastly set His face to go to

Jesus two of His disciples, saying unto them, Go into the
village over against you : and as soon as ye be entered
into it, ye shall find an ass tied, and a colt with her,
whereon yet never man sat; loose him, and bring *him*

Jerusalem." (See Luke xiii. 22, xvii. 11, xviii. 31, xix. 11, 28.) Greswell states, that whilst Bethphage lay on the direct road to Jerusalem
from Jericho, Bethany did not, but was a little way off the road;
though the two villages were contiguous. Bethphage, in the direct
route, is specified, as our Lord halted there. (See App. X.)

5. *then sent.*—These disciples were two of the twelve, as the
narrative of St. Mark seems to decide; and not a certain two of the
multitude (Luke xix. 37) of believers, who were gathering about Him
at this crisis of His ministry.

6. *two of His disciples.*—We find that amongst the disciples, our
Lord often selected one or two for the discharge of certain duties.
To Jude was entrusted the common purse; Philip and Andrew seem
to have had charge of provisions (John vi. 5, 7, 8), and also to have
received those who desired to speak privately to our Lord (John xii.
21, 22); Peter, James, and John were His chosen attendants on several
occasions, at the raising of Jairus's daughter, the Transfiguration,
and the Agony in the garden. Peter and John were sent by our
Lord to prepare the room for the Passover (Luke xxii. 8), and the
probability is that they were the "two of His disciples" sent to
Bethphage on this occasion. S. Mark's account seems like that of
an eye-witness, and so might designate Peter as one of the two.
The early writers attach a significance to the disciples being sent two
together, as signifying the two testaments, the spirit and the letter;
or theory and practice, that is, knowledge and works. The allegorical
interpretations of these writers may seem occasionally overstrained,
but their *principle* of interpretation is one recognized by apostolic
writers, and in the Holy Scriptures generally, and deserves our most
respectful attention.

7. *the village over against you.*—Bethphage.

8. *as soon as ye be entered.*—Our Lord gives, in this exercise of His
foreknowledge, a proof that He was acting under the direct influence
of Divine Providence, upon a pre-arranged plan. He shows also that,
under this influence, He could incline the wills of men to further
" the determinate counsel and foreknowledge of God." (See note 11;
and xxiii. 3; App. I.)

9. *an ass tied.*—As if it were ready prepared for them. The ass is
mentioned by the prophet and by S. Matthew, as well as the colt; it
was, however, upon the colt that our Lord rode, and no doubt the
ass followed of her natural instinct. The prophet, in his sacred vision,
beheld them thus, and so minutely recorded what he saw.

10. *whereon yet never man sat.*—This is in accordance with the

unto Me. And if any man ask you, Why do ye loose *him?* say ye, The Lord hath need of him; and straightway he will send him hither. And they went their way, and found the colt tied by the door without, in a place where two ways met; and they loose him. And as they were loosing the colt, the owners thereof said unto them, Why loose ye the colt? and they said, The Lord hath need of him: and they let them go. And they brought him to Jesus, and cast their garments upon the colt, and they set Jesus thereon. And as He went, they spread their clothes in the way. All this was done, that it might be fulfilled which was spoken by the prophet,

ancient rule (itself, no doubt, typical designedly of this event), by which there was a sacredness attached to such animals, things, and places as had never been put to any service or occupation. (See Numb. xix. 2; Deut. xxi. 3; 1 Sam. vi. 7.) So also for our Lord's use was a sepulchre chosen "wherein never man before was laid" (Luke xxiii. 53). (See also xxxii. 8.)

11. *The Lord hath need of him.*—Our Lord could incline the hearts of all men to give effect to His commands (note 8); and at this festival, very especially, all houses were open, and all services freely rendered by the dwellers about Jerusalem, to those who came up to keep the feast. An early writer, speaking of Christ's power thus influencing the owners, says, "By this He instructs His disciples that He could have restrained the Jews, but would not." But "the Lord's service" seems to be the password here, and there is reason to think that the owners of the colt recognized His authority, as themselves either His disciples, or at least well disposed towards him. The title "Lord" is significant, and is in keeping with the royalty He was now assuming. It contrasts with the order for a room for the Passover, where our Lord, in His more ordinary character, says, "the Master saith" (Matt. xxvi. 18). The two occasions are interesting, both in coincidence and in contrast. (See xxiii. 3, 6.)

12. *tied by the door.*—This, together with the locality (Gk. "the place"), is detailed with extreme minuteness, and is intended to show the importance attached to our Lord's choice of the animal on this occasion, which His prophet had foretold, and which He so carefully signified as designed. (See notes 18, 19.)

13. *cast their garments,* etc.—This action, and their spreading of their garments to carpet the road which He traversed, were signs of their recognition of Christ's royalty. (See 2 Kings ix. 13.)

14. *that it might be fulfilled.*—Jesus thus fulfilled, on the occasion pre-ordained, the prediction of His own Spirit by the prophet. He

saying, **Tell ye the daughter of Zion, Behold, thy King cometh unto thee, meek, and sitting upon an ass, and**

foreshowed what He proposed doing; and He now fulfilled that purpose, and the declaration of it which He had given by Zechariah. But the disciples acted their part, not knowing at the time the significance of their own actions. (See John xii. 16.) This is ever the course of prophecy; which is an evidence to the age of its fulfilment, and to subsequent ages, of God's foreknowledge of His actions, and of those of men, long before: it is (as Herbert says) " a letter sent sealed to posterity." When the appointed time comes, God and man do not combine to act as the prophet has bespoken of them, in order to make God's word true; but God acts as He has foreshown, and, in the undisguised coincidence of men's actions, the verification of prophecy ensues; and then men see, in what has happened, the fulfilment of what was written. And this evidence of God's providence, and of the unchangeableness of His decrees, is perhaps a greater manifestation of His power and truth, than even the most striking miracle. See S. Peter's comparison of the assurance of prophecy to the truth of Christ, with that given by the word of His eye-witnesses, themselves convinced by sight of His miraculous power, and of His majesty in transfiguration, and by the testimony heard by them from heaven itself (2 Peter i. 16–21). He says that we have, in prophecy, the "more sure word" of witness.

15. *daughter of Zion.*—A personification of the city of Jerusalem, which was founded on Mount Zion : a common figure in Scripture.

16. *behold, thy King cometh.*—Cometh " unto thee if thou believest; against thee if thou believest not." (*Chrys.*) A reference to the exact words of Zechariah (ix. 9, 10) will show the nature of this kingdom. It was to be one of peace. The chariot and horse of war, and the bow of battle were to be cut off, and the king was to inaugurate an era of peace; His mission was to be that of a Saviour, His personal attributes justice (*i.e.* righteousness) and humility; He was to reign over the heathen world, and His sovereignty to be universal: a picture the very reverse of any kingdom of earth. The words are—

Rejoice greatly, O daughter of Zion;
Shout, O daughter of Jerusalem :·behold, thy King cometh unto thee:
He *is* just, and having salvation ;
Lowly, and riding upon an ass,
And upon a colt the foal of an ass.
And I will cut off the chariot from Ephraim,
And the battle-bow shall be cut off :
And He shall speak peace unto the heathen:
And His dominion *shall be* from sea *even* to sea,
And from the river *even* to the ends of the earth.

17. *sitting upon an ass.*—The judges of Israel, representatives not of a kingdom of warriors, but of God's theocracy of peace, rode thus.

a colt the foal of an ass.   These things understood not

(See Judges v. 10, x. 4, xii. 14.)   And so rode at least the two first kings of Israel, so typical of the Messiah.   The horse was associated in Israel with the idea of war; the ass, with that of peace and humility (prominent characteristics of our Lord, and of the subjects of his kingdom upon earth), but still with that of royalty.   Justin Martyr shows a reference in Gen. xlix. 11, to this Advent and Passion of Shiloh, and the gathering of the people to Him.

18. *and a colt.*—Though it appears that both the ass and her colt were brought to Christ, as spoken of by the prophet, the word "*and*" may be used, not as expressing addition, but as explanatory—" an ass, even a colt the foal of an ass;" for certainly the latter only was required by our Lord.   Some writers have pointed out the deeper humility which was manifested in the choice of the colt; but no doubt the true reason was that stated by S. Luke: it was that "whereon yet never man sat." (See note 10.)   Ancient writers have seen in the ass the representative of the Jewish Church, long accustomed to bear the burden of the Divine law; and in the colt that of the Gentiles, as yet unbroken to the yoke of Christ, who was now sanctifying it : they were standing where two ways met, the way of life and the way of death, undecided which to take.   S. Matthew, who more especially wrote for Jewish readers, alone mentions the ass; it follows after our Lord, as does the Jew follow the Gentile, to receive in turn the Gospel, when the times of the Gentiles are fulfilled.   S. Jerome also notices that " the Jewish nation is, towards God, the mother of the Gentiles."   Pseudo-Chrysostom further sees in these animals, types of the degradation of those who are in the humiliation and bondage of sin, "drudges under the load of error" laid upon them in their ignorance of God : " Therefore He saith to His disciples, ' Loose them,' that is, by your teaching and miracles, for all the Jews and Gentiles were loosed by the Apostles; and ' bring them to Me,' that is, convert them to My glory."   These thoughts, which, with its figuring the kingdom of peace and humility, give to our Lord's riding upon the colt of an ass the character of a parable in action, are well worthy of consideration, where the whole of our Lord's progress is so highly significant, and so minutely impressed upon us by all the Evangelists.

19. *understood not.*—It was a remarkable exercise of candour which prompted the disciples, who have handed down our Lord's religion to the end of time, to confess that they, of all men, did not understand their Master and His doctrines, whilst they were conversant and associated with Himself.   And yet, though a few hostile minds may wing a shaft against the religion they affect to ridicule, from this admission of the ignorance of the first teachers of Christianity, and their want of self-assertion ; the whole of Christ's Church has found cause to thank God for their sincerity and truthfulness, and for the evidence their candid admission, and their unwillingness to screen

His disciples at the first: but when Jesus was glorified,
then remembered they that these things were written of
Him, and *that* they had done these things unto Him.

And when He was come nigh, even now at the descent

their own shortcomings and ignorance, give to the fact that their
illumination was of the direct influence of the Holy Spirit (see John
xiv. 25, 26), who not only recalled to them our Lord's recorded
teaching, but prompted the inferences they deduced from it. In the
present instance, the disciples neither thought of the prophecy they
were in the act of fulfilling, nor perceived how significant of a spiritual
kingdom of peace, were the very steps they took to hail the dawn
of their visionary reign of Christ, over the Roman oppressor, and over
the heathen, upon the restored throne of David's temporal sovereignty:
a proof of the remarks made above (see note 14) on the unconsciousness
of human agents in the fulfilment of prophecy.

20. *glorified.*—When Jesus had ascended to the throne of His
glory, and had poured down upon the disciples the Spirit from on
high, the promised Comforter, the Holy Ghost, then there opened to
their minds the true bearing of what they had taken part in. One of
the gifts then bestowed on them, was the gift of prophecy, and of
the understanding of ancient predictions. We may suppose that
other quotations, cited and illustrated by the Evangelists, became impressed on their minds in this way (see John ii. 17, 22, viii. 28, xiii.
7, xvi. 12, 13); though some may have been expounded to them by
our Lord Himself (as in Matt. xvii. 11–13; Luke xxiv. 27, 32). We
notice, too, that very much of His teaching must have been an-
ticipatory of this period of spiritual illumination, before which it was
as a parable to them. See their confession of this in John xvi. 29:
"Now speakest Thou plainly, and speakest no proverb."

21. *they had done these things.*—The setting Him upon the colt,
and spreading their garments upon it, and along the road, and their
saluting Him so royally, "Hosanna to the Son of David;" which the
disciples and the multitude did.

22. *at the descent.*—(See App. X.) Dean Stanley's description of
this progress, though so often cited, is too remarkable to need apology
for insertion here. "Gradually the long procession swept up and
over the ridge where first begins 'the descent of the mount of Olives'
towards Jerusalem. At this. point the first view is caught of the
south-eastern corner of the city. The Temple and the more northern
portions are hid by the slope of Olivet on the right. What is seen
is only Mount Zion . . . and the angle of the western walls . . .
surmounted by the castle of Herod, on the supposed site of the palace
of David, from which that portion of Jerusalem, emphatically 'the
city of David,' derived its name. It was at this precise point, 'as He
drew near, at the descent of the Mount of Olives'—may it not have

of the mount of Olives, the whole multitude of the disciples began to rejoice and praise God with a loud voice for all the mighty works that they had seen; saying, Blessed *be* the King that cometh in the name of the Lord, peace in heaven, and glory in the highest. And some of the Pharisees from among the multitude said

been from the sight thus opening upon them?—that the shout burst forth from the multitude, ' Hosanna to the Son of David ! '"

23. *multitude of the disciples.*—Certainly many more than our Lord's personal followers.. Bartimæus (Luke xviii. 43) and Lazarus were doubtless with them ; and other grateful recipients of His healing grace, who may have been going to return thanks at Jerusalem at this festival ; and probably a large number of those who were, more or less decidedly, His followers, who were gathered on the performance of those mighty works that they had seen (especially the restoration of sight to Bartimæus, and the raising of Lazarus, so recent and so notable), in the hope that Christ was now going to assume the throne, and to claim the government of Israel.

24. *rejoice and praise God.*—Their united ascription of 'praise has almost the appearance of a set form of thanksgiving ; such were known to the Jews.

25. *the King.*—They, like others, hoped that "the kingdom of God was now immediately about to appear." (See Luke xix. 11.)

26. *in the name of the Lord.*—Consciously or unconsciously, they were fulfilling His words in Luke xiii. 35.

27. *peace in heaven.*—(See Luke ii. 14.) We may well suppose that some of these disciples were familiar with the words of the angels' song, and that they were then echoing it.

28. *glory in the highest.*—*i.e.* in heaven; the same as " Hosanna in the highest." S. Luke, writing to Gentile readers, translates an expression which they could not understand. They thus invoke God's approval and ratification of their act, from the highest heaven.

29. *the Pharisees.*—(See App. II.) They were there on a malicious errand. Already they had held one secret council, at which they consulted to put both Christ and Lazarus to death, and so to silence both the preacher and witness of accredited truth (John xii. 10, 11) ; and they kept sitting, at frequent intervals during this week, at Jerusalem, with the same intent. They were now watching our Lord, and no doubt were well pleased at first with acclamations, which they could easily represent as seditious. But as the enthusiasm increased, they began to fear its results; and, carried away with passion and jealousy—just as they were moved next day, when the voices of children did Him honour in the Temple (Matt. xxi. 15, 16)—they desired our Lord's own interference. They thus showed how clearly they

unto Him, Master, rebuke Thy disciples.   And He answered and said unto them, I tell you that, if these should hold their peace, the stones would immediately cry out.

Much people that were come to the feast, when they

at least, understood the general purport of His mission; for they would not else have asked Him to repress enthusiasm, whose hopes they well knew He did not purpose realizing. It was their crowning sin, that they saw (John ix. 40, 41), more clearly than other men, what Christ's real pretensions were; and they would not acknowledge Him as more than an ordinary teacher. They were, however, soon obliged to whisper amongst themselves, how vain at present were their insidious efforts against the Christ (John xii. 19). It is sad to be unable to give them credit for mistaken zeal in God's service. The whole narrative shows malice, and plotting, and murder, and perjury, and blasphemy, to have been sins to which they were no strangers; these sins would have discredited the cause of any religious zeal, and they were sins which were distinctly branded, in the law of the God whose word they dishonoured. If we require further evidence of their utter worthlessness, we have but to read the account given by Josephus of their conduct, a few years later, within the walls of their besieged city: his studied suppression of all fair notice of Christianity (App. III.) shows him a witness prejudiced in their favour.

30. *the stones.*—An expression of proverbial mould, which has many illustrations among sacred, and classical writers, but is scarcely a proverb. (See Ps. xcvi. 11–13; Hab. ii. 11, iii. 10–13; Matt. iii. 9.) The kingdom of nature would own the presence of her Maker, though men might appear unmoved. So "the rocks were rent" at Christ's crucifixion (Matt. xxvii. 51). Bede points out the convulsions of nature at our Lord's crucifixion, as instances of the actual fulfilment of this remark of our Lord; men either disowned Him, or stood afar off, but nature felt what was being done on earth, and owned her Lord. S. Gregory thus expresses this sympathy of nature with her Lord's presence: "the heavens knew Him, and forthwith sent out a star, and a company of angels to sing His birth. The sea knew Him, and made itself a way to be trodden by His feet. The earth knew Him, and trembled at His dying. The sun knew Him, and hid the rays of its light. The rocks knew Him, for they were rent in twain. Hades knew Him, and gave up the dead it had received. But though the senseless elements perceived Him to be their Lord, the hearts of the unbelieving Jews knew Him not as God; and, harder than the very rocks, were not rent in pieces by repentance." (See xxi. 29; II. i. 5.)

31. *that were come to the feast.*—Jerusalem was full of people at this time; the people of Galilee, so accustomed to His progresses through

heard that Jesus was coming to Jerusalem, took branches of palm trees, and went forth to meet Him. The people therefore that were with Him when He called Lazarus out of his grave, and raised him from the dead, bare record. For this cause the people also met Him, for that they heard that He had done this miracle.

their towns and villages, amongst the number : and the fame of the mighty miracle wrought lately at Bethany, had spread throughout the city. And now the news had come, that Jesus was setting out to go to the city; and so "they went forth to meet Him," carrying palm branches, emblems of victory—a most significant action (see Rev. vii. 9, 10)—to grace His triumph. This crowd went forward, until they met the procession coming in from Bethany, with Christ in their midst; they then turned round, and headed the procession towards the city : so becoming, in S. Mark's words (xi. 9), "they that went before :" whilst those who had conducted Christ from Bethany now became "they that followed." (See note 38, 39).

32. *when He called.*—Many of the best MSS. have "*that* He called." The change in the original, of the vowel "e" for "i," gives this reading; the sense then is, " The multitude that was with Him bare record that He called Lazarus out of the grave, and raised him from the dead." These were willing and prompt to join the acclamations of the "multitude of the disciples," and their loud hosannas expressed their praises. These shouts of triumph are mentioned by all the Evangelists, though S. John alone give account of the miracle which immediately prompted them, so guiding us to the reason ; probably because Lazarus was alive when the other three wrote (tradition says he lived at least 30 years after he was raised from the dead), and because the malice of the rulers against him (John xii. 9–11) still continued. Another instance of this caution is given in the case of the disciple who cut off the ear of the servant of the high priest, at the arrest of Jesus. S. John alone mentions the name of the disciple, Peter, and that of the servant, Malchus, writing when both were dead, and therefore when nothing was to be feared ; whilst all the other Evangelists merely record the fact, without mention of names. If the rendering of the A. V. in this passage is retained, it still equally connects the reason for their rejoicing with the fact which all record.

33. *bare record.*—Of the miracle, of which many had been eye-witnesses, and which was accepted by all as a notorious fact ; to the multitude which crowded forth from Jerusalem to meet them, moved very much with anxiety to know the circumstances of this mighty act, and to see Lazarus.

34. *the people met Him.*—This was apparently the other division of the multitude who issued from Jerusalem, in consequence of the news

And a very great multitude spread their garments in the way; others cut down branches from the trees, and strawed *them* in the way. And the multitudes that went before, and that followed, cried, saying, **Hosanna**

of the great miracle being spread through the city, and of the announcement that Christ and Lazarus were approaching.

35. *a very great multitude.*—Lit. "the greatest part of the multitude." The outer crowd now caught up the enthusiastic plaudits of the disciples, and those immediately about them; and, like some mighty chorus, pealed it forth, until it rose on every side of Jesus, and perhaps reached the distant city. And as it swelled up from the thousands of hearts and voices, it grew more definite in its ascription of glory to Him as the Messiah; "Blessed is He that cometh;" "Blessed is the King of Israel;" "Blessed be the kingdom of our father David, that cometh in the name of the Lord;" "Hosanna in the highest."

36. *spread their garments.*—Not only imitating the action of the disciples, but emphasizing it; they also ascribed regal honours to the Christ.

37. *branches.*—The palm branches, no doubt, chiefly. The spreading of the king's path with leaves and flowers, was a well-known emblem of rejoicing, and one connected, in the Jewish mind, with joy and thanksgiving (Lev. xxiii. 40). Their song of praise was part of that which belonged to the thanksgiving service of the Feast of Tabernacles, which was celebrated in the autumn, and was the most joyous festival of the year. The use of the word "Hosanna" became so general in connection with this thanksgiving, that it was given to the palm branches used at this festival. From the use of these branches, thus significant, we derive the name by which this day is now designated, "Palm Sunday."

38. *they that went before.*—(See note 31.) Those who had come from Jerusalem to meet Him, and turned back towards the city on joining the procession. The Greek here marks emphatically the two great divisions of which the procession was composed: "And the multitude, those that went before, and those that followed," etc.

39. *they that followed.*—Those who had come with Christ from Bethany; including, doubtless, very large accessions of those who were on their way from the upper provinces to Jerusalem, to keep the Passover. The ancient writers see here an intimation, that believers before our Lord's advent, and Christians, praise and confess Him with one harmonious voice.

40. *Hosanna.*—*i.e.* "Save, I pray." The words of Ps. cxviii. 25, 26, here quoted, are—"Save now, I beseech thee, O Lord. . . . Blessed be He that cometh in the name of the Lord." They were always interpreted of the Messiah, and therefore so used by this multitude.

to the Son of David: **Blessed** *is* **He that cometh in the**

41. *the Son of David.*—This expression proved that the multitudes now hailed Jesus as the promised Messiah, promised to Adam, to Abraham, and to David; and to whom all the prophets gave witness; in whom all the services of their religion were centred, and to whose kingdom their "twelve tribes, instantly serving God day and night, hoped to come." This was really their recognition of Christ as the promised Messiah; though His was, to their minds and hopes, a temporal sovereignty, connected with the delivery of the Church from Roman rule, and with their national exaltation to the empire of this world. Their rejection of Him, a few days later, was caused by their persuasion that He would not so deliver them; and that He was not therefore, as they had supposed, the true Messiah. The reaction of opinion, the evil guidance by which they were led, and their national excitability, may explain much; the fact that then was the hour of the powers of darkness, and that they were given up to their delusion, because they had suffered themselves to be led to reject the truth which they might have perceived, may explain the rest of their extraordinary perversity, and wickedness.

42. *blessed is He that cometh.*—Bishop Horne has striking remarks in connection with this subject: "At the time predicted by the prophets, not only Jerusalem looked for a completion of the prophecies, but the whole earth sat still, expecting that Judæa should give her a King. And, lo, the promised King of the Jews is come of the royal house and lineage of David. All the circumstances of His birth, the words of His mouth, and the actions of His life, demonstrate Him to be the Messiah, foretold by the prophets from the beginning of the world. He cometh to His own; and Jerusalem is commanded to rejoice and shout: but His own received Him not; and Jerusalem turns a deaf ear to the voice of all her prophets, not suffering herself to believe that anything said by them could refer to Jesus of Nazareth. Her heart was depraved and hardened; she demanded to be put in possession of the empire of the world; she despised the appearance of her King with the acclamations of an ignoble multitude, and soon nailed a spiritual monarch to the cross. With how different sensations are the members of the Christian Church affected, when they hear the words of Zechariah, 'Behold, thy King cometh unto thee.' We join His train; we attend Him in His progress towards Jerusalem, and seem to enter with Him into the holy city, while the whole multitude of those who go before, and who follow after cry, 'Hosanna to the Son of David: Blessed is He that cometh in the name of the Lord.' When we behold the scene, we are taught to conceive by it a noble idea of the Messiah, at His first advent, ushered into the Church as her Lord and King; the prophets going before, and Apostles following after Him: all proclaiming and bearing testimony to Jesus, all singing 'Hosanna to the Son of David!' all pronouncing the blessedness of Him who cometh

name of the Lord: Hosanna in the highest ; Blessed *is* the King of Israel that cometh in the name of the Lord. Blessed *be* the kingdom of our father David, that cometh in the name of the Lord : Hosanna in the highest.

The Pharisees therefore said among themselves, Per-

in the name of Jehovah. We know that this is He 'to whom give all the prophets witness,' and that He hath fulfilled those things which were written of Him. We know that He hath overcome our enemies, and triumphed gloriously ; that He hath erected a universal and ever-lasting kingdom, and given laws to the world; nay, that He doth govern all things in heaven and earth." Dr. Geike notices, that this ascription of praise is said to have been sung as a hymn in the early Church.

43. *in the name of the Lord.*—With the power of God, and in fulfilment of His continuous promises. The words may be rendered, " Blessed in the name of Jehovah be He that cometh," *i.e.* Messiah.

44. *the Pharisees.*—(See App. II.) Referring to the council of the Sanhedrim, which had been held to consider the question of putting Jesus and Lazarus to death (John xi. 47–50); at which Caiaphas, with plausible craft, proposed to give up Christ to the Roman power, as a mover of sedition. It seems that the Pharisees now despaired of effect-ing their purpose through the agency of the Sanhedrim, as a court for taking cognizance of offences against the national religion, and there-fore determined to give in to the policy of the Sadducees, under Caiaphas, and to press the charge of political treason, which eventually brought Christ to His death by Roman executioners. This also, and not any mitigation of their malevolence, may partly explain the circumstance, which is so noticeable with regard to the Pharisees at this crisis, that having been our Lord's enemies actively during the whole of His career, they now seem to retire into the background, and leave the chief priests to be the prominent agents in the closing scenes of His life. The conduct of the leaders of the great Jewish sects, and of the chief priests, is very extraordinary; there is no parallel to it. Wherever Christianity has come in contact with the priests and leaders of any other religion, it has been opposed vigorously, and often insidiously ; but scarcely with the avowed intention of putting out the true light. It has never been brought into collision with any other religion which, like that of the Jews, came direct from God, the Author also of Christianity ; which was essentially introductory to Christianity (Gal. iii. 23–26), and whose intelligent advocates should therefore have recognized, and hailed its advent. Our Lord's decision must have been the true one : " He that is of God heareth My words : ye therefore hear them not, because ye are not of God." The Sadducee's consciousness of wrong is shown in his anxiety to put to death the Author and the witness of the resurrec-tion (John xii. 10, 11), rather than refute what he professed to disbe-

ceive ye how ye prevail nothing? behold, the world is gone after Him.

And when He was come near, He beheld the city, and

lieve, by fair arguments; or, failing this, renounce his error, and embrace the manifest truth. The Pharisee, too, strangely gave up the opportunity of making a point against the rival sect, with the aid of Christ's doctrine. But these, and other sects of the Jews, were found to forego their bitter hostility, in order to become confederate against Christ (Matt. xxii. 15, 23, 34). This object made them, for the time, associates in evil, just as Herod and Pontius Pilate "were made friends together," on the day of their mutual persecution of Christ (Luke xxiii. 7, 12).

45. *prevail nothing.*—It was useless, in the face of this general defection, to arraign Christ on a charge of false doctrine: "they feared the people."

46. *the world.*—The exaggeration of discontent and rage. They did not think it so far gone in devotion to Christ, as to be beyond recall to their allegiance. They thoroughly understood the power of their own influence, and the temper of the people whom they ruled.

47. *when He was come near.*—The glimpse of the city which was gained "at the descent of the Mount of Olives" was lost, as the road dips for a short distance "behind the ridge of Olivet. A few moments and the path mounts again, it climbs a rugged ascent, it reaches a ledge of smooth rock; and in an instant the whole city bursts into view. . . . It is hardly possible to doubt that this rise and turn of the road, this rocky ledge, was the exact spot where the multitude paused again, and He, when He beheld the city, wept over it. Nowhere else on the Mount of Olives is there a view like this. . . . Here His eyes beheld what is still the most impressive sight which the neighbourhood of Jerusalem furnishes, and the tears rushed forth at the view." (*Stanley.*) (See App. X.)

48. *He beheld the city.*—The sight of the city, "beautiful for situation, the joy of the whole earth," was a most impressive one. It has exercised a strange fascination over travellers in every age; but never could it have looked more grand and striking, than at this time. The fortifications of Herod, and of the Romans, gave it the appearance of impregnable strength, especially from the point of view from which our Lord beheld it. It seemed to rise up in towering majesty directly from the valley below; and if the Temple then standing, was deemed less sacred than that of Solomon, it was probably far more magnificent in proportions, and in external detail. (See App. X.) But though the hosannas of the multitude were ringing in His ears, He beheld the city with the omniscient eye of God; it was before Him a guilty and abandoned city, about to be God-forsaken, full of souls for whom He should give His own life in vain. He saw before Him the scenes of

wept over it, saying, If thou hadst known, even thou, at least in this thy day, the things *which belong* unto thy

His Passion, the cross of His agony; and He heard the frenzied cries of popular execration, and rejection. A little further distant in time, were the Roman eagles, gathering to devour the carcase of the dead Church of the Jews. (See xviii. 81.) It has been noticed how peculiarly this passage proves the union of the two natures of Christ: He weeps as man, over the woes which He adjudges and foretells as God.

49. *He wept over it.*—The original word is much stronger than that used by S. John (xi. 35), to express the weeping of Jesus at the grave of Lazarus. Here He wept for the ruin of the city of God, and, far more, for the souls perishing therein. In the present instance, He poured forth His lamentations with His tears; He wept aloud: in the former case, the tears flowed from His eyes, but He wept in silence. We must not overlook the analogy, between the fair and guilty city, long so full of promise, so often warned and entreated, on which so many hopes had centred; and the human soul, heir of such excellent promises, and of such high aspirations. For thus, when its doom is imminent, after its rejection of all warnings and of its Saviour's love, He weeps over the ruin which He may not avert. And so angels, in whose presence " there is joy over one sinner that repenteth," weep at the thought of the depths of woe, in which he must be for ever engulphed from their view.

50. *over it.*—It was over the city, and its coming doom, and its determined impenitence, its unatoned-for sin, but not over the prospect of His own sufferings, that our Lord sorrowed; these wrung from Him neither tears, nor cry of agony, nor expression of pain, nor word of entreaty.

51. *if thou hadst known.*—Or, "O that thou hadst known." This is the breathing of the Saviour's earnest desire, now despairing of its fulfilment.

52. *in this thy day.*—The day of grace, when Christ would repeat, with fullest assurance, all the offers of mercy He had made to His people. The disciples (Luke xix. 37) had recognized this day, as the Psalm they had quoted in their ascription of praise taught them. The whole passage runs thus: " This is the day which the Lord hath made; we will rejoice and be glad in it. Hosanna. . . . Blessed is He that cometh in the name of the Lord." (Ps. cxviii. 25, 26.) There is a connection apparent in our Lord's mind, between the fulfilment of this passage in the action of the multitude of disciples, and in that of the reckless city, in whose Paschal Hallel it would presently be sung: " *We*" (the disciples) "will rejoice and be glad in it." "O that *thou* (Jerusalem) hadst known, *thou also*, in this thy day, the things that belong unto thy peace!"

53. *the things which belong to thy peace.*—Ancient writers have noticed an allusion to the name of Jerusalem, in our Saviour's words. It means,

peace ! but now they are hid from thine eyes. For the days shall come upon thee, that thine enemies shall cast a trench about thee, and compass thee round, and keep thee in on every side, and shall lay thee even with the ground, and thy children within thee ; and they shall not leave in thee one stone upon another ; because thou knewest not the time of thy visitation.

And when He was come into Jerusalem, all the city

"They shall see peace." Christ Himself was the "Prince of peace," who now came to offer true peace to His royal city : " Would thou wert indeed *Jerusalem*, and hadst seen the things which belong to thy peace."

54. *hid.*—Not by the removal of Christ's grace, for His religion was continually offered first to the Jews, wherever it was preached ; but "hid" by their own wilful blindness, and by the darkness of their own prejudices, which have now brought down the impenetrable gloom of God's wrath.

55. *thine enemies.*—The Roman armies, which minutely fulfilled these words of our Lord ; who, a day or two later, repeated with additional distinctness, this prophecy of doom upon the city, Church, and nation of the Jews. Our Lord's words were literally fulfilled. Titus encircled the city with a mound and trench, lines of circumvallation whose circuit was nearly five miles, and he levelled the buildings. (See xviii. 53–57, 67.)

56. *the time of thy visitation.*—The day when Christ personally visited the city with the offer of salvation. Again we notice the analogy to the human soul ; how Christ's visitation of mercy may not be neglected. For, like Jerusalem, men perish not necessarily for their sins, but for their blindness, and for their rejection of the day of their gracious visitation ; their perverseness blinds them alike to present opportunities, and to the evils which are coming. If men thought deeply, like our Lord, of this danger, how earnestly and frequently they would pray that the day might never come to them, when " the things which belong to their soul's peace should be hidden from their eyes," and when " the acceptable year of the Lord " should have given place to " the day of vengeance of our God."

57. *all the city was moved.*—She should " lift up her gates " to welcome the " King of glory ;" but she knows Him not yet. The entrance of so vast a procession, into a city so crowded with Jews of every district of Palestine, and with those of other lands, who were gathered at the city to the festival, must have attracted considerable attention. Perhaps its approach had been descried from the distance ; and some, it may be, derisively, and some in the eagerness of warm and friendly enthusiasm, asked whose coming was so royally

was moved, saying, Who is this? And the multitude said, This is Jesus the prophet of Nazareth of Galilee.

And Jesus entered into Jerusalem, and into the temple : and when He had looked round about upon all

greeted. There were, however, many minds ever on the stretch for indications of the Messiah's advent; and, familiar as the Jews were with the letter of Scripture, some of them may have thought of Zechariah's prophecy, as the procession entered Jerusalem.

58. *who is this?*—"Ask Moses, and he shall tell you, The seed of the woman that shall bruise the serpent's head. Ask our father Jacob, and he shall tell you, The Shiloh of the tribe of Judah. Ask David, and he shall tell you, The King of glory. Ask Isaiah, and he shall tell you, Emmanuel, Wonderful, Counsellor, The mighty God, The everlasting Father, The Prince of peace. Ask Daniel, and he shall tell you, The Messiah. Ask John the Baptist, and he shall tell you, The Lamb of God. If you ask the God of the Prophets, He hath told you, 'This is My beloved Son, in whom I am well pleased.' Yea, if all these be too good for you to consult with, the devils themselves have been forced to say, 'I know Thee who thou art, the Holy One of God.' On no side hath Christ left Himself without a testimony; and accordingly the multitude have their answer ready, 'This is Jesus the prophet of Nazareth of Galilee.'" (*Bishop Hall.*)

59. *the prophet of Nazareth.*—This answer is peculiar, from the lips which had so lately hailed Him as King, and Son of David, titles of higher meaning. There may, however, be an allusion in " *the* prophet " to Him of whom Moses wrote (Deut. xviii. 18). S. John describes those who formed the front of the procession as it entered the city (and by whom, therefore, the inquiry of those within it could be answered), as "much people were come to the feast." Very probably many of them had come from Galilee, and now claimed Jesus as the especial Prophet of their own country, in which He had done so many mighty works.

60. *looked round.*—Our Lord entered His Father's House, and presented Himself before God. See His declaration of Himself, and the fulfilment of His mission (Ps. xl. 6–11). He thus fulfilled the prophecy of Malachi iii. 1; the Lord had "suddenly come to His Temple." The precincts of the Temple were now crowded with those who had been worshipping there; but the hour of sacrifice was over; they that bought, and they that sold, and the changers of money were leaving its courts; and, beyond the gesture of survey, and disapprobation doubtless, which the Evangelist remarks, Christ took no notice of what He saw until the morrow. He could not conclude in anger this day of rejoicing. And as the evening closed on this eventful day, the multitudes dispersed; and He returned with His personal followers to the quiet village, which He had left a few hours before, on His triumphal progress to the city. It seems indeed strange that He could

things, and now the eventide was come, He went out unto Bethany with the twelve.

𝕸onday in 𝕳oly 𝖂eek.

II. *THE BARREN FIG TREE.*

S. Matt. xxi. 18, 19 ; S. Mark xi. 12–14.

Now in the morning, as He returned into the city from Bethany, He was hungry : and seeing a fig tree afar off

have departed so quietly, after so demonstrative an entry. The interest of the multitude speedily droops, and they quickly melt away. They sought their homes, and left Him to seek His. There is no mention of any hospitality being offered Him, in the city which He had just entered as a King. Bede, who delights to press words, and actions, and names, for any significance latent in them, notices a fitness in our Lord's sojourn at *Bethany* (" the house of obedience ") with the family so devoted to Him there ; for that in the heart of obedience Christ will ever make His dwelling-place.

Lightfoot explains the melting away of the multitude who had attended Christ, by a rule that travellers, with their unwashen feet and soiled garments, might not approach the precincts of the Temple.

Our Lord's example of going to God's House on entering a town, or city, is oftener followed in the letter, than in the spirit. Men often go to inspect architectural beauty, or antiquities, or decorations in God's House ; but do they as often go to seek God's presence there ?

1. *He was hungry.*—It is interesting to notice the indications of our Lord's humanity, as He approaches the end of His mission. Though the example of His life is now perfected ; and though His divinity is more clearly displayed ; and we see that His sacrifice for sins is a Divine sacrifice, through all the awe and mystery which surround the closing act of redemption ; we gain now a more distinct impression of His humanity, than at any period of His life. In His friendship with the family at Bethany, amongst whom He spent so much of this week ; in His appreciation of acts of personal devotion, such as the anointing by Mary ; in His closer intimacy with His disciples ; in the tenderness of His sorrow ; in His true manliness in suffering ; in His filial affection as manifested on the cross ; in the exhaustion which hastened His death ; and in many other instances, we see that He was as truly the Son of man, as in other respects it was patent that

having leaves, He came, if haply He might find anything

"truly this man was the Son of God." On the present occasion,
vigils of prayer, and the deep anxiety of His mind, had wearied and
exhausted Him; and the prospect of the cooling fruit, which belonged
to a more genial season, rather than to these days of affliction and
agony, caught His fancy, and He hungered for it. Several of the
ancient writers see a spiritual allusion, to Christ's hunger for the
fruits of righteousness amongst His people, the Jews; and His punishment of their great and flourishing pretence, combined with their utter
want of reality. (See note 2.)

2. *a fig tree.*—S. Matthew, with an emphasis which our translation
has missed, says "a *single* fig tree." Early writers have noticed
several senses, in which this tree, and its fate, are a parable to the
world. It was that one tree of our Lord's choice, fair to see, and full
of religious promise, which God had graced, and watched, and warned,
and tended under the dispensation of the law, by priest and by prophet, by judge and by king; the tree from which, during these three
years of His own ministry, He had come seeking fruit, and had found
none; on which the sentence had gone forth, "cut it down;" over
which, after His efforts in vain to avert the end, He had lately wept,
for it knew not the time of visitation. The fig tree is a symbol and
parable throughout the Scriptures. Our Lord hungered for the fruits
of righteousness from the chosen tree, from this Jewish Church of
many and great professions; and it bore no fruit now, nor were there
the gleanings even of fruitfulness, under its late history (see note 5);
it flourished only in external show. He deposed it from its trust, and
destroyed it. The Jewish Church should no more hereafter for ever
be the representative guardian of God's truth. And, as this act of
destruction is a parable of the end of the Jewish Church, so it is a
warning to every branch of the Church of Christ, and further, to
every individual member of the Church, that Christ must find fruit
where He sees profession; or the same sentence will pass from Him,
of utter doom. "All this was done in figure: in this act of Thine I
see both an emblem and a prophecy. How didst Thou herein seem
to teach Thy disciples how much Thou hatest an unfruitful profession; and what judgment Thou meantest to bring upon that barren
generation? Once before hast Thou compared the Jewish nation
to a fig tree in the midst of Thy vineyard, which, after three years'
expectation and culture yielded no fruit, was by Thee, the Owner,
doomed to a speedy excision; now Thou actest what Thou then saidst.
No tree abounds more with leaf and shade; no nation abounded more
with ceremonial observations, and semblances of piety. Outward
profession, where there is want of inward truth and real practice, doth
but help to draw on and aggravate judgment." (*Bishop Hall.*)

3. *having leaves.*—This was a significant fact. The fruit of the fig

thereon : and when He came to it, He found nothing but leaves ; for the time of figs was not *yet*. And Jesus

tree comes out before the leaves appear, which then grow over to shadow and protect it : so do rites and ceremonies defend and guard the truths they present to us. The leaves, therefore, supposed the fruit; the ceremonies, truth. It was a type of the Jewish Church, which was adorned with all that external profession could offer to the eye, but whose promise was a false pretence.

4. *nothing but leaves.*—The fact of there being leaves, showed that there might, and ought to have been fruit ; the sap that produced the one, should have formed the other. The grace of God, which gives men knowledge of His ways sufficient to produce the outward appearances of true religion, is sufficient to produce the fruits of righteousness in their integrity, and the reality of religious life. The truth must be natural and possible, or the counterfeit would never be able to obtain currency. Christ does not expect what He has no right to look for; for He has made it true of religion within the conditions of His Gospel, that it is easer to be, than to seem.

5. *the time.*—The precocity of the tree brought on its ruin. It was in advance of all other trees; and, at a time when, under usual circumstances, fruit could not have been expected, it offered fruit. The Jewish Church stood in advance of all the world, in religious profession, rather than in truth. The Jews claimed God as their Father, and boasted His especial favour; but yet the hour of the fulfilment of their trust had not come. They should have been the first to learn the truth of Christ, as they had ever the first offer of His Gospel; they had been trained under the guardianship of the law, that the Gospel of Christ might be committed to their charge, in order that they should promulgate it amongst the nations. But they assumed to have already the *final* dispensation of God, and to be the exclusive inheritors of His promise; thus, they professed not only to have more than they had, but more than they were expected to have. We see this precocity in religious profession in individuals also; it promises too much: in the days of growth it professes maturity. Its danger is shown here: God does not expect of those young in the faith, the ripe maturity of elders; it is enough that they be ready to learn, and prompt to obey, that they offer the early fruits of righteousness. There is an unhealthiness about a too flourishing profession ; it may rob the life of fruit, and the soul may be withered in its unreality. For there is time and season, growth and maturity, in the religious life; and precocity is often the herald of decay. Farrar notices that this tree was "hopelessly barren;" there were neither the gleanings of the autumnal figs, nor the first ripe spring figs; "but on this fruitless tree there was neither any promise for the future, nor any gleanings from the past."

answered and said unto it, No man eat fruit of thee hereafter for ever. And His disciples heard it.

III. *THE CLEANSING OF THE TEMPLE.*

S. Matt. xxi. 12, 13 ; S. Mark xl. 15-19 ; S. Luke xix. 45, 46.

And they come to Jerusalem : and Jesus went into the

6. *answered.*—Answered the voice of assertion of fruitfulness, in the flourishing profession of the leaves.

7. *No man eat fruit.*—" Let this which is thy fault be thy punishment; that since thou bearest no fruit at all, never mayest thou more bear any fruit." (*Bishop Hall.*) It was characteristic of Christ's mercy that He gave this severe lesson to mankind in the instance of a tree only. It was His one act of judgment, the sole exertion of His miraculous power in destruction ; and it was no human life that was sacrificed : none of the many false ones who surrounded Him were withered as an example. It loses none of its force, however, in contrast with the fact that whenever He saved it was man that received the grace of salvation. Bengel observes, " The Old Testament has many miracles of destruction, the New Testament but one ; " or, as Archbishop Trench happily expresses it, " Christ's miracles of mercy were unnumbered, and on men ; His miracle of judgment was but one, and on a tree." Bishop Jeremy Taylor mentions an ancient fancy that this was the tree " in the eating of whose fruit Adam made an inlet to sin."

8. *for ever.*—Yet with a limitation as to the spiritual interpretation; for as in Ezek. xvii. 24 we read, " I the Lord have dried up the green tree, and made the dry tree to flourish," so we read (Rom. xi.) that there is a restoration ordained for the house of Israel, coupled with a mighty extension of the Church of Christ.

9. *the disciples heard it.*—They remarked and reflected on a manifestation of power so unusual on their Lord's part. It is the object of a parable, spoken or acted, to lead to this observation and reflection; for so, when the meaning is found, its lesson is indelibly engraven on the mind.

1. *Jesus went.*—There is a close connection between the doom just pronounced upon the fruitless fig tree, and the action of our Lord in the Temple. The disciples, who had in their thoughts the act of unusual severity which they had but now witnessed, might perhaps see one lesson, of many which it was intended to convey by parable. The cleansing of the Temple itself was in a high degree figurative : it foreshadowed a far more important cleansing of the House of God

temple of God, and began to cast out them that sold

for all time, than even that of the Temple of Jerusalem, important as it was; and the lesson thus doubly impressed, must have entered deeply into the hearts of those whose office it was to found the Church of Christ, when all things that He had spoken to them were brought to their remembrance, and made clear to them.

2. *the temple of God.*—(See App. IV.)   Though our Lord was in His Father's House, it is not likely He ever went beyond the court of the Israelites, to which He had legal access.   The court which was the scene of this cleansing, was exterior to that of the Israelites, and was called the court of the Gentiles, to whom the profanation of holy places by those who held holy offices must have been a great stumbling-block, and scandal.   (See xvi. 1, 7.)

3. *began to cast out.*—This is the second time our Lord had performed this most significant act; once at the commencement of His public ministry, as related by S. John only, and now again at its close, as the other Evangelists narrate.   There is in certain respects a great difference in these acts, which have such strong points of resemblance.   There is the same zeal, which "even consumed Him," and gave to our Lord a dignity, and irresistible power to carry out what no ruler might have dared to attempt, nor even avowed force could have scarce effected.   None might meet His look, and resist His will; nor could men then question the right He assumed, to exercise authority in His Father's House; for this was one of those occasions when the Divinity of His nature asserted itself, and men fell backward before Him.   S. Jerome accounts that, of all the signs of our Lord, this was the greatest manifestation of power, greater than the raising of Lazarus, or than even the Transfiguration; speaking of His thus confronting so many enemies, he says, "Surely a flame and starry ray darted from His eyes, and the majesty of the Godhead was radiant in His countenance."   But there was this difference in the two occasions: in the first instance, He cleansed the Temple and pointed out the sin of those who desecrated it, calling them to repentance, and exhorting them to amendment, saying, "Make not My Father's House a house of merchandise;" but now the sentence is pronounced, "Ye have made it a den of thieves," and they are cast forth without reprieve.   This was the fulfilment of God's word by the mouth of Malachi (iii. 1–5); the Lord, whom they professed to seek in the elaborate ceremonial of their worship, had unexpectedly come to His Temple, and sat there as a Refiner, and Purifier, and as a Judge.

The account of S. Matthew seems to place this cleansing of the Temple, on the day of our Lord's public entry; but a careful comparison of the passage with the parallel passages, in S. Mark especially, and S. Luke, shows, as most writers agree, that it was on the following day.   As our Lord "looked round about upon all things" in the Temple, on the evening of His entry, He could not see this profanation

and bought in the temple, and overthrew the tables of
the moneychangers, and the seats of them that sold
doves ; and would not suffer that any man should carry
any vessel through the temple. And He taught, saying

of it in action, though the stalls and tables of the traders might be
there; for the services of the day were over, and these " thieves " of
the sanctuary had gone forth.

4. *them that sold and bought.*—It is thought that these were priests,
who derived much unfair profit from traffic in the sacrifices of God ;
this trade was at least authorized, and protected by the priests. From
S. John we learn that sheep and oxen were bought, and sold in the
Temple. It was, no doubt, a great convenience to the majority of the
worshippers, that they could find fitting sacrifices for purchase, instead
of their having to bring them with them, from the distant parts of the
land. But there can be no justification of the desecration of God's
Temple, by its being made the seat of this traffic ; nor of the extor-
tionate charges, and unjust rates of exchange, which were exacted from
the necessities of the buyers.

5. *moneychangers.*—Those who changed the Roman, or Greek currency, for that which alone might be offered in the Temple, the Jewish
half shekel of the sanctuary (Exod. xxx. 13). It may be supposed how
gladly those who came from foreign lands, and those who had only the
money of Cæsar, would resort to tables of exchange ; but, again, there
was no need to place these within the Temple of God, nor to derive an
excessive and unjust gain from the barter.

6. *doves.*—(Gk. " *the* doves.") The offerings of the poorest classes
(Lev. v. 7). An exorbitant rate was charged even for these, and the
poor man was robbed in the exercise of his religious duties, even under
the very shadow of the House of his God. If we think how great an
addition to the difficulties, and fatigues of the journey to Jerusalem
from the more distant provinces, would be the charge of the sacrifices
they must offer, we shall see at once the desirableness of their sale
upon the spot ; but, then, how men must have " abhorred the offering
of the Lord," when, rather than thoughts of peace and holiness, they
took away the recollection of the unrighteous charges made upon them,
within God's House, by the very priests of His Temple, or under their
license, and for their profit. Corn. à Lapide says, those who sold doves
were women, but on what authority is not apparent.

7. *any vessel.*—Any vessel of ordinary use, not belonging to the
services of the sanctuary. In addition to the profanation of the Temple
by the usurer and the extortioner, the priests were accustomed to
allow the House of God to be made a common thoroughfare ; than
which nothing could be more destructive of the feeling of reverence, on
the part of those amongst whom they ministered, or more insulting to
the dignity of Almighty God. A parallel has been noticed (though it

unto them, Is it not written, My house shall be called of all nations the house of prayer ? but ye have made it A den of thieves. And the scribes and chief priests

should not be pressed) between the profanation and destruction of old S. Paul's Cathedral in London, and those of the Jewish Temple.

8. *He taught.*—A teaching which admonishes all ages, all clergy, and all worshippers. God's House must not be the resort of business and merchandise, much less of unjust license and gain. Those who, being in charge of sacred things, sell, trade, and seek ungodly gains, through the holy offices, and sacred influences, which they exercise in God's trust, are obnoxious to the punishment with which our Lord will surely visit them, and are ministering in a Church which their own act is degrading, and bringing to ruin ; for God will drive out such abominations from under the shadow of His House and Name. And (to take a more general view of the lesson here taught), if men bring their distractions of mind, their business, merchandise, daily work, pleasure, into the House of God, and mingle them with the utterance of worship and service ; if their hearts are offering these things before God, instead of the pure and hearty worship of the Spirit ; they will eventually be cast out of Christ's Church—if not from His House of Prayer on earth, surely from the Temple of the living God above, in the day when He shall sit as a Refiner and Purifier, and as the Sovereign Judge, upon the throne of God.

9. *of all nations.*—*i.e.* " for all nations." (See Isa. lvi. 6–8.) Perhaps S. Mark quotes these words of the prophet, which the other Evangelists omit, as writing especially for Gentile readers ; but we cannot but see the propriety, which would dissociate from the minds of Gentile men the idea of such profanation of the House of God, as that of which the court of the Gentiles had been the daily scene, under the authority of the priests of the Temple ; and, at the same time, express to them the catholicity of the pure Church of Christ, in which there should be no outer court, partitioned and profaned, which might be good enough for the Gentiles, who came thus near to the presence of God ; but, for Jew and Gentile, one Church of Christ, who came and preached peace, to the Gentile which was afar off, and to the Jew which was nigh, and who had " made both one, and had broken down the middle wall of partition between them " (Eph. ii. 14–17). The words were certainly significant words, as spoken by our Lord in the court of the Gentiles.

10. *a den of thieves.*—The words of Jer. vii. 11, alluded to by our Lord, are these : " Is this house, which is called by My name, become a den of robbers in your eyes ? Behold, I have seen it, saith the Lord." He then goes on (*vv.* 12–16) to show that as, in the case of Shiloh, profanation of God's House had led to final rejection, so would it be in this instance ; for this was a sin which should not be pardoned, and for which there should be no intercession. Nothing could be more detri-

heard *it*, and sought how they might destroy Him : for they feared Him, because all the people was aston-

mental to the cause of true religion, than that God's own priests should be looked on as robbers, by those who came to worship, and a visit to God's House as invested with the dangers of a stronghold of robbers, and this under the shadow of His great Name. This was one of the ways in which they made their proselytes twofold more the children of hell than themselves. (See xiv. 10.) The original word used by Jeremiah is a strong one. It means more than simple *thieves;* our word "robber" is nearer, which implies violence and murder. Luther's translation gives "den of murderers;" a fit description, if the term includes those who permitted, and profited by the profanation of the Temple. It might appear to them that their sin would be concealed in the sanctity of the Temple, as the robbers are hid in their den ; but our Lord foresaw their violent purposes, and foretold them, on the occasion of His first purification of the Temple, "Destroy this temple, and in three days I will raise it up." (John ii. 19.) In the siege of Jerusalem this designation became fearfully expressive; the Temple was indeed the stronghold of robbers and assassins.

Associating the lesson of the doom of the fig tree, with this that followed the abuse of the House of God, we cannot fail to see how justly the great pretence, and profuse ceremonial of the Jewish Church, covering, not fruits of holiness, and the nourishment of the nations in true religion, to those hungering after righteousness, but rather such nefarious and scandalous profanations, received the sentence, " No man hereafter for ever eat of thee the fruit of righteousness; receive from thee the ministration of eternal life."

11. *heard it.*—They may not themselves have been present when the cleansing of the Temple took place. If so, when intelligence was brought them, they renewed their consultations against His life, taking much thought how to compass this; for they could not openly seize Him in the present state of popular feeling; they were baffled for the moment. If present, however, when Christ drove out those who profaned the Temple under their license, they must have felt bitterly the reflection on themselves, which the popular approval evidently endorsed, in the judgment pronounced on the sellers, and money-changers. They considered that they only, who sat in Moses' seat, possessed the right to control the affairs of the Temple ; and Christ not only overruled this, but assumed publicly the authority of the Son of God, in the Temple of God.

12. *they feared Him.*—They had that sort of fear which evil men have of that which is good; and, in their consciousness of His being in the right, and themselves in the wrong, they sought to kill Him. They wished to have to themselves, without further chance of His interference, the authority, and the right which were His. Our Lord

ished at His doctrine: and could not find what they
might do: for all the people were very attentive to
hear Him.

And the blind and the lame came to Him in the
temple; and He healed them.   And when the chief

expressed this feeling against Himself, in His parable: "This is the
heir; come, let us kill Him, and the inheritance shall be ours."

13. *astonished.*—They were under the awe of that feeling which
Christ in other instances inspired; the awe in the presence of One
who "spake as never man spake," and who uttered words and truths,
which appealed to the consciousness of right within the hearers.   They
also understood the argument, grounded on their own witness of His
actions, "If this man were not *of God*, He could do nothing."

14. *very attentive.*—S. Luke's word is expressive of very intense
feeling; they "hung upon" His utterance.

15. *the blind and the lame.*—(See Keble's beautiful lines on this
subject in "Lyra Innocentium.")   No sooner had Christ cast out those
who desecrated the Temple, for whose exorbitant charges probably few
poor and afflicted persons could afford to offer any sacrifice, except
prayer, the "calves of their lips" (Hos. xiv. 2; Heb. xiii. 15), than
these persons of many and great necessities saw their opportunity,
and discerned the hope of acceptance: there was room made for them
in a Temple purified of abuses; and they come in numbers before
Christ, to implore His gifts of salvation.   The contrast between His
gracious acceptance of their prayer, and the severity which He had
just shown, in the case of those who "profaned the Temple" in their
sight, and were "blameless" in the eyes of the rulers, is very noticeable.   The poor and the devout are keen to recognize the abuses of
God's House, and prompt to occupy their own place therein the
moment these are swept away, and His church renovated and thrown
open to them.   It is one of the rules connected with the House of
God, and should never be forgotten, that, if we wish to see the poor
and the mass of the people in their place in our churches, we must
keep these clear of the exclusive usurpations and proprietory distinctions of the rich, who thus thrust them forth.   The abuses condemned here, and in James ii. 1–5, rather than any questions of
doctrine, are the causes of dissent and schism.

16. *He healed them.*—(See note 3.)   S. Matthew seems to place
this act also on the day of our Lord's triumphal entry; but it is
generally thought that it occurred on the following day.   S. Matthew
is not narrating facts in their exact chronological order of occurrence,
but placing them in groups bearing upon each other.   One instance
of this is in the cleansing of the Temple, which he associates, as he
does this scene of healing, with Christ's entry into the Temple.
Another is in the anointing at Bethany, which he seems to place within

priests and scribes saw the wonderful things that He did, and the children crying in the temple, and saying, Hosanna to the Son of David ; they were sore displeased, and said unto Him, Hearest Thou what these say ?   And

the Holy Week (Matt. xxvi. 6–13), apparently to show the connection between the disappointed avarice of Judas, and his resolve to get money by the betrayal; in which case, a careful comparison with the accurate arrangement of S. Mark, and with S. John, shows that it really took place as early as the Friday, or Saturday, before the public entry into Jerusalem.

17. *saw the wonderful things.*—If the rulers were not present at the cleansing of the Temple, they were witnesses of many of these miracles of mercy and power subsequently performed, which accredited our Lord's right to exercise an authority superior to theirs, in the House of God.   It is a sign of their utter degeneracy, that these undoubted works of God only affected them with displeasure. No other House of God ever had, or could have, such glorious indications of His Presence as these.   The rulers knew well how unprecedented, and how genuine were these acts of salvation; but they would far rather Christ had never come to visit His Temple, and that these sufferers had remained in their afflictions, unhealed, than that their own evil teaching and influence should be exposed and endangered, by the manifestation of Christ's truth and power.

18. *the children.*—Gk. masculine.   Like "the blind and lame" in their necessity, the children, in their innocence, were not afraid because of the severity of Christ's rebuke to those who profaned the Temple; they well knew their place in His heart.   Some writers think the words of praise which these children uttered, must fix the occurrence on the day of our Lord's entry, in the order of S. Matthew's Gospel; but there is little in the argument.   It is, at any rate, as possible that, when the account of our Lord's progress had been discussed in many a household at the close of the day, these children, recognizing Him in the Temple on the following day, took up the acclamation, with which they had heard that the multitudes had so universally greeted Him, as they brought Him in from Bethany on the preceding evening.

19. *hearest thou.*—The voices of the children in our Lord's praise, were more than the rulers could bear : their guilelessness and unconsciousness were so strongly in contrast with the deep passion of anger and malice, which swayed themselves ; and the ascription of Messiahship to Christ, neither disclaimed by Himself, nor distasteful to those who were gathered round Him, and so obviously true as He now stood in the midst of those whom He was healing, affected them with the same feelings of apprehension and wrath, with which those present in the procession of the day before, had listened to the voices of the enthusiastic multitudes.

Jesus saith unto them, Yea ; have ye never read, **Out of the mouths of babes and sucklings Thou hast perfected praise ?** And He left them, and when the even was come He went out of the city into Bethany ; and lodged there.

20. *yea.*—Our Lord not only signifies His consciousness of the children's homage, but His acceptance of it as truth from their lips, and as matter of prophecy.

21. *babes and sucklings.*—Our Lord had frequently shown His love and regard for children. They were the first martyrs in His cause. To those who would enter His kingdom, He proposes the unquestioning faith and trust of children. When describing heaven, and the temper and holiness of its inhabitants, He finds no illustration within human experience, but that of children : " Of such is the kingdom of heaven." When showing the terrible sin of those who mislead others to their ruin, and cause them to stumble and to wander from the way of truth, He sums up all the different grades of this sin, in the instance of him "who shall offend one of these little ones which believe in Me." Certainly children have their place in the Church, and kingdom of Christ; and it is perhaps the brightest place. There should be, amongst the services of every church, occasional services in which children are specially concerned, plain and simple, within reach of their capacity ; they will thus, soon and eagerly, see that theirs also is the House of God. S. Ephrem considers that "children that as yet knew not the speech of man, sung praises from the arms, because they saw He rode upon a foal ; " taking literally the words "babes and sucklings."

22. *perfected praise.*—These words are from the LXX. version, so often authorized by the quotations of our Lord and His Apostles ; the Heb. has "founded strength." Whether, as in the latter case, the weakness of their physical powers is clothed in the strength of God, when they invoke His name and express His praise, and so "His strength is made perfect in their weakness ; " or whether, as in the former, the heartiness and simplicity of their devotion, which is unfettered by the thought of sin, or by any want of faith, is the perfect type of true adoration ; the sense is still the same, that the utterances of children in the praise of God are breathings of heavenly voices, and that in their simplicity, and earnestness, are the solid foundations of eternal and acceptable service. " Did these murmurs recall the sequel of the verse, ' *because of Thine enemies*, that Thou mightest still the enemy and avenger ' ? " (*Farrar.*)

23. *He left them.*—In displeasure certainly, for themselves and their sentiments were utterly dissonant to the feelings which actuated Him ; and in judgment. (See Hos. ix. 12.)

24. *lodged there.*—He appears to have resided here with His disciples,

Tuesday in Holy Week.

IV. *THE WITHERED FIG TREE: LESSONS OF FAITH AND FORGIVENESS.*

S. Matt. xxi. 19–22; S. Mark xi. 20–26.

And in the morning, as they passed by, they saw the fig tree dried up from the roots. And Peter calling to remembrance saith unto Him, Master, behold, the fig tree which Thou cursedst is withered away. And Jesus answering saith unto them, Have faith in God. For

at any rate during the first two or three days of the week; but from Luke xxi. 37, we may conjecture that the hours of the night were not spent beneath any roof, or in repose, but in prayer, in the solitude of the Mount of Olives; as we read of Him elsewhere going out by night " into a mountain apart to pray."

1. *in the morning.*—S. Matthew gives the incident of the destruction of the fig tree as a continuous story, showing at once the action of our Lord, and its consequences, and the teaching which He founded upon it. S. Mark tells us that there was an interval of a day, between the sentence upon the tree and the remark made by S. Peter, declaring—apparently on behalf of his fellow-disciples (Matt. xxi. 20)— the impression made on the Apostles; for they would not notice it in the gloom of the evening, on their way out to Bethany.

2. *behold, the fig tree.*—S. Peter does not notice this as illustrating the great lesson it was designed to teach, but as an instance of the power of our Lord's words; the miracle fills his thoughts, as he is speaking. Perhaps it was not until much later, that the disciples understood the lesson conveyed by it (ii. 2–5), and drew the still more obvious inference, that a word could have effected the same immediate destruction of all who compassed His ruin in Jerusalem, had He willed to put forth His power, instead of going voluntarily to His Passion and cross.

3. *have faith.*—This answer is to the remark of S. Peter. Our Lord does not interpret His own action, or unfold its teaching; these are left enshrined in the parable of the action. But He says to Peter that, in the defence and furtherance of the cause of Christ, all necessary power will be given to the Apostles to work miracles, provided they have themselves faith. The remembrance, therefore, of this miracle of destruction, would be coupled in their mind with the admonition, " Have faith in God."

verily I say unto you, That whosoever shall say unto this mountain, Be thou removed, and be thou cast into the sea; and shall not doubt in his heart, but shall believe that those things which he saith shall come to pass; he shall have whatsoever he saith. Therefore I say unto you, What things soever ye desire, when ye pray, believe that ye receive *them*, and ye shall have *them*. And when ye stand praying, forgive, if ye have

4. *this mountain.*—It was not probable that any occasion would arise, to demand the literal removal of any mountain; but figuratively the expression is one well known to the Church of Christ. (See Matt. xvii. 20; 1 Cor. xiii. 2.) Any difficulty in the way of faith, any form of evil (either inherent in the heart of man, or external, as the powers of evil), though strong and deep-seated as a mountain, should be levelled or uprooted by the power committed to them: "Every mountain and hill should be made low." Origen says, "There is in every unbeliever a mountain, great in proportion to his unbelief, which is removed by the word of Christ's disciples." The terms of our Lord's grant contemplate no eccentric or destructive exercise of miraculous might, though it is a grant without limitation, except that it must be according to the will of God (1 John v. 14), and accompanied by absolute faith that God will give effect to His servant's word; such a faith will shape its requests in submission to God's will. The disciples would recognize the expression as a familiar Jewish one: many of their great Rabbis were spoken of as "removers of mountains."

5. *what things soever.*—Not exactly a repetition, with emphasis, of the former ample and distinct promise; but rather the carrying down of that promise, that the mountains of difficulty should be removed, to the assurance that their every prayer, in every need, should be fully granted, and that their every word and act should stand, so long as it was in accordance with His way and will, and was the fruit of a living faith. Within such limits nothing should be impossible to them. The passage recalls that in Matt. vii. 7–11, where the promises attached to prayer have a general and perpetual application; they have here pointed reference, though they are not confined, to the wants of the Apostles.

6. *forgive.*—The subject of prayer brings up that condition of acceptance so solemnly annexed to it, when our Lord first taught His disciples their distinctive prayer. (See Matt. vi. 12, 14, 15.) But its special meaning here, with reference to the gifts of miraculous power bestowed on the disciples, appears to be that, though our Lord exercised His judicial power in the instance of the fig tree, in the rejection of the Jewish Church, in the destruction of Jerusalem, in the final judgment—occasions either within their knowledge, or revealed to them—yet they

ought against any: that your Father also which is in heaven may forgive you your trespasses. But if ye do not forgive, neither will your Father which is in heaven forgive your trespasses.

V. *CHRIST ASSERTS HIS AUTHORITY. THE BAPTISM OF JOHN.*

S. Matt. xxi. 23–27 ; S. Mark xi. 27–33 ; S. Luke xx. 1–8.

And they come again to Jerusalem : and when He was come into the temple, the chief priests, and the scribes, and the elders of the people came unto Him, as He was teaching, and said, By what authority doest Thou these

were not to touch prerogatives which were His only. Their miracles were to be chiefly miracles of forgiveness, mercy, love ; not those of vengeance against their adversaries. (See Luke ix. 55.) Such an abuse would entail a forfeiture of the grace given to them, and might even shut them out from Christ's forgiveness of their sins, and so from eternal life. In a more universal sense, prayer, to be successful with God, must be offered in a spirit of love and faith. We are not to pray angrily against the enemies and opponents of any good and holy cause which we have at heart, but in full faith in God, " without wrath and doubting " (1 Tim. ii. 8). " The secret of successful prayer was faith ; the road to faith in God lay through pardon of transgression ; pardon was possible to them alone who were ready to pardon others." (*Farrar.*) (See App. V.)

1. *as He was teaching.*—Christ followed up His acts of the cleansing of the Temple, and of healing the sick, by direct teaching of the truth. " I sat daily with you teaching in the Temple," He says of His own work during these days. It was His desire to give to the multitudes who assembled there, as clear a knowledge of His Gospel as they were able to receive.

2. *By what authority.*—His questioners were the high priest and heads of the twenty-four courses, or their representatives. Is the authority Divine ? they would know ; for certainly it was not human. None but themselves, the legal guardians of the Temple, could have conferred such a commission. And, if Divine, who directly gave it on God's behalf ? Such a question had been asked when our Lord had before cleansed the Temple (John ii. 18.) There was a fair semblance of what was right in their demand ; it only needed to have been made in good faith, not in the hope of turning His reply into a charge of

things ? and who gave Thee this authority ? And Jesus answered and said unto them, I will also ask you one thing, which if ye tell Me, I in like wise will tell you by

blasphemy, or otherwise against Himself. They were answerable, as those who sat in Moses' seat, for the House of God, and for the observances connected with it ; they were also, on this occasion, representatives of that great council which took cognizance of all questions regarding religion. Our Lord's act of the previous day, and His sitting there as a teacher, naturally suggested some such inquiry ; and of those present when it was asked, He alone knew that the question put by this august and venerable deputation, was the result of secret plotting against. His life (see Luke xix. 47), though it may be that the people knew that the general feeling of the rulers was antagonistic to Christ. Farrar says " they sternly and abruptly asked Him " this question. Certainly the words of S. Luke, "came upon Him," suggest a sudden action, though they may only imply their action in concert; for would not an angry demand of this nature lose much of its point with the people, and much of its plausible character? The triumph of yesterday showed that matters were not yet ripe for open violence ; and it seems more likely that the result of consultation and plotting, would be an outwardly courteous, though earnest and pressing (see *Greek*), demand, that they would fall back on what was right and due from themselves in their official capacity, under such circumstances of unusual character, rather than set every mind against them, by an exhibition of irritation and rudeness. It is evident that, on the following day (much more, therefore, on this day), the deputation which came to our Lord advanced with marked courtesy ; nor can it be argued that they had learnt from bitter experience the wisdom of doing this, for it was their obvious interest to do so, and thus to curry popular feeling on this occasion also.

3. *one thing.*—Gk. "one word," *i.e.* of inquiry ; one proposition. To many a question, and trial, and sign had they subjected Him ; but their answer to one single question will suffice for His purpose ; and this was not the putting off of their question, to which they might claim the prior answer, because our Lord's question was itself the reply to theirs. He might have appealed to the popular voice in His favour ; but the rulers had a reply ready for such an answer—"This people, who knoweth not the law, are cursed." (See the results of any appeal to popular decision in His favour in John vii. 45–52, ix. 22, 28–34.) If He appealed to his miracles in support of His own assertion of Sonship with God, they had already attempted to stone Him as a blasphemer (John x. 30–39 ; Matt. ix. 32–34). It was therefore useless to give any direct answer to their question ; nor was it our Lord's way to give other arguments in support of His mission, than those which God had ordained as sufficient. These were the testimony of John, the

what authority I do these things. The baptism of John,
whence was it? from heaven, or of men? Answer Me.
And they reasoned with themselves, saying, If we shall
say, From heaven; He will say unto us, Why did ye not
then believe Him? But if we shall say, Of men; we
fear the people; all the people will stone us: for all hold

voice of the Father from heaven, the witness of the prophets, and the
evidence of miracles. (See John v. 33, 36, 37, 39.)

4. *the baptism of John.*—The whole ministry of John is included in
this its initiatory rite; but it is noticeable that John's testimony to
our Lord's was chiefly given when he was baptizing, so careful was he to
certify, at that important solemnity, that he was but the herald of the
Gospel. (See Matt. iii. 11, 14; Mark i. 5–8; Luke iii. 3–18; John i. 19–28.)

5. *from heaven, or of men.*—*i.e.* direct from heaven, or of any human
origin or commission. As John was the accredited messenger sent
from God to prepare the way before the Christ, the consequence of
acknowledgment of his Divine mission, would be the virtual acknowledgment of the truth of the commission and person of Christ; for
John's words were, " I saw, and *bare record* that this is the Son of
God" (John i. 34). The answer, therefore, to their own question would
be obvious. They were ready enough to deny the Divine authority of
our Lord's commission; but dared not publicly deny that of John,
about whom there was one universal opinion, and persuasion amongst
the people: they " all held John as a prophet." But it is likely that
our Lord's question was directed to the people also; since a dis-
passionate answer, after fair inquiry, might bring conviction to the
mind of some of them.

6. *they reasoned.*—It is sad to notice how these, the chief religious
teachers of the day, gave no moment's thought to the question of
truth or right; but merely to what was most expedient to say before
the people, in reply to this, to them most embarrassing question.
They had already predetermined the case against Christ (Luke xix.
47, 48). The people would not know what their " reasoning" was,
but still, hesitation even was discreditable to them; they ought to
have been ready, by this time, with a decision on a subject of so much
notoriety and importance as the mission of John the Baptist.

7. *will stone us.*—They were ready enough to stir up the people to
this outrage on others, and had a just reason to fear it themselves. It
is evident that they had little reliance on their real influence with
those they ruled; but, in the instance of Christ's death, as on various
occasions during His life, we see that they understood the fickleness
and fanaticism of the multitude, and were skilled in exciting their
worst passions. Farrar strikingly remarks, " ' Answer Me,' said Jesus,
interrupting their whispered colloquy; " supposing a very probable interval between " From heaven, or of men," and the words "Answer Me."

John as a prophet.   And they answered Jesus, and said, We cannot tell.   And He said unto them, Neither tell I you by what authority I do these things.

VI. *THE PARABLE OF THE TWO SONS.*
S. Matt. xxi. 28–32.

But what think ye ?   A *certain* man had two sons :

8. *we cannot tell.*—This was a profession of ignorance by the leading theologians of the nation, whose especial province it was to decide on questions concerning religion, and on the pretensions of any who rose up as teachers or prophets (Mal. ii. 6 ; Matt. ii. 4).   The people were deeply interested in the question ; the rulers had sent a deputation long ago to John to inquire about it (John i. 19), and the reply, " We cannot tell," would only cover them with public confusion and disgrace. Our Lord, however, was aware that they could tell well enough, and meant, " We *will not* tell."

9. *neither tell I you.*—Christ does not say, "I cannot tell," as they said ; His straightforwardness and truth is in contrast with their disingenuousness : He says, " I do not tell."   We may well suppose there was not one bystander who did not feel the justice of our Lord's rejoinder.   If these men were unable to decide the nature of John's mission, which was introductory to that of Christ, and could not say whether he was true prophet or false, they were evidently not fit persons to judge of the authority of Christ ; and were not, therefore, entitled to question it.   And to give them any direct answer, at this time, to their question, would simply be the " casting of pearls before swine," who would " trample them under their feet, and turn again and rend Him."   They had owned, before the people, their incompetence to decide the point, and that was final.   " There are two seasons when the knowledge of the truth should be kept back from those who ask ; either when he who asks is unfit to receive, or, from his hatred or contempt of the truth, is unworthy to have that which he asks opened to him."   (*Bede.*)

1. *what think ye.*—These words mark the close connection of the parable with what had just been said ; and the question as to what they *thought*, is a reproach to those from whom it was useless to ask a decision.   Those who had shown themselves unworthy to judge of our Lord's commission, shall now condemn themselves as disobedient to God's command through John.   Our Lord's parable gives the answer to the question He had proposed to the rulers, which they had declined ; the repentance which God gave to men, in connection with John's baptism and preaching, attested his mission from God.

2. *two sons.*—Representatives of two great classes : those who profess

and He came to the first, and said, Son, go work to-day in
my vineyard. He answered and said, I will not : but

to do God's will, and those who openly refuse to follow it. As the
result of the parable is, that the latter are found to be in a better
position, it may be noticed how infinitely superior, really, is the man
who promises obedience to God's will, as he knows it, to him who
defies it. It is impossible to deny that the man of careful religious
practice and profession (for we cannot judge the heart) is better than
the notorious and wilful sinner. But the want of spiritual truth and
reality, beneath the external show of excellence (the lesson of the
fig tree above mentioned), is always more dangerous to the soul, than the
audacity of one whose conscience may startle him into reflection and reformation. Repentance seems more possible to him than to the formalist.

The " two sons " have been identified by the ancient writers with
the Gentiles, and the Jews; the former of whom abandoned God's
service, and took up the worship of idols, and, at the preaching of the
Apostles, threw them aside and returned to the true God ; whilst the
Jews, with every profession of religious knowledge and obedience,
deliberately rejected the Messiah. But the parable, though it undoubtedly bears such an application, is more immediately true of the
two classes amongst the Jews of our Lord's day—the Pharisees and the
publicans, the formalists and the notorious sinners. And it has a still
more extensive scope than even these ; as it is true to nature in every
age, its lessons are world-wide.

3. *the first.*—There is apparently nothing in the order in which the
Jews are spoken to, though the summons, to reconsider and repent,
naturally first greeted those who refused obedience, and lived in sin.
The actual disobedience of those who so loudly professed to obey,
would not be so speedily noticed. And it was not until the multitudes
of those who had sins to confess, had brought John's cry in the
wilderness to the ears of those who lived in Jerusalem, that they sent
down scribes and Pharisees to his baptism ; who saw the remarkable
reformation which was taking place, and even then did not repent
and become obedient to the will of God, and work in the cause of
His Son.

4. *Go work to-day.*—The exhortation of religion to a life of service
to God, which God makes to man through the dispensation of His
word : " To every one of us is given grace, according to the measure of
the gift of Christ ;" and to every one of us is assigned his proper
personal work. The force of the word " to-day " is very marked : God
desires that we should not tempt Him by delay in fulfilling His will
(Heb. iii. 7–15).

5. *will not.*—*i.e.* I have no will for it ; I prefer not. The bold and
wilful refusal to serve God, howsoever expressed—in the life, or in
profession ; in defiance of God's commands, or in the neglect of them.

afterward he repented, and went.   And he came to the second, and said likewise.   And he answered and said, I *go*, sir ; and went not. Whether of them twain did the will of *his* father ? They say unto Him, The first. Jesus saith unto them, Verily I say unto you, That the publicans and the harlots go into the kingdom of God before you.   For

6. *repented, and went.*—This son felt at last ashamed of his unfilial conduct, and now did his best to atone for the past, by a life of compliance with his father's will. Conscience had slept, but it was now fully roused. And thus, in terror of the consequences of sin, men of evil or negligent life see the error of their way, and with hearty repentance and true faith turn unto God, and do works worthy of repentance; they endeavour to serve God for the future, as earnestly as they have neglected Him wilfully in the past, and heaven is opened to their after-obedience. This was the case with the publicans, in the direct application of the parable.

7. *I go, sir.*—Or, "my lord." Nothing could be more respectful and prompt, in the way of professed obedience, than this reply. It promised everything, with the utmost deference to all commands; and nothing could be more hollow than the promise. For there was wanting everything like sincerity and heartiness in intention ; and virtual disobedience was the natural result.

8. *did the will.*—Comparatively, that is; for neither was a doer of the will of God, after the example of Christ.

9. *the first.*—They thus gave judgment in their own cause against themselves, not intentionally, but it was immediately seen to be so, on their hearing the application of the parable. They saw plainly enough what was right and true, in a supposed case, but they would not act as they could judge. The conviction is clear and without appeal, like that of the parable spoken by Nathan (2 Sam. xii. 5–7; see also 1 Kings xx. 39–41.) The manner in which Christ thus made them judges against themselves, was too consonant with Eastern figures of speech and habit to leave room for reply.

10. *the publicans,* etc.—All the vilest and most despised, and the most notoriously wicked, who came down in shame and penitence to Jordan, where John was baptizing ; and when they heard the message, "Repent ye," many of them amended their lives, and did their best to live after God's commands.

11. *Go . . . before you.*—The true force of the original word is not brought out in this rendering, which *seems* to mean, "Sooner shall these reach heaven than you shall reach it ;" the word really implies that these should *precede* them, or "show them the way" into the kingdom of heaven. It is one of those instances of the merciful character of the religion of Christ, and its suitableness for sinners,

John came unto you in the way of righteousness, and
ye believed him not; but the publicans and harlots
believed him: and ye, when ye had seen *it*, repented not
afterward, that ye might believe him.

that, even to these formalists, there is not the door of hope quite
closed. It may be no easy task for the Pharisee to follow the publican;
but, if he can lay aside his pride, and take up the humility of the
penitent sinner, he will find the door left open to himself, by which
the other has entered heaven, and he will not be refused entrance.
Whenever is the door absolutely shut in the face of those who would
come to Christ, until the very last? It is often the case that such
mercy and love underlie the *words* of Christ; as if, where He had
passed along, seeking the sinner, He left some track of kindness, which
he might discern, and take comfort. Christ only could understand
the full force of words; but we should follow Him better, if we weighed
more carefully our words (especially our words of severity). We often
repel when, with some gentler and more kindly-chosen expression, we
might draw to our side, some one whom Christ is seeking to save by us.

12. *the way of righteousness.*—John came with all the unreserved
obedience to the letter of the law, and all the austerity, that the most
ascetic professor of the "straitest sect of the Jews" could desire; he
ought to have satisfied them in this respect, but they said of him,
"He hath a devil" (Matt. xi. 18). They did not see any beauty in
the way of legal righteousness, when they saw it carried out from the
heart; for John was sincere.

13. *when ye had seen it.*—This extraordinary scene of repentance,
on the part of those apparently most hardened and reprobate, should
have convinced the rulers. These men had sent a select deputation
from Jerusalem, to examine John about his mission; they had
witnessed its effects, and the presence of God's Spirit with His work;
for repentance, followed by reformation of life, must be work of God.
They heard also the testimony which he gave, of his own office in
subordination to Him who should come, and the rumour passing from
mouth to mouth, that the promised Messiah was immediately to
appear. It was with an eye to this prospect that the multitudes were
receiving baptism from John. But they witnessed this extraordinary
scene in vain; they would have nothing to do either with the baptism
of John, or the repentance he proclaimed, or the message of which
he was the herald. The words of his parable recall those of S.
Luke vii. 29, 30: "All the people that heard Him" (*i.e.* Christ giving
testimony to John's character), "and the publicans, glorified God, being
baptized with the baptism of John. But the Pharisees and lawyers rejected the counsel of God against themselves, being not baptized of him."

14. *repented not afterward.*—Unlike the son who "repented afterwards," and returned to his duty, they were equally unaffected by

VII. *THE PARABLE OF THE WICKED HUSBAND-MEN.*

S. Matt. xxi. 32–46 ; S. Mark xii. 1–12 ; S. Luke xx. 9–19.

Hear another parable : There was a certain house-holder, which planted a vineyard, and hedged it round

the call to true repentance, and by the example of those who, in such numbers, and from such depths of sin, were brought to God. This is true of the religious formalist of every age ; he has made such a profession of external religion, that he has no deep-seated feelings which can be touched. There is no appeal to conscience, for it is voiceless under the pressure of that perfect self-satisfaction which possesses him ; besides, his careful counterfeiting of the truth evidences the absence of all reality. The deceiver of others often becomes a self-deceiver as well. Such a man is impenetrable, except after the destruction of his whole system of religion.

1. *Hear another parable.*—Our Lord immediately proceeds to this second parable, in which, having before shown what the testimony of John was concerning Him, He now pourtrays His own relationship as the heir, the Son of God, towards all who had previously exercised stewardship within His kingdom, and over His Church. The scope is wider than that of the preceding parable, which had reference to two classes of Jews, as called to God by the dispensation of the law ; this refers to the Jews and Gentiles, as called by the dispensation of the Gospel. The parable was spoken certainly (as S. Matthew declares) to the Pharisees, being so closely consequent on that preceding it ; but also (as S. Luke says) to the people, "against" (*i.e.* with reference to) the rulers. Our Lord, in thus addressing them, marks the un-willingness of these rulers to listen further.

2. *householder.*—The same figure is used elsewhere. (See Matt. xx. 1.) "The household of God" is wide and extensive. (See Eph. ii. 19–23.) But the Jews chose to understand it only in the restricted sense mentioned in Isaiah v. 7, where "the vineyard of the Lord of hosts is the house of Israel." The parable of the labourers in the vineyard (Matt. xx.), and, more especially, this parable, give a far more general meaning.

3. *a vineyard.*—A very usual figure in Holy Scripture. The great-ness of the returns (Cant. viii. 11), the unremitting care necessary in cultivation, and many other points of resemblance to God's Church, have been pointed out by ancient writers. The reference in this parable to Isa. v. 1–7, is very remarkable. There is, however, a difference in the meaning of the term "vineyard," which there represents the Jewish Church, and is destroyed for its unfruitfulness ; whilst here it

about, and digged a winepress in it, and built a tower,
and let it out to husbandmen, and went into a far

represents the Catholic Church of God, from which the unfaithful
Jewish "husbandmen" are removed, and are destroyed for their
wickedness, whilst the living and reformed Church is given to the care
of others, who will render the fruits of righteousness in due season.
We may therefore take the "vineyard" to represent, in a general sense,
God's visible Church on earth.

4. *hedged . . . tower.*—There has been a meaning attached to each
of these several precautions for the protection and management of the
vineyard. The "hedge" has been interpreted to mean the fence of
special ordinances, which God placed round the Jewish people in the
law (Ps. lxxx. 12), thus keeping them carefully separate, and protected
from the rest of the world ; both by geographical position, and by His
guardianship, they were fenced from the outer world. (See Ps. cxxv. 2 ;
Isa. xxvii. 2, 3). The "winepress" has by some been identified
with the prophetical inspiration which filled men with the spirit of
God ; by some with Jerusalem, where the fruit of the Church might be
said to be expressed ; by others, again, with the ministration of doctrine
and discipline, or with the sacrifices of the altar as the fruits of devotion
by others : the "tower," again, with the Temple, or (as by S. Hilary)
with the law, which rises towards heaven, looking to the coming of
Christ ; by others, with the civil institutions for administrating justice,
and control, and protection. Of these meanings the explanation
given by Theophylact is very intelligible : he says the hedge is the
law ; the winepress the altar ; the tower the Temple. But the
hedge of protection to the vines, the winepress digged beneath the
ground to receive the juice of the pressed grapes, and the tower of
observation and guard, are all familiar objects in vineyards of the
present day ; and, without pressing the figurative meaning closely, we
may take these natural circumstances as conveying the idea, that
every care and precaution had been taken, all necessary arrangements
provided, everything done by God's providence, that could have been
done (Isa. v. 4), to ensure the protection and maintenance of the
fruits, and of all concerned in giving in a plentiful return from the
vineyard.

5. *let it out.*—The expression supposes an agreement by which a
portion of the profits accrued to the husbandmen. It always must
have been so. Those who minister in holy things are participators in
the excellence of those things (1 Sam. ii. 28 ; 1 Cor. ix. 13, 14) ; they
would profit in the advance of the people in true religion ; and themselves would be had in honour before God and men, and their own
souls would be enriched also—"for he that watereth shall be watered
also himself." The "righteous man's reward" and "the prophet's
reward" were definite and coveted honours.

country for a long time : and when the time of the fruit drew near, he sent his servants to the husbandmen, that they might receive of the fruits of the vineyard.   And the

6. *husbandmen.*—The authorized teachers and guardians of religion ; those whose office it was to minister, within God's visible Church, the ordinary means of grace ; and, in a widening sense, those who ministered to each other, in any social or domestic relationship, the cultivation and training of religious life.   These were, at first, within the Jewish Church, but only whilst the limits of the Church of God were those of the land and children of the promise ; the promise through Abraham, though a world-wide heritage, being restricted to their guardianship (Gal. iii. 15–19) as a temporary measure.

7. *a far country.*—The "land which is very far off," where dwells " the King in His beauty " (Isa. xxxiii. 17), and where our hopes rest. Its present distance from us can only be estimated from comparison of the language of Scripture ; and, in stating the exceeding greatness of God's mercy, we read, " As the heaven is high above the earth, so great is His mercy towards them that fear Him " (Ps. ciii. 11).

8. *for a long time.*—Gk. " sufficient ; " some considerable time, sufficiently long for the accomplishment of his purpose.   God left the Jewish nation to be the guardian of His spiritual kingdom on earth, for many ages ; leaving them, during that period, apparently to their own discretion, within the limits of His law and theocracy.

9. *time of the fruit.*—When it was time to look for the fruits of righteousness, from those who had been so carefully furnished with ordinances of religion ; when it might be expected that the faith and example of the chosen and representative race, should have begun to leaven the world ; and the light of Divine truth, on the candlestick of their Church, to lighten the moral and spiritual darkness of other lands.

10. *his servants.*—These were, perhaps, the great judges and seers of old ; and also, generally, God's servants the prophets, whom in long series God had sent, " rising up early and sending them," but in vain (2 Chron. xxxvi. 15, 16 ; Jer. xxv. 4, 5).   They came with God's demand that men should cast away iniquity, and bring forth the fruits of righteousness, which God requires.   The " servants " are distinguished by eminence of office and spirit, and by occasion, from the " labourers," who are the ordinary ministers and stewards of religion. SS. Mark and Luke give " *a* servant," specifying that the office was an individual one, not bestowed at the same moment upon many. S. Matthew gives them in their full numbers, without specifying that they came one by one, or, at the most, comparatively few in the same age.

11. *fruits of the vineyard.*—(See note 9.)   The Gk. of Matt. xxi. 34 gives " *his* fruits," *i e.* the share of the produce belonging to the owner of the vineyard ; the rendering, however, of the A.V. follows Mark xii. 2.

husbandmen took his servants, and beat one, and killed another, and stoned another.   Again he sent other servants more than the first; and they did unto them likewise.

Then said the lord of the vineyard, What shall I do ?

12. *beat, killed, stoned.*—This last suggests a charge of blasphemy. The other Evangelists, giving the separate instance of one or two of these, describe their being generally "shamefully handled" and wounded, but not killed. They were sent home to their lord repulsed and wounded, and without the fruits they came to seek ; but others were slain on the spot. See our Lord's summary of these outrages in Matt. xxiii. 34, 35, and that in Heb. xi. 32–38.

13. *other servants.*—It has been noticed that there are three distinct embassies spoken of here, which have been likened respectively to the law, the prophets, and the Gospel ; the earlier period including Moses himself (who declared of the people, "They be almost ready to stone me "), and Gideon, Barak, Jephthah, Samson, David, Samuel (Heb. ix. 32), and perhaps also the earlier prophets who prophesied under the kings, with the great prophets Elijah and Elisha. The second series might include the mighty prophets, from Isaiah, and those who wrote under the Captivity, more numerous than the first, and of great power. These also the Jews treated even worse than the first. (See Neh. ix. 26.) If, however, these messengers be not grouped, as S. Matthew's version of the parable seems to allow, into these main divisions, we may at least see that God's servants, in continued series, were sent on this mission in every age, to exhort and warn, and to demand the fruits of righteousness on God's behalf ; and that, with very few exceptions, they were maltreated in the discharge of their office, so that none was able to take, to Him that sent him, those fruits which he was bidden to require. There is an excellent remark of Rabanus, quoted by Corn. à Lapide : " A servant is sent whenever the law, or a psalm, or a prophet is read ; he is cast out whenever such is despised or blasphemed. He kills the heir who treads under foot the Son of God, and does despite to the Spirit of His grace. The vineyard is given to another whenever the humble receives from the proud the grace despised by him."

14. *then said.*—The Lord takes counsel with Himself. His messengers have been repulsed, and Himself insulted ; but His forbearance and goodness are infinite. What shall He now do which will bring these rebels round to better feeling ? He will treat them with distinction and honour, so great that they must be shamed into a return to their duty and allegiance. Here, and in the expression " They will reverence my Son," God is speaking as a man. He well foreknew the result of His Son's mission, and it was with the fullest consciousness of what lay before Him in the Divine appointment, that the " Lamb slain from the foundation of the world " went forth to do the will of

Having yet, therefore one son, his well-beloved, he sent him also last unto them, saying, They will reverence my son.   But when the husbandmen saw the son, they said

God, as it was written of Him. But God's plans, and God's foreknowledge, do not coerce human will. It is a mysterious contact, whenever God's plans and human free will come together; it is never possible for us to define their several limits. We can only state and feel, that as God leaves man's action free, unfettered by the fact of His own foreknowledge, and unrestrained by His compulsion, so it is left possible to man to act better than he does act; the Almighty power is in suspension, not to compel, but, on man's prayer, to assist him. And thus God speaks as if hesitating or uncertain, or as repenting, or being grieved; in fact, as if actuated by human feelings and sentiments. He speaks thus in the language, and within the comprehension of man. In the present instance, not only had all been done in His vineyard that could be done in it, but all that Christ could do, during the period of His ministry, was done to win the Jews to the better way, and done in vain. Christ did not pretend that He attempted, what He knew God had determined should not succeed; but in good faith He dealt with them, as those who might be brought to the Gospel. God did not compel the Jews to disown, reject, and crucify our Lord, nor Judas to betray Him; the sacrifice for the world's salvation might have been otherwise as efficiently accomplished, though God foreknew what would result, and arranged accordingly. The truth is stated by S. Peter, though not defined (Acts ii. 23): "Him being delivered by the determinate counsel and foreknowledge of God, ye have taken, and by wicked hands" (lit. by the hands of men without law, *i.e.* the Gentiles) "have crucified and slain;" a deed as deliberately resolved, and responsible, as God's foreknowledge was infallible; and what He foreknew was, by His determinate counsel, permitted without the exercise of His resistless might in interference. Further than by such general outlines, we cannot explain or comprehend a difficulty, which runs through the whole of Scripture, the difficulty of reconciling God's eternally devised action with the free will He has permitted to man.

15. *one son.*—The only begotten Son of God (John i. 18); "His own Son" of Rom. viii. 32. His infinite superiority to all God's messengers is here expressed. Even the highest of the prophets is inferior to the "One Son." They are "servants;" He is the "Son." (See Heb. iii. 5, 6.) He is spoken of here anterior to His birth into the world as "My Son;" He is therefore necessarily Divine.

16. *well-beloved.*—See Matt. iii. 17, and xvii. 5.

17. *last.*—Not merely last in succession to these other messengers, but as charged with God's last dispensation and covenant.

18. *they will reverence.*—See note 14.

19. *saw the son.*—Our Lord prayed for those who crucified Him, as

among themselves, This is the heir; come, let us kill
him, and let us seize on his inheritance. And they

for men who "knew not what they did" (Luke xxiii. 34; see also Acts
iii. 17); that is to say, they did not see the full bearing and consequences,
nor even the full wickedness, of their action—not because they could
not have seen, but because "their eyes have they closed .... lest
they should see with their eyes." And yet they saw enough to make
their recognition of the Son a matter of certainty, and their rejection
of Him deliberate. (See John ix. 41, and xi. 47–52.) The difficulty
here is lessened, if we apply the same blindness, to the consequences of
folly and sin, to more trivial and ordinary instances. Who sees the full
consequences of any act of wilfulness or indiscretion, especially when he
has resolutely shut his eyes to the consideration of these? and yet, who
is really the less guilty for such blindness? It is impossible that the
rulers did not see the force of the miracles, example, and doctrine of
Christ, and of the coincidences of His life and mission with the predictions of the prophets, and with the types of the law. They had, however, determined that the Messiah should be a temporal prince, and
they had attributed Christ's miracles to Satanic power; and the deliberate refusal of evidence of course kept them ignorant of the fulness of
that which they might have seen, had they as resolutely looked towards,
as they did away from, the light of truth. Such obstinacy is worthy
of all condemnation; but such sad perversion of mind, and of the
moral nature, is indeed mournful and pitiable.

20. *they said.*—This is the reading of the thoughts of man's heart
by the eye of God; such counsel would not be owned even to themselves, much less confided to each other, but yet it was their secret
thought. This must be considered as our Lord's testimony to the fact
that the Jewish leaders did generally recognize His mission as that of
the Christ.

21. *the heir.*—The heir is the Son of Man. (see Heb. i. 2.) As the
Son of God (Heb. i. 8, 10), He was the Creator of all things; but
He is the heir of the kingdoms of this world, and of the kingdom of
redemption.

22. *let us seize.*—In the East the tenancy of land is often hereditary
in the tenants' family, so long as the rent is paid. In the absence of a
legal heir, the tenants may have thought they should have the best
claim to possession of the land. There is expressed here their assertion of their knowledge of the badness of their own cause, which at all
hazards they elected absolutely to maintain. They could not bear the
thought of losing their influence and position, even though their
giving way was the advance of the truth. And not only this, but they
had an unreasoning dread of the destruction of their national existence
and Church, by the Roman power, if they should own our Lord and
embrace His cause. For this reason also they resisted the conviction

caught him, and cast *him* out of the vineyard, and slew
him.   When the lord therefore of the vineyard cometh,
what will he do unto those husbandmen ? They say
unto Him, He will miserably destroy those wicked men,
and will let out *his* vineyard to other husbandmen,

of truth, and refused obedience to the will of God; their personal and
official interests, as well as their fanatical devotion to their system of
religion, were thus enlisted in opposition to Him.   The advice of Caiaphas was acceptable to them all : it was " better that one man " (so
they professed to regard our Lord) " should be put to death," be His
claims as a Teacher what they might, " than that the whole nation
should perish " by acknowledging them to be just, and advocating them.
The strong coincidence has often been noticed, between the treatment
of Joseph and his brethren, and this recognition of the Son, as they saw
Him approaching the vineyard ; and between the fulfilment of the predictions of God through Joseph's dreams, which his brethren strove by
their wicked act to prevent, and this attempt of the Jews to prevent
the destruction of their Church, by taking those evil precautions which
eventually caused it to perish. (See Gen. xxxvii. 19, 20, xlv. 5, 7, l. 20.)
    23. *cast him out.*—As the vineyard was the Church, this must
imply that they excommunicated Him, and disowned Him as if he were
an alien.   Jewish writings assert the formal excommunication of Christ.
But there appears to be also a reference to His being borne to "suffer
without the gate " of the city (Heb. xiii. 12).
    24. *the lord ... cometh.*—In His visitation of judgment. This took
place at the destruction of Jerusalem, for the punishment was national
and temporal.
    25. *what will he do.*—Our Lord here asks a question, the answer to
which will again convict the rulers by self-condemnation.   (See vi. 9.)
    26. *they say.*—In SS. Mark and Luke, our Lord seems to speak this
sentence, which, in S. Matthew's circumstantial account, the rulers
give as their answer to our Lord's question. He evidently adopts their
reply, as His own sentence.   The discrepancy, if any, is reconciled by
supposing Him to have repeated their words, in tones which brought
conviction of the meaning of the parable to the minds of his hearers :
" Yes ; He *will* destroy the husbandmen, and will give their vineyard to others."   And it may be that conscience, for the moment
active, prompted the cry, " God forbid ! " for no warning or prediction
of judgment could be so convincing, as this bringing them to pronounce
sentence in their own case, and so judge themselves.
    27. *miserably destroy.*—No misery in destruction of human life, ever
exceeded that of the misery which accompanied the siege of Jerusalem
(Matt. xxiv. 21).   (See sect. xviii.)
    28. *other husbandmen.*—The Apostles and their successors, *i.e*, the
rulers and teachers of the Christian Church. The vineyard, the Church,

which shall render him the fruits in their seasons.
And when they heard *it*, they said, God forbid.　And He
beheld them and said, What then is this that is written,

remains the Church of God; but a new dispensation of religion is to be
given; new doctrine, that of Christ, is to be inculcated; and new
stewards of the mysteries of God are to be set in charge with that
trust.　These shall never more confine all the advantages of religion to
themselves; they shall render the fruits of holy living to Christ, the
Head of the Church.　The rendering of these fruits is seen in the conversion of the world to God; the fruits are the graces and virtues of
Christian life and character, in living action.

29. *their seasons.*—These, as well as the fruits, are various.　There
are seasons of trial and suffering, when the fruit of righteousness is
patience and resignation to God's will.　There are seasons when the
fruit is that of an active and diligent life, which can effect mighty
things in the accomplishment of God's work.　These are scenes of
quiet life, when example and peace do their work in His behalf, training the mind in habits of faith and trust, which are mainstays in
times of trouble; for "the work of righteousness shall be peace; and
the effect of righteousness quietness and assurance for ever" (Isa.
xxxii. 17).　There are seasons of life also when these fruits are
different: even "from the mouth of babes and sucklings God has
perfected praise;" "even a child is known by his doings."　And so,
through life, with changing seasons, and through the varied opportunities of life, the required fruits are varied, until perhaps that old
age comes, when the virtues and graces of a well-spent Christian life
are matured, and crown it with honour (Prov. xvi. 31).

30. *when they heard it.*—S. Luke, who tells us the parable was
spoken "to the people," seems to say that this was *their* remark.
Some of the bystanders, however, whether of the rulers or of the general
audience, who now saw the meaning of the parable, thus deprecated
the terrible doom which had been pronounced by their fellows, and
endorsed by our Lord; who took up their words, and applied them
personally to themselves, with the declaration of Scripture to point
them.

31. *beheld them.*—Or "looked upon them," thus drawing their
attention towards Himself.　Our Lord's habit of earnestly regarding
those to whom He was speaking with solemnity, evidently impressed
itself on the minds of the Evangelists.　In this instance He doubtless
looked on the rulers with indignation and sorrow, for they were now
trifling with their latest offers and warnings; and the terrible consequences were within His sight. (See also Matt. xix. 26; Mark. x. 21,
23; Luke xxii. 61.)

32. *what then is this.*—You say, "God forbid!" but what is the
meaning of this Scripture so familiar to you, so often quoted?　God's

**The stone which the builders rejected, the same is
become the head of the corner: this is the Lord's**

will lies in the opposite direction; God has decided that He whom you
now reject, shall become the Head over all. It is to be noticed that the
words our Lord now cites, are taken from the same Psalm with those
which were so lately upon the lips of those who had hailed Christ as
the Son of David.

33. *the stone.*—There is a change here from the lesson of the parable
to another almost proverbial figure. The transition is simple and easy,
and the idea in many points closely parallel with that of the parable.
The son in the parable was slain, and the narrative ends with the
assurance that the householder would come to avenge his death. It
would have been a strained and unnatural continuation of it, and
wholly unsuitable to the minds of those who heard it, to have represented the son as rising again to sit in judgment upon the rebels. But
there is a well-known saying which supplies the sequel, "What then is
this that is written, The stone which the builders rejected is become
the head of the corner?" That Christ against whom, when He lay low
upon the ground in His humility, they stumbled, will yet be chiefest of
all. The son, rejected, cast out, and slain, is yet therefore reserved for
fullest triumph. Benham quotes a Jewish legend, which, whatever be
its authority, is interesting: "When all the materials prepared by
David for the building of the Temple were brought to Moriah, and
the work begun, the place for each stone was found without difficulty,
excepting in one case. One stone was left apparently misshapen,
'having no beauty that it should be desired;' while other stones
were chosen, it lay neglected, and passed into a jest. But at last,
when the work was all but complete, the corner stone was wanting.
Every effort was made to fill the vacancy without avail. At last,
'the stone which the builders rejected' was tried: it fitted exactly;
and by it the whole building, fitly framed together, became the habita-
tion of God."

34. *the builders.*—"How could they remain builders any longer, when
the whole design of their workmanship was thus deliberately overruled, and set aside? Did not their old Messianic prophecy clearly
imply that God would call other builders to the work of His Temple?"
(*Farrar.*) S. Peter, in his address to the "rulers of the people, and
men of Israel," gives a personal application in his use of their
passage: "This is the stone which was set at nought of *you builders*"
(Acts iv. 10, 11).

35. *head of the corner.*—Many of the early writers agree in interpreting this to mean that the corner stone, occupying the angle of the
wall, and so uniting two walls, represents the union of the Jew and
Gentile in the person of Christ. (See in Eph. ii. 18–22 a beautiful
illustration of this passage.)

doing, and it is marvellous in our eyes? Whosoever
shall fall upon that stone shall be broken; but on whom-

36. *the Lord's doing.*—Nothing in look, or tone, would be wanting
to point this central truth to the hearts of those who heard our Lord
apply the passage. The stone was despised, rejected, but finally
graced with eternal honour; and God's providence was evident in the
whole matter. It was the most solemn appeal to the consciences of
those who were now being found " even to fight against God."

37. *in our eyes.*—Those who could understand and own that it was
the Lord's doing, would wonder at, and admire, the working of His
providence. No human plans would have been so laid, none thus
accomplished. The humility of Christ's advent and life, His rejection
by the people of the promise, His suffering a death of such ignominy,
His exaltation to supreme glory, and the history of the salvation of
those who, like Him, are " made perfect through suffering," will be
events for ever marvellous in the eyes of all His people.

38. *whosoever shall fall.*—Two punishments lie in the way of Christ's
adversaries: a greater and a lesser. Both are ruinous; as opposition
to His cause must ever be. One, however, is temporal and reparable;
the other is eternal and fixed. Whosoever shall so stumble at the
doctrine and offers of Christ, at His words and example, which are
lying ever in his path for acceptance or rejection, as the foundation
of his faith; and, rejecting Him, shall turn to any other source of
happiness—" shall be broken," shall suffer terribly and severely. All
his hopes shall perish; all that he has built up for himself shall be
shattered against that " stone of stumbling and rock of offence," on
which the strife and passion of his life have been striking: " The
adversaries of the Lord shall be broken in pieces." But this may be
a temporal ruin only, and may teach him, before it be too late, to
cling to that rock for salvation, which stands firm, whilst all that
clashes upon it is broken up. It may be written of many such,
" Have they stumbled that they should fall (*for ever*)? God forbid;
but rather, through their *fall*, salvation is come." But the case is
different with those " on whomsoever it shall fall." Eternal wrath will
overtake them when Christ appears in judgment; there shall be no
escape or reprieve; their destruction will be complete and final. It
will be, in this case, as it was in the vision of Daniel (ii. 34, 35);
where, before the stone cut out without hands, all opposing powers
were " broken in pieces together, and became like the chaff of the
summer threshing-floors; and the wind carried them away, that no
place was found for them; and the stone that smote . . . became a
great mountain, and filled the whole earth." The scribes were fulfilling
one of these conditions; they were resisting Christ, and their labour
would be frustrated, they would lose it: if they persevered, they would
come within the second condition.

soever it shall fall, it will grind him to powder.　Therefore I say unto you, The kingdom of God shall be taken from you, and given to a nation bringing forth the fruits thereof.

And when the chief priests and Pharisees had heard His parables, they perceived that He spake of them. But when they sought to lay hands on Him, they feared the multitude, because they took Him for a prophet. And they left Him, and went their way.

39. *Therefore.*—Gk. " because of this," *i.e.*, because of your rejection of Christ, the chief corner stone; and as your own sentence upon yourselves proceeds, and as God's decision warns you, I now pronounce judgment.

40. *the kingdom of God.*—The Church of God, and the privileges of His covenant, and of the promise, and your office of stewardship therein, shall be taken from you by God; and given to others, to a true people of God gathered out of all nations, who shall bring forth, what you have refused to Him, " fruits worthy of repentance," " fruits of righteousness."　Bede gives to this parable a personal application: " To every one of the faithful is let out a vineyard to cultivate, in that the mystery of Baptism is entrusted to him to work out.　One servant is sent, a second, and a third, whenever the Law, the Psalms, and the Prophets are read.　But the servant who is sent is said to be treated despitefully, or beaten, when the word heard is despised or blasphemed.　The heir who is sent, that man kills as far as he can who by sin tramples under foot the law of God.　The wicked husbandman being destroyed, the vineyard is given to another when, with the gift of grace which the proud man spurned, the humble is enriched."　(See note 13.)

41. *He spake of them.*—They were fully aware of this, with regard to both His parables: it was impossible to miss the application so unreservedly stated.　Even if at first they chose to repress the conviction of their conscience, as the parable proceeded He had spoken so plainly that they could not misapprehend Him.

42. *to lay hands.*—S. Luke says that " the same hour they sought to lay hands on Him; " they were for arresting Him on the spot, in execution of the secret resolution they had already passed.　But, even if they stepped forward menacingly to attempt this (as the words of S. Luke almost seem to imply), a glance at the bearing of the multitude around made them hesitate.　They saw things were not ripe for their purpose; the popular feeling was still in Christ's favour; and so " they feared the multitude, because they were taking Him for a prophet."

43. *they left Him.*—There is something saddening and awful in this

VIII. *THE PARABLE OF THE MARRIAGE OF THE KING'S SON.*

S. Matt. xxii. 1-14.

And Jesus answered and spake unto them again by

wilfulness; we follow them in thought, passing away from Christ's presence with unsoftened hearts, and with every evil resolution confirmed. They knew not that the system of their theology, and their hopes were shattered, and there impended over them the menacing gloom of eternal ruin. They thus retire from every offer of mercy, and from all hope; and so go forth to fulfil that doom which His words had just spoken, not yet in judgment, but in the last utterance of merciful warning and admonition; for, as S. Augustine remarks, "He has no wish to strike you, who cries out, Beware!" No; he would fain have gathered them to Him even there, but " they would not " (willed it not).

The history of our Lord's dealing with the Jewish rulers from first to last, through admonition, and warning, and distinct declaration of the prospect before them, is the history of a wonderful forbearance, of unwearied patience and gentleness in the face of opposition and misconstruction, and of the employment of every means, which power and goodness could suggest, for bringing them within the fold of truth. We may hence see what is also His mode of dealing with individuals. To take an extreme instance, that of Judas. There is the same constant and anxious warning and exhortation, continued through a long season, and urged with increased earnestness during those closing scenes when the traitor had taken his resolution, and was setting forth on his wicked errand to the chief priests. Even then our Lord did not give him up; from his own mouth He convicts him, as he asks, " Lord, is it I ? " and the Lord answers, " Thou sayest it ! " just as He convicted these rulers, and then plainly spoke of their doom. The last chance is given, strengthened by every consideration of occasion and deepened feeling; but Judas sets forth to his evil work. These must be examples of His general dealing with mankind; of His unwillingness to leave them whilst there is any remote hope of them, and of his ever strengthening and multiplying His warnings as men advance in hardness; of His making more distinct and plain before them the danger they are daring. It is only when men " leave Him and go their way " to their evil purposes, that they pass from the range of His mercy. (See note 14.)

1. *answered.*—No questions on the part of the multitude are recorded ; but our Lord frequently answered the thoughts of the heart; and many great questions were at this time agitating all hearts, more

parables, and said, The kingdom of heaven is like unto

than one of which is met by these three parables. Definite ideas
were eagerly sought after on the great subjects of John's baptism, of
the mission and office of Christ, of the kingdom of the Messiah,
of the condition of the nation under His kingdom. We read also of
various points of doctrine and discipline, subjects of controversy
between rival sects, the solution of which was hoped for from the
Messiah; and when such questions were brought before Christ, the
people hung upon His answer.

2. *again by parables.*—The three parables, of which this is the last
in order, form a series of great interest; each is intimately connected
with the other, and it is wonderful how distinctly and clearly our
Lord speaks in them. The first gives the call of the Jewish people,
both of the professedly religious, and of the notoriously abandoned
and outcast classes: the former complied with all the seeming devotion
of formal profession, but were utterly disobedient so far as practice
was concerned; the latter refused to obey God, going boldly off into
sinfulness of life, but afterwards repented, and came in to the Gospel.
The second gives the stewardship of the Jews in their trust within
the Church of God, and their disregard of all God's messages to
them; and, finally, their refusal of Christ, and their putting Him to
death, followed by the doom of the faithless stewards of God's
mysteries, and the transfer of their commission and privileges within
the renovated Church of Christ to others. And last, *this* parable gives
the setting forth of the Gospel dispensation, and the summons of those
to whom it had been so long promised, to enjoy its liberty and
blessings: it shows their contemptuous disregard of it, both before and
after the covenant was sealed with the Blood of Christ; then the
call of the Gentiles, far and wide—the more civilized and cultivated,
as well as the wild and savage heathen—to fill the places, vacant and
prepared for them, at the Table of the Lord; then the fate of any
who pressed into the presence of the King of kings, except through
the covenant of Christ. This third parable seems more especially
addressed to the multitudes by way of warning; for the rulers, represented by those who had refused to come, had gone away: to the
rest, therefore, their danger is declared. Thus, in each parable there is
the unfolding of a further and progressive truth, and a more extended
scope, until the last brings us to the very kingdom of God in heaven.

3. *The kingdom of heaven.*—The kingdom of the promised Messiah,
first as offered to the Jewish nation, but with an after reference to
all ages. The meaning is not exactly the Gospel of Christ, or His
dispensation of religion, but a rather more extended sense; for the
parable begins with the days of the earlier dispensation, and continues
through that of the Gospel, and closes within the kingdom of heaven.
It is less restricted than that of the vineyard in the second parable,
which represents the Church of God on earth only.

a certain king, which made a marriage for his son, and
sent forth his servants to call them that were bidden to

4. *a marriage.*—Gk. a "marriage feast;" the use of the plural
word, in the original, generally implies the continued festivities of a
wedding. This figure of a marriage festival is used by the prophets
to express the relationship of the Church to God: with the New
Testament writers it is employed to represent "the spiritual marriage
and unity betwixt Christ and His Church." The latter part of the
parable, with the assemblage of the guests, each in his wedding
garment of fine linen, and the marriage blessing when the king comes
in to see the guests, finds a counterpart in the vision of S. John
(Rev. xix. 5–9).
There is a parable in S. Luke xiv. 16–24, which has many points
of resemblance with this; and no doubt intentionally so, for it refers
to the invitation of the Gospel. The two have been taken as different
versions of the same parable by several authors; but a careful attention to the points of difference will show that, whilst the former refers
to individuals, this latter one refers more especially to the rejection
of the Gospel by the Jewish nation, and their punishment; and it is
not an amplification even, of that of S. Luke, but distinctly and
originally different in object. The similarity of subject may be
accounted for by the principle of our Lord's teaching during this week,
His resetting and repointing of former parables and truths with new
applications, which has been noticed in i. 1.
5. *His son.*—Our Lord still keeps before His audience, and unfolds
the truth of His Sonship with God. It was pointedly expressed in
the preceding parable, and they saw that He was speaking of themselves, and their rejection of His mission; and therefore they comprehended that He was Himself "the son" of whom He spoke in that
parable. He now asserts this royalty, as the Son of the great King;
and (as they well understood), in the application of the parable, as the
Son of the King of heaven, the Divine Son of God.
6. *His servants.*—Apparently John the Baptist, the seventy, and
the twelve disciples on their first mission, as heralds of the Gospel
(Matt. x.), and who were sent to those who were already prepared
to receive such a summons; their message was, "The kingdom of
heaven is at hand."
7. *them that were bidden.*—The Jewish Church, which had long
been in preparation for this invitation, is now reminded of God's
promise, and summoned to its fulfilment. By Moses and the prophets,
and in every page of the earlier Scriptures, they had been made aware
of this marriage feast; and they had been taught to look to the
coming of the Messiah from the very dawn of their nationality; and
earlier even, from the time when the first promise was given to Adam,
there was an invitation to come. In fact, the Lamb of God had been

the wedding: and they would not come.   Again, he sent
forth other servants, saying, Tell them which are bidden,
Behold, I have prepared my dinner: my oxen and *my*
fatlings *are* killed, and all things *are* ready: come unto

"slain from the foundation of the world" in the purposes of God;
and God's invitation to the future feast of the Gospel had been made
intelligible to man from the beginning, as we read in the bright instances of faith in Heb. xi.

8. *they would not come.*—The rulers had just turned away from Him
in final refusal; the people generally rejected Him when they desired
the release of Barabbas, and invoked upon themselves and their
children the consequences of shedding His blood.

9. *other servants.*—If the servants first sent were those above
mentioned, these must be the Apostles, and subordinate ministers of
the Gospel after the Ascension; and, thenceforward, their successors
to the end of the dispensation.   Perhaps we may take a more general
view of them, than this primary and particular one; for as the Holy
Spirit was given to the Church for all time, so was His Presence to be
universally diffused; and therefore the Apostles, and all inferior ranks
of teachers and ministers, the Church in her formularies and rules of
faith, and every one to whom it is given to train and instruct others
in the faith, all these proclaim the invitation, "Come to the marriage."
(See vii. 6.)   In Rev. xxii. 17, the commission is given at the least as
widely as this: "The Spirit, and the bride" (the Church, by her formularies, organization, and ministers) "say, Come. And let *him that heareth*
say, Come."   Bede takes a different view of the "servants" in this
parable.   He makes the first to be Moses, the second David, the third
the company of the prophets; but it is better to take these amongst
the servants who had originally bidden to preparation for the promised
festival; although it must be owned such an interpretation continues
the invitation beyond the coming of the Son, concerning whose first
advent the parable is silent.

From this point the parable becomes prophetic, as it deals with
times future to those when it was spoken.

10. *my dinner.* . . The original word implies an earlier meal than
this; in fact, a meal introductory to the grand festival itself, as the
guests are gathering; and answers to those foretastes of future happiness which the Church on earth can afford, in anticipation of the
great gathering in heaven.

11. *all things are ready.*—Nothing remained to be done; the great
sacrifice was now accomplished, and their remained no more offering
for sins yet to be made: all provisions of the Christian covenant were
complete, and open to the invited.   The sacrifice was slain, the "table
furnished," the guests are called in.   There is an extraordinary parallel
to this parable in Prov. ix. 2, 3, 5, where Wisdom (who from ch. viii.

the marriage.   But they made light of *it*, and went their ways, one to his farm, another to his merchandise : and the remnant took his servants, and entreated *them* spite-

22-31, we gather is a prophetical personation of the Divine Son, in the beginning with the Father, but setting His love on man) summons mankind to her feast of heavenly things.   The bread and wine which she offers are further types of the heavenly Supper of our Lord, and prophetically illustrative of His great institution; itself introductory (see note 10) to the grand and perfect festival of heaven.

12. *made light of it.*—Not derided, but took no account of it. Nothing could be more disheartening than this utter indifference and unconcern ; it is perhaps even a greater difficulty to encounter than open hostility, which, however, draws down counter force in opposition.   But little can be said, or done, against those who have nothing to say for, or against the invitation, but who quietly and decidedly act as if it was no concern of theirs in the remotest degree.   As there is nothing to record of their opposition, so nothing is said of their punishment, further than this, that they "were not worthy."   The parable leaves them; it does not descend into that depth of gloom, where those who have counted themselves unworthy of eternal life, and rejected the counsel of God against themselves, and have made light of His offers, bewail the folly in which they have turned away to the transitory engagements and distractions of life.   (See Gk. in Heb. ii. 3.)

13. *farm . . . merchandise.*—One was intent on the improvement of that on which he had settled himself for his life's occupation : the Gk. gives "*his own* farm," as marking proprietary right.   Another was absorbed in the anxieties and ventures of trade and speculation, which left but little time or thought for any other interest.   The one was settled on riches already acquired; the other absorbed in the acqui- sition of wealth.   Perhaps the call was not altogether unheeded, even in the ardour of the pursuit of these objects of immediate preference ; for the time only, they may have set it aside, intending to consider it at a convenient season.   For the present, however, there was no hesitation in their action ; each gave his whole mind to his particular occupation, and not one thought to the king's gracious invitation.   It is worthy of notice, that these representatives of multitudes, perish in their misuse of what is, within due limit, laudable.   The business of the world could not progress unless men were absorbed in it with all their heart. But yet the work-days of life are no less God's days, than the sabbath; and all true work is His, all talents are His, and all mankind His agents.

14. *the remnant.*—There was a smaller section of those invited, not specified amongst the generality occupied in their own concerns. These were animated by determined hostility to the king, and looked as little to any earthly occupation, as to their heavenly call ; their avowed and resolute object was, to do all they could in the way of

fully, and slew *them*. But when the king heard *thereof*, he
was wroth ; and he sent forth his armies, and destroyed
those murderers, and burned up their city. Then said
he to his servants, The wedding is ready, but they which

opposition. The rulers were, for the most part, of this class ; the
people generally ranked amongst those careless, indifferent, irreligious.

15. *took . . . entreated spitefully . . . slew.*—Some were seized and
shut up in prison, like Peter ; others, like S. Paul, were subject to
every cruel violence and indignity ; and many, like Stephen, and
James the brother of John, were put to death for their proclamation
of the Gospel invitation.

16. *wroth.*—Yet He continued His invitation and His offers of reconciliation for forty years, until nearly every one of Christ's Apostles
had been hurried into His presence by his enemies, to tell the result
of their mission and their violent death. And "when the King heard
this," His wrath recalled the offers of His mercy.

17. *his armies.*—The armies of avenging powers (though heathen
powers, and intent merely on their own objects in conquest) are often
styled "God's armies" (see Isa. x. 5); and never had Divine commission so undoubted been delivered to such agents, as was entrusted
to the Roman armies against Jerusalem. With regard to the Jews'
refusal of Christ, Bishop Latimer observes that "ambition, covetousness, and cruelty would not let them come. God is angry with
covetous men, with ambitious men, but most of all with cruelty. This
cruelty the King would not leave unpunished, but sent forth His men
of war ; His men of war came at His commandment. Titus and
Vespasian were sent of God to punish those covetous Jews, ambitious
Jews, cruel Jews, that would not credit Christ, nor believe the preaching of salvation." But theirs was not the only army of God gathered
against the doomed city on His mission of destruction. Famine, pestilence, and the horrors of war are all so termed in the pages of Scripture ;
and these were arrayed against Jerusalem, as they had never been
against any city, or people, in the world's history.

18. *murderers.*—(See Matt. xxiii. 34–36.) But before execution was
done upon them, they had added to their list the blood of our Lord, and
of His martyrs Stephen and James, and of many other of the Apostles
and prophets of the Lord Jesus.

19. *their city.*—Jerusalem. Our Lord gives a fuller prophetic
description of the terrible afflictions of the siege and destructio n of
Jerusalem, later in the same day (sect. xviii.). It has been noti ced
how God's rejection of the city is made apparent in the use of the pronoun " *their* ; " it is *His* no longer. There is the same emphasis in the
term " *your* House," in speaking of the desolation of the Temple (Matt.
xxiii. 38.) (Sect. xiv. 48 ; see also in Exod. xxxii. 7.)

20. *his servants.*—See note 9.

were bidden were not worthy. Go ye therefore into the
highways, and as many as ye shall find, bid to the
marriage. So those servants went out into the highways,
and gathered together all as many as they found, both bad
and good : and the wedding was furnished with guests.

21. *were not worthy.*—See note 12 ; Acts xiii. 46.

22. *the highways.*—Rather, those places where main roads met, than
which there could be no more likely places of public resort. "Cross-
roads" or " thoroughfares " would be nearer the sense, but would not
be quite close to the original word, which occurs only in this single
passage in the N. T. ; the classical use of the word gives generally the
sense of " openings of ways," passages out, ways of entrance and exit.
A number of these might meet in some great square, market-place, or
forum ; and in such places the preachers of the apostolic era proclaimed
the Gospel. The gatherings in Eastern bazaars are most numerous, and
heterogeneous. Another, and more general sense, would include those
great centres of public concourse, in the wide world of God, where
population congregates, and where men of different nations come and
go, on their business between land and land. At these, the capitals of
provinces and kingdoms, and at all great cities of commerce and trade,
the invitation of the Gospel was published. In these " highways " they
would meet the Jews of the Dispersion, the Samaritans, and the Gentiles, who thus would hear the Gospel. Farrar, referring to Lightfoot,
points out how the servants, though bidden to go thoroughly into these
" highways," only went into the main roads. This delicate reference
to the imperfect work of human agents is lost in our version.

23. *bad and good.*—There was no exception or limitation, whether
of number or fitness ; " as many as they found, both bad and good,"
expresses a call that is universal. So the great net of the Gospel,
broadcast over the world, gathered into the visible Church " of every
kind ;" and the separation between bad and good was made at the end
of the world (Matt. xiii. 47–50). (See P. II. vi. 18.) The commission to
the servants was, to " preach the Gospel to every creature ;" for none are
so good as not to need Christ's salvation, none so wicked as to be impossible of restoration by it. Indeed, the further men have gone from the
way of salvation, the greater their need of grace. As we look upon
the world, we see how true it is, that " both bad and good " come
under the influence of the Gospel. In one sense none are *good* until
they receive it, for the only goodness current with heaven is that of
the standard of Christ ; and those are beyond redemption *bad*, who
wilfully and persistently reject it. But there is a vast difference in
the excellence, or wickedness, of those who hear the Gospel call ; some
are " not far from the kingdom of heaven ;" others outrage the law of
nature, " written in their hearts." But, as our Lord declares, sometimes " the first are last, and the last first." Like the sons in the first

And when the king came in to see the guests, he saw there a man which had not on a wedding garment: and

parable of this series, some profess obedience and never really obey, whilst those who have at first flatly refused, afterwards repent and become obedient; or (like the Jewish stewards of God's vineyard in the second parable, and in this), the great privileges which were theirs are forfeited, and those last called, and least endowed, become first in the kingdom of Christ.

24. *to see the guests.*—The word rendered "*to see*" is one which expresses scrutiny or inspection; by no means only the meeting, or welcoming His guests. To the good His eye would brighten with the expression of welcome, and approval of what He saw; to the bad it would be a terrible glance, which would read their every fault and deficiency. The word rendered "*guests*" is lit. "those reclining," or sitting at table. They were no longer simply "those bidden;" for they had now come in, and seated themselves at the king's table, an open profession of acceptance of His invitation and call.

25. *a man.*—He is one only in number; but, from the command to gather in "all, both bad and good," and from the closing remark, "many are called," we see that he is the representative of a large class who are in the same condemnation. There is a particular comprehensiveness in his being represented singly; it shows that each one individually attracts the eye of the king, not one escaping in the multitude of those similarly deficient. It is the declaration of individual responsibility, and of the judgment of individuals: "Every one of us shall give account of himself to God" (Rom. xiv. 12).

26. *a wedding garment.*—In illustration of this passage, see Isa. lxi. 10; Zeph. i. 7, 8, where guests are bidden, and the princes and rulers punished for contempt, and "such as are clothed with strange apparel" degraded. It is in the East, if not exactly a common custom, not an unusual practice to give, on special occasions, a dress of honour to the guests at a high festival. If such a gift were offered *by the king*, the refusal to put it on would be a mark of extreme contempt and disaffection, an intended insult. It was natural to offer such robes, in the present instance, to guests gathered in from the highways and by-ways.

Many are the interpretations attached to the "wedding garment," especially by ancient writers. Some called it faith, charity (Col. iii. 14; 1 Tim. i. 5), holiness (Heb. xii. 14), mercy (Col. iii. 12), humility (1 Pet. v. 5), the new man (Eph. iv. 24), and other Christian graces; others, the confession of Christianity (Rom. x. 9, 10; Matt. x. 32), or the Sacraments, especially that of Baptism. It is difficult to say that any of these are wrong, though none alone may be right; they are all included in the garment of Christ's righteousness, the "putting on of the Lord Jesus Christ" (Rom. xiii. 14). The man who had not on the wedding garment, showed his decided intention to enter heaven in

he said unto him, Friend, how camest thou in hither not
having on a wedding garment?　And he was speechless.

some other way, vested in excellence and worthiness of his own.　The
essential idea of the garment is *personal* apparel, and its fitness, or the
contrary, is personal respect, or contempt; there being here a choice
between appearing in royal, or degraded attire.

27. *friend.*—This word is thrice used by our Lord, in the sense in
which we find it here; there is distance, distrust, and disapprobation
conveyed in it, as thus used; though it includes the recognition, with
reproach, of former relationship and intimacy.　The two other instances are Matt. xx. 13, and xxvi. 50.　The original word is also
capable, like this term "friend," of a much warmer signification than
that in which it is here used.

28. *how camest thou.*—"He was discovered by the Lord, who
escaped the notice of the servants." (*S. Augustine.*)　There is no
such question asked, or answered, within the visible Church on earth;
its members take upon themselves the responsibility of the truth of
their profession and membership, to which man's scrutiny cannot
penetrate.　It is only when indifference, or irreligion, or the want of
orthodoxy, pass beyond the wide limits which may be assigned to
private judgment, that action may be taken against a lukewarm or
offending member; his conscience, however, may forecast the question
of his Lord.　In all her services the Church of Christ addresses *sinners*,
those who are in need of a Saviour; like her Lord, she seeks those that
are lost, and embraces those not yet fit for heaven, not yet clothed with
the wedding garment.　There are, therefore, many such within her
pale; it is hers to invite, rarely to judge; and perhaps, to any age of
her mission, the want of the true garment is not perceptible, in the case
of many of her "guests."　But it will be different at the last.　Those
who are nominally Christian, but not really such, must encounter this
terrible question from the mouth of the Judge: "How camest thou in
hither?"　Under what pretence, with what authority, dost thou take
thy place at My Table, assume My holy Name, refusing the true
character of My people.

29. *speechless.*—He had not one word to answer; he was self-convicted, and he knew that no plausible excuse, nothing but what was
absolutely true, could for one moment be offered.　There was no plea
for one who had refused, with intention of insult, or with careless contempt, the garment offered to him.　It will, no doubt, be thus at the
end.　There are many who are eloquent enough in expressing their
doubts, difficulties, and theories about religion; who have every sort of
plausible reason to offer for themselves, whenever any rule of Christianity, or any ordinance of their Church, crosses their inclination, or
clashes with their peculiar views (see Luke xiv. 18): but they will not
dare to offer one of these pleas before the Judge; they will be " speech-

Then said the king to the servants, Bind him hand and foot, and take him away, and cast *him* into outer darkness: there shall be weeping and gnashing of teeth.

For many are called, but few *are* chosen.

less." "In this speechlessness all the objections ever raised against Christianity must vanish at the last."

30. *the servants.*—The original word here is quite different from that rendered " servants " earlier in this parable. These are ministers of the king, "the angels" of Matt. xiii. 49; their work and office is distinct from that of those, whose commission it was to give the king's invitation to the guests. These are the guards of the royal household, who encircle his throne,—the angels therefore; not, as in the former case, the preachers of the Gospel. The difference in the original terms may be expressed as *servants* (or rather, slaves) and *ministers :* the human agents were slaves to sin, now ransomed servants to God; the angels are freeborn sons of lights, and intelligent ministers of the Almighty's purposes.

31. *bind him.*—He is now within the bonds of irresistible power; no efforts will avail to release him, nor can he now walk in the way in which he should have gone, nor do the things which are pleasing in God's sight. The power of free will, so greatly abused, is taken from him; he has been the bond-servant of evil, tied and bound with the chain of his own sins, and now he is judicially bound, by the sovereign decree of the Judge.

32. *outer darkness.*—From the light of the Gospel, and from the brightness of the kingdom, will be excluded all "that obey not the Gospel of our Lord Jesus Christ; who shall be punished with ever-lasting destruction from the presence of the Lord, and from the glory of His power, when He shall come to be glorified in His saints" (2 Thess. i. 8–10).

33. *weeping and gnashing of teeth.*—These words occur frequently in S. Matthew's Gospel; and they are our Lord's description of the misery of those, whose unhappy lot it is to mourn hopelessly over the glorious destiny which they might have shared, and from which they have excluded themselves; and of their despair and agony, as they find themselves bound to the companionship, and punishment, of those altogether alien to themselves: for the world in which they have cast their own lot, is the "everlasting fire, prepared for the devil and his angels." For themselves a far different place had been prepared by Christ; but, of their unutterable folly, they rejected it, and have so come into a place not prepared for them, and for which they were not intended. They can never be at home in the world of lost spirits, though it be their dwelling-place for ever.

34. *many are called.*—(See Matt. xx. 16.) This is one of those sententious sayings of our Lord, which recur in a variety of con-

IX. *QUESTION OF THE PHARISEES AND HERODIANS CONCERNING TRIBUTE TO CÆSAR.*

S. Matt. xxii. 15–22 ; S. Mark xii. 13–17 ; S. Luke xx. 20–26.

Then went the Pharisees, and took counsel how they

nections, and which therefore may be assumed to be rules of His kingdom, differently illustrated. Other examples of these rules will be found in App. VI. There may, at first sight, be an apparent contradiction, between the lesson here drawn, and the actual instance in the parable ; as the many are accepted, and but the one rejected. But, considering the universal nature of the call to the feast (for the servants " gathered together all as many as they found, both bad and good "), and that the one rejected is the representative of a large class individually illustrated (see note 25), we must gather that the meaning here is, that the call to the inheritance of the heavenly world, is to all who had lost their inheritance in Adam's fall ; but that God's choice of those worthy of it, is limited to those who accept His offer of mercy, and who do not add to the loss, for which they are not solely responsible, that rejection of the restoration of their privileges, which is wilful. They are chosen of God, or not chosen ; but His choice is, between those who refuse, and who accept His terms, rather than of some to be called, and others not to be called. His choice is therefore, to a great extent, the ratification by Him of their own self-election, or self-rejection. For, however insuperable may be the difficulties which surround the subject of election, predestination, choice, or whatever we may term the exertion of God's sovereign will concerning us, this much stands out clear and distinct—that all who hear the Gospel have the call to salvation through Christ, and that it is a call obedience to which is impossible to none ; it is not crossed by any arbitrary bar of God, which prevents any man's acceptance of His offer. God's choice is against those who put not on the wedding garment furnished to them, but in favour of those who accept it.

35. *few chosen.*—We must not omit to notice, that the reference in this sentence is to those who had refused to come, as well as to the man who had refused to put on a wedding garment ; to the indifferent, as well as to the daringly contemptuous.

1. *Then went the Pharisees.*—The action of the Pharisees is here resumed from the close of sect. VII. (Mark xii. 12). When Christ had finished the parable of the wicked husbandmen, and pointed it against them, they would have laid violent hands on Him immediately (vii. 42) ; but fear of the people prevented them ; so they left Him, to deliberate on their measures. We now see that they returned to the

might entangle Him in *His* talk. And they sent out
unto Him their disciples with the Herodians, spies which

council chamber, probably one of the large chambers within the courts
of the Temple, named Gazith (though the general session of the great
council was, at this time, held outside the Temple), and so were
assembled at no great distance from where Christ was speaking.
Their resolution was speedily taken; or, rather, they now gave orders
for the adoption of measures already well discussed (i. 29).   They
send forth a carefully selected deputation, instructed how, with artful
questions, to make Him commit Himself, before the people whom
they so dreaded, by His own replies.

2. *entangle Him in His talk.*—Tried by every, even heathen,
standard of what is fair and honourable, this action is truly despi-
cable; but no words can adequately stigmatize the malignity of this
proceeding on the part of Jewish rulers.   That the chief teachers
of the then purest religion upon earth, should insidiously tempt, and
then watch the words of, One whom they all believed to be at least "a
Prophet come from God," and who claimed, under the voice of prophecy,
and by sanction of such miracles as had never yet been seen in Israel,
to be the Messiah, the Son of God; in order that they might put Him
to death by the hands of a heathen power which the nation hated,
seems indeed of deeper than human malice.   This is an illustration
of our Lord's words (John viii. 44): "Ye are of your father the devil,
and the lusts of your father ye will do" (lit. "it is your will to
do ").

3. *Herodians.*—(See App. II.)   The present union of these two
parties, is one of those instances where contending sects, or parties,
have for the moment laid aside their hostility to each other, to crush
excellence, which is counter alike to each. History furnishes many
parallels.   Thus the Pharisees, Herodians, Sadducees, and others combined against Christ; thus also Herod and Pontius Pilate were made
friends together (xxx. e. 6).   These new-made allies, the disciples of
the Pharisees and the Herodians, had little enough in common: the
former were theologians of the straitest sect of the Jews' religion;
the latter were the political partisans of Herod, and therefore more or
less friendly to Roman interests.   Corn. à Lapide cites the opinion of
many of the ancient writers, who say that they were an heretical Jewish
sect, who had at one time taken Herod the king for the Messiah
foretold by Jacob, and that he, on his part, felt a personal vengeance
against any who was received as Christ; and therefore he slew the
Innocents.   He also rebuilt the Temple, to rival that of Solomon.
To the same effect is the opinion of Theophylact, who mentions the
Herodians as "a certain new heresy, who said that Herod was the
Christ, because the succession of the kingdom of Judah had failed."
They were generally Sadducees, which alone was sufficient to make

should feign themselves just men, that they might take hold of His words, that so they might deliver Him unto the power and authority of the governor. And when they were come, they say unto Him, Master, we know that Thou art true, and carest for no man : for Thou

them adversaries to the Pharisees. Their alliance was formed in the council chamber, and was not intended to be public; and the deputation thus composed came before our Lord, to beg Him to decide a question naturally at issue between their sects. It had both a religious and political aspect; and they hoped that He would be entangled on one or both sides.

4. *spies.*—Lit. "suborned men." They had got their instructions beforehand, and were set upon their appointed task.

5. *just men.*—The original word, though a general term, has here a somewhat technical character: it refers to " the righteousness that is of the law." These men professed great zeal for the law, and for all questions arising out of its interpretation. They must have seemed "just men" to the multitude; they pretended to be very anxious for our Lord's opinion on a question of undoubted importance. They were men of official weight, representatives of the great council; they approached our Lord with professions of deference, and in great apparent anxiety about the matter they laid before Him. The impression they produced must have been decidedly favourable.

6. *might deliver Him.*—We notice the indignity they proposed against our Lord, Himself a Son of Israel, in invoking the aid of a hostile heathen power to destroy Him, by a death in their law held accursed. There was in it also the moral cowardice that dared not oppose popular opinion, but did this dark and underhand work, that the responsibility might appear to lie with the Roman power, not with themselves.

7. *were come.*—They now join the throng around our Lord; and room, no doubt, was respectfully made for this distinguished deputation, and all voices were hushed, in reverence for their character, and in the interest of their present approach to Christ. For they at once, apparently, open their mission,—not request to be heard.

8. *Master.*—A term most respectful, and expressive of high rank as a teacher of theology. (See John iii. 10.) They must have addressed the flattery of their deferential words to the ear of the multitude, as they could scarcely expect that of Jesus would be caught by it.

9. *Thou art true.*—Declaring the truth, and exposing whatever is false, not allowing it to pass unchallenged; " neither concealing what is true, nor speaking what is false." It was impossible to make fuller admission of our Lord's sanctity and excellence; and they *felt* the truth of the character they assigned to Him. But the speech was worthy, in its deep hypocrisy, of that arch-spirit of evil, of whom it

regardest not the person of men, but teachest the way of God in truth. Tell us, therefore, what thinkest Thou ? Is it lawful to give tribute unto Cæsar, or not ? Shall we give, or shall we not give ? But Jesus perceived their wickedness, and said, Why tempt ye Me, *ye* hypocrites ?

has been well said, that "he never lies so profoundly, as when he speaks truth."

10. *the person of men.*—Neither the weight and authority of the sacred office of the rulers ; nor the influence of sects ; nor the rank and power of Cæsar, and his representative, the governor ; nor yet the royalty of Herod.

11. *lawful for us.*—Is it in accordance with a right interpretation of God's law, and of His rights of sovereignty over Israel, for us, who are Jews, heirs of the promise and subjects of a theocracy, to pay homage and yield fealty to any foreign prince, especially to one who is an idolater ?

12. *Cæsar.*—The imperial designation of the Roman power. Tiberius was the "Cæsar" at this time.

13. *shall we give.*—Their question is thus more closely put. The former might be resolved by some casuistry, an art in which the Jewish doctors were adepts. They therefore put the plain point, "Is it God's will that we pay this tribute, or that we withhold it, and rise against it ?" The craft of their question was cleverly veiled ; it was a deeply interesting question to every Jew, and one which our Lord ought to decide, as the Messiah. These men, too, had every right to ask this question. Had they done it in good faith, they would have received the clear decision of Christ, and His reasons for it. The question was the more subtle, since (if we follow Jerome) there was a very current opinion at that time in Galilee, that it was not lawful, according to the precept issued by Judas of Galilee, which was still cherished by many persons.

14. *their wickedness.*—There was death in the answer, whether "Yes" or "No." Did our Lord decide that tribute must be given, it was equivalent to saying that He had no deliverance to offer to Israel, and that He acquiesced in the degradation and subjection of the nation, to even heathen powers—an answer which must make every Jew, in whose heart burned "the hope of Israel," from the Pharisee downwards, His enemy. If He decided that it was unlawful to pay tribute, the Herodians would at once report His answer to the Roman governor ; and there could be no doubt of His being immediately seized, and put to death, as instigating a most dangerous insurrection against Rome. Pilate had already done stern execution on several of our Lord's reputed fellow-countrymen, the Galilæans, who had been concerned in insurrection lately ; and he would not be likely to inquire further, if he heard that Christ was a Galilæan, and had given such a decision with all the weight of His sacred character. Judas of Galilee (Acts

Shew Me the tribute money. And they brought unto
Him a penny. And He saith unto them, Whose *is* this
image and superscription ? They say unto Him, Cæsar's.
Then saith He unto them, Render therefore unto Cæsar
the things which are Cæsar's ; and unto God the things

v. 37) had raised the standard of revolt, during the census of Cyrenius
(Luke ii. 2); and even in that day, and so late as the destruction of
Jerusalem, his followers formed a powerful and well-organized political
sect, which gave the greatest anxiety to the Roman governors—an
important fact, if we couple it with that of the popular excitement on
the occasion of our Lord's entry into Jerusalem, in illustration of the
opinion that, would He but speak the word, He might immediately
ascend the throne of David, and call out the nation in insurrection ;
as more than one pseudo-Christ aspired to do.

15. *tribute money.*—Lit. "the authorized coin of the census."

16. *a penny.*—Josephus says that the Roman provincial poll-tax of
a penny (*denarius*) a head was imposed on Judæa by Pompey.

17. *this image.*—"Lightfoot quotes the following saying of the
Rabbis :—'Wheresoever the money of any king is current, there the
inhabitants acknowledge that king for their lord; and hence Christ
answers the treachery of the question propounded out of the very
determination of the schools.'" (*Bishop Goodwin.*) It was not necessary
for Him to say "Yes" or "No;" appeal to the political maxim of
their own school was sufficient. Their habitual practice had already
decided the matter; they had accepted, and were using currently, the
coin of the Roman empire.

18. *render.*—These are not to be "*given*" (as they asked), but
"*rendered*" as of right. The word "*render*" implies the giving of
what is justly due. "Render therefore to all their dues," is S. Paul's
comment on this decision" (Rom. xii. 6, 7). The question is not
a new one. "Shall we give, or shall we not give?" is not a fair view
of the case. This has been long decided; it now remains merely to
render the right. Our Lord does not touch on the question, whether
the rule of the Romans was right or wrong, a tyranny, or of God's
sanction; He took the fact as it was, and stated simply what was the
true duty under existing circumstances.

19. *things which are Cæsar's.*—Our Lord does not specify these,
further than the tribute supposed, and implied them; but He would
not allow (and His decision is for all nations, in all ages of time) that
the profession of religion is any plea for rebellion against the lawful
ruler. The interests concerned in His reply were, therefore, far more
extensive than they appeared; and His words were spoken for many
inquirers, of purer conscience than these. For men labouring under
real anxiety as to what was right, in the conflicting claims of religion
and loyalty, they decided for ever, that no follower of His might object

that are God's. And they could not take hold of His words before the people : and they marvelled at His answer, and held their peace ; and left Him, and went their way.

to live under the civil laws of the country in which he resided ; or might, in the name of Christianity, take up arms against the State, for the assertion of his views.

20. *things that are God's.*—These the Herodians especially, were apt to lower to the convenience of political exigency. But the answer concerned both parties of His questioners ; for the Pharisees also lowered the law of God, to the traditions of their sect. And our Lord's rule echoes down all ages of Christianity. He decides that, whilst the civil powers have their dues and honour, God has His also ; and that the interests of religion may not give way to any earthly consideration whatever—there can be no political necessity superior to them. If there is interference with God's sovereign claims, on the part of the State, men must follow Daniel's example (vi. 10) ; and in such a case the rule of Matt. x. 28 holds good. For "in like manner as Cæsar demands of us the stamp of his likeness, so does God also : and if that which bears Cæsar's image is reckoned to him, men, who bear the likeness and image of God, are duly His ; body, soul, and spirit are His ; His claims on men are paramount." Therefore, "thou must give thy money indeed to Cæsar, but thyself to God." (*Tertullian.*) There may be here also a further connection between the things of Cæsar and of God. The Jews were manifestly under Cæsar's rule, and tribute was due to him ; their not rendering to God the things that were His, was the real cause of their being subjected by God to a foreign yoke. If they gave God His due, and turned to Him with repentance, therein would lie their true hope of deliverance from that yoke, and from the hated tribute ; which it was, at present, not only lawful, but necessary, to pay.

21. *before the people.*—They took, however, fatal hold of His words, when not restrained by their presence, and by that of Christ. It was not too bold a falsehood for them to plead before Pilate, "We found this fellow . . . . forbidding to give tribute to Cæsar" (S. Luke xxiii. 2) ; whilst they made, on the other hand, such use of His real words, "Render unto Cæsar the things that are Cæsar's," that they brought Him to His death. They sent their emissaries throughout the city, spreading, secretly and diligently, the information that Christ had decided for the Roman yoke, and was therefore no true Messiah ; so that the fickle multitude, which had so joyously hailed Him as "the King that cometh in the name of the Lord," five days later cried with equal energy, " Crucify Him ; His blood be on us and on our children ; we have no king but Cæsar." (See xxx. *d.* 10, *f.* 13.)

22. *held their peace.*—They were self-convicted of hypocrisy, and it

X. *QUESTION OF THE SADDUCEES CON-CERNING THE RESURRECTION.*

S. Matt. xxii. 23–33 ; S. Mark xii. 18–27 ; S. Luke xx. 27–39.

The same day came unto Him the Sadducees, which say that there is no resurrection, and asked Him, saying,

was impossible to answer a single word to our Lord's reply, and they read no sympathy, at present, in the faces of the multitude ; so once more they retired, baffled (vii. 43), and to make way for those whose subtle questions were to succeed theirs, but not the less resolutely set against Him.

1. *the same day.*—A day of peculiar trial to our Lord, when Satan, who had " departed from Him for a season " (S. Luke iv. 13), gathered adversaries against Him.   There seems to have been some interval after the departure of the Pharisees, during which, no doubt, their report was taken to the council, and the order given for the Sadducees to essay the part assigned to them ; during which also our Lord continued His teaching in the Temple.

2. *the Sadducees.*—(See App. II.) The question proposed by these Sadducees is thoroughly characteristic. They do not take hold of our Lord's words, in order to place His life in danger ; they merely try to lower His public reputation as a teacher. They were not so bitterly opposed to Him personally, as the Pharisees ; they were too sceptical, and indifferent to any strict views of religion, to feel, as the Pharisees did, on the subject of His growing reputation and success. There is a sneer in their question, and also the hope of bringing Christ's doctrine into a position of great absurdity. The extreme earnestness and spirituality of Christ's character, and the strictness of His views on every point of morality, were probably an offence to them, sufficient to make them unite with the Pharisees, for the occasion, in opposition to Him. Many MSS. omit the word "*the*" before "Sadducees," and render " which say " simply " saying ;" but the question seems one by the sect generally, as proposed by its chief representatives, and the best MSS. support the usual reading.

3. *no resurrection.*—" The Sadducees say there is no resurrection, neither angel nor spirit " (Acts xxiii. 8) ; and therefore there was not much self-restraint in their lives, nor reference to any state hereafter. Their views were necessarily low and crafty, and (to use a modern term) " rationalistic ; " their appreciation of Scripture was very limited, and they could little understand the deep spiritual nature of Christ's doctrine. In His reply He points out this, and challenges their doctrines, both as to the resurrection and the spirit world. The term

Master, Moses wrote unto us, **If a man die having no
children, his brother shall marry his wife,** and raise up
seed unto his brother. Now there were with us seven
brethren : and the first, when he had married a wife,

" resurrection," of course includes a state of being to which mankind
are to be raised.

4. *Master.*—See ix. 8.

5. *Moses wrote.*—(See note 17.) The Sadducees are charged with
receiving only the books of Moses, but there seems no real ground for
such an imputation. They no doubt venerated those books, much
more highly than they did other portions of Scripture; but so did the
Jews generally. Their very material views of religion, however, and
their denial of a future state, might make them less able to appreciate
the spiritual teaching of the Psalms and the Prophets, and therefore
less ready to refer to, quote, or study these ; but this appears to be the
extent of their rejection of these Scriptures. The avowed rejection of
the greater portion of the received canon of Scripture, would constitute
a heresy, which would have summoned all men to its forcible extirpa-
tion ; but there is no imputation of heresy against them, which would
have been the case had they been decidedly heretical.

6. *unto his brother.*—This, known as the " levirate law " (from the
word " *levir,*" a brother-in-law), was one of the many instances of the
incorporation, by Moses, into the law, of a very ancient maxim, an
earlier allusion to which is found in Gen. xxxviii. 8. It is supposed to
be of Cushite or Chaldæan origin, and is prevalent amongst African
tribes; it has been a law common to many Oriental nations. The
brother (or nearest kinsman) took to wife the widow of his deceased
brother, whose name and property were inherited by their first child.
The importance of this law in Israel is apparent; every man had his
inheritance in the land of promise, and the extinction of a name in
Israel was a subject of deepest sorrow. There was one amongst the
immediate ancestors of David, and therefore of our Lord Himself, who
was descended from such a marriage. (See Ruth iv.)

7. *seven brethren.*—This seems to be a supposed, though certainly a
possible, case ; the point in question would be equally valid were there
but two brothers concerned, but the confusion apprehended by the
Sadducees, is much more strongly illustrated in the case of seven
brothers, all rising to claim the same wife in the resurrection. Their
object was, not so much to refute our Lord's doctrine, as to ridicule it ;
that being a far more efficient way of discrediting it with the multitude, and one more in accordance with their principles, which forbade
their working themselves up to frenzy, like the Pharisees; and also
easier and more direct, than trying to argue, or prove their case. They
took the shorter method, of denying doctrines to which they objected,
and of making them appear absurd ; leaving their opponents to prove

deceased, and, having no issue, left his wife unto his brother: likewise the second also, and the third, unto the seventh: and they left no children, and died. Last of all the woman died also. In the resurrection, therefore, when they shall rise, whose wife shall she be of them? for the seven had her to wife. Jesus answered and said unto them, Ye do err, not knowing the scrip-

them, and to demonstrate their graver aspect. It is worth while noticing, how exactly parallel is the method of scepticism and rationalism, in denying and ridiculing orthodox truth; it requires neither much learning nor ability, and it is usually a mark of the want of earnest feeling on the subject of religion. The " shallow infidel " is the popular designation of a large and mischievous class, of those who cast reproach on the name and truth of Christ, and who do more injury to the convictions of others, than is done by men of large mind and profound learning, and of infinitely greater earnestness, who write and argue in misconception of the truth. It pleases the " shallow infidel " to be able to propound theories which are unanswerable, and to demand proof which cannot be given, by the wisest and the best. There is no answering this " fool according to his folly; " he is supremely, as Scripture brands him, " *the fool*."

8. *no children.*—Neither born before their death, nor posthumous; so there was no claim on the part of any one brother, stronger than that of another. The Pharisees had, however, a decision which would have accounted the woman the wife of the first brother, which probably gave colour to their anxiety for Christ's decision.

9. *when they shall rise.*—The Sadducees emphasize the great point on which their schools were at issue with those of the Pharisees, and with Christ, whose doctrine they hope to show so unnatural a notion.

10. *ye do err.*—Whatever may be the source of error in the case of others—whether prejudice, zeal for ancient faith, political partisanship, or even active hostility to the Gospel—you, at least, have no claim to respect for your opinions. You come to cast ridicule on the truth before the people, and your argument is founded on ignorance of Holy Scripture; you are talking about that of which you know nothing; and you are not in earnest either, nor have you any worthy conception of the power of the Almighty God of Israel. Nothing could more effectually cover with well-merited confusion, these men who had designed to overwhelm Christ, than His convicting them of ignorance; for, among the Jews, knowledge and learning were confined to the Scriptures, and to the Rabbinical writings, and traditions founded on them. One ignorant of Scripture was, on the other hand, held to be an ignorant and uninformed man. They despised all learning connected with other nations and countries, as they did those nations themselves;

tures, nor the power of God. The children of this world marry, and are given in marriage : but they which shall be accounted worthy to obtain that world, and the resurrection from the dead, neither marry nor are given in marriage : neither can they die any more : for they

scarcely any of the Jewish Rabbis permitted the study of the Grecian literature, though they spoke Greek vernacularly, and though communication with the Alexandrian schools was familiar. But they knew more of the letter, than of the spirit, of Holy Scripture; and Tertullian says well, he " would rather be somewhat less versed in Holy Scripture, than misunderstand it.". We note our Lord's reply, as showing the true way to meet the objections of those (see note 7) who, in the shallowness of their knowledge, and in their want of true conception of the gravity of religion, cast their idle words of doubt, or denial, on its truths. Dean Burgon remarks, " To *quote* the Scriptures is not to *know* them."

11. *power of God.*—The immediate anger of the audience would be roused, against any one who underrated the power of the great God of Israel. The words "power of God" are generally taken to refer to the resurrection; the Sadducees did not comprehend that power which could put aside all difficulties : Christ may, however, referring to the Scriptures generally, mean that they. knew them aright, neither in their letter nor their spirit. The exercise of God's power in the resurrection has been likened to the art of an analyst, or refiner, who can detect the component parts of a mixed mass of chemical compound, or of metal, and bring them out distinctly and severally, and reunite them. So can God resolve our bodies into their component substances, and recall these from being blended with other substances, and reunite them at His pleasure. Amongst comparisons of great things with small, this is a good comparison.

12. *accounted worthy.* — Very forcible words, which, by their solemnity, must arrest the attention of all who hear them, and must have touched the conscience of those who had addressed our Lord; for they would gladly hope that there was no resurrection, knowing themselves unworthy of a better life.

13. *from the dead.*—Gk. " from amongst the dead." A resurrection within the general resurrection; that of those, namely, accounted worthy to rise to endless life, from amongst those who shall rise to the immortality of death.

14. *neither can they die.*—Therefore there is no need of marriage, as *they* viewed it, (and of this only our Lord speaks,) nor of any provision, for replacing those departed; much less any necessity for such a law, as that which occasioned the Sadducees such embarrassment. Our Lord's silence with regard to the higher, and nobler view of married life, does not lead us to infer that the spiritual end of so close a relationship, does not find its perfect realization in the future and better life.

are equal unto the angels ; and are the children of God, being the children of the resurrection. Now that the dead are raised, even Moses shewed at the bush, when he calleth the Lord **the God of Abraham, and the God of Isaac, and the God of Jacob.** For He is not a God

15. *equal.*—Gk. "equals, or peers, of the angels." It is not here implied that they are in power, equals of the angels, "who excel in strength," and they are not of the same nature; but as sharers of the gift of immortality. They will doubtless be equal in dignity, for the perfection of the *present* nature of man is described as "a little lower than the angels;" and it is hereafter to be inexpressibly glorified through Christ, who "took not on Him the nature of angels, but took on Him the seed of Abraham." S. Augustine holds that the children of the resurrection will supply the "loss which the fall of the devil had brought on the fellowship of the angels."

16. *children of God.*—The relationship of children and parents, cannot exist in a world where there are no parents : and sonship with God is one of the declared blessings of the Christian covenant; even "now we are the sons of God" within its provisions. Our Lord also calls us "brethren," and speaks of God as "My Father and your Father, My God and your God." He is Himself not merely the *Author* of the resurrection, but declares "I am the Resurrection and the Life." S. Paul (Gal. iii. 26) says to Christians, "Ye are all the children of God through faith in Jesus Christ." Immortality of life is an attribute of the Being of God, and those who enjoy it are thus partakers of His nature, and His true children. There is therefore a deep mystery, which connects the subjects of our sonship with God, and our resurrection to the life eternal.

17. *even Moses.*—The fact that our Lord passed over the much more direct assertion of this doctrine in the Psalms, in Isaiah, and in Daniel, may give apparent support to the charge alluded to in note 5. But it was most natural that He should refute an objection founded on a law of Moses, by the words of Moses himself. And these words show also, that the revelation of the resurrection lies at the very threshold of the Jewish covenant, and of those Scriptures supremely venerated by every Jew. In passing over passages so pointed and distinct as those of the prophets, and resting His arguments on these words, our Lord took ground that only He could have taken; none but God could have declared the intention of Him, who made the covenant with Israel, to include in it the revelation of this doctrine.

18. *at the bush.*—Probably in the portion of his book containing the record of God's appearing to him in the bush, and its result.

19. *the God of Abraham.*—In the other Evangelists these words are quoted, more directly than by S. Luke, from Exod. iii. 6, as the words of God. And many commentators, following Theophylact, have

of the dead, but of the living ; for all live unto Him : ye
therefore do greatly err.   And when the multitude heard
this, they were astonished at His doctrine.   Then certain
of the scribes answering said, Master, Thou hast well
said.

argued from the words, "I am the God of Abraham," etc., that God
would have said, "I was the God," if there were no resurrection.   But
the verb is not expressed in the original of the passage in Exodus ; and
the argument really rests, on God's revelation of, Himself as the God of
Abraham, Isaac, and Jacob (not of their *spirits*, but of themselves, the
men), centuries after they had died, to earth and its inhabitants.   His
doing so showed that they were alive to Him, and that He could raise
them again from the sleep and dust of death.   He adds, "This is My
name for ever, and this is My memorial to all generations" (Ex. iii. 15).
(See the apostolic comment on this truth in Heb. xi. 16.)

   20. *of the dead . . . living.*—Gk. "of dead men, but of living."

   21. *live unto Him.*—To the eye of God life is continuous, being
unbroken by what seems to man so definite a limit, that of our stay
upon earth.   Therefore, though dead to men, they are living to God.
Their bodies were in the keeping of their descendants, at that very time
manifestly dead; but God is the Author of perfection, and if their
spirits were in His safe keeping, thus separate from the body, He would
certainly, in His good time, reunite body and spirit in fulness of
perfection; for body and spirit are inseparable in perfect humanity.
It has been objected, that the passage which our Lord quotes does not,
in proving the present existence of Abraham, Isaac, and Jacob, prove
also their resurrection.   But it must include this, as God would not
associate with Himself, for eternity, those whom He had deprived of a
material necessity of life ; the body is a necessary part of perfect man.

   22. *the multitude.*—Our Lord's doctrine was "not as the scribes"
taught; not involved in verbiage and uncertainty, leaving no definite
impression on the mind; but He spoke with the authority of God, and
with such clearness that the multitude easily understood Him, and
wondered at the hidden riches of their Scriptures, as He brought them
to light : and their astonishment was that of men who were at once
surprised, delighted, and convinced.

   23. *certain of the scribes.*—They were not all equally actuated by
malice, for these men were frank enough to own the excellence of
Christ's answer, and the truth of the hitherto unknown meaning, of the
familiar words which He had interpreted.   Their so admitting it shows
that it was, at the same time, an interpretation unknown to the schools
of religious knowledge, in which they were deeply versed; it was the
flashing of a new light upon their minds, the light of the spiritual meaning of Scripture, upon those whose superstitious veneration for the letter
of Scripture, blinded them to that deeper meaning.

XI. *QUESTION OF THE LAWYER CONCERNING THE FIRST AND GREAT COMMANDMENT.*

S. Matt. xxii. 34–40 ; S. Mark xii. 28–34.

But when the Pharisees had heard that He had put the Sadducees to silence, they were gathered together. Then one of them, *which was* a lawyer, having heard them reasoning together, and perceiving that He had answered them well, asked *Him a question* tempting

1. *put to silence.*—The original word is a strong one, expressive of the utter discomfiture of the Pharisees ; it means literally, " to *muzzle.*"

2. *gathered together.*—Gk. " were collected together at the same place." They had been in council ; but now, on hearing of the disgrace of the Sadducees before the multitude, they appear to have collected together around our Lord, listening to Him, or rather watching Him intently. His refutation of the errors of the Sadducees, must have given them satisfaction at any other time, for they professed belief in the existence of angel and spirit, and in a future state. But their thus grouping themselves around our Lord, attracted the attention of the Evangelist, as he notices it repeatedly (Matt. xxii. 34, 41) ; we may suppose, therefore, that this gathering was regarded as a proof of combined action, for some purpose hostile to our Lord, although the consultations of the council were, no doubt, secret. The Psalmist foresaw such a gathering of Christ's foes, and their becoming confederate for such malice. (See Ps. lxxxiii. 2–5.)

3. *a lawyer.*—(See App. II.) In Mark xii. 28–32, it is said he was a scribe ; and the two designations have often been identified : but there appears to be really a distinction between them. The scribe was a man holding an official post ; the lawyer was one honourably known, and designated for his learning in the law. Here, and no doubt often, he held the office of a scribe. There is this apparent distinction in Luke xi. 44–46, where the lawyers feel themselves included in our Lord's denunciation of the scribes ; and appeal to Him against it, as being, perhaps, more deeply versed in God's law than the ordinary scribes.

4. *having heard them reasoning.*—He therefore had not returned with the rest of the Pharisees (Matt. xxii. 22), nor taken part in their council. He was, no doubt, one of the most candid of Christ's audience. (See x. 23.)

5. *tempting Him.*—From S. Mark's narrative (ch. xii. 28) we gather that this was not from purely evil motives. It may have been one of the preconcerted questions, but evidently this lawyer was in earnest about it ; and our Lord answered him as one who was sincere. The question he proposed was one much debated, and hotly, amongst rival

Him, and saying, Master, which is the great commandment in the law?   And Jesus answered him, The first
of all the commandments is, **Hear, O Israel ; the Lord
our God is one Lord : and thou shalt love the Lord thy**

schools of theology ; and this learned man must have been deeply interested in such a question, and, from our Lord's remark in Mark
xii. 34, not merely from party motives.   To *tempt*, therefore, in this
instance, means to try, or put to the proof; he wished to know if
Christ could give a satisfactory solution of a difficult question.

6. *Master.*—See ix. 8.

7. *the great commandment.*—Gk. "Which commandment is great in
the law?" an Hebrew idiom.   It is very easy to suppose how questions
of this sort would arise amongst learned men, whose studies were confined to the Scriptures and the Talmudic writings, and what importance any such points would assume to them.   Some, for instance,
contended that the law of sacrifice was the great law ; and at this the
very reply of the lawyer to our Lord's question seems to glance.   Others
advocated the pre-eminence of the law of circumcision; others, of the
sabbath ; and other principal laws of Moses had their prominence in the
teaching of the rival schools of theology.   Some of their learned doctors
declared that Moses delivered 365 prohibitions and 248 commands; in
all, 613 precepts, which could not all be of the same vital importance.
But they contended which were the greater, which the minor, and
which *the* great commandment in the law.   They failed to see the
unity of the law, and that he who offended in one point was guilty
of all.

8. *our Lord.*—The unity of the Godhead was the great feature of
distinction in the Hebrew faith, which separated it so entirely from all
idolatrous nations, who were polytheists.   When once in the history of
their nation, they came in contact with a people, the Persians, who recognized one great principle of good, and one of evil, the consciousness
of a cognate belief produced a mutual kindliness of feeling, which the
Jews perhaps never felt for, or experienced from, any other Gentile
nation.   Cyrus the Great, King of Persia, is spoken of in Scripture, and
his actions towards the Jews are marked by the greatest goodwill and
generosity, and by profound veneration for the name of the God of
Israel. (See Isa. xliv. 28, xlv. 1, 13; Ezra i.)   Our Lord places this
doctrine of the unity of the Godhead in the foreground, as the very
essence of the law ; the lawyer is prompt to acknowledge that this was
the truth of God's law.

9. *thou shalt love.*—This principle is as distinctive of Jewish worship, as is the Object of their faith distinct.   Other nations might strive
to propitiate, or appease ; some might even desire to please their gods;
but *love* in worship—love, reverence, and trust—were unknown to the
heathen.

God with all thy heart, and with all thy soul, and with all thy mind, and with all thy strength. This is. the first and great commandment. And the second *is* like unto it, **Thou shalt love thy neighbour as thyself.** There is none other commandment greater than these. On these two commandments hang all the law and the prophets. And the scribe said unto Him, Well, Master, Thou hast said the truth: for there is one God; and

10. *all thy heart.*—With every power of life and love; with every spiritual and rational faculty; with the fulness of the intellectual powers, and with every physical energy through which these powers can find expression; with "body, soul, and spirit, which are His."

11. *first and great.*—*First* in order and dignity; *great* in importance and results. The love of God will ever be the first and greatest motive that can engage and inspire the immortal spirit, which He has given to man. The teaching of S. Paul is founded on this, when (1 Cor. xiii.) he places love foremost amongst Christian virtues, because it "never fails;" it is eternal, for it is the temper of the blessed inhabitants of heaven, and God Himself is love.

12. *the second.*—The second is inferior, as it regards an inferior object, man; but it is "like unto it" in this respect, it occupies the same prominence with reference to our duty to man, as the first with regard to our duty to God. And as there are but two great duties of life, our duty to God and our duty to our neighbour, in which all the interest and work of life centre; so are there but two great commaudments in the law. All others are but varied aspects of these two.

13. *thy neighbour.*—Our Lord, in His parable of the "good Samaritan," defines this to include any fellow-creature who may need our help and kindness, or who may have any claim upon us; and in giving the extreme instance of a "neighbour" in one of alien and hated race, and an outcast in religion, lower than even the heathen in a Jew's sight, He evidently includes all mankind.

14. *as thyself.*—If this is our rule of life, we shall never break any injunction or prohibition of the Decalogue, referring to our neighbour; nor fail in any social or moral duty towards him.

15. *hang all the law.*—The precepts of the law and the exhortations of the prophets are but necessary variations of these supreme laws; and every rule and interpretation, every promise and menace, are grounded only on these. Their whole weight and importance are derived from them; they are, in every instance, dependencies of the first or second great commandment. This, therefore, is a just summary or abridgment of the law and the prophets.

16. *the truth.*—The lawyer, in his skill and learning, detected no flaw in this decision; in his conviction it was not more nor less than

there is none other but He : and to love Him with all
the heart, and with all the understanding, and with all
the soul, and with all the strength, and to love *his* neighbour as himself, is more than all whole burnt offerings
and sacrifices.　And when Jesus saw that he answered
discreetly, He said unto him, Thou art not far from the
kingdom of heaven.

" the truth."　Trained as he had been from childhood, deeply versed in
all the knowledge accessible to the wisest, in all traditions of the schools
of the prophets (once the great seminaries of religious teaching), and of
the fathers of the Jewish Church, he now admitted our Lord's resolution
of all questions on this debated subject, as " the truth."　It is very
noticeable how, during this solemn week, our Lord's enemies, and those
who were no professed adherents of His, multiply testimony to the
truth of His office, and ascribe praise to His character.　The multitudes
of the people hail Him as King and Son of David ; " the world is gone
after Him ; " " the whole city is moved " at His advent ; fear of the
people, who so confessedly hold Him in veneration, stands repeatedly as
a barrier to the malice of those who would take His life ; the blind, and
the lame, and the sick recognize Him as their Saviour ; the children
offer Him perfect praise ; the rulers are obliged tacitly to admit, for
they dare not deny, His right to cleanse the profanations of the Temple
and to restore the worship of His Father's House ; none can gainsay His
parables ; those who came from the Sanhedrim to question Him, preface their subtleties with the admission that He is, in truth, a Master
in Israel, a Teacher come from God—that He is true, and teacheth God's
way in truth, with utter impartiality and fearlessness of men ; He
refutes all who question and disparage Him, and wrests from certain
of the scribes, and from this learned and candid lawyer in particular,
the admission, " Master, Thou hast well said ! "　Throughout the week
there are these constant testimonies to His truth, and therefore admission of wrong on the other side ; they occur incidentally, and they form
the strongest witness in His favour. (See II. iii. 17.)

17. *more than all.*—This was a triumph of the spirit over the letter
of the law, in the mind of one of its most skilled and earnest votaries.

18. *burnt offerings and sacrifices.*—Whether of larger, or lesser
value ; for more serious, or more venial offences ; whether against God
directly, or for the violation of His social and moral laws.　The whole
system of sacrifice would be cancelled by the reign of perfect love.

19. *discreetly.*—With some discernment of the spiritual truth and
meaning of the law.

20. *not far.*—" You have come as far as the law can bring you ;
you see that the love of God and of your neighbour is the end of the
law."　(*Bishop Goodwin.*)　This man's step was now on the threshold

XII. *JESUS QUESTIONS THE PHARISEES CONCERNING THE CHRIST.*

S. Matt. xxii. 41-46 ; S. Mark xii. 34-37 ; S. Luke xx. 40-44.

While the Pharisees were gathered together, Jesus asked them, saying, What think ye of Christ? Whose son is He? They say unto Him, *The Son* of David.

of the Gospel; he was near it in his understanding of the real mission of law, and in the comprehensiveness and intelligence of his mind. One stage more, and he might see all the law, with its sacrificial ordinances and types, all the predictions of the prophets, fulfilled in Christ, and the principle of love to God and man illumined with the light of the Gospel. What a crisis in his life lay in his advance, or recession from this point! It is not indeed said if, being so near, he went further onwards towards the truth, and found it; but none of our Lord's words fell to the ground, nor did He ever leave any sincere inquirer standing on the verge of the discovery of truth. We may be sure that now, or subsequently, he had the invitation to advance; or that He receded from the kingdom to which He was now so near.

1. *gathered together.*—(See xi. 2.) S. Mark adds, "while He taught in the Temple," which further defines the occasion of this question.

2. *asked them.*—The result of this question was, that they were completely silenced; not daring to reply to it, after their recent defeats, and not venturing to put any further subtle questions. But this was a result very inferior to the primary purpose of our Lord; the question was asked by Him in true concern for their infatuation, and in the last hope (for it formed His last word of doctrine to them) that they might see the truth to which they were closing their eyes. They were rejecting Christ, because He did not accord with their prejudices. He draws from them, therefore, the confession that Christ is the son of David; and this was His own descent, according to authenticated genealogies. He then would lead them on to the inevitable conclusion, that David ascribed a Divine nature to his son; but they evaded this point, and kept silence. He brought them to the light, and they shut it out from themselves.

3. *what think ye?*—What is the received opinion? What say the scribes, and the theological schools? What is your individual belief? and this last is Christ's question to every individual in every age, "What thinkest *thou* of Christ?"

4. *Christ.*—Gk. "*the* Christ;" the promised Messiah.

5. *Whose son is He?*—This is not merely an inquiry as to His earthly descent, but suggests the question, "Is He more than that?"

He saith unto them, How then doth David in spirit call Him Lord, saying, **The Lord said unto my Lord, Sit Thou on My right hand, till I make Thine enemies Thy footstool.** If David then call Him Lord, how is He his son?

The Jews confined their thoughts and expectation to the humanity and temporal dignity of the Messiah.

6. *of David.*—This answer was obvious to any Jew; our Lord would scarcely have asked the question of such a deputation, and on such an occasion, to receive merely an answer which one of their children might have given, which they had already virtually given in the Temple (iii. 18–22). It was not a sufficient answer to give, either to such a question, or in the presence of those whose teachers in religion they officially were; they had, however, given that answer which must involve them, on being further questioned.

7. *how then.*—If this is all, if the Christ is only the son of David, how do you explain the words of David himself, which are universally interpreted of the Messiah.

8. *in spirit.*—*i.e.*, "by the inspiration of the Spirit." S. Mark distinctly says, "by the Holy Ghost." S. Luke adds, "in the Book of Psalms"—an incidental testimony to the inspiration of that sacred book, which was our Lord's manual of devotion whilst on earth. He was constantly quoting the Psalms, and applying them to His own circumstances, very specially during the last week of His ministry; and His last words, as He died upon the Cross, were words from this book.

9. *the Lord.*—There is a marked distinction in the original Hebrew version of these words; it is literally, "Jehovah said unto Adonai." "Jehovah" is the sacred and incommunicable name of the eternal God; "Adonai" means, more simply, Lord, and is used in many parts of Scripture as a translation, or representation, of that great Name which the Jews hesitated either to write, or to pronounce. It is used with sufficient frequency, as expressive of Divinity, to arrest the attention of the Jews, especially as they understood the passage of the Messiah.

10. *sit.*—Expressive of the enthronization of Christ, after His ascension, upon His throne as Mediator, at God's right hand, or in the exercise of that supreme power given to Him in earth and heaven. Such enthronization of a son, by the king, had not been uncommon in Hebrew royalty, and was therefore nationally intelligible.

11. *my Lord.*—The emphasis rests on the word "Lord;" not, as it is sometimes mistakenly read, on "my."

12. *thine enemies.*—It was manifest, therefore, that the Messiah would have foes. The Jews thought them their own national enemies; but with these He scarcely came in contact, until they became His executioners, at the instance of His own people. But now, as He

And no man was able to answer Him a word, neither durst any *man* from that day forth ask Him any more *questions*.

And the common people heard Him gladly.

pointed the passage, and following upon His teaching of this day, they must have seen something of His view of the case, namely, that prominent amongst His foes were " they of His own household ; " and that their purpose was ordained to fail. And for all His people, in time to come, these concluding words of His public teaching in the Temple declare that His cause will triumph, by the decree of Jehovah ; and that even now He is enthroned in power, waiting for the hour of final victory.

13. *if David.*—If David *himself*, in the inspired consciousness of the truth, calls Christ his Lord, what view could he hold of Christ as his *son ?* If He came merely by descent from David, as David did from Abraham, Israel, Judah, and others specially designated as ancestors of the Messiah, how could be be his *Lord* (" Adonai ")?   There could be no one in Israel greater than the king ; and David, as king and father, could not be inferior in dignity of office to any son of his, who might succeed him upon his throne. To be David's Lord (Adonai), He must be David's God also ; and, in speaking of Him as at *that time* his " Lord," he expressed the eternity of His being. The only solution of this question must be that which Christ declared, that He was Himself the Son of God, as He was the son of David. His being David's son, and Lord, includes the mystery of the union of the manhood with the Godhead, in Christ. It was not to be expected that this could be seen by the Jews of that day, as clearly as now by Christians ; but yet, had the Jews been content to lay aside their prejudices, and to give Christ a fair hearing on His own claims, they must, with Him as their Teacher, have learnt and accepted the truth. As it was, their silence on Christ's question was a confession, that they did not understand the Scripture testimony to the Divinity of Christ, although they were the authorized expositors of holy Scripture ; or that, understanding it, they rejected it. Theodoret (quoted in the " Speaker's Commentary ") draws the conclusion on this point clearly and concisely : " If David, the king and prophet, calls Christ his Lord and Master, then He is not a mere man, as the Jews madly maintain, but God and Lord ; and David His creature and servant."

14. *neither durst.*—No one had any subtle question which he dared propose ; and, apparently, no one had any desire to ask, in good faith, for any further information concerning the doctrines and claims of Christ, whilst He was now ready and anxious to reveal them. (See note 2.)

15. *the common people.*—To these the plain and direct teaching of One, who was so merciful and condescending to them as Christ, and who solved those deeply interesting questions, which their own teachers and

XIII. *CHRIST REPROVES THE SCRIBES AND PHARISEES.*

S. Matt. xxiii. 1–12 ; S. Mark xii. 38–40 ; S. Luke xx. 45–47.

Then in the audience of all the people spake Jesus to the multitude, and to His disciples, saying, The scribes and Pharisees sit in Moses' seat : all therefore whatsoever

scribes only mystified and disputed about, gave great satisfaction: their error was in forsaking the teaching of Him who, they perceived, spoke to them as " having authority, and not as the scribes."

1. *then . . . spake.*—Our Lord at once perceived that He had spoken in vain to the Pharisees and rulers, whose deputation probably now retired; and He well knew that the great obstacle to the mind of the multitude (glad for the moment to hear Him, and tractable) was that their teachers, in whom they had ever believed with an hereditary trust, one and all rejected His claims as Christ. He therefore at once proceeded to denounce the hypocrisy and sin of these teachers. He can keep personal terms with them no longer, now that they are hopeless in themselves, and the cause in others of a fatal obstinacy. There was this further fitness in the present opportunity (which the word "*then*" marks), that the victories Christ had gained over the subtleties of His opponents, were so strong a confirmation of His claims as the Teacher come from God, that the minds of the people were bent on Him. The words " in the audience of all the people " have a marked significance.

2. *multitude . . . disciples.*—The people had now to form a judgment for themselves, and to decide between right and wrong influence, as their fathers had to pronounce between Elijah and the prophets of Baal, and to follow the truth. It was a sad effect of this bad teaching, that they " loved to have it so." They are therefore now solemnly warned and addressed. The disciples also had to take that place in the Church of Christ, which the rulers had occupied under the dispensation of Moses ; they, therefore, must be especially cautioned and exhorted. It is likely also that many of the scribes remained near Him, as they had done before (ix. 22), and listened to this uncompromising condemnation of erroneous teachers, and were thus warned. The " audience " here present was truly representative of the nation, whether in influence, metropolitan and provincial, or in numbers. Farrar states that some of the Temple courts held about 6000 persons.

3. *Moses' seat.*—-They occupy the official position of authorized teachers of the law of Moses, and are his successors in dignity and honour, as leaders of religious thought and practice.

they bid you observe, *that* observe and do; but do not
ye after their works: for they say and do not. Beware
of the scribes, for they bind heavy burdens, and grievous

4. *all therefore.*—From Matt. xxiii. 16–26, we see that our Lord
does not mean absolutely all they teach; the word "therefore" (meaning in consequence of their official position) gives the necessary limitation of the precept. Whatever, as authorized teachers of the law of
Moses, they teach agreeably to the spirit of that law, is to be respected;
whatever, as exponents of their own tradition, they add to the law of
God, is not binding. (See Mark vii. 6–13.) They sit in Moses' seat
to teach the truth, and so must be reverenced; but they may not take
advantage of that high dignity, to make the law of God of none effect
through their traditions. Our Lord thus shows Himself superior to
any feeling of enmity against those who, by custom and position, had
what He demanded for his own pure teaching, the attention of the
people; He condescended to no disparagement of their office, to exalt
His, or to degrade them from their chair.
5. *observe and do.*—Receive with reverence of spirit, and perform
with obedience, what they officially enjoin. Our Lord's command to
regard with due honour the office of the authorized teachers of religion,
though their personal character be not equally worthy of respect, is
very decided and remarkable. If they be personally unworthy of their
office, and "give occasion to the adversaries of the Lord to blaspheme,"
they receive so heavy a condemnation from the Lord, that men equally
frail, and perhaps less tried, may well spare their own words and acts
of reprobation; and be careful how they add to the evil, by taking
advantage of the unworthiness of the priest, to point scorn against the
office, and against their Lord's Church; for if they take the "occasion
to blaspheme," they are not guiltless of the blasphemy, and they thus
rank themselves in the number of the "enemies of the Lord."
6. *their works.*—Their practice was very different from their preaching. They were habitual violators of the sacred laws, whose guardians
and expounders they were appointed to be. Their "leaven," the mass
of their traditions which were contrary to the true spirit of the Lord,
and their iniquitous practices, spread most injuriously through the
religious life of the nation.
7. *say and do not.*—They said that the law must be obeyed in its
every minutest detail, and yet (Matt. xxiii. 23) they lived in the constant neglect of the weightier matters of the law. Compare Acts i. 1,
and Mark vi. 30, with this passage, where the *doing* of Christ and
His Apostles, not only kept pace with, but preceded their *teaching*.
8. *heavy burdens.*—S. Peter, speaking to the disciples (Acts xv. 10),
describes the law of Moses, as expounded by the scribes, as "a yoke
upon their neck, which neither they nor their fathers were able to bear."
To this they added the intolerable weight of their own tradition. But

to be borne, and lay *them* on men's shoulders ; but they *themselves* will not move them with one of their fingers. But all their works they do for to be seen of men : they desire to walk in long robes, they make broad their

they themselves knew the hopelessness of attempting to practise it ; so they did not attempt it, beyond the general principle of doing all their works to be seen of men. To give one instance. The sabbath, as prescribed by them, became a day of vexatious restraint, which was then proverbial in the world. In no single way did they do more to destroy the life of their Church, and to encourage irreligion. And it is worth while for those who, from austerity of views or disposition, contrive to make the Lord's day a day of restraint, and misery, to those around them, especially to the young, to consider the very dangerous tendency of that practice, which makes the yoke of Christ a "burden," and the special day of His service a day of gloom ; they are really destroying religious life at its very fount and source.

9. *fingers.*—Unlike the Apostles, in Acts xv. 28, who imposed only the burden of " necessary things " on the Church. They bind up burdens impossible for the shoulders (the full bearing power) of other men ; they will not bear the burden of a finger themselves ; or perhaps they will not put out a finger, to raise, adjust, or relieve their load. (See the Christian rule in Gal. vi. 1.)

10. *to be seen of men.*—The whole principle of the law, and of God's true religion, under any of its dispensations, has been to teach men so to live as " seeing Him who is invisible." The principle of the scribes, therefore, to live to the popular eye, is utterly opposed to God's way ; " they loved the praise of men more than the praise of God." They did " outwardly appear righteous unto men," but our Lord tells us what they were before God : they were " like whited sepulchres ; " they were " full of hypocrisy and iniquity." They had thoroughly forgotten the original duty of the scribe, as given in Ezra vii. 10.

11. *desire.*—It was not their wearing of the long flowing robes of their office, which our Lord reprobates, but rather their making this a matter of essential moment ; it was the expression of the pride and assumption of their spirit, through this external channel, which is condemned. The robes of the theological professor, as also the vestments of the priest, may be regarded as matters of indifference, or may be held expressive of a reverence for the sacred duties they discharge ; but when they become party symbols, marks of spiritual pride, or when the vestment engrosses the mind of the priest or people, they are to be utterly condemned. They have lost all right significance ; they are no longer " holy garments for glory and for beauty." These, as matters of ancient prescription and ritual, and their assumption as peculiarities or novelties, as significant of party or sect, are two very different matters in the sight of God.

phylacteries, and enlarge the borders of their garments,
and love the uppermost rooms at feasts, and the chief
seats in the synagogue, and greetings in the markets,
and to be called of men, Rabbi, Rabbi.   But be not ye

12. *phylacteries.*—Lit. "safeguards." They were intended as outward
memorials of the duty of laying up, and keeping safely, the commandments of God, in their heart and in their lives; and also they were
sometimes superstitiously supposed to preserve the wearer from the
evil eye, and from evil spirits.   Both senses are included in the term.
They were small amulets containing written portions of the law, and
were bound upon the forehead, between the eyes, by a leather strap.
The custom of wearing them on the part of males, from 14 years and
upwards, was founded on a literal compliance with the words of
Deut. vi. 8—an example of that ready preference of the letter to the
spirit of a command, which was the root of so many errors and absur-
dities in their religious system.
13. *borders.*—In Num. xv. 38–41 the Jews are commanded to wear
a border and fringe of blue, for a memorial before God.   The scribes,
by way of showing themselves more mindful of God's will, and holier
than other men, gave their fringe a greater depth, and in some instances
embroidered the upper portion with texts of Scripture.
14. *rooms.*—Or *seats*. The Jewish tables were arranged in two parallel
lines, connected across their upper end by a third table, and leaving
a passage, between the two side lengths, for the admission of servants;
since, from the width of the seats, on which the guests reclined at
length, with their feet outwards (John xiii. 25, xii. 3), nothing could
be placed on the table, or removed from it, except in front of the guests.
The master of the house sat at the upper table, in the centre; the
"uppermost seats" were those immediately on his right and left hand,
at the same table.
15. *greetings.*—*i.e.*, salutations. They desired, in all these places of
public resort, to be saluted by their disciples with the title " Rabbi,
Rabbi;" it was considered disrespectful to address them by name.
Whenever they appeared in public, whether on social, religious, or
official occasions, they expected to be noticed in such a manner, that
they stood personally between the honour due to their host, their God,
or to the business which brought them into the presence of the public.
16. *Rabbi.*—Master; in the sense of superiority over the mind of
others, both as a teacher and as a spiritual superior.   The more appropriate title, in the case of Christian teachers, is that used by S. Paul—
" minister of Jesus Christ " (1 Cor. iii. 5). Similarly, S. Paul forbids
disciples to boast themselves in the name of their particular teachers.
(See 2 Tim. iv. 3.)
17. *be not ye.*—The prohibition is not against these teachers being
addressed by titles of respect and reverence—the very nature of their

called Rabbi : for one is your Master, *even* Christ ; and all ye are brethren.   And call no man your father upon the earth : for one is your Father, which is in heaven.

duties, and the high interests with which they are associated, entail this—but against the love of these titles, and the multiplication of them, the spiritual pride and exclusiveness they foster, as making men " lords over Christ's heritage." All Christians are " brethren in Christ ; " and therefore " be ye not many masters " is a right rule.   There will be but one Lord and Master in heaven ; and the nearest possible approach to this example, consistent with the relative position of those who sit in the seats of the Apostles and elders, and of those who sit before them " in the room of the unlearned," or of those who receive from them God's message, is what Christ enjoins.   It cannot, however, be binding as an absolute prohibition, as S. Paul (1 Cor. xii.), describing the fraternal unity of the Church, and the necessary difference in the endowments of each member of Christ, expressly tells us (*v.* 28) that God has ordained divers orders in His Church ; and, in Eph. iv. 11–13, that these were for the edifying of the body of Christ's Church, during its continuance on earth, until it attains to Christ's kingdom of glory. These, however, are *official* distinctions and titles.   Our Lord's prohibition is against *personal* titles, which must minister to the pride of the individual so distinguished above his equals ; or the ambition of those titles which are official, *i.e.*, " be it not your ambition to be masters."

18. *your father.*—To take this prohibition in the most literal sense (a sense in which it must often have been read by converts to Christianity), it teaches that no authority or tie upon earth, however natural and binding, may intervene between us and God's commands.   The claims even of a parent are inferior, in every respect, to those of " our Father which is in heaven ; " hence His uncompromising declaration, " He that loveth father or mother more than Me is not worthy of Me " (Matt. x. 37 ; Luke xiv. 26).   The Pharisees understood this principle, but they perverted it.   They admitted that if property, for instance, is dedicated to God's service, it is not liable to ordinary claims ; but, after vowing it, they paid to God a very small portion, and recovered the rest to themselves,—resisting, nevertheless, natural claims, on the excuse of its being *Corban*, dedicated to God ; so repudiating the fifth commandment of the Decalogue (Mark vii. 10–13).   Our Lord, in pointing this out, adds, " And many such like things ye do."   It was an instance of the ordinary effect of the traditions and doctrines of the Pharisees, upon the pure word of God.   But the terms " Rabbi," " Father," and " Master," were titles assumed by the scribes, as expressive of spiritual supremacy ; and in this sense, rather than the literal one, the precept is to be understood.   The title of Pope (*Papa*), as universal father over the Church, would seem a direct breach of this command.

Neither be ye called masters, for one is your Master, *even* Christ.   But he that is greatest among you shall be your servant.   And whosoever shall exalt himself shall be abased ; and he that shall humble himself shall be exalted.

XIV. *THE EIGHT WOES.*

S. Matt. xxiii. 13-39.

But woe unto you, scribes and Pharisees, hypocrites !

19. *greatest.*—The example of this humility was distinctly given by our Lord, who, being Lord of all, came amongst men "as he that serveth." The constant stress laid by Him upon this necessity of true humility, is a very leading feature in His doctrine, and a mark of distinction between Christianity and every other religion.   The opposite vice, pride, is the source of more evil and misery than perhaps any other. God declares He will not suffer or tolerate it ; and it sets every created spirit immediately in opposition to Him, wherever it is manifested.   It is a low and degrading vice, though so common to man ; its natural tendency is to drag the spirit downwards, to *abase* it.   We see that true and noble minds are less actuated by it, and that humility is the virtue of those who are truly great.   In our Lord's life, in His perfect manhood, we never see that there is want of true manliness in His great humility ; nor is any legitimate ambition crossed by it.   The counterfeit is truly loathsome.   Nothing is more unmanly than mock humility ; by contrast it gives to pride and ambition almost the air of virtue.

20. *exalt himself.*—(See sect. viii. 34, and App. VI.)   This is the most frequent, and varied in illustration of these rules of the kingdom, in accordance with the remarkable prominence given to this subject in our Lord's doctrine.   Its application is stated as invariable, "*Whosoever*," etc.

1. *woe unto you.*—Our Lord's public ministry ends mournfully, with denunciations of judgment ; all the more so because in contrast with the blessings, with which He opened His mouth at its commencement, in the Sermon on the Mount.   It was the close, in gloom and sadness, of that which had opened so brightly.   "They which had sat in darkness had seen a great light," and had turned from it to their congenial darkness ; they had neglected the warning to "the proud," and had refused the Saviour in His humility.   Now their feet were "stumbling upon the dark mountains" in their error ; the shadow of death overhung them ; the "gross darkness," judicial upon their wilful blindness, lay before them.   (See Jer. xiii. 15, 16.)   In Luke xi. a short and earlier version of some of these woes is given : our Lord now recapitulates and

for ye shut up the kingdom of heaven against men : for

defines, what He before had spoken in brief; but the neglect of the earlier expression of His indignation, gives a sad and terrible emphasis to this.

2. *hypocrites.*—The original word means *an actor*, whose impersonation of other characters than his own, masking his countenance, and adoption of the dress and habit of other men, and his often exaggeration of them, gave rise to the metaphorical and bad sense, in which the word is current in our language. A man who acts, or professes a virtue which he possesses not, is a "hypocrite;" and hypocrisy in religion is sin of deeper dye, than perhaps any open and manifest act of wickedness. As a habit of the mind, it is perhaps more deadly to the soul than those wilfulnesses which so often know repentance and amendment. The character of a hypocrite is best seen in the instance of the scribes and Pharisees, whose name is for ever associated with this very awful brand. Following our Lord's revelation of their true character, we may see what hypocrites are, unmasked. They do not act up to what they profess; "they say and do not." They bind men's consciences with precepts, which they totally ignore in their own practices. Their principle is to catch the eye of man. The good deeds they do are for ostentation's sake only. They are ambitious of vain titles, of precedence, and of domination over men's minds; they exalt themselves. They exclude men from heaven, by their perversion of religious knowledge. They enrich themselves, under the guise of charity. They are zealous to proselytize, and engraft their own vices upon those of their converts, rather than reclaim them from evil. They profane God's Name, by senseless and superstitious oaths. They profess the most minute regard for the literal requirements of the law, and live in constant neglect of its highest spiritual obligations. They are "whited sepulchres;" they affect great sanctity of life, that they may sin in secret with the greater impunity. They bewail the sins and error of their neighbours and fathers, and go to greater excesses, in the same sins which they denounce. They obscure the truth, with the mists of tradition and sophistry, and with pomp of outward ceremonial. They censure in other men the most trivial errors, whilst guilty themselves of the grossest. These, and other similar particulars, are characteristic of hypocrites, as our Lord sees them; but as man sees them, they are often, as the Pharisees were, outwardly scrupulous of all external duties of religion— "righteous over much," in fact, as the acting of a part is usually the overdoing of it.

3. *shut up.*—In S. Luke xi. 52, they are described as having "taken away the key of knowledge," and so prevented the entrance into the kingdom of God's truth, of those who had diligently sought the way, who were so near as to be upon the very threshold, being "they that are entering."

4. *Against men.*—Gk. "in front of," *i.e.,* they shut the door of

ye neither go in *yourselves*, neither suffer ye them that are entering to go in.

Woe unto you, scribes and Pharisees, hypocrites ! for ye devour widows' houses, and for a pretence make long prayer: therefore ye shall receive the greater damnation.

heaven in their very face, that door which they had already reached. This is the eminence of sin, attainable by one who holds the sacred office of a teacher of God's truth, and is, in schism or in hypocrisy, a teacher of false doctrine; for he can mislead men from the very gate of heaven, and so pervert and deaden their appreciation of truth that the gate may be closed against them for ever. *They* are not without sin ; but his is the greater sin, and worthy "the greater damnation."

5. *widows' houses.*—They took advantage of the desire of women of rank and substance, to devote themselves to works of religion and mercy, who naturally were ready to take advice from those who were the authorized teachers of religion. Their long and frequent prayers gave them credit in the eyes of these women, who were imposed on by their pretence of sanctity. They so misused the influence they thus gained, that they reduced them to the utmost distress and contempt. Our Lord's career furnishes incidental notices of this readiness, on the part of the women of Israel, to devote themselves to good works; such was Anna the prophetess, a widow of fourscore years. S. Luke (viii. 2, 3) gives the names of several of those who forwarded the interests of Christ's cause, and "ministered to Him of their substance;" of such also were Martha (whom tradition ranks amongst the widows) and Mary, the sisters of Lazarus. S. Paul gives a grave caution to Timothy (2 Tim. iii. 5–7) to watch against the evil effects of the abuse of their trust by teachers of the Christian Church, which he must have seen often enough in that of the Jews; he shows the terrible consequences of the perversion of those "silly women, ever learning, and never able to come to the knowledge of the truth," who had been "led away captive " by their blind trust in those who seemed to them to have a "form of godliness."

6. *for a pretence.*—To give themselves a fictitious credit, in the minds and hearts of those whom they intended to ensnare. There is here one reason for our Lord's condemnation of those who stood conspicuously praying in the corners of the Temple; perhaps also His eye fell, at the same time, upon some of these silly victims of credulity.

7. *the greater damnation.*—A condemnation now, which impenitence would make eternal and irreversible. God revealed Himself in Israel as "the God of the widow;" such were therefore under His immediate eye, and injury done to them would certainly draw down the Divine vengeance. Of how much heavier condemnation and sorer punishment were they worthy, who assumed the guise of sanctity, and "devoured widows' houses" under the cloak of religion. Of such says S. Augus-

Woe unto you, scribes and Pharisees, hypocrites! for ye compass sea and land to make one proselyte, and when he is made, ye make him twofold more the child of hell than themselves.

Woe unto you, *ye* blind guides, which say, Whosoever shall swear by the temple, it is nothing; but whosoever

tine, "Many persons devour upon earth what they must digest in hell." Gregory declares that "a feigned sanctity is a double iniquity," deserving "the greater damnation."

8. *compass sea and land.*—A figurative expression, denoting the most intense zeal and energy, and suggesting manifold agencies.

9. *one proselyte.*—Such was their ardour to gain proselytes to their sect, rather than to their faith, that they spared no pains or outlay; and the gain of a single convert was reckoned worth their utmost exertion. It would have been well had their laudable ambition been to bring him to God, rather than to their party; they would have read a noble lesson to the Church of Christ, of the excellence of missionary zeal. As it is, we see it by contrast with them; just as our Lord bids His servants emulate the superior wisdom of the children of this world over the children of light, in the pursuit of their best interests. Thus, *fas est et ab hoste doceri.* On the position of *proselytes* in Israel, see the article in Smith's "Dict. of the Bible."

10. *twofold more.*—He is not made a convert to true religion, but to party purpose; and therefore, not being reclaimed from any of his natural errors by any good example or grace set before him, he simply adds, to the vices of his former state, those derived from his new teachers, with all the hypocrisy and pretence which distinguished them. The conduct of these proselytes greatly lowered the reputation of the Jewish religion in the eyes of other nations, amongst whom it became proverbial. This was an old reproach. (See Ezek. xxxvi. 20).

11. *the child of hell.*—A common Hebraism, denoting worthiness of the punishment of hell. "Children" or "sons of Belial," "son of perdition," "son of wickedness," "children of light," "children of darkness," etc., are other instances of this usage. Perhaps the exact opposite of "the child of hell" is the phrase, "the children of the kingdom."

12. *blind guides.*—Teachers indeed of others, but having themselves the most inaccurate and senseless views of truth. Yet, as they directed the Magi to Bethlehem, or as a sign-post points but moves not, so could these blind guides give some useful directions to the children of light, who so far might look to those who occupied "Moses' seat."

13. *nothing.*—A mere vain form of words, not binding in the least degree. The Jewish sophistry about oaths was proverbial among the heathen; they professed to be scarcely able to ascertain or frame the oath, which would bind a Jew's conscience.

shall swear by the gold of the temple, he is a debtor!
Ye fools and blind: for whether is greater, the gold, or
the temple that sanctifieth the gold? And, Whosoever
shall swear by the altar, it is nothing; but whosoever
sweareth by the gift that is upon it, he is guilty. *Ye*
fools and blind: for whether *is* greater, the gift, or the
altar that sanctifieth the gift? Whoso therefore shall
swear by the altar, sweareth by it, and by all things
thereon. And whoso shall swear by the temple, sweareth
by it, and by Him that dwelleth therein. And he that
shall swear by heaven, sweareth by the throne of God,
and by Him that sitteth thereon.

14. *debtor.*—He is bound to the fulfilment of his oath. The same
original word is repeated in the next clause, and is translated " guilty,"
where the margin of the A. V. gives " debtor, or bound."

15. *the gold, or the temple.*—This gold was especially that of offerings (Corban), rather than that of the sacred vessels, or of decoration.
The scribes had reasons of their own for attaching superior sanctity to
costly religious offerings. Our Lord does not here mean that the
Temple which sanctifies the gold, furnishes a more binding oath than
that taken upon the gold directly offered to God, and which, if not
offered in the Temple, would not be sacred. His object is not to give
a gradation of the consequence of inferior oaths, but to show the folly
and wickedness of rash swearing altogether. Oaths are not binding
according to any scale of estimation; the oath by the gold or the
Temple, by the gift or the altar, or even by heaven itself, are equally
profanations of that great Godhead which invests all these abodes and
instruments, of God's service and presence, with the sanctity which
they possess.

16. *the gift.*—This exaltation of man's gift was made in the very
spirit of self-righteousness; what was offered to God was thus reckoned
as of higher value than God's holy altar. Christ's valuation is a very
different one. He regards not the consequence of the giver, the munificence of the gift, or the sanctity of the altar, or of the Temple itself;
but rather looks to the purity of the heart and motive of the giver, and
the cheerfulness of his devotion. These, rather than any cost or locality,
constitute an acceptable gift.

17. *Him that sitteth thereon.*—This solemn declaration is so very decided against the sin of rash and profane swearing, that no thoughtful
man can allow himself to be guilty of such folly. He is indeed a " fool
and blind," who does not perceive the importance of his lightly spoken
words. He may mean nothing, for instance, when he says " By
Heaven!" as a kind of seasoning of his remark; but God decides that

Woe unto you, scribes and Pharisees, hypocrites! for ye pay tithe of mint and anise and cummin, and have omitted the weightier *matters* of the law, judgment, mercy, and faith : these ought ye to have done, and not

this light and common phrase is the invocation of His own great Name and presence, as He sits in high majesty upon His throne of glory. However "blind," therefore, to this view of the value of his words, however meaning nothing, he is a "fool" to trifle with the Name and dignity of One so holy, and so jealous of the "honour due unto His Name." A right sense of the folly and senselessness of swearing, may deter many minds from that wickedness ; but one who takes a true view of the majesty of God, and of the dignity of his own nature, and the sacredness of his own word, will never affect to strengthen what he denies or affirms, in this way. If he does invoke the Name of God, it will be only as one may invoke it with a full perception of the gravity and solemnity of his admiration.

18. *pay tithe.*—They were so scrupulous in following out the letter of the law, that they offered the tenth even of the commonest herbs in their garden, lest there should be a tenth of *anything* which was not duly given to God. This was a small matter, but it showed great scrupulosity. Provided their dues of higher importance had been paid also, there would be no better example of rendering " to God the things that are God's," than that of the scribes and Pharisees. Our Lord expressly decides, " These things ought ye to have done."

19. *the weightier matters.*—Those great and profound truths which underlie the requirements of the law, and of which these requirements are but illustrations. They exhibit the spirit of God's law, and, in their perfection, descend from the highest to the lowest details of practice ; they embrace things great and small.

20. *judgment.*—That judgment of self, and of outward things, and of God's claims, which recognizes true value and just rights. Men who possess this principle will be *just*, just towards God and towards man.

21. *mercy.*—S. Luke (xi. 42) has "the love of God." It is that love of God and of man which makes men merciful in thought and act. God desires that the requirements of His law should be obeyed in the spirit of love ; it is one of the rules of Christ's kingdom, " I will have mercy and not sacrifice." (App. VI.)

22. *faith.*—*i.e.* faithfulness towards God and man, sincerity and truth. Our faith in God and man will lead us to act in this good faith in the discharge of our relative duties. The prophet Micah (vi. 8) gives as a summary of the spirit of the law of God, " What doth the Lord require of thee, but to do justly, and to love mercy, and to walk humbly with thy God ? "

23. *these ought ye,* etc.—It was a matter of debate whether God's law required obedience in such minute details. If, however, the conscience

to leave the other undone. *Ye* blind guides, which strain at a gnat, and swallow a camel.

Woe unto you, scribes and Pharisees, hypocrites! for ye make clean the outside of the cup and platter, but within they are full of extortion and excess. *Thou* blind Pharisee, cleanse first that *which is* within the cup and platter, that the outside of them may be clean also.

of the Pharisees felt bound in this respect, it was quite right they should be thus particular; for no man can be too careful in his obedience to God. It would have been a very admirable feature in their character had they shown equal care in things of higher moment; but these they left undone; and therefore their great pretence of faithfulness in these matters was an insult, rather than a devotion to God's law.

24. *strain at.*—Early English versions have "strain out," which is the proper rendering. The gnat and the camel both belonged to classes of animals unclean by the law; they stand at either extremity of the list for comparative size. Our Lord thus speaks proverbially to show that the extreme scrupulosity of the Pharisees in minor matters is only to be paralleled by their utter indifference to those of the highest importance. They were very careful to guard against the smallest legal contamination and pollution, but utterly reckless as to the most serious acts of moral pollution. They had a code of instructions and penalties, bearing on the accidental pollution of what they drank by the presence of small insects, and carried it to a point of extreme minuteness. The Buddhists have a similar custom of straining out small insects from what they drink, at the present day.

25. *the outside.*—This was another of the scrupulous acts of the Pharisees, which attracted much attention; they had traditions enforcing very strict rules about the washing of their hands before eating, lest by accident, or unwittingly, they should have touched any unclean thing. The same care was taken to wash before using all cups and vessels connected with their food, though previously cleansed, and apparently clean, lest anything unclean, any insect even, should have touched them, and so conveyed legal pollution.

26. *within.*—The wine and food within these vessels, about whose external cleansing so much prescribed anxiety was shown, were too often tainted, to God's sight, by the fraud and violence and extortion by which they were procured.

27. *are full.*—i.e. "are filled by." The delicacies of their festivities are the proceeds of their extortion, and are consumed in excess—sins in bold and terrible contrast with the scrupulous cleansing of their vessels of food.

28. *cleanse first.*—Thus the Pharisees, so particular about external cleanliness, if they would be really clean to the standard of the law,

> Woe unto you, scribes and Pharisees, hypocrites! for
> ye are like unto whited sepulchres, which indeed appear
> beautiful outward, but are within full of dead *men's*
> bones, and of all uncleanness. Even so ye also out-
> wardly appear righteous unto men, but within ye are
> full of hypocrisy and iniquity.

must be free from the sins of rapine and wrong, of which their hearts
and lives were full. Our Lord gives (Luke xi. 41) one instance in
which they could reform themselves: "Give alms of such things as ye
have" (Gk. "the things within"); "and, behold, all things are clean to
you." If alms are given, not as the Pharisee generally gave, with
ostentatious hand, but from the heart within, in the spirit of love and
mercy, the very heart is purified in the exercise of such loving charity;
for many a generous and kindly thought must accompany the liberal
and cheerful act.

29. *whited sepulchres.*—It was a custom amongst the Jews that, on
a given day in the year (the 15th day of the month Adar), all sepulchres should be whitewashed; and even the ground where graves were,
was marked with white, that people might know where they were, and
so avoid pollution. This pollution was a serious one; it continued for
seven days. (See Num. xix. 11–16.) Our Lord has another application of this figure to the Pharisees, likening them to ground which
had not been so marked for caution: "Ye are as graves which appear
not, and the men that walk over them are not aware of them" (Luke
xi. 44). So deadly was the influence, example, and teaching of these
hypocrites, so soul-polluting, and yet so fair to see, that men took
them for what they appeared to be. Again, their faults were so carefully hidden from view, that those who came in contact with them
never suspected what lay hidden beneath, in the depths of their heart,
and in the retirement of their life; yet those who learnt from them
learnt contamination, and were not aware how utterly it was barring
them from the presence of God.

30. *appear righteous.*—Our Lord here speaks of the popular impression of the character of the Pharisees. They were generally supposed
to be most conscientious and scrupulous, in the discharge of every
religious duty. We should remember, in thinking of them, that our
knowledge of their true character is by revelation of our Lord Himself.
They appear to us the extreme of all that is evil—hypocrites, bigots,
narrow-minded, persecutors, murderers; but in forming this estimate
we are looking on them with that true judgment in which we shall
be able to read all characters, on whom our Lord passes sentence at the
last day. We are admitted to read their *hearts*, and to learn the secret
of their lives; and the sight is so ghastly a one, that we forget almost
to think of what they *seemed* to be. Our Lord says here that they

Woe unto you, scribes and Pharisees, hypocrites! because ye build the tombs of the prophets, and garnish the sepulchres of the righteous, and say, If we had been

"outwardly appeared righteous." Their great zeal for the law, their ostentatious piety, their long and public prayers, did not seem so over-done, to a nation who considered them as doing their part to set publicly a good example, and who were very tolerant (as most Eastern people are) of outward display, and who had been brought up from childhood in a belief in the views and standard of the Pharisees. A fair consideration of their high reputation for righteousness, will account for many of the difficulties in the way of the advance of Christ's cause, notwithstanding the strong impression He constantly made upon the multitude; and also for any surprise with which even the disciples heard that these men of high pretensions and great wealth could scarcely be saved, and that their own righteousness must *exceed* that of the scribes and Pharisees, if they would enter the kingdom of heaven. The same consideration points with greater clearness the lesson which these professors of religion, who stand so constantly in the foreground of the Gospel, read to the Church of Christ.

31. *tombs of the prophets.*—This age was one of great spirit in public buildings. It had seen the restoration of the Temple, with many magnificent additions, and massive fortifications. It had also under-taken the building of the long-neglected sepulchres of the prophets on a scale of great grandeur. Whatever their own generation may have considered them, and however treated them, the Jews of this era established their name as one of the chief glories of the nation. Our Lord does not reprove them for thus honouring the memory of the just; but for planning far greater excesses in the same direction as their fathers had sinned in, whilst they are thus building. And seeing that these prophets were the bold reprovers of sin and all hypocrisy in their day, there must have been a certain consciousness on their mind, that it was very much more satisfactory to build to their memory, as dead; for they would have been most inconvenient witnesses to Christ, and opposers of their own pretensions, had they been still living.

32. *if we had been.*—A very self-righteous reflection, and not at all without parallel, in the history of many people. How common is the thought that had we lived in the days of our Lord, how we should have eagerly listened to Him, delighted in His miracles and parables, cor-dially supported His cause at all risks, and at every sacrifice; how we should have brought to Him our difficulties and grievances, and sub-mitted to His decisions—never have betrayed, denied, or forsaken Him; but have followed Him, whithersoever He went, even unto death. And yet we are not, perhaps, the more earnest in studying His word written; in praying to Him in our times of need, and forwarding His cause by self-denial, by work, and with our heart and substance; in owning Him

in the days of our fathers, we would not have been
partakers with them in the blood of the prophets.
Wherefore ye be witnesses unto yourselves, that ye are
the children of them which killed the prophets. Fill ye
up then the measure of your fathers. *Ye* serpents, ye

before men in the ways most practical in our days, and in following the
blessed steps of His most holy life, and in showing forth the Lord's
death till He come, in the way appointed for us. This appreciation of
the lives and times of former witnesses for the truth, rather than those
of the present day, and of God's means of grace of their day, is well
rebuked by a modern writer: " Ask in Moses' time, Who are the good
people? they will be Abraham, Isaac, and Jacob; but not Moses: he
should be stoned. Ask in Samuel's time, Who are the good people?
They will be Moses and Joshua; but not Samuel. Ask in the times
of Christ; and they will be all the former prophets with Samuel, but
not Christ and His Apostles." And thus the present age sighs after
other times, other witnesses, old saints, other agencies, other means
of grace, than those that are common and appointed: something novel
or something ancient is demanded; the opportunities and agencies that
exist are too often overlooked and depreciated.

33. *witnesses.*—The self-righteous and proud spirit of this boast is
the very spirit of their fathers, in which they rejected and destroyed
the prophets of old, and their testimony.

34. *the children.*—In the sense of being inheritors of the same spirit,
and therefore capable of the same actions. There is a moral relationship amongst all evil men, as there is also a communion and fellowship
amongst the good. They must be closely united at heart, who are guilty
of the same crimes; they are cognizant of the same principle and the
same aims, and employ the same means to their end. These Pharisees
were far in advance of the wickedness of their fathers; capable, therefore, of appreciating and perpetrating any of the minor gradations of
the sins, in which they were themselves eminent. The alliance between
these fathers and their children was as close and natural in the relationship of iniquity, as in the descent of race.

35. *the measure.*—Possessed of the same spirit, active in the same
wickedness, go on and complete the fulness of your iniquities. This
is Christ's sentence of judicial abandonment. He had done His best
with them, and in vain; henceforth they are left to themselves, unrestrained, unwarned, and with the avenging angel of wrath to speed
them to ruin. Thus was the sentence spoken to Judas: " What thou
doest, do quickly " (John xiii. 27).

36. *ye serpents.*—Our Lord repeats the denunciation of John the
Baptist. But John had spoken half hopefully, though in much astonishment, that any influence had succeeded in " warning them to flee from
the wrath to come." Our Lord has done with hope; and speaks in

generation of vipers, how can ye escape the damnation of hell ?

Wherefore, behold, I send you unto prophets, and wise men, and scribes : and *some* of them ye shall kill and crucify ; and *some* of them shall ye scourge in your synagogues, and persecute them from city to city : that upon you may come all the righteous blood shed upon the earth, from the blood of righteous Abel unto the

the grief of seeing their house left unto them, their Temple God-forsaken, their opportunities forfeited, their condemnation imminent. He has exhausted the means of grace, and foresees no further probability of gaining them back ; and now, in the despair of the Saviour who has in vain offered life, He forecasts the sentence which He must pronounce as the Judge : " How can ye escape the damnation of hell ? "

37. *generation of vipers.*—Compare His words, " Ye are of your father the devil, and the lusts of your father ye will do " (ye are purposed to do). " He was a murderer from the beginning, and abode not in the truth " (John viii. 44). In Rev. xx. 2 he is named " the dragon, that old serpent, which is the Devil, and Satan."

38. *wherefore.*—Since you so fully evince the spirit of your fathers.

39. *I send.*—Christ speaks with authority, in the position which His parables had just claimed, as the Son of God, the Head of the Church of God.

40. *prophets*, etc.—The Apostles and other witnesses of the New Testament. To many of these the gift of prophecy was distinctly assigned, as well as to the Apostles. The seven deacons were men " full of the Holy Ghost and wisdom " (Acts vi. 3, 10). In Matt. xiii. 52, our Lord designates the Apostles and ministers of His Gospel, " scribes instructed unto the kingdom of heaven ; " and the title may, with great propriety, be given to Apollos (Acts xviii. 24–28), and to others like him.

41. *kill and crucify.*—As James, and Stephen, and Peter, and many others. The Apostles, in Acts v. 40, were scourged ; so was Paul, five times by the Jews, thrice by the Romans—he was also driven from city to city. All these persecutions were, however, common to the first preachers of the Gospel. It has been well noticed that, though mention is here made of Apostolic and other Christian martyrs, none is made of Christ. His death was the life of the world ; His blood, " which speaketh better things than that of Abel," calls down grace and pardon, and the cleansing of the world's sin, rather than vengeance.

42. *Abel.*—The first martyr in God's cause in the history of the world, slain in exactly the same spirit of malicious enmity to his witness for the right, as that in which the prophets were slain, and Christ Himself, and His martyrs, put to death. The object, in every

blood of Zacharias son of Barachias, whom ye slew between the temple and the altar. Verily I say unto you, All these things shall come upon this generation.

case, was to silence a troublesome witness to truth, whose life was also a continued protest against sin.

43. *son of Barachias.*—The prophet Zechariah is so called (Zech. i. 1), but there is no account or tradition of his having experienced this terrible death. But Zechariah the son of Jehoiada was so put to death (2 Chron. xxiv. 20–22); and the circumstances of his death made an impression which was never effaced. He, like Abel, died for his witness to the truth of God in the face of error; he was the last in order of those specified in the Old Testament as slain for the truth's sake, as Abel was the first. As he died, he said, "The Lord look upon it, and require it;" to which there seems to be a reference in Luke xi. 51, which strengthens the view that this is the prophet alluded to. It is difficult to say why S. Matthew gives his name as "the son of Barachias;" it may have been an early error on the part of a transcriber, or an instance of the somewhat common practice of having two names amongst the Jews. Dr. Hammond gives another— Zecharias the son of Baruch, slain immediately before the siege of Jerusalem, in the Temple, near the altar, and thus the last, as Abel was the first martyr; and as he was not slain when Jesus spoke, he proposes to read, as the Greek will allow, "whom ye shall have slain," etc. (See Josephus, "Wars," iv. 5, 1.) But the general opinion inclines in favour of Zechariah the son of Jehoiada, the last prophet slain by the Jews before they ceased to be a thoroughly independent nation.

44. *between the temple,* etc.—Between the most holy place and the great altar of sacrifice, in the court of the priests.

45. *this generation.*—We see the truth asserted here, which history has so often illustrated, that the existence of nations through their various generations, is a distinct national life. A national character forms and grows, until it becomes as clearly defined, in its degree, as is the character of any individual man. The parallel between individual and national life is a very close one: and God deals with either upon the same general principles. As the individual character forms slowly from infancy, under various influences, and grows with the man's strength, until it becomes a clear and defined personality, with which God deals, if wicked, with various chastisements during its progress, by way of check and warning, until at last judgment falls upon no single act, but upon the culmination of the whole life, when there is no further hope of amendment; so is it also with national life, and with the life of a Church. To take the illustration of Israel: the whole course of their career, as a nation and Church, shows how God dealt forth various punishments and warnings, of greater or lesser force, in the hope of reforming them from sins in

O Jerusalem, Jerusalem, *thou* that killest the prophets, and stonest them which are sent unto thee, how often would I have gathered thy children together, even as a hen gathereth her chickens under *her* wing, and ye would not! Behold, your house is left unto you desolate. For I say unto you, Ye shall not see Me hence-

which generation after generation trod in the steps of their fathers; and it was not until the Captivity that even the spirit of idolatry was extinguished, whose infancy was in the Syrian exile of Jacob's household, and in the captivity of Egypt. But there were other sins than this, which unfitted them for God's work in the world; their bitterness, exclusiveness, waywardness, actuated them still, until the Jew of our Lord's day was a sadder proverb in the world, than ever his father had been. And before God's eye there was the most ostentatious hypocrisy, added to the fully developed national faults, which made their character utterly hopeless; it had grown through many generations, and fully reached maturity when judgment fell. It would be easy to trace the same growth and development of national character, the same rise and fall, of nations to whom the end of eternal corruption has come by means of external foes, though the hand of God is less specially revealed than in the instance of the Jews; but the parallel between the individual and the nation is an invariable rule of life.

46. *O Jerusalem.*—(See I. 48–56.) The contrast is most touching, between the loving solicitude of our Lord, in His unwearied goodness sending so long a continuance of messengers and prophets, and the bitter and persistent malignity of those whom He so deeply loved, and for whose salvation He had endured so much.

47. *how often.*—Not alone in the experiences of His own active and constant zeal, whilst on earth amongst them, but in the person also of every prophet and messenger, of the long succession whom they had rejected and slain.

48. *your house.*—No longer " God's House." (See viii. 19.) The Temple is meant in the first instance, but not excluding the city, or land of promise. These had been severally the " House of God," the " City of the Great King," " the land which the Lord thy God careth for." He now disowns and cast them off. The word " behold " has the sense of propinquity of time: " Look! this disolution immediately impends."

49. *left . . . . desolate.*—Left and abandoned by God; desolate in the deepest reality, being bereft of His gracious presence; and soon to be desolate of its inhabitants, who would fall by famine, pestilence, or the sword, or mourn in the land of hopeless captivity. The Temple, their boast and centre of strength, would be destroyed in the general ruin.

50. *see Me.*—These were the concluding words of Christ's public ministry; they saw Him no more as the Messenger of salvation.

forth, till ye shall say, **Blessed** *is* **He that cometh in the Name of the Lord.**

XV. *THE WIDOW'S MITE.*

S. Mark xii. 41-44; S. Luke xxi. 1-4.

And Jesus sat over against the treasury, and beheld how the people cast money into the treasury : and many

51. *till ye shall say.*—Some writers explain that the Jews will at last be compelled to make the unwilling admission, that Jesus was the Christ,—when they see Him whom they pierced, invested with the attributes of Divinity, at His second advent. No doubt there is this signification : but yet there lies beneath it another and brighter meaning; for, although our Lord's words were words of doom and awe, they still promise hope. It has been so with every denunciation of God's wrath during this week (see vi. 11, vii. 43); and now, when He is leaving them for ever, He sets His seal to those bright promises which the long line of His martyred witnesses had declared, that there shall come a day of repentance and salvation to Israel, when they shall acknowledge and welcome the truths which they now despised. How distant that day may be, we cannot tell; but it is a distinct and assured word of prophecy, and it will be fulfilled in God's time. Again shall the nation hail "The King that cometh in the Name of the Lord," and rejoice in His advent ; and it is also declared that this shall be an event of fuller blessing to the whole world, than the Christian dispensation has yet seen (Rom. xi. 15).

1. *Jesus sat.*—Our Lord did not at once leave the Temple. His sitting there gave any one who desired it an opportunity of addressing Him, which, if I am right in the date of their interview, was embraced by certain Gentiles. (See xvi.) Perhaps He lingered thus, for some late expression of penitence or devotion. S. Luke says He "looked up" from the group around Him, and so noticed what was passing near Him.

2. *money.*—The voluntary offering of those who gave gifts for the repairs and service of the Temple.

3. *the treasury.*—From 2 Kings xii. 9, we find that a chest was placed besides the altar, at the entrance of the court, for the reception of voluntary offerings. It is said that in our Lord's day there were thirteen of these coffers, placed in the court of the women, for such purposes. It is not certain whether the "treasury" here spoken of was one of these chests, or a special part of the court of the women so designated, or a room in the Temple; as in John viii. 20 we read, "These words spake Jesus in the treasury, as He taught in the Temple," which seems to specify a certain locality. It could not, how-

that were rich cast in much. And there came a certain poor widow, and she threw in two mites which make a farthing. And He called *unto Him* His disciples, and saith unto them, Verily I say unto you, That this poor widow hath cast more in, than all they which have cast

ever, have been further within the Temple than the court of the women, or the widow would not have been admitted within it. It was likely that our Lord would be found teaching in a court to which women were admitted, and where they could therefore listen to Him.

4. *cast in much.*—There was the usual ostentation on the part of the Pharisees, in making these gifts: but many rich men gave large and noble gifts of their abundance, with real devotion ; and our Lord speaks in acceptance, and comparative approval of these, as large gifts from ample means.

5. *widow.*—The extreme representative of a large class, and varied in the experience of misery, the desolate poor. She must have included every phase of desolation; since one in the solitary and unprotected state of widowhood like hers, so destitute as to possess only one farthing, could have no inferior in the gradations of such misery.

6. *two mites.*—It is to be noticed that she threw in the only money she had in the world for her own necessities. She certainly had a strong faith in the God of the widow; and there must have been thorough purity of motive in her offering, or she would not have met this unqualified acceptance from our Lord. Farrar says, "She had given two *prutahs*, the very smallest of current coins; for it was not lawful, even for the very poorest, to offer only one."

7. *He called.*—This gesture shows His strong feeling on the occasion, and His anxiety that the case should be recorded, and published. We notice, too, that His discourse and remarks are now confined to His disciples, or addressed primarily to them ; He had ceased to address the multitude of the Jews, as a teacher.

8. *more.*—If her offering was slight, there was munificence and piety in her heart; none other had given so unreservedly. However large a sum the rich had given, it was not all their wealth. Our Lord does not, of course, advocate the giving of all that we have, or of any improvidence, even in almsgiving. The giving up of that on which other claims lie, to the cause of religion, is no virtue ; God would reject the " Corban," at the price of the breach of the fifth commandment. He only speaks of the true faith, and genuine piety, of this poor widow ; and shows how God receives, nay requires, His dues from the very smallest means, and does not regard the amount of the gift, so much as the means and heart of the giver. It is the same act of gracious acceptance as that which acknowledged the giving up of the comparatively little "all that they had," on the part of the Apostles, with the splendid reward of the twelve thrones at His right hand. But there is little

into the treasury: for all these have of their abundance cast in unto the offerings of God, but she of her penury did cast in all that she had, *even* all her living.

XVI. *GREEKS DESIRE TO SEE CHRIST. HE FORETELLS HIS DEATH.*

S. John xii. 20–36.

And there were certain Greeks among them that came

need for elaborate explanation of an incident, which is so true and simple that it touches all hearts, and is for ever fresh in interest, and is thoroughly intelligible to all readers.

9. *the offerings of God.*—We see that God accepts and appropriates the gifts we give of our substance with which He has blessed us. Little perhaps do those, who so offer, reflect that Jesus is sitting over against the treasury of His Church, as carefully beholding them, as He beheld, unknown and unheeded, these givers of the offerings in His Temple; and that He scrutinizes the motives and heart of each, as he offers his gift, and makes His award, as He did in the case of these Jewish worshippers, according to the truth and purity of their motives. It is very possible that the poor widow neither saw Him, nor heard His precious words concerning herself, but in her heart only received His answer; the careful mention of the disciples only, as hearing what He said, almost decides that she was not permitted to know it. And this only strengthens the parallel between this case, and the offertories of God in our own day; the acceptance of our gifts, in proportion to the purity of our motives; and the oversight of the Lord, to whom ostensibly they are offered. The lesson is an important one, in days when the offertory of God is not only gathered for the repair and decoration of that House in which it is offered, but embraces, like the Christian religion, the Catholic Church in the world; for all causes of piety, of charity, of missionary enterprise, come within the scope of the Christian treasury. We therefore hence learn these several weighty truths: that God requires gifts from us all, even from the very poorest and most desolate; that He accepts them graciously, with a regard to the means of the giver, and to his motives in offering, rather than to the actual value of the gifts; that He exercises a personal oversight over what is offered in His House; and that no one of insignificant means may fear the rejection of the humblest gift, by Him, who graciously, for the sake of all such, has recorded His acceptance of the widow's mite. The use of the phrase, "*my mite*," by those who ought to "cast in much," is a misapprehension of the lesson of this incident; their *mite* is in such strong contrast with that of the widow, that it were better not thus to challenge rejection of their offering.

up to worship at the feast: the same came therefore to Philip, which was of Bethsaida of Galilee, and desired him, saying, Sir, we would see Jesus. Philip cometh and

1. *Greeks.*—Foreigners, Gentiles, and probably "proselytes of the gate," who might worship in the "court of the Gentiles." Such was the eunuch of Acts viii. 27. The Jews called such by the common name of Greeks, they being the leading people known to them, and the Greek language being common to the civilized world. There is some uncertainty as to the day on which this incident occurred. (See iii. 3.) Some place it on the day of our Lord's triumphal entry, when, however, there was no particular word spoken, or act performed, which specially might encourage the Gentiles to approach Christ; and when it would appear that our Lord confined Himself to observation of all things. (See i. 60.) Others place it on one of the two succeeding days. The weight, however, of opinion places it on this day, and almost as the last discourse of our Lord in the Temple. There seems a fitness of occasion in favour of this. After the cleansing of their court, our Lord's assertion of His claims before those who questioned them, His parables, so evidently leaning from the Jews towards the call of the Gentiles, and His final rejection of the Jews, these Gentiles might discern their hope and interest; and, after conference, send to Him where He now sat, to come and speak with them. These were the representatives of the Gentiles, at the close of our Lord's life on earth, as were the Magi on His coming into the world. (See note 9.) On the tradition concerning King Abgarus, of Edessa, see App. VII.

2. *to worship.*—Apparently as a matter of annual custom; if proselytes, certainly so.

3. *the feast.*—See App. VIII. A.

4. *to Philip.*—There have been many conjectures as to their choice of Philip. His name, being of Greek origin, denotes a certain alliance with the Gentiles, many of whom were settled in Galilee. And these Greeks, or some of their relatives or fellow-countrymen, may have been residents of Bethsaida; the mention of Philip's town here may suggest so much. Philip had been instrumental in bringing Nathanael to Christ, as he now introduces these Greeks. He seems to have appropriated to himself, as a life's duty, the bringing of others to the Saviour; thus fulfilling, in his own and other cases, the Saviour's words, addressed to him first among the disciples, "Follow Me."

5. *sir.*—They address him with marked respect, but not with the familiarity of personal acquaintance: it would therefore appear that it was either from the fact of some local association, or from his undertaking this duty towards inquirers, that these Greeks approached Christ through Philip.

6. *see Jesus.*—Gk. "the Jesus," the Saviour. They desired a personal interview with Himself. They had, no doubt, seen and heard Him, in the course of His public ministrations during this week.

telleth Andrew : and again Andrew and Philip tell Jesus.
And Jesus answered them, saying, The hour is come, that
the Son of man should be glorified.   Verily, verily, I say
unto you, Except a corn of wheat fall into the ground and

7. *telleth Andrew.*—We find Philip and Andrew engaged together
in another instance (John vi. 7, 8). Their names are coupled, in
two of the lists of the twelve Apostles ; and when our Lord sent out
His disciples two and two before His face, these two fellow-townsmen
may have gone together as fellow-evangelists. The name of Andrew,
like that of Philip, is of Greek origin. Philip probably now consulted
him, as being uncertain whether he might properly, or judiciously
bring the request of these Greeks to Christ, where He now was, in the
Temple ; as the habit of His preaching, and His repeated strong
injunctions to the disciples, were against addressing themselves at
present to the Gentiles (Matt. x. 5). Bishop Ellicott thinks that the
request was brought from the court of the Gentiles, where these Greeks
had admission, to our Lord, whilst still teaching in the inner court.
(See xv. 3.) The two disciples may have approached and spoken, as
our Lord continued sitting in the treasury.

8. *answered them.*—*i.e.* the two Apostles : but no doubt our Lord
had gone where these Greeks desired to see Him ; and that they
heard the words which He spoke with reference to their having come
to seek Him, and to do Him honour. (See note 10.)

9. *the hour is come.*—The expression is a solemn one ; it has reference
to that last hour of the final witness and struggle against the world,
when the work of Christ's Messiahship was summed up and consum-
mated. (See xxiv. *d.* 24, xxvi. 5.) But there is another reference
here, immediate on the present circumstances, for it had been formerly
against Christ's design to admit the Gentiles to the privileges of the
Gospel ; but now the time had arrived for that, upon the Jews' rejection of it. It is difficult to trace the thought suggested to our Lord
by the arrival of these representatives of the Gentiles, to claim their
share in the common Saviour (note 6) ; but their coming was probably
influenced by the triumphal entry of Christ into Jerusalem, His
miracles in the Temple, His parables and addresses to the people, so
distinctly foreshadowing the mission of the Gospel beyond the pale of
the Jewish Church : and so He may have taken up their desire to
share in His glorious kingdom, and assured them that He was in truth
about to be glorified, but not (as they supposed) as an earthly sovereign, but by death ; and that, if they embraced His cause, they must
follow it even to the death. If they thus dared for His sake, they
should be where He was, and be the honoured of His Father. Then
follows the remembrance of how this glory is to be won.

10. *a corn of wheat.*—This, in its varied forms, is a constant
figure in our Lord's discourses. The seed of the word ; the wheat

die, it abideth alone : but if it die, it bringeth forth much
fruit.   He that loveth his life shall lose it ; and he that
hateth his life in this world shall keep it unto life eternal.

growing up amidst the tares; the silent growth, the blade, the ear,
and final reaping of the grain ; the mission fields of the world, as fields
ripe to harvest; elsewhere the bread of life ;—all these meet us as
illustrations of our Lord's teaching.   Here we have the figure (so
amplified by S. Paul, with reference to the resurrection) of the sowing,
and dying, and springing again in increase, of the grain of corn.
Stier notices our Lord's appeal to the prophetic mysteries of nature,
rather than to the word of God's prophets, as an argument for the
presence of the Greeks whilst He is thus speaking.

11. *abideth alone.*—Its vitality is fruitless ; there is no increase
from it.

12. *much fruit.*—Thus would Christ die, and from His death would
spring the world's life.   "That corn was He; to be mortified in the
unbelief of the Jews, to be multiplied in the faith of the Gentiles."
(*Augustine.*)   In every age, both Jews and Gentiles, and especially the
mighty harvest of the Gentile world, would rise to the life immortal
through Him,—all of the children of the resurrection.   He might die
alone, as He must tread alone the winepress of God's wrath ; but He
should rise with many brethren, the increase of His death.   Looking
into the future of even a very few years of the Church, how far more
glorious would be the results of Christ's death, than ever His life on
earth had been, or might be.   This is His answer to those Gentiles
who came to see Him.   Their hopes lay in the death which, in a few
days, He would suffer for their sakes.   If they would follow Him to
the end, He foreshowed them both the immediate and future prospects
of His cause.

13. *he that loveth.*—(See App. VI.)   This is another of those rules
of Christ's kingdom so variedly illustrated in the teaching of His life.
Here He tells all who would follow Him, that His is a cause in which
they must be prepared to peril life, or, at least, to lead lives of self-
denial for His sake.   As he that hesitated to risk the corn of wheat by
committing it to the earth as seed, should lose it, and never reap its
produce, while he who ventured it in the hope of a future harvest should
receive it again with abundant increase ; so Christ's followers, if they
loved the present life, and its enjoyments and prospects, too dearly to
put all to the hazard, if necessary, they would lose it so far as the
prospects of eternity are concerned.   If they *hated* life (so valued it
as second in comparison with Christ's cause, and its offers), they might
indeed encounter persecution, or even lose their life in this world, but
they would inherit eternal life ; and their death, like the dead corn of
wheat, or the dead Christ Himself, would be productive of a plentiful
harvest of life.

If any man serve Me, let him follow Me; and where I am, there shall also my servant be: if any man serve Me, him will *My* Father honour.   Now is My soul troubled; and what shall I say?   Father, save Me from this hour: but

14. *serve Me.*—If any one desires, as these Greeks for instance, to enter into My service, he must follow Me in My life of patience, self-sacrifice, and benevolence; and if he has to follow Me through death, he shall find Me beyond the grave, and share My glory there. And as the consequence of My service may be, on earth, the contempt and reprobation of men, and his name may be cast out as ignominious, My Father shall grace that despised name with the favour which is His to grant; it shall be had in honour before angels and men, when all earthly honour ceases for ever.

15. *troubled.*—(See xxiv. *d.* 1, xxviii. 8.) A sudden wave of sorrow seems to roll across the Saviour's spirit. Here only, and in the agony in the garden (Matt. xxvi. 38), does He use the word translated *soul.* He speaks not of the spiritual being, but of the human soul, which here was agonized, and, in Gethsemane, so utterly prostrated that His very life was stricken with sorrow, and there was necessity for an angel's ministration. He now forecasts the agony, and the sorrow, and the death before Himself, and before those followers whom He seeks to lead upwards to the Father. The glory of future triumph, of the union of both Jew and Gentile in the gift of a common salvation, is fully in His view; but all that must befall Himself and His disciples, of struggle unto death before the final victory, darkens the immediate foreground.   Never is Christ more fully shown to be perfect man, than in the prospect and hour of death. As naturally as any of the sons of men, does He humanly shrink from the hour of death. " As He draws near to the cross, His human nature appears, a nature that did not wish to die, but clave to this present life." (*Chrysostom.*) "In that He was troubled, He considers the weak members of His body, the Church, that they may not think themselves reprobate, should they be troubled at the approach of death." (*Augustine.*) The LXX. use the original word (which our Lord perhaps quotes here), to express extreme horror and dismay, in Ps. vi. 3, and xxx. 7.

16. *what shall I say.*—As the conflict between these two absorbing prospects almost convulses our Lord's spirit, so does it check utterance of words.   What shall He adequately say, in the struggle between the prospect of terrible death before Him, and the brightness of glory to be won by death?

17. *save Me.*—" Let this cup pass from Me;" put it aside, and devise other means.   It was not surely the common horror of death, or that our Lord feared to die in His own cause. He was not less fearless than the heroes of our race; but much more is veiled, in the agony of His spirit, than we can express to ourselves. His was death in the person

for this cause came I unto this hour. Father, glorify
Thy Name. Then came there a voice from heaven, *say-*

of the sinner, with the punishment of the guilty sinner weighing upon
His pure and innocent soul; and in sight of all that the refusal of His
salvation would bring upon those who despised reconciliation through
His blood. It was not surely that Christ feared the pain of death, but
that His spotless soul shrank from the imputation of the sins of the
world before His Father. As we could not undertake this burden, and
as sin is not alien to our souls as to His, we cannot conceive of His
agony, and of the trouble of His soul, in prospect of the sacrifice He
had to offer. It has been proposed to read these words interrogatively,
as suggesting the conflict of thought: "What shall I say? Shall I say,
Save Me from this hour? No! for this cause came I unto this hour."

18. *for this cause.*—Some modern critics have suggested that our
Lord came to this hour for the cause of being saved through the path
of endurance, *i.e.* that in endurance would lie the victory—a sense
which includes so much truth that it deserves consideration; as the
path of safety in danger, and certainly in spiritual danger, lies often in
facing it, and standing firm. But the simpler and more direct meaning
is always preferable, in the interpretation of our Lord's words; and we
read in the whole life of Christ, and in His own account of His mission
to the world, the truth that He came upon earth for the very purpose
of encountering the struggle of this hour. For this cause came He to
this hour, that He might die for the world's sins. He must not seek,
therefore, safety in flight from these difficulties, but meet them. "The
cup which My Father hath given Me, shall I not drink it?"

19. *Father, glorify,* etc.—"I do not say, 'Save Me from this hour,'
but I say, 'Father, glorify Thy Name;' though agitation would force
the utterance of the former, I say the reverse, 'Father, glorify Thy
Name.'" (*Chrysostom.*) The mainspring of the life of Christ was obedience to the will of His Father; it immediately asserts its influence here :
"I came down from heaven, not to do Mine own will, but the will of
Him that sent Me" (John vi. 38); therefore, "Thy will be done;"
"whatever Thy glory demands from Me, be it done in Me and by Me."
We see here, as in the agony, the assertion of the two wills in Christ,
which we should carefully notice as bearing upon the mysteries of this
struggle. (See note 16, and xxviii. 12.)

20. *a voice.*—Thus, for the third time, God spake from heaven in
attestation of the mission of His Son; and each voice marks an occasion of the fullest importance. God spoke from heaven at His baptism,
at His transfiguration, and now at this hour of crisis. "In the
enclosure of the Temple itself, the voice of the Father solemnly declared
before all the people that the first revelation is closed and completed;
that now is beginning the second, and therefore higher one, the glorification of His Name through Christ." (*Lange.*) This manifestation,

ing, I have both glorified *it*, and will glorify *it* again. The people therefore, that stood by, and heard *it*, said that it thundered: others said, An angel spake to Him. Jesus answered and said, This voice came not because of Me, but for your sakes.　Now is the judgment of this

and our Lord's previous declaration that the hour of His glory had now come, give very much more significance than we might have supposed, to the arrival of these representatives of the Gentiles.　Whether they perceived that the Jews had rejected the blessings of the Gospel, and that our Lord, in His parables, declared that these might now be theirs, and that they had, therefore, come to claim them (see notes 6, 9), we cannot say; but there must have been much more in the occasion, than the suggestion of a passing train of thought to our Lord's mind, in the agitation produced by their coming.

21. *I have both glorified it*, etc.—In the previous manifestations of the Divinity of Christ, in His miracles and teaching, and in His life, and now especially in its casting out of the prince of this world, which was the *crisis* of the world's history; again it shall be glorified in His Passion, in His death, resurrection, and ascension, and in the future supremacy of His Gospel kingdom.　This is the evident and primary sense; but it may also include this, that as God's Name has been glorified in the dispensation of the law that is past, now it shall be exceedingly glorified in the dispensation of the Gospel of Christ.

22. *it thundered.*—Compare Rev. i. 15; Dan. x. 6.　They all heard a mighty sound of awe, but it was not equally intelligible to all; some thought it thunder, some the voice of an angel.　(See Dan. x. 7; Acts ix. 7.)　The bystanders appear to have understood, very much as they had faith in Christ, or otherwise.　To some it was an ordinary phenomenon, perhaps unexpected, or out of season; but still, to them, natural causes were a satisfactory solution of anything unusual.　To others, it was a voice from heaven for certain, but they thought it the voice of God's angel; for they recognized a certain fitness of occasion, and, in the person of Christ, one worthy of Divine interposition.　And this is a true type of the ordinary comprehension of God's voices about us, of warning, encouragement, and mercy.　Some see natural causes and natural effects, in every accident of their lives; others delight to trace God's presence, controlling and directing their varied fortunes in the issues of their lives, and to hear the voice of God addressing them by various outward means and agencies, which, unconscious of His influence, gives them direction.　"All things work together for good to them that love God," because God's providence oversees and directs their working.

23. *this voice.*—Our Lord's words are thus decisive of its true nature.

24. *for your sakes.*—Christ had prayed, but the answer had come

world : now shall the prince of this world be cast out.

to Himself spiritually.   He needed not any visible or audible sign from heaven, to tell Him of what He was fully conscious ; but, for the sake of those who stood around, and especially of those who were fastening their highest hopes upon Him, this third time God spake from heaven. And however the powers of evil might seem to prevail against Him, and however momentary fear might unnerve human confidence, those who heard the voice, had heard the decision of the Almighty ; and His was a voice which must reassert itself in their memories and hearts.   (Cf. John xi. 42.)

25. *the judgment.*—Gk. " *crisis.*" The point of decision, when judgment is given with regard to the future of this world, who shall possess its kingdoms and sovereignty ; and discernment and separation (for this sense also is included in the word) is given amongst its inhabitants, and they are ranged as subjects of its true Lord, or the usurper " prince of this world." Now is freedom granted to the world in bondage to sin and death, for now the judgment is given against the prince of this world ; he shall be cast out of his usurped dominion, and " He whose right it is " shall take it. The death of Christ was the point whence this restoration dates, which includes both Jew and Gentile in the brotherhood of the Gospel—a restoration which will be completed in the hour of final judgment ; and, therefore, hence dates the peculiar glory of the Redeemer Son, and of the Father glorified in Him. The world would not at once discern this : it might be very long before the Jew perceived it ; it might be long even before the fulness of the Gentile world would rise up to follow their representatives, who now sought Christ's presence. It would be the special work of the Holy Spirit, in succeeding ages, to convince the world of judgment, namely, that the prince of this world is judged (John xvi. 11), as He implants this conviction in the spirit of those whom He influences. (See xxv. e. 7, 13.) S. Chrysostom and others consider this statement as the interpretation by Christ of the words of the voice from heaven, that thus the Son would be glorified.

26. *the prince of this world.*—Who is in usurped occupation of dominion amongst men.   " The prince of the power of the air, the spirit that now worketh in the children of disobedience" (Eph. ii. 2) ; whose is the " power of darkness," from which God " has translated us into the kingdom of His dear Son " (Col. i. 13). There is another interpretation, which (Tittmann argues) may probably be included as subordinate to the main and primary, which regards the Jewish world of prejudice, error, and hypocrisy (an utter subversion of the purity of the Mosaic religion) : all this Jewish world was cast out before the face of Christianity, and judged, together with " the prince of this world" (John xiv. 30), who had used these agents to oppose the introduction of Christ's kingdom. Dean Burgon (quoting Dr. W. H. Mill) has the following note :—" All the Fathers, from Ignatius

And I, if I be lifted up from the earth, will draw all *men* unto Me. This He said, signifying what death He should die.

The people answered Him, We have heard out of the law that Christ abideth for ever: and how sayest Thou,

to Bernard, represent Satan as snared by his own success; and by taking away the life of the One immaculate human subject, losing for ever that proprietary right over the lives of all the rest, which had been his through the penal consequences of the first sin." See also Ælfric.

27. *lifted up.*—Our Lord had used this expression before (see John iii. 14, viii. 28), to express His being lifted up on the cross of His crucifixion.

28. *draw all men.*—Not force: "I drew them with cords of a man, with bands of love" (Hos. xi. 4; Jer. xxxi. 3). Our Lord "commendeth His *love* towards us," in that He died for us (Rom. v. 8). It is the cross of Christ's death that is the point of union of all elements of human discord in the harmony of God's world; the conviction that He died for men, draws all human hearts around Him. The Gk. "unto *myself*" is here very emphatic. It is not the revelation of hell that scares men from it, nor the picture of heavenly happiness that allures them; the great thought of interest for every life is, that Christ gave His life for our life. "All men" means men of all nations and generations; the Gentile world, as well as the Jews; all individuals of the human family. Our Lord makes this grand assertion of saving might, in the very face of death.

29. *out of the law.*—The word of God, as the Jews possessed it; including the Psalms and Prophets, in which are the clearest declarations of the everlasting royalty of the Messiah, and of the eternity of His kingdom. There is no passage, which refers to Him, which gives any impression of a temporary sovereignty; wherever its declaration is alluded to, it is as a dominion that shall be wide as the world, and that endureth throughout all ages.

30. *Christ abideth for ever.*—Clearly they understood that our Lord claimed the Messiahship, because they immediately add, "How sayest Thou, the Son of man must be lifted up?" They quote the title by which our Lord so usually spoke of Himself, but which He had not now used. His own words just uttered were, "I, if I be lifted up." (See also John iii. 14.) By associating Him, therefore, with the designations "Son of man," and "the Christ," they distinctly gave to Him the position which He claimed. But yet they did not quite understand how He could die a disgraceful and ignominious death, and yet abide for ever. "See how maliciously they put the question. They do not say, 'We have heard out of the law that Christ *doth not suffer*,' for in many places of Scripture His Passion and resurrection are spoken of together; but 'abideth for ever.' And yet His immor-

The Son of man must be lifted up? who is this Son of man? Then Jesus said unto them, Yet a little while is the light with you. Walk while ye have the light, lest

tality was not inconsistent with the fact of His suffering. They thought this proved, however, that He was not Christ." (*Chrysostom.*) These words are an interruption of the crowd around, to whom Christ was not exactly speaking, but who could not look on His gracious address to the Greeks with favour.

31. *this Son of man.*—The emphasis here should be placed on the word *this*. Is He the same as spoken of in Dan. vii. 13, to whom eternity of being is ascribed? The passage is a remarkable one; and it must have been impossible for a Jew to misunderstand the significance of the title " Son of man," however expressive it may have appeared to be of His genuine human sympathy, and true manhood. " Behold, one like the Son of man came with the clouds of heaven, and came to the Ancient of Days, and they brought Him near before Him." *They* appear to be the ministering angels who attended His ascension; for, immediately before, we read, " The Ancient of Days did sit . . . and thousand thousands ministered unto Him, and ten thousand times ten thousand stood before Him." (See II. viii. 18, 25–28.)

32. *yet a little while.*—The answer appears to be thus: The Son of man, the Christ, who must be lifted up, is eternal; He " abideth for ever;" although with you He is manifest only for a little while, as " the Light." You know that it said that " the Son of man came with the clouds of heaven, and came to the Ancient of Days;" this is going to be fulfilled: from earth He will be lifted up upon the cross, and die; but angels will conduct Him to the Father in the clouds of heaven, after His resurrection. What is seen on earth and in heaven are but different phases of manifestation which concern the same Son of man, Myself, the Christ. I am now present as the Light of the world; yet a little while, and I shall be lifted up upon the cross, that I may draw all men unto Me, by My love in dying for them—then I ascend to My Father, the Ancient of Days. " Yet a little while is the light of My personal presence with you, and the light of My personal doctrine shines forth unto you: make use of this happy opportunity while it lasteth." (*Bishop Hall.*)

33. *the light.*—Christ speaks of Himself, and of the truths which He reveals and illustrates. (See also John viii. 12, ix. 5, xii. 46.)

34. *walk.*—Rouse yourselves, and be in earnest; look to your footing, lest in the advancing darkness you wander from the right way. (See Jer. xiii. 16.) The Jews were much given to disputations about religion, as were also the Greeks (1 Cor. i. 22, 23), and this came very much in the way of decision and earnestness in the matter. Later on, it became necessary for the apostolic writers to give the most pointed warnings against this evil tendency. We have seen how much pre-

darkness come upon you : for he that walketh in darkness knoweth not whither he goeth. While ye have light, believe in the light, that ye may be the children of light.

These things spake Jesus, and did hide Himself from them.

XVII. *THE DISBELIEF OF THE JEWS; AND THE DOCTRINE OF CHRIST WHICH THEY REJECTED.*

S. John xii. 37-50.

But though He had done so many miracles before

occupied the Jews were with absorbing questions about subjects of secondary importance, such as tribute, fasting, tithes, the great commandments in the law, and other such questions. Our Lord put before them the practical example of a consistent and active life, in the service of God ; and it is the very epitome of His own life in words, when He says, " *Walk* in the light."

35. *darkness.*—The darkness of those who have rejected the light. " There is internal evidence at *vv.* 35, 36, that as this application to Him was apparently the last event of the day, so was it made when the night was at hand. The allusion at least, in those verses to the approach of the night, besides its spiritual meaning, becomes so much more striking and impressive if it contains a sensible meaning also." (*Greswell.*)

36. *come upon you.*—Steal over you unaware of the imminence of danger, which, for want of light, you cannot see. It will come unawares therefore ; you will not know whither you are going. " Quite benighted were they at the time of the siege of their city." (*Burgon.*)

37. *hide Himself.*—He withdrew Himself from those who rejected, disbelieved, or disregarded His words. He probably went away to Bethany, where during the week He resided. This appears to mark the close of His public and personal ministry as a teacher. He would still be set forth by His Apostles as the Light of the world ; but after a few years the light would be withdrawn finally from the Jewish people, and the darkness of destruction come upon them. Christ gave this warning as He now withdrew from preaching to them. The way in which the passage concludes, forms an argument for placing the visit of the Greeks to Christ at the close of this day (see note 1), instead of (with Dean Milman, Dr. Farrar, and others) on the day of the entry to Jerusalem. Christ would scarcely be said to hide, or withdraw Himself, if He reappeared the next morning ; there was also nothing in the

them, yet they believed not on Him : that the saying of
Esaias the prophet might be fulfilled, which he spake,
Lord, who hath believed our report P and to whom
hath the arm of the Lord been revealed P Therefore
they could not believe, because that Esaias said again,

events of that day to necessitate His hiding Himself, but everything
to encourage Him to return to the people.

1. *but though.*—This passage (John xii. 37-50) appears to be a
summary of the effect of Christ's preaching upon the Jews, and of His
declaration of His Messiahship.   As such, it fitly follows on His with-
drawal from that work. So very extraordinary was the consequence of
the prejudices of the Jews against our Lord, so inexplicable their blindness, that S. John gives this notice and comment upon it, before com-
mencing that portion of his Gospel which immediately concerns the
Apostles.   He shows that there had been no failure in the power put
forth for their conviction, and that their obstinacy is no argument
against the cause of Christ ; for it was foreseen, and, in the eternal
councils of heaven, provided for.   Isaiah had foreshown how it would
be with them. S. John gives also words of our Lord in support of His
own claims, which were probably spoken during this week, but which
contain the sum of many discourses on these points.

2. *might be fulfilled.*—(See i. 14.) The object of the Evangelist
is to show that this was foreseen and arranged for, and that therefore
it in no way disconcerted the plans of the eternal Trinity. The Jews
were in no respect compelled to act as they did, in order to the fulfilment of prophecy, and were certainly quite as guilty as if God's foreknowledge had not foreseen, and provided for the difficulty ; more
guilty, in fact, for they were distinctly warned by the declaration of
His foreknowledge, the monition of the prophet being a caution and
prohibition against unbelief.

3. *who hath believed.*—They are so few in number that they can
scarcely be pointed out.   The prophet's vision was not keen enough to
discern them.   He knew that there must be some few ; God's word
could not be spoken in vain ; but who were they ?   The spirit of this
inquiry was different from that of Elijah, who assumed that, as he
knew none, there were no worshippers of God left in Israel, whilst the
eye of God noted and numbered them by thousands (1 Kings xix.
14, 18).

4. *the arm of the Lord.*—A title of Christ, in whom the power of
Divinity was manifest and revealed in His miraculous works. He was
the Arm of the Lord made flesh.

5. *because that Esaias said.*—(See note 2.) This is the most distinctly
and strongly expressed, of those passages which speak of the predictions
of the prophets, and the necessity that events should happen accord-

He hath blinded their eyes, and hardened their heart ; that they should not see with *their* eyes, nor understand with *their* heart, and be converted, and I should heal them.   These things said Esaias, when he saw His glory, and spake of Him.

ingly.   We have only to think of the numerous acts of unbelief, of which this paragraph is a summary, to see how entirely faithful was the witness of the prophecy.   It is impossible for God's foreknowledge to be at fault in the minutest particular ; it is equally impossible that God should compel men to act wickedly, in order to fulfil His words by the prophet.   If ever power is exerted in this direction, it is when grace is taken away from the reprobate, and judicial vengeance is already hurrying them on in the path from which they have refused to turn.   The following may serve as showing the opinion of the Fathers upon this point : "The Evangelist says 'Could not,' to show that it was impossible that the prophet should lie, not that it was impossible that they should believe ;" and, again, "they did not disbelieve, because Esaias said they would, but because they would disbelieve, Esaias said they would." (*Chrysostom.*)   "If any ask why the Jews could not believe, I answer, because they would not." (*Augustine.*)   We cannot tell how comforting to the disciples, and to the early Church, it must have been thus to know from the beloved disciple, that things had happened with regard to Christ, exactly as they had been foreshown ; and that no mistake had been made, nothing omitted that was not provided for.   There is a peculiar fitness in S. John's thus pointing the witness of prophecy to the age of its fulfilment, as he wrote later than the other Evangelists, and to readers who were keenly critical of the claims of Christ as "the power of God and the wisdom of God."

6. *hath blinded.*—Judicially, as the consequence and punishment of their persistent refusal to see.   The whole passage, as given by the prophet (Isa. vi. 9–13), is remarkable ; it is repeatedly applied to the Jews of that day by our Lord and His Apostles.   The prophet is commissioned to declare the sentence given by God upon the people for their iniquity ; it is, however, accompanied by words of hope of restoration after the lapse of long ages.   Besser here quotes words of Augustine, which afford an admirable explanation of this and similar passages : "God *hardens*, not by imparting wickedness, but by withdrawing grace ; He hardens by not softening, and blinds by not enlightening." Tittmann reads, "He" (*i.e.* this people, not God) "hath blinded." This is not grammatically incorrect, but it is opposed to the general interpretation of the passage.   It is better to say that God hardens and blinds, by permitting men to have their own wicked way ; for it is thus that, in all generations, unbelieving men frustrate the grace of God, and His counsels, against themselves.   Their own habits of unbelief have formed

Nevertheless among the chief rulers also many believed on Him; but because of the Pharisees they did not confess *Him*, lest they should be put out of the synagogue: for they loved the praise of men more than the praise of God.

such a barrier that they cannot now believe; and then God's rule interposes, that from those who will not have His grace, shall be taken away even the power to believe, so far as their free will would enable them to do so. He thus confirms the unbelief of those who refuse to know Him.

7. *saw His glory.*—*i.e.* the glory of Christ. The passage above quoted is one of those which shadow forth the doctrine of the Holy Trinity and the Divinity of Christ; we find in it also, remarkably, the ascription of glory, "Holy, holy, holy, Lord God of hosts," which we meet with in Rev. iv. 8. The prophet exclaims, upon this vision of heaven's glory, "Mine eyes have seen *the King, the Lord of hosts.*" Here S. John tells us that Isaiah had seen the glory of *Christ*; but in Acts xxviii. 25, we read that, "Well spake the *Holy Ghost* by Esaias the prophet unto our fathers," instead of the sentence, as in Isaiah, being ascribed to "the Lord of hosts."

8. *chief rulers.*—The word "chief" is not particularly specified in the original. These were members of the Sanhedrim, and others of note. We know from S. John the names of one or two of them, who were believers in Christ, but not adherents—they were secretly His disciples—Nicodemus, and Joseph of Arimathea. But they are spoken of with favour, and therefore no doubt they had found ways and means of showing their sympathy with the cause of Christ. But S. John, writing long after the event had revealed those who owned and disowned Christ, appears to refer here to somewhat different men—to believers at heart, but who kept their belief to themselves, and took public part against Christ, or at least did not favour Him. The remark, "They loved the praise of men more than the praise of God," is one of heavy reprobation. S. John seems to have had some personal facilities for ascertaining this; he was known to the high priest, and doubtless, therefore, to others of note amongst the rulers. He, more than the other Evangelists, gives prominence to the fact that the crowning sin of the rulers was, that "they saw" the truth which they refused to follow.

9. *put out.*—This was one of the most powerful impediments in the way of the confession of Christ. It entailed terrible disgrace and suffering; the excommunicated was cut off from religious and social privileges, and regarded as an outcast from the hope of Israel. This had already been used against the spread of Christianity. (See John ix. 22, 23.)

10. *they loved.*—"As their faith grew, their love of human praise grew still more, and outstripped it." (*Augustine.*)

The Doctrine.

Jesus cried and said, He that believeth on Me, believeth not on Me, but on Him that sent Me. And he that seeth Me seeth Him that sent Me. I am come a light into the world, that whosoever believeth on Me should not abide in darkness. And if any man hear My words,

11. *Jesus cried*, etc.—This expression is very emphatic, and denotes very earnest and distinct enunciation of these truths. It seems to mark something different from His usual calm intonation of voice and gesture in His public teaching. The same word is used of the loud and commanding voice with which He summoned Lazarus from the grave ; and again of His own last cry, in which He yielded up the ghost. It is here His emphatic declaration of His office of Saviour, and of His desire to be known as the Saviour, rather than as the Judge of the world.

12. *he that believeth.*—The doctrine given in the following words seems to be a summary of Christ's teaching upon these points, and no doubt in words frequently and forcibly uttered, and probably repeated during this week. They are, then, the words which He made clear and distinct to the Jews, and supported by His miracles ; they are intimately connected with the summary of the unbelief and rejection, just given by the Apostles. The doctrines contained in this summary are found in the following passages, and in many others : Mark ix. 37 ; John xiv. 9, viii. 12–15, iii. 17 ; Luke x. 46 ; Mark xvi. 16 ; John viii. 38, etc.

13. *not on Me.*—Not on Me only. The union of the Son with the Father was so intimate, that belief in Christ was belief in the Father, seeing Christ was seeing the Father, and hearing Christ was hearing the Father ; therefore the reception or rejection of the Son, was the reception or rejection of the Father. (See John xiv. 9, x. 30.) Those who receive and believe in Christ as the Son of God, believe that as there is the Son, there must be the Father also ; "as if He said, He that taketh water from a stream, taketh the water, not of the stream, but of the fountain." (*Chrysostom.*)

14. *a light.*—See xvi. 33.

15. *abide in darkness—i.e.* in his original darkness. The expression denotes that all men are in darkness, until they receive the light of Christ. This was a most unpalatable truth to the Jews, who claimed superior illumination for themselves. (See John ix. 39–41.) They could not, however, help receiving light from Christ ; their especial sin consisted in their shutting out and turning from the light. The words seem also to apply especially to those of the rulers who believed in Christ, and yet did remain in darkness ; they would not confess Him for fear of excommunication, and for love of the praise of men.

and believe not, I judge him not: for I came not to judge the world, but to save the world. He that rejecteth Me, and receiveth not My words, hath one that judgeth him: the word that I have spoken, the same shall judge him at the last day. For I have not spoken of Myself; but the Father which sent Me, He gave Me a commandment, what I should say, and what I should speak. And I know that His commandment is life everlasting: whatsoever I speak therefore, even as the Father said unto Me, so I speak.

16. *I judge him not.*—I am not answerable for his condemnation and judgment; this is not My present mission to the world; I am now a Saviour, not a Judge. Christ will, however, at the last day sit as the Judge of all mankind; and this high office is committed to Him because He is the Son of Man, and so One who knoweth what is in man, able to appreciate the force of all our temptations and trials, and to make allowance for our infirmities; and therefore His judgment of men is just. (See John v. 22, 27, 30; Heb. iv. 15.) But yet it is His desire to commend Himself to us rather as the Saviour. (See xxi. 5, 10, 12.)

17. *hath one.*—*i.e.* hath a judge. God and Christ alike refuse the character of the Judge. God hath committed all judgment to the Son, who is the Saviour; and He will but pronounce the sentence already given by His word of truth. God desires to be known as our Father; Christ, as our Saviour. "Who is he that condemneth?"

18. *the word.*—Our Lord ascribes the highest force to the written word of God, though delivered by Moses (John v. 45–47). He represents the words of Moses as accusing them before God of unbelief in Him; much more must the word of Christ Himself be a witness against them, and a judge of those who refuse to hear it. That word must prove the word of life or of death, for it is the word of truth. He that is of God heareth it; others hear it not, because they are not of God. So all must stand or fall before the word of Christ. He will but pronounce the final sentence according as that word has already judged, or as mankind have decided for themselves by that word, which searches and tries all hearts and consciences; for the commandment, the word of God, to the world through Christ is life everlasting. (See II. iii. 13.)

19. *what I should say . . . speak.*—The former may refer to Christ's private discourses with His disciples, and what He said in the house of His friends; the latter to His more formal public teaching. The original words mark a difference. It is, however, somewhat forced to define the distinction; but the evident meaning is that both His private and social discourses, equally with His public preaching, were inspired and "commanded" by the Father: "*Whatsoever* I speak therefore, even as the Father said unto Me, so I speak."

XVIII. *CHRIST'S GREAT PROPHECY OF THE DESTRUCTION OF THE JEWISH CHURCH AND NATION; AND OF HIS OWN COMING.*

S. Matt. xxiv. ; S. Mark xiii. ; S. Luke xxi. 5-38.

And Jesus went out, and departed from the temple. And as He went out of the temple, one of His disciples saith unto Him, Master, see what manner of stones and what buildings *are here!* And Jesus answering said

1. *went out.*—Jesus now quitted the Temple for the last time; His public teaching was ended, and there was nothing further for Him to do in the House of God upon earth. S. Matthew, with some disregard of the sequence of time, gives us what is very valuable, the connection of certain events with each other. We see here an illustration of this. He passes by certain minor incidents (xv.–xviii.), in order that he may point out the connection between our Lord's denunciation of doom to the Temple, and this question of the disciples. The twelve could not but hear with astonishment and sadness, His words of desolation. They thought of the Temple, its memories and its glories, so representative of their religious and national life : and now one of them, speaking the sentiments which engrossed them all, pointed out to Him (S. Matthew says they "came to show Him ") its magnificent proportions and details, and its massive structure, as if to urge some reversal of His sentence ; and it seemed to them as if the end of the Temple must be the end of the world, or at least of the age and dispensation. Another instance of this peculiarity of S. Matthew's Gospel is his placing the incident of the anointing of Christ four or five days later than its actual occurrence, to show its influence on the act of Judas. (See xxii. 8.)

2. *stones.*—The blocks of marble, of the purest white, were of very large dimensions ; some of them are said by Josephus to have been from sixty to seventy feet in length—a size quite extraordinary, but not wanting confirmation from modern travellers, who speak of stones of sixty-four feet in length amongst the ruins of Baalbec. (See App. XI.) The late explorations of the Palestine Fund prove the vast size of the stones still lying *in situ ;* though these are none of the stones pointed out by the disciples, as those were all thrown down.

3. *buildings.*—(See App. IV.) The dimensions and details of the whole building were extremely magnificent and costly. From the distance the Temple "looked like a mountain of snow," so great was the purity and dazzling whiteness of the marble with which it was built. Portions of it were covered with plates of gold, which, in the full rays of the sun, were brighter than the eye could bear to rest on. The word may also mean "building materials," which must now

unto him, Seest thou these great buildings ? there shall
not be left one stone upon another, that shall not be
thrown down.

And as He sat upon the mount of Olives, over against
the temple, Peter and James and John and Andrew
asked Him privately, Tell us when shall these things

have been spread around, as the work of building was still in progress,
and was continued for many years, until nearly the time of the destruction of the Temple. It seemed strange and sad to the disciples
that so grand and splendid a work, not even finished as yet, should be
doomed to utter destruction. S. Luke makes mention (ch. xxi. 5) of
the " gifts," or votive offerings, with which the Temple was adorned ;
these were partly gifts from the rich and pious Jews, and also from
foreign kings and princes, some of them being gifts from Roman
emperors, testifying to the esteem and veneration in which the great
Temple of the Jews was held in the world, and how unnatural, therefore, it seemed to be, that any should design its destruction. We
learn from Josephus, that the most positive orders were given by the
Roman general, to preserve it from injury at the taking of the city ;
and its destruction was the result of apparent accident. " The value
of the plunder was so great that gold fell in Syria to half its former
value." (*Milman.*)

4. *seest thou.*—Regard them well, in all their present glory and
magnificence, and in their massive strength. Not one of these noble
buildings shall survive the great overthrow ; not one massive stone
shall rest upon another. The fulfilment of this was literal; the Romans
dug up the very foundations of nearly the whole of the site of the
Temple, and actually, now or after the revolt in the reign of Hadrian
(App. IX.), drove a ploughshare across them. (See Micah iii. 12.)

5. *mount of Olives.*—(App. X.; see i. 22, 47, 48.) There was a very
striking view of the Temple and city from this height. Here the
Tenth Legion under Titus took its station, being the first point occupied
by the Roman army which invested Jerusalem.

6. *asked Him.*—The questions asked by the disciples read, as if they
partly comprehended the different eras distinguished in our Lord's
answer ; but they can scarcely have done this. It is probable that
they thought that some striking sign would mark the first event, and
that our Lord's coming would close the then present age ; and that on
His coming (probably to inaugurate the monarchy, which they had not
quite ceased to expect), the punishment upon the nation which now
rejected Him, would be the destruction of their government and capital.
Both the question and the answer seem to mark three events—the
destruction of Jerusalem, the coming of Christ, and the end of the
world ; these divisions should be borne in mind in any consideration of

be ? and what *shall be* the sign when all these things shall be fulfilled ? what shall be the sign of Thy coming, and of the end of the world ?

And Jesus answered and said unto them, Take heed

the subject. It is said that four of the disciples asked this question *privately*, that is, apart from all others; there was so much danger attending any question which referred to the destruction of the Temple, that common prudence dictated such conversation being restricted to very few. S. Andrew, on this occasion, is added to the three, who on three other occasions enjoyed special revelations of Christ, who called him first as an Apostle.

7. *Thy coming.*—The disciples apparently understood that the destruction of Jerusalem would be coincident with an advent of Christ in power; and they probably thought this would be followed by the proclamation of the kingdom of Christ, of which His parables had spoken so specially during the day's teaching.

8. *end of the world.*—Gk. " end of the age " or dispensation; which, probably, is all that the disciples understood of Christ's fuller meaning; though some writers think that they literally supposed the fall of the city, and the end of the world, would come together. The vagueness of the term well expresses their undefined apprehension.

9. *Jesus answered.*—Bishop Ellicott's words are striking: " In a prophecy in which at first the fate of the holy city, and the end of the world, are mysteriously blended, but which gradually, by means of the solemn parables of the ten virgins, the talents, and the revelation that follows, unfolds itself into a distinct declaration of the circumstances of the last judgment, the Saviour of the world vouchsafes an explicit answer to the question of His amazed hearers; yea, too, and on the slopes of that very mountain where mysterious prophecy seems to indicate that He who then spoke as our Redeemer, will hereafter appear as our King, and our Judge." The predictions which are now delivered are in the highest strain of prophecy, but, like prophecy in general, they are veiled in a certain obscurity—less so, no doubt, than the predictions of the prophets; but still there is a veil drawn over the distant events shown. Prophecy is a witness to the age of its fulfilment that God foreknew the exact truth in the age of its delivery, and is therefore not likely to be perfectly clear as a narrative of facts before its fulfilment. The portions of this prophecy which specially refer to the desolation of Jerusalem, and the signs preceding it, are necessarily more distinct, being so immediately near, and being designed to warn the disciples of the dangers attending that time of trouble. And yet the whole prophecy is so blended, that it is difficult to distinguish exactly what event is spoken of. Very possibly the troubles attending the coming of Christ in one instance are typical of those of the other. Bishop Wordsworth (on Matt. xxiv. 3) gives an

that no man deceive you.   For many shall come in My
Name, saying, I am Christ; and the time draweth

appropriate and beautiful illustration of the distances, and the involved
aspect of prophecy; and especially of this prophecy of our Lord's two
advents in judgment.   "Future *events* in time may be compared to
distant *objects* in place.   In a mountainous country, two ridges of hills
rising the one above the other, are seen in the horizon almost as one,
although there may be many miles between them; and it is only when
the spectator arrives at the summit of the first ridge that he is aware
of the chasm between them.   So is it with future events.   The prophets of the Old Testament pass rapidly from describing the first
advent of Christ to the second advent, so that the two advents seem
blended together; but when the predictions concerning the first advent
had been accomplished by the manifestation of Christ in the world,
then the prophecies concerning the second advent became more distinct.
Yet, even *then*, the coming of Christ to judge Jerusalem seemed to be
blended with His coming to the universal judgment."   Those who are
familiar with any mountain scenery will appreciate the justness of this
illustration; it is, however, most striking to those who have seen the
magnificent ranges (for this word must be substituted for ridges) of
eternal snow, rising one beyond another in the mighty Himalayas.
There is an outpost from which the highest peak in the world is visible
as a small cone, apparently part of an infinitely lower range (in the
foreground the second and third highest of known mountains are prominent), until, as the traveller approaches to the nearer range, the vast
height and solitary grandeur of that peak become more distinct.   This
highest of all mountains, as yet untrodden by man, is thus an illustration to the world of that still distant event, the most sublime and the
grandest which the spirit of prophecy has ever declared.   Farrar has
another figure very apt, in illustration: "Jesus turned the thoughts of
His disciples to two horizons, one near, and one far off.   The boundary
line of each horizon marked the winding up of an *æon*.   Each was a great
ending; of each it was true that the then existing 'generation,' first
in its literal sense of *generation* (the ordinary life of man), then in its
wider sense of 'race,' should not pass away until all had been fulfilled.
And the one was a type of the other; the judgment upon Jerusalem,
followed by the establishment of the visible Church on earth, foreshadowed the judgment of the world, and the establishment of Christ's
kingdom at His second coming."

10. *take heed.*—Watch and beware.   This warning runs through the
whole prophecy, and is sounded like a refrain, whenever our Lord
speaks of the future.   Be it now, or distant, we are to be watchful,
and on our guard; for if we do not attain to the day of Christ's
advent, yet, in the day of our visitation, and in the hour of our death,
He will come to us personally.

near; and shall deceive many: go ye not therefore after them.　And ye shall hear of wars and rumours of wars: see that ye be not troubled: for these things must

11. *deceive you.*—This warning includes even the Apostles themselves, as well as the Christians of the apostolic age; for this manifestation of error would precede the destruction of Jerusalem.　These false Christs would have a large following (see John v. 43), but "go ye not after them."

12. *many shall come.*—(See App. XI.)　The names of Simon Magus, Theudas (not the Theudas of Acts v. 36), Dositheus, and Borchochab are mentioned, as also "that Egyptian" (Acts xxi. 38), together with others not specified by name, as rising up and drawing away multitudes after them, in the vain hope of their being the Messiah who should deliver them from the Roman yoke.　The Jews thus acquired the character of being thoroughly disaffected and turbulent, and gave constant offence to their Roman rulers by their following these pretenders, until it became necessary, as an example to their colonial empire, to destroy Jerusalem.　This desolation, therefore, was the direct consequence of their following *false* Christs; and their rejection of the true Christ naturally opened the way to the pretensions of those to whose lies God now abandoned them.

13. *in My Name.*—The original is not "*in*," but "upon;" *i.e.* taking their stand upon My Name, assuming it without warrant.

14. *wars,* etc.—By these prophecies the first three Gospels, published before the destruction of Jerusalem, were put on trial before the world, within the first century of the Christian era; for they were verified by the exact fulfilment of the prophecies which concerned this advent of Christ.　It is remarkable that S. John, writing after that era, omits this wonderful prophecy; perhaps designedly, to avoid the imputation of writing it after the events had happened.　Nothing could more truly express the character of the times, than the words "wars and rumours of wars."　Josephus describes the constant strife between the Jews and Syrians, and the inhabitants of various cities in which Jews were living.　They were generally turbulent and disaffected; and several of the Roman emperors, in succession, threatened them with war.　Outside also, in the Roman world, there were wars proclaimed against Syria, though the danger passed.　Again, Otho and Vitellius were in strife for the empire; nothing was settled and sure.　S. Luke uses the words "wars and commotions," to characterize the great wars, and the seditions and insurrections which *threaten* war.

15. *troubled.*—If this caution against being agitated by signs of alarm and trouble, applied to the times of the destruction of Jerusalem, it has also a wider and more extended meaning.　The same undefined fear which prevailed at times, in the early days of Christianity, against which our Lord and His Apostles warned the Church, has

first come to pass; but the end *is* not by and by. Then said He unto them, Nation shall rise against nation, and kingdom against kingdom: and great earthquakes shall be in divers places, and famines, and pestilences; and fearful sights and great signs shall

disturbed the world in many ages; notably so at the close of the tenth century, when so general an impression of the approach of the end fell upon men, that it interfered with much of the business and enterprise of the world. For instance, few large and notable religious buildings, and few great undertakings, were entered on, until the eleventh century was well forward, and the mind of the Church re-assured. Even in later times there have been panics and renewals of this "trouble" in various localities. Any undue agitation on this subject is unwholesome to the Christian mind, and injurious to the cause of Christ; it tends to weaken in the world's mind the force of His own prediction. S. Peter (2 Pet. iii.) pointed out the danger of the derision thus excited. The publication, therefore, and perusal, of sensational works (of which this century has had a surfeit) on the interpretation of prophecy in connection with these events, is to be deprecated. It is a laudable study only so far as it may lead men to regard thoughtfully the signs of the day, and God's word in history, and may minister to the strengthening of faith.

16. *not by and by.*—Not immediate. These signs are heralds of approaching change; but the end (a term general and indefinite) itself is still distant. They would long precede the destruction of the Jewish Church; and there would be a long interval also, of the same general character, before the end of the world should come. In connection with this intimation, and contrary to the expectation of a more im-mediate advent, we may regard with interest the interpretation of the author of the Epistle of Barnabas, which may date from the earlier part of the second century; who, taking the type of the six days of creation, and the seventh day of rest, says, "The Lord will finish all things in six thousand years ... when His Son coming again shall destroy time, and judge the ungodly, and change the sun, and the moon, and the stars; and then shall He truly rest the seventh day." There was also a similar opinion current amongst the Jews, as to the duration of time, and the end.

17. *then He said.*—For these signs, etc., see App. XI.

18. *earthquakes.*—Josephus and other historians mention great and terrible earthquakes in Judæa, in Asia Minor, in Crete, at Rome, and in Phrygia. This prediction had a thorough fulfilment; and especially so in countries where the Jews were dwelling. (See App. XI.)

19. *famines and pestilences*—The latter are generally the con-sequence of the former; hence the current Greek proverb, "After famine pestilence." To give an instance only of each, where several

there be from heaven. All these are the beginning of
sorrows.

But take heed to yourselves : before all these, they

might be cited : we read, in Acts xi. 28, of a famine in Judæa, in the
time of Claudius ; and Josephus mentions the great importation of corn
into Judæa during its prevalence. Tacitus records a pestilence at
Rome, A.D. 66, which swept off 30,000 people. (See App. XI.)

20. *fearful sights and great signs.*—Record is made, in Josephus, of
a comet which overhung the city for a whole year ; of a light which
shone by night round the Temple and altar ; of the opening of itself of
the great gate of the Temple ; of large armies contending in the clouds
over Jerusalem ; and of the mysterious voice, as of multitudes, within
the Temple, which said, "Let us go hence !" Many of these are also
confirmed by the historian Tacitus. (See App. XI.)

21. *beginnings.*—There would, therefore, be worse than these behind
them.

22. *sorrows.*—Gk. " birth-pangs." The prelude of the coming desolation, but, more justly, of the regeneration. The word is a strong one,
and shows with what troubles and disquiet the birth of the new era of
Christianity was ushered into the world ; what terrible portents and
trials will also precede the creation of the " new heavens and the new
earth, wherein dwelleth righteousness." There is also signified the
death agony of the Jewish Church and dispensation, and of the dying
world that now is. Elsley thinks there may be, in the use of this
term, an allusion to Isa. lxvi. 7, 8, as the Jews interpreted the passage
to mean that, before times of trouble and desolation came upon Israel,
the Messiah should be born.

23. *take heed.*—Part of this warning is a repetition, in substance, of
our Lord's first charge to His disciples (Matt. x. 17-22). He bids them
guard their words and actions. As the rulers had watched His words
to entangle Him in His speech, so would they also encounter risk of
charges of sedition and disaffection, which the magistrates would take
immediate notice of, though they might disregard mere questions of
religion. They must, therefore, be "wise as serpents, harmless as doves."

24. *before all these things.*—Before the destruction of the city and
Jewish Church, there was much work and much success, with much
persecution also, before the Apostles of Christ. In those few years
there would be shown, in epitome, the history of the Church in all ages ;
home and missionary labour ; the testimony of martyrs to the truth ;
the faith rising triumphant over difficulties ; persecution itself turning
from being an adversary, to become an agent in infusing new life and
strength, and in propagating the faith. It was the first persecution at
Jerusalem which dispersed the Apostles amongst the Gentiles, driving
them into the highways and hedges of the world, to gather in converts
to the faith.

shall lay their hands on you, and persecute you, and shall kill you: they shall deliver you up to councils; and in the synagogues ye shall be beaten; and ye shall be brought before rulers and kings for My sake, for a testimony against them. And it shall turn to you for

25. *persecute you.*—The warning here given was most minutely fulfilled in all parts of the world, wherever the Gospel was preached. It will be enough to trace the beginnings of this system of persecution, in the "Acts of the Apostles," in which, and in the Epistles, sufficient evidence is offered of the energy of the spirit of antichrist. The life of S. Paul embraces nearly every one of these particulars of experience.

26. *kill you.*—Acts vii. 59, xii. 2.

27. *councils.*—Acts iv. 1–22, v. 21–41, vi. 12, xxii. 30.

28. *beaten.*—Acts v. 40; 2 Cor. xi. 24.

29. *rulers and kings.*—The quotations above cited might be greatly multiplied by references to the Epistles; but to extend them beyond the representative experience of S. Paul, and to verify them, in the case of the noble army of martyrs, from early ecclesiastic writers, and from contemporary historians, would be to narrate the whole history of the Church, in the first three centuries, and onwards.

30. *for My sake.*—This is the point on which the reality of martyrdom turns. It must be *for Christ's sake,* not from the obstinacy which refuses to consider the opposing side of doctrine, which, not from principle, but prejudice, will neither change nor yield. It must be in the true " defence and confirmation of the Gospel," not from rashness and intemperate zeal; it must be in the cause of truth, and not of party. There have been those claimed by Church, and party, and sect as martyrs, because they have died rather than change, who have had as much claim to that high title, as the Jew who fell in the ruins of his Temple. We may respect their courage and devotion, but they are not true martyrs.

31. *against them.*—Or, " to them." These persecutions shall bring the cause and gospel of Christ before witnesses whom it would never else have reached; and the constancy of Christ's servants under suffering and trial, will win those who never else would have been won. It was a trite but true saying, " The blood of the martyrs is the seed of the Church." If they rejected this testimony borne *to them,* the words of Christ which they rejected would witness *against them,* and condemn them (see xvii. 17); but the object of preaching the gospel of salvation is not to witness *against* those to whom it is offered.

32. *turn to you.*—In like manner, these times of trouble will give you opportunities and advantages of bearing testimony to the cause of Christ; and the success which will attend your advocacy of it, will testify to your devotion and diligence.

a testimony ; and ye shall be hated of all nations for My Name's sake. But when they shall lead *you*, and deliver you up, take no thought beforehand what ye shall speak,

33. *hated.*—Tacitus calls the Christians a race hated for their crimes. All kinds of terrible superstitions and evil practices were vulgarly attributed to them by their enemies ; and the horror of these, coupled with the domestic disruption caused in any family, one of whose members became a Christian, combined to make the name of Christian hated in the world. But no false witness, or misrepresentation, or family trouble, could alone account for the hatred of the world against a religion which had such promises, and which could produce such transformation of character, and which inspired its worshippers with such strength of soul, and such peace. Nor could the fact of its being a new religion, account for the opposition it met with in the Roman empire ; for it was the policy of Rome to adopt all national religions, however gross, within their dominions. As they conquered a country, so did they adopt its gods, and erect a new statue to the new god. Why Christianity alone should not be tolerated and adopted, and why it should raise a storm of ill feeling which no other ever did, can only be explained by the fact that it alone opposed the usurped dominion of the prince of this world ; it alone testified to the world that the deeds thereof were evil ; it alone (because it was not of this world) concentrated against itself all the powers, manifestations, and systems of evil and of error dominant in the world, and in the hearts of the " children of this world." It could make no compromise with evil, or with false religion. Its mission was to subvert all wrong, and error, and falsehood ; and therefore the world has hated it, as it has hated its Author, Christ.

34. *My Name's sake.*—See note 30.

35. *take no thought.*—This injunction is to the same purport as that more general one given in Matt. vi. 25, 31, 34 ; which does not countenance any unnecessary precipitation of one's self into danger—for that would be tempting God's providence—but such a fearlessness in the front of actual danger as Christ showed. Here there is to be no rashness or intemperance of speech, for our Lord had just bidden them " take heed to themselves," and to watch opportunities of speaking to advantage in His cause, in the presence of those who persecuted them ; and this presupposes all possible prayer, thought, and deliberation. But Christ now tells them to dismiss anxiety about what they should say, and not to study how to put unpalatable doctrines with more prudence than straightforwardness ; but to put their trust in Him, and " speak the truth with boldness," not in the " enticing words of man's wisdom." For God's Holy Spirit will inspire His witnesses, in their hour of need, with the words fittest to the occasion in the sight of Him, who beholds every heart and temper of those who hear their

neither do ye premeditate; but whatsoever shall be given you in that hour, that speak ye : for it is not ye that speak, but the Holy Ghost : for I will give you a mouth and wisdom which all your adversaries shall not be able to gainsay nor resist. And then shall many be offended, and shall betray one another, and shall hate one another. Now the brother shall betray the

proclamation of the Gospel, and who will Himself give that sanction and authority to their utterance which is best, wisest, and most convincing.

36. *I will give.*—A promise of Christ's presence with them, and of the taking upon Himself the responsibility of their actions and words.

37. *wisdom.*—The first difficulty of which they would become conscious, was one which is but seldom felt amongst missionaries of modern times. These go forth to the heathen as the possessors of a civilization and learning superior to their own. But these "fishermen of Galilee" had to teach the way of life to those who were the most thoroughly trained theologians, and who sat in the seat of Moses, invested with all the dignity of their sacred office; they had also to dispute and argue with the scientific and subtle dialecticians of Greece. They could not, therefore, possibly stand forth before these, much more plead the cause of Christ with success, without the direct inspiration of the word and wisdom of God. (See App. XII., XIII.)

38. *your adversaries.*—Christ gathers them round Himself, not merely as servants fighting in His interests, but as identified with those interests. His enemies are their enemies, just as His God and Father is their God and Father.

39. *gainsay nor resist.*—See the first of countless instances of the fulfilment of this promise in Acts iv. 13–16.

40. *offended.*—This is another sign, and a sad one, of these days of trouble. Not only would there be opposition from without, but defection also from within. Many would stumble at the demands made on them by the cause of Christ, and shrink before the fiery trial of persecution.

41. *betray.*—A yet deeper degradation. Some of those possessing the faith of Christ would purchase their own safety by the betrayal of their brethren in the faith. Judas would not be the only traitor in the confraternity of Christians; for the reference here is to these, not simply to heathen relatives.

42. *the brother.*—(See Micah vii. 6.) The pages of early Church history are full of instances in which the profession of Christianity seemed to cancel the nearest domestic obligations. The Christian was given up to the magistrates, and to death, by husband, wife, parent, brother, and by the closest friends. Tacitus records that, in the reign

brother to death, and the father the son ; and children shall rise up against *their* parents, and shall cause them to be put to death. And ye shall be hated of all *men* for My Name's sake. But there shall not an hair of your head perish. In your patience possess ye your souls.

of Nero, Christians were delivered up by their parents, brothers, kinsfolk, friends. This refers to heathen relatives; the former statement to *lapsed* traitors.

43. *hated of all men.*—(See note 33.) But this is a more personal hatred; not only would Christians be a hated race amongst all nations, but every Christian convert would be a man hated by every other man, for the sake of the Name which he bore, and the religion which he professed.

44. *an hair of your heads.*—(Cf. Matt. x. 30 : "The very hairs of your head are all numbered.") Christ discloses the minuteness of His personal care and providence over them. Nothing could happen to them unseen by God ; and if they did die in His cause, not even a hair should fall from them in vain, and unvalued. If death came upon them, they should in no wise *perish.* Perish is not a term to apply to those who are heirs of immortality. We cannot carry the expression to its lowest and minutest particulars. No *man* could have thought of speaking of the loss of anything so insignificant ; but Christ, who does number the hairs of our head, knows best the full and particular blessings included in the immortality of life promised to us.

45. *patience.*—The " patient waiting for the coming of the Lord " is set forth as a chief virtue by all the apostolic writers; it is a great exercise of faith. If the hour of Christ's coming were definite, multitudes would be watching for it, but in high-wrought, overstrained excitement (see note 15); and all God's work in the natural ways of life would be paralyzed. That patience which was so eminent in Christ, would never " have her perfect work." S. Augustine declares strongly, that no one can guard the hope of the future life, who has not patience in the trials of this life. This has been a necessary virtue in every age of Christianity ; and never more so than now, when it is a protest against the bustle, fever, and excitement of life. And, no doubt, as patience became more and more characteristic of Christ's true disciples, as the troubled life of the Jewish Church drew towards its end ; so will it be, as the end of the world draws on, on the part of those who discern the spirit and aid of Christ. So the good seed, cast into good ground, " brings forth fruit with patience ; " and we shall " with faith and patience inherit the promises."

46. *possess ye.*—This is equivalent to the promise that thus they should possess their life ; and especially the life of the soul, the truer and inner life. The promise had a fulfilment in the destruction of Jerusalem, in which not one Christian perished. They continued

And many false prophets shall rise, and shall deceive
many.   And because iniquity shall abound, the love of
many shall wax cold.   But he that shall endure to the
end, the same shall be saved.   And this gospel of the
kingdom shall be preached in all the world for a witness
unto all nations; and then shall the end come.

patient and watchful, and observant of their Lord's words; they knew,
therefore, when to leave the doomed city, and to seek their safety as
He had directed.   But the promise is general, to all ages.

47. *false prophets.*—(See 1 John iv. 1: "Many false prophets are
gone out into the world.")   They were numerous in the apostolic age,
especially before the destruction of Jerusalem.   (See note 12.)

48. *iniquity.*—Or, "lawlessness."   This is within the pale of the
Church itself; the consequence partly of the evil teaching of these false
Christs and false prophets, partly of the unsettled state and agitation
of the world around.   The apostolic writings abound with warnings
against this spirit of lawlessness, which is irreverent of sacred things,
and impatient of discipline and control.   The natural result would be
the relaxation of attachment, on the part of those less in earnest about
their religion.   Our Lord's view of those whose love has waxed cold,
is shown in the exhortation to the Church of the Laodiceans (Rev. iii.
15, 16); they are utterly abhorrent to Him.

49. *to the end.*—(See note 16.)   In the first place, to the end of
the present trial, until the Jews can no longer raise persecution against
them.   All who survived the rage of their opposition, and maintained
their faith in Christ, were preserved for the overthrow of the Jewish
Church (Rev. iii. 10). (See note 46.)   But, in a wider sense, to all who
should fall as the first martyrs to the cause of Christ, and to all
who should be His devoted witnesses, in all ages of the faith, by life or
by death, it promises the crown of eternal life.   (See Rev. ii. 10.)

50. *in all the world.*—Like most of the expressions in this prophecy,
there is here a double reference.   First, the Gospel should be preached
in all the Roman world ("all the world" of Luke iii. 1); and this, we
gather from history, was actually the case.   The writings of S. Paul
also express as much as this.   (See Rom. x. 18; Col. i. 6, 23.)   And
then also it appears to be God's will, that a like proclamation of the
truth of the Gospel should be made in every nation of the world, during
the present dispensation, before the second advent of Christ.   This
has nearly attained an actual fulfilment in our own times.

51. *for a witness.*—Not apparently for the thorough evangelization
and conversion of all nations, but so that believers are numbered from
all.   The Church did little more than give her testimony in all portions
of the Roman world, before the destruction of Jerusalem; conversion
to the true faith was not national, but individual, or at most within

And when ye shall see Jerusalem compassed with armies, then know that the desolation thereof is nigh. When ye therefore shall see the abomination of desolation,

limited numbers. Reasoning from this typical advent, it may be that we are not to expect the entire conversion of the heathen world to Christ before He comes again—a reflection which may console many a missionary Church for her apparent want of success, and may urge her to further efforts in her Lord's behalf; for He fixes no limit to the extent of her witness in any nation. He asks, "When the Son of man cometh, shall He find faith upon the earth?" The answer must chiefly rest in the activity or negligence of His servants.

52. *the end.*—The end of the Jewish dispensation, as the conclusion of the witness of the apostolic age to the Roman world; the end of time, as the conclusion of that of the Church of Christ to the human race, during the generations of her era.

53. *compassed.*—The Governor of Syria, Cestius Gallus, invested Jerusalem with a large army, about four years before the final destruction; when suddenly, without apparent cause, but really in consequence of political difficulties in the empire, he raised the siege, and retired with his forces from the neighbourhood. The Christians, remembering our Lord's words, escaped at once, and fled to Pella, on the east of Jordan, in a desert district within the mountain country, though not itself on the mountains. Bede speaks of Pella as being "under the protection of Agrippa, the King of the Jews, of whom mention is made in the Acts, and who, with that portion of the Jews who chose to obey him, always continued subject to the Roman empire." (App. XI.)

54. *is nigh.*—Our Lord spoke forty years before the final desolation, and He gave this sign of warning, which preceded the end by about three years and a half.

55. *abomination of desolation.*—Very various have been the interpretations of this expression. It has been identified with the Roman armies which compassed the city, as if S. Luke gave (ch. xxi. 20) an expression which would be intelligible to Gentile readers, which the words of Daniel would not; and, in order to make the two signs coincide, which are really separate, the "*holy place*" has been explained to mean the precincts of the holy city, especially the Mount of Olives, where the Roman army first took up position. But the presence of the Roman army without, could scarcely give such a signal for immediate flight as that spoken of in Matt. xxiv. 16–20, where it is evidently spoken of as a matter of the present hour; and four years nearly elapsed before the army stood in the holy place, meaning the Temple. It has also been explained to mean the Roman eagles, which were the objects of idolatrous worship; but these were commonly seen in its vicinity long before the event. Various other meanings have been assigned, but one only seems to deserve especial mention, and it is

spoken of by Daniel the prophet, stand in the holy place, (whoso readeth let him understand;) then let

probably the right one. No doubt, the words of Daniel had several fulfilments, as, for instance, when Antiochus Epiphanes set up an image of Jupiter in the Temple (in 1 Macc. i. 54, the words of the prophet are applied to that profanation). And our Lord's application of it may have had also various fulfilments spiritually, with regard to profanations of the Christian Church, and as a sign of the great end, which we cannot yet verify with it. But it appears necessary to look for a verification of it as a sign separate from, and subsequent to, the compassing of Jerusalem with the Roman armies, and one near to the end. And this may be done by supposing (with Dean Alford and other writers) that it refers to the seizure and occupation of the Temple by the Zealots, under their leader John, three years and a half after the war began; who took away the daily sacrifice, and thoroughly profaned the Temple, which became his stronghold, and the scene of hideous excesses, crimes, and plots. The expression in Daniel, both in ch. ix. 27 and xii 11, is coupled with the cessation of the daily sacrifice. Bishop Wordsworth, who has an exhaustive note on the expression, points out that the original of Dan. ix. 27 literally means "the abominable wing" (or, the wing of abomination), "the desolator"—a happy description of the Zealots, who, under plea of defending the Temple (the wing being the emblem of defence and covering: see Ps. xxxvi. 7; Matt. xxiii. 37), really made it more desolate. Dr. Pusey ("Lectures on Prophet Daniel") gives a different meaning—"pinnacle of abominations," in the sense of *acme*; but he says the application must be sought within the Temple. Another argument in support of the above interpretation may be found in the fact that the Zealots, directly they were in possession of the Temple, prohibited any of the inhabitants of Jerusalem from leaving the city—a circumstance which verifies the haste with which our Lord directed the Christians to depart from it, without even coming down into the house from the housetop; so immediate would be the danger on the appearance of this sign of the end. (See App. XI.)

56. *Daniel the prophet.*—The inspiration of the prophet Daniel has been strangely questioned; our Lord here expressly ranks him amongst the prophets.

57. *the holy place.*—The Temple; and, more exactly, the court in which the great altar of sacrifice stood. No less definite interpretation of these words is satisfactory, because *the holy place* was a term which had its distinct meaning from the times of the Tabernacle downwards. It could scarcely be now used by our Lord in a new and general sense, to include the district round the city occupied by the Roman armies (see note 55); especially as His object was to give a sign so definite and intelligible, that it could be at once recognized, when the emergency

them which be in Judæa flee to the mountains ; and let
them which are in the midst of it depart not ; and let
not them which are in the countries enter thereinto :
let him which is on the housetop not come down to take
anything out of his house ; neither let him which is in
the field return back to take his clothes. For these be
the days of vengeance, that all things which are written

arrived. The interpretation objected to, seems to have originated in
the identification of the "abomination of desolation" with the armies
of Rome compassing the city. But this only confuses two clearly
separate signs, between which there was an interval of three years and
a half. (See notes 53–55 ; App. XI.)

58. *in Judæa.*—In the whole country which became the theatre of
war.

59. *the mountains.*—They fled to Pella, many of them at the first
outbreak. (See note 53.) In a spiritual application of this, to troublous
times in the Church of Christ, warning is given to those who fear God,
to escape from the midst of the world. As God's saints of old—Lot,
Moses, Elijah, Daniel, and others—found safety and protection in
the wilderness (see Ps. lv. 6–8) ; so, in times of danger and trouble, we
must fly to God's presence from the turmoil of life,—to God, who is our
Rock and Mountain of defence ; not from the post of difficulty into the
retirement of solitude, but, in heart and soul, to the spiritual protection
of Christ. (See App. XI.)

60. *the midst of it.*—The midst of the devoted city.

61. *the countries.*—The country districts ; the fields around. Safety
would not be found within the city walls ; though they were so strong,
by position and art, that the Roman general said that God alone had
given him the city, as it could never have been taken without the
Divine aid.

62. *housetop.*—The houses in the Holy Land had frequently an outer
staircase, communicating with the roof directly (see Mark ii. 2–4) ; by
this a more hurried and secure flight might be possible, than by going
down through the house, and from the door. In many instances it was
easy to run from housetop to housetop, along entire streets, and so to
escape by the roof staircase of some house distant from the point of
danger. Such an escape from danger has often been made in Eastern
cities.

63. *in the field.*—Working in the fields, and so having laid aside
his upper garment.

64. *the days of vengeance.*—The day of Him who hath said, "Vengeance is Mine." No event is recorded of equally terrible magnitude
since the beginning of the world ; no era has been of equal consequence
with this, which at once closed the Jewish dispensation, and established

may be fulfilled. But woe unto them that are with
child, and to them that give suck, in those days! for

the Church of Christ as the true Church of God upon earth. As Jerusalem was but the capital of a people politically and commercially insignificant, proverbially bigoted, and universally detested, this must
have appeared, at the time, an event less interesting to mankind than
many of the convulsions of the civilized world; but for concentration
of woe and suffering there has been nothing equal to the miseries of the
vanquished in this war; and certainly nothing has so influenced the
destinies of the world, as the overthrow of the Jewish, and rise of the
Christian, supremacy in religion. No transfer of imperial power from
one nation to another has ever so changed the civilization of the world,
its standards, and its codes. Our Lord Himself contrasts the days of
His advent to overthrow the Jewish state, and of His final advent,
blended as they are in the double interpretation of prophecy, with the
age of the Deluge : "As the days of Noe were, so shall also the coming
of the Son of man be." But yet He places the convulsions and sufferings of these periods superior to those of the Deluge itself, though it
submerged the world and its entire population : "Then shall be great
tribulation, such as was not since the beginning of the world to this
time, no, nor ever shall be " (Matt. xxiv. 21–39).

65. *written.*—See Dan. ix. 26, 27; Zech. xi. 1; Ps. lxxiv. 1–3;
Deut. xxviii., especially *vv.* 32, 37, 48–57, 64–68 ; and many other passages throughout the writings of the prophets.

66. *woe . . . with child.*—"Our Lord foreshows, not imprecates,
their woe." (*Bengel.*) So far as this refers to the Christians, it
expresses the necessity of celerity, and unencumbered flight, and the
difficulties of a journey so hurried and perilous, on the part of those
whose young children must share it; and thus our Lord's words are
words of compassion for the suffering which He foresees. Ancient
writers have also seen in them a spiritual allusion to the state of mind
of those in the troubles of the "new birth " into the faith of the
Gospel. They will be distracted by the strain from either side, and
utterly want the patience of those who possess their soul in reliance on
Christ's word, assured of their safety under His protection (see notes
45, 46); they are not yet quite convinced of the new faith, whilst adrift
from their old persuasion, and know not what to do. S. Augustine
considers them verified in those who have hopes and expectations in
the present world, amidst the things of the world, and amidst the
interests which their hopes have brought forth. There is yet another
sense in which these words have been understood, in relation to those
within the city; their sufferings may be summed up in the case of
extremity, foretold in Deut. xxviii. 56, 57, which Josephus narrates
of a noble Jewish lady, once well known for her tenderness and refine-
ment. (See App. X.) These applications of the words must all have

there shall be great distress in the land, and wrath upon
this people. And they shall fall by the edge of the sword,
and shall be led away captive into all nations : and
Jerusalem shall be trodden down of the Gentiles, until
the times of the Gentiles be fulfilled. But pray ye that

been realized in the distresses of this time; and, such is the pregnant
meaning of prophecy, they must receive other verifications in those of
the end of the world. (See App. XI.)

67. *the sword . . . captive.*—Josephus gives 1,100,000 as the round
number of those who perished in the siege of Jerusalem; many of
them by famine, and by crucifixion, but multitudes by the sword.
He also states that 97,000 were led away into captivity. Dean Milman
states the total number killed throughout the country, during the whole
war, as 1,356,460; of prisoners, 101,700. There has been scarcely a
country in the world, east or west, where the Jews have not been
settled in a state of subjection, and inferiority. (App. XI.)

68. *trodden down.*—This has been thoroughly verified in the state
of Jerusalem in every age, to the present time ; whether the rulers of
the land have been Roman, Saracen, or Turk, it has been a city
trodden down. Nor can the Christians, in tolerated possession of the
various shrines and reputed holy places, in and round the city, be said
to have at all bettered her state. There have been such disgraceful
feuds between rival Churches, and such " lying wonders " and legends,
and falsification of sites sanctioned, and such bitter strife and crime,
to the disgrace of the Christian name, that the ruling heathen power
has learnt, in Jerusalem, to despise the name both of Christian and
Jew. " The city of the Great King," " the joy of the whole earth," in
which such bright and happy prophecies centred, and still rest, has
been, and now is, trodden down and desolate; " she being desolate shall
sit on the ground " (Is. iii. 26 ; Lam. ii. 10, 15).

69. *the times of the Gentiles.*—There is here, as in all prophecy, a
limitation of the period of degradation, and a promise of future restoration. S. Paul speaks to the same point : " Blindness in part is happened
to Israel, until the times of the Gentiles be come in " (Rom. xi. 25).
Under the Divine impulse, the possession of Jerusalem by an alien
power has always been maintained ; but it has been more than once a
political question, whether the establishment in the Holy Land of a
nation like the Jews, distinct and separate, great in numbers, strong
in ancestral claims, yet not likely to complicate questions of the day,
and against whose land no Christian power dare lay violent hands,
would not naturally compose various difficulties, which have reference
to the guardianship of the land, and the " Eastern difficulties " founded
on them. But no such policy has come to any definite issue. It has
been also stated that the Jews—so wealthy, collectively, that no great
enterprise, nor even war, can take place without their aid—have offered

your flight be not in the winter, neither on the sabbath
day.   For *in* those days shall be affliction, such as was
not since the beginning of the creation which God
created unto this time, neither shall be.   And except
that the Lord had shortened those days, no flesh should

more than once to buy the land of promise, acre by acre, but in vain ;
and that on one occasion, the Government in possession replied in terms
most significant, though merely as an expedient for denying an inconvenient application, that they were set in trust of the land of God,
whose alone it was, and that they could not therefore sell His land for
money.   However much, or little truth may be in these reports, this
much at least is certain, that the restoration of the Jews to their own
land has been considered by more than one Christian sovereign ; but
that it must remain unsettled "until the times of the Gentiles be fulfilled," the times during which God gives to them lordship over His
heritage for their own opportunities of salvation; however dear be the
thought of restoration to all who wish well to Jerusalem, or however
politically desirable it may seem.   The exact meaning of this term is
generally thought to be the time when the Gentiles shall have had fully
made to them the offer of the Gospel, which the Jews refused ; that is
to say (with Farrar), "their whole opportunities under the Christian
dispensation."

70. *in the winter.*—When the inclemency of the weather, the cold
and wet, would fearfully aggravate the difficulties of those who fled for
their lives, homeless and destitute, over a country devastated by the
enemy, and upon the trackless mountains.   Spiritually, we must not
defer to the winter of life, our flight to the mercy of God, from the
destruction which comes upon evil-doers.

71. *sabbath day.*—When the prejudice of the inhabitants of the land
(and even of the Jewish Christians themselves, not yet emancipated
from the observances of the sabbath) would regard a long and hurried
march a sin, and would array every hindrance, forbid assistance, and
close every house, against those whose flight was a violation of the
sacred day.   Corn. à Lapide thinks that this also includes the Judaizing
scruples of some Christians, who still bound themselves by the strict
ordinance and traditions of the sabbath, as delivered to them by the
Jews, and refused to fly beyond the legal limit.

72. *in those days.*—In the days of trouble and war, when those who
would save their lives must fly.

73. *beginning.*—Expressly, therefore, including the terrible sufferings
of those who perished in the waters of the Deluge (see note 64); and
consequently the destruction of Sodom and Gomorrah, and that of the
Babylonish captivity, and the horrors under Antiochus Epiphanes.

74. *shortened.*—Providence, therefore, would interfere to stay the hand
of the avenger, before the fury of the invading army was satisfied.   They

be saved : but for the elect's sake, whom He hath chosen, He hath shortened the days. And then if any man shall say unto you, Lo, here is Christ; or, lo, *He is* there ; believe *him* not : for false Christs and false prophets shall rise, and shall shew signs and wonders,

would not overrun the whole land, and destroy all cities, as they had destroyed Jerusalem. Although many large towns experienced their wrath, the destruction of the land was not absolute, else there had been an extermination of the whole nation, and the entire destruction of their nationality.

75. *the elect's sake.*—For the sake of Christians, who must else have been involved in the general ruin ; and who, to the eye of God, possessed the spiritual life of the nation. It is noticeable how the presence of those who are God's servants, is ever a protection against the extremity of evil, even to those who hate and oppose them ; they are a safeguard, "the salt of the earth," a principle of life. (See Isa. vi. 13 ; Acts xxvii. 24.) So the presence of "ten righteous within the city" of Sodom, would have sufficed to preserve the cities of the plain ; so Lot's presence preserved Zoar. Another interpretation makes "the elect" those Jews hereafter to be gathered into the fold of Christ —an inferior meaning, but true in the sense in which God refuses to root up the tares growing in His field, lest the growing wheat be rooted up also, and so prematurely exterminated. The destruction of Jerusalem is said to have turned very many Jews to the Christian faith.

76. *lo, here is Christ.*—This seems to be a warning of later deceptions than the former. (Cf. note 12.) Those were the false Christs of the early apostolic age; these may be of the siege of Jerusalem. They promised deliverance from that terrible danger (App. X.). The rumour was sometimes that he was in the desert, preparing to march to their relief; sometimes that he was secretly present amongst them, ready to manifest himself, and to lead them forth to victory. And it is probable that there may be, in the last days, a further fulfilment of this warning; for scarcely any very notable event transpires, but the cry of the hasty interpreter of prophecy is raised, "Lo, He is there!" whereas Christ is perpetually present in the changes of the world's fortunes. (See note 15.)

77. *signs and wonders.*—*Signs* that herald some further manifestation, and these would address themselves to men of thought and influence ; whilst the multitude would be struck by the *wonder,* and at once follow one who could apparently suspend any common and known law of nature, and produce effects beyond their experience and comprehension. These two words are often used together of our Lord's miracles, as showing the aspect under which they were viewed— by some as signs that they should see far greater things than these;

to seduce, if *it were* possible, even the elect. But take ye heed : behold, I have foretold you all things. Wherefore if they shall say unto you, Behold, He is in the desert ; go not forth : behold, *He is* in the secret chambers ; believe *it* not. For as the lightning cometh out

by others as convincing proofs of present power, and as suggestive of things spiritual which underlie them. There is no reason to explain these signs and wonders of Antichrist as mere tricks of magic, for we read of real wonders wrought in support of his false cause, of "the working of Satan with all power and signs, and lying wonders" (2 Thess. ii. 9); and even the drawing down of fire from heaven, the great sign of God's answer to solemn invocation, will be counterfeited (Rev. xiii. 13). S. Paul supposes the case even of angels preaching another gospel, and therefore evidently determines that the signs and powers of evil must be tried by the standard of the word of God. (On the use together of " signs and wonders," see Archbishop Trench, " Notes on Miracles," p. 2.)

78. *if it were possible.*—"One of two things is implied : that if they are elect, it is not possible ; and that if it is possible, they are not elect. This doubt, therefore, in our Lord's discourse expresses the trembling in the mind of the elect." (*Gregory.*) (See John x. 28.) But reading this in connection with other passages of Scripture (such, for instance, as 2 Tim. ii. 10, where the salvation even of the elect may be endangered by the relaxation of S. Paul's efforts), we conclude that our Lord does not state the impossibility that the elect should fall away. He does not teach that after election there is no further danger from temptation ; He merely declares His foreknowledge that they would stand firm, and promises His special aid to that end. He immediately adds the words of caution, else unnecessary, "Take ye heed ; behold, I have foretold you all things." The key-note to this prophecy as a warning is, "*watch and pray ;*" "he that *endureth* to the end, the same shall be saved."

79. *desert . . . secret chambers.*—(See note 76.) Christ's presence will not be local as now ; He will not be found in any one given place, nor will there be any mystery about His presence. You need not go forth to meet Him, nor expect that He will come forth from some place of secresy to hail you.

80. *as the lightning.*—Christ's presence will be manifest from east to west—"in His universal Church," the ancient writers explain. "*Wherever* two or three are gathered together in My Name, there am I in the midst of them." He is visible by His gracious influence, as the power of electricity is visible in the flash of lightning. At the same time, to Christ's enemies, the Jews who rejected Him, He will be plainly and evidently visible in judgment. Even the Romans saw the judgment of God in the desolation of the people. Titus, naturally

of the east, and shineth even unto the west; so shall
also the coming of the Son of man be.   For wheresoever
the carcase is, there will the eagles be gathered together.

a man of humane feelings and character, justified the unprecedented
cruelties of the siege, by saying he did not dare to spare those upon
whom the wrath of God rested. So far as the words refer to the
second advent of Christ to judge the world, they speak of the suddenness of His coming, and of the universality of His presence : "Every
eye shall seek Him."   The words "cometh out of the east" have given
rise to customs connected with *orientation* which prevail in the
Christian Church : every church, and every congregation worshipping
therein, look towards the east; and so do the bodies of the Christian
dead lie eastward, as if to face their Lord, when He shall summon them
from their graves to meet Him.

81. *the carcase . . . the eagles.*—This verse has received several interpretations, and has exercised the ingenuity of commentators, both
in ancient and modern times. The ancient writers almost unanimously
interpret it of Christ; and their view, being thus general, is entitled
to the most respectful credit. They explain that Christ, who gave
His life for us, is the Body to which all Christians congregate from
every nation under heaven, as if by a common impulse. There are
passages in the prophets, and elsewhere, which ascribe the name and
characteristics of eagles to God's people, as Isa. xl. 31; and so also,
in all Christian congregations, the memorial of the Lord's Body is the
common bond of union amongst His saints. This interpretation holds
whether we consider it generally, with reference to Christ's body, as
being the bond of union of the Christian Church; or specially, with
regard to the Eucharist; or, as some have done, with regard to the
assembling of the saints to meet the Saviour, as spoke of by S. Paul
(1 Thess. iv. 17). The margin of the A. V. gives a reference to
Job xxxix. 27–30, which is a significant passage under this aspect.
We have there "the eagle," the saint, at God's command mounting
up; setting her affection on things above; dwelling and abiding in
the Rock of ages; seeking from thence her sustenance; discerning
spiritual mysteries; beholding the heavenly things at present far off;
and "where the *Slain* is, there is she." Another interpretation holds
that the body is the Jewish Church and people, chiefly congregated at
Jerusalem, but also wherever else found ; the eagles, the Roman armies,
whose well-known standard is here alluded to. A third interpretation is a very general extension of the second : that wherever the
dying body of the Jewish Church might be, there should the swift
and unerring agents of God's wrath be gathered from afar to the prey.
The spiritual meaning of these views, and their reference to the final
coming of Christ, are obvious. Of the first, that, as Christ's presence
is universal in His Church, and as His advent will be instantaneously

Immediately after the tribulation of those days there

recognized from east to west; so will assemble, with unerring certainty and speed, all who have hope in His coming. Of the second, that wherever God's enemies are found, whether they be the dying Jewish Church, or the dying world, nominally Christian, which may be rejecting Him at the last, or the sad decay of a dying Church, the agents of God's vengeance upon the impious and wicked will, " with unerring and irresistible impulse, hasten to their prey, and assemble for their destruction." Either sense (for the second and third are really as one) gives a plain and intelligible interpretation. Both may have been present in the meaning of our Lord; for it is a characteristic of prophecy to be intelligible in various ways, and to have reference to various periods, as God's eye sees many events combined to His view, and so speaks as to refer to all. But we cannot surely err in leaning towards that of the early Fathers of the Church, who probably may give us the sense of the tradition of apostolic preachers, for it is supported by the great names of Irenæus, Hilary, Origen, Chrysostom, Jerome, Ambrose, Gregory, Theophylact, and others. There is also a support given to their view by the words of our Lord Himself, in the parallel passage in Luke xvii. 37, which appears to be an earlier mention of several of the particulars gathered into this prophecy. He is describing how, of two companions occupied in the same life's duty, one shall be caught away to meet Him at His coming, and the other left; and the disciples ask, "Where, Lord?" He replies, "wheresoever the body is, thither will the eagles be gathered together" (wheresoever Christ may be, thither will His saints assemble)—a passage in which the interpretation of the ancient Church decidedly has the advantage over that of many modern commentators; for evidently those who are gathered to Christ are " the eagles," whilst His enemies are left.

82. *immediately.*—To understand the definite meaning of this word, we must know that there will be no cessation of these troubles until the end comes—nothing of any striking and separate character will intervene; and that, therefore, upon their conclusion, "immediately" will these signs that follow be seen. As soon as the Roman armies compassed Jerusalem for the second time, there came signs and wonders in the heavens and on the earth, which are detailed by Josephus. (See App. XI.) But with regard to the supreme end, we may suppose that the troubles and afflictions which still rest upon the Jewish people, and which mark the progress of the Christian era, will continue without further direct interruption, or without any further intervention of our Lord's presence, " until the times of the Gentiles be fulfilled;" and then, "immediately" on the conclusion of these, the end will come. Bishop Ellicott says, "Modern critics recognize a change of subject here: what is *above* is mainly, but not exclusively, to be referred to the destruction of Jerusalem; what *follows*, mainly, but not exclusively, to the second advent and final judgment."

shall be signs in the sun, and in the moon, and in the
stars, the sun shall be darkened, and the moon shall not
give her light, and the stars shall fall from heaven ; and
upon the earth distress of nations with perplexity ; the
sea and the waves roaring; men's hearts failing them for

83. *signs in the sun*, etc.—The testimony of Josephus may be cited
to the literal fulfilment of these several portents during the siege of
Jerusalem (see App. XI.): what fulfilment they will have at the last
of all, we cannot say until the event declares them; but the words of
S. Peter (2 Pet. iii. 10, 12) certainly point to a literal fulfilment.
The passage has from ancient times been interpreted also in a spiritual
sense, to show that there will be troubles in the Church of Christ.
Even the light of the " Sun of righteousness " will be obscured, as well
as that of the Church and her teachers, " the moon and the stars "
which borrow their light from Him, and reflect it upon the world.
Our Lord's question, " When the Son of man cometh, will He find faith
upon the earth?" seems to imply that some branches of the Church
will fail in this respect. It is probable that, coincident with some
literal and typical fulfilment of our Lord's words, this spiritual signification will be realized ; for signs of trouble in the powers of nature, are
ever significant of distress and evil amongst those who dwell upon the
earth. Bishop Goodwin gives the sun, and moon, and stars as the
religion of the Jewish Church, the government of the Jewish state, and
the judges and officers in both respectively. This may apply to the
primary fulfilment of our Lord's words, and such an interpretation is
in accordance with the usage of prophecy.

84. *stars shall fall.*—The ancient writers agree that, with regard to
stars falling, the fulfilment may be according to the Scripture rule, that
" Scripture often speaks of things, not as they are in themselves, but
as they seem and are apparent to men."

85. *upon earth.*—These words, and those below, " the tribes of the
earth," both seem to distinguish " the children of this world," whose
hopes and interest are in the things of this life, from those who are
Christ's own, the objects of His care, and subjects of His spiritual and
eternal kingdom.

86. *failing them.*—The natural consequence of the disturbance and
insecurity of the social and political world, the troubles which attend
any great convulsions of these, and of the strange portents of the
heavenly bodies coincident with these. Those who have nothing to
hope, but everything to dread, from the coming of Christ, must feel an
undefined but real fear when both heaven and earth are full of signs of
trouble. Those whose hopes are centred upon earth cannot but feel
things which affects its stability, and they will also have an instinctive
dread of further terrors impending, " of those things which are coming
upon the earth." The words of false prophets, and those who bring

fear, and for looking after those things which are coming on the earth : for the powers of heaven shall be shaken : and then shall appear the sign of the Son of man in heaven : and then shall all the tribes of the earth mourn,

out sensational volumes and pamphlets upon prophecy, and who conjure up all the old sayings of various countries, which seem to point to present troubles, will only add to the distraction of the public mind; for it is not to be expected that, when our Lord's signs of final trouble are visible, the minds of many will be able to find refuge in scepticism. To take an illustration from the end of the Jewish age, that type of the supreme end : it is not likely that the inhabitants of Jerusalem, in the last days of that city, were quite so satisfied and free from apprehension, as when they invoked upon themselves the blood of the Saviour whom they rejected. And so also, in these days of trouble, the votaries of all false religions will feel their inability to offer comfort, or to inspire confidence. Those who cannot look to a Saviour they never heard of, will not know the apprehensions of those who have rejected, or neglected, the Christ who was declared to them ; but yet there can be no sense of relief in any heart upon earth, to which Christ has not said amidst such troubles, "Lift up thine head; thy redemption draweth nigh."

87. *the powers of heaven.*—This may mean, not merely the greater heavenly bodies which would be included in "the sun, and moon, and stars," but the laws which govern these with regard to earth, the force and influences which they exercise upon it, and perhaps also those which belong to, and control, the atmosphere which surrounds us. Spiritually, the controlling, purifying, and sustaining influences of the Church upon the world will be shaken and weakened.

88. *sign of the Son of man.*—This also appears to have a double reference to the troubles which ended the Jewish state, and to those of the final doom. The Jews, whether or not they interpreted of Christ's advent the various signs recorded by Josephus, must have seen, in the destruction of their Church and city, the triumph of Christ who foretold it ; and, in the crucifixion of so many thousands of their countrymen outside the city gates, the fulfilment of their imprecation upon themselves of the responsibility of His blood. It was evident then to multitudes of them, that they had rejected the true Christ, for it is impossible that the hopes and warnings of the Christians, and their entire freedom from these troubles, should altogether escape the notice of the inhabitants of a city wherein Christ had been so long preached, and His words proclaimed. But its fulfilment in the latter days must be interpreted by the event; whatever it may be, every one living upon earth who has heard of Christ, will recognize it as "the sign of the Son of man." Most ancient, and many modern, commentators concur in the conjecture that this sign will be the sign of the cross, the early

and they shall see the Son of man coming in the clouds
of heaven with power and great glory.　And when
these things begin to come to pass, then look up, and

Church being almost unanimous in this opinion ; and certainly nothing
is to us so distinctive a sign of Christ, as that of which He says Himself, " Whosoever doth not bear his cross and come after Me, cannot
be My disciple."　"The sign of the cross shall be in heaven," says T.
à Kempis, " when the Lord shall come to judgment.　Then all the
servants of the cross who in their lifetime conformed themselves to
Christ crucified, shall draw near unto Christ the Judge with great confidence."　Those who abuse the sign of the cross to superstitious purposes must be utterly worthy of condemnation, as abusers of the mark
of Christ ; but, on the other hand, the bigotry of those who cannot bear
to look upon a cross, whether represented pictorially, or as a decoration
of their Church, or as worn by any Christian personally, to whose
mind it speaks only of superstition, is scarcely less to be condemned.
There is not much to choose between the excesses of superstition and of
Puritanism.　Both should remember that our Lord speaks of the cross
as a distinction of discipleship, and therefore it should neither be made
a sign of superstition, or of party, or a sign that is spoken against ;
and they should remember also that the early Church expected (though
the expectation may *possibly* be erroneous) that this sign will be also
" the sign of the Son of man in heaven."　When Christianity became
the religion of the empire, the cross was assumed as its standard.　But,
however spiritually, or literally, it may be regarded as the sign or
the emblem of our redemption and our profession, to no one who
abuses it superstitiously, or who repudiates it puritanically, can it be
heartily said, " *In hoc signo vinces.*"　Those who are not influenced by
either of these errors will most charitably judge those who are so, by
remembering how differently human minds are constituted ; some being
keenly sensitive to the expression of the thing signified in the sign,
others being affected in an entirely opposite direction.　Dean Mansel
sees an earlier verification of this sign in the spread upon earth of the
religion of the cross ; he also interprets " *the angels* " of Matt. xxiv. 31
of the preachers of the Gospel.

　89. *coming in the clouds.*—Here our Lord speaks of His second
advent.　(See Matt. xxv. 31–46 ; and sect. xxi.)　The expression
" *clouds* " sometimes signifies angels.　(Cf. Ps. civ. 4, lxvii. 17 ; Rev.
i. 7 ; Matt. xvi. 27.)

　90. *look up.*—That which every soul of man, and every system of
religion, and every earthly enterprise and interest which is uncon-
nected with Christ—that which causes all the tribes of the earth to
mourn for the knowledge that they are none of His, will be the sign
of triumph and assured happiness to all who love His Name.　The day of
the world's doom will prove the day of their redemption (Isa. xxv. 9).

lift up your heads; for your redemption draweth nigh.
And He shall send His angels with a great sound of a
trumpet, and they shall gather together His elect from
the four winds, from one end of heaven to the other.

Now learn a parable of the fig tree; When his branch
is yet tender, and putteth forth leaves, ye know that
summer *is* nigh : so likewise ye, when ye shall see these
things, know that it is near, *even* at the doors.   Verily I
say unto you, This generation shall not pass away, till

91. *a parable.*—Gk. "*the* parable," *i.e.* its own proper lesson.   S.
Luke gives "the fig tree and all the trees;" there is thus this parable
from nature in every land.   The "putting forth of leaves" is the unfolding of indications of the approaching advent of Christ; the development
of Antichrist, and the signs and troubles above referred to, are indications of the event in its several senses.

92. *it is near.*—*i.e.* "the kingdom of God is nigh at hand" (Luke
xxi. 31).   The advent of the Gospel was nigh at hand in the hour of
the destruction of Jerusalem; the approach of the heavenly kingdom
will be nigh at the last hour of time upon earth.

93. *this generation.*—This prediction was literally fulfilled; the destruction of the Jewish Church took place within forty years from the
date at which our Lord foretold it.   There was also, no doubt, a reference to the great end; and in the earliest ages it was so understood.
But the misconception of the term *generation*, in the extended sense of
prophecy, led Christians of those days to suppose the end immediately
near; and it needed all the exhortation of SS. Peter and Paul to convince them that it was not immediate.   The word rendered " generation "
is, by the best critics, allowed to have the wider sense of *race ;* and so to
imply that the Jewish race, now distinct even in its degradation, would
not pass away from earth as a separate people until the second advent
of Christ.   The same use of the Greek word which is rendered " generation " both in the Latin and English version, is found in Deut. xxxii. 5,
" A perverse and crooked generation;" Ps. xiv. (Greek version, xiii.) 5,
" God is in the generation of the righteous;" Ps. xxiv. 6, " This is the
generation of them that seek Him ;" Jer. vii. 29, " The generation of Thy
wrath" (the reference is probably to Deut. xxxii. 5, as is more clearly
marked in the Greek and Latin versions); and in Ps. lxxiii. 15, " The
generation of thy children," where the Latin version has " nation."
Our Lord seems to use the same word in its extended sense in Luke
xvi. 8: " The children of this world are in their generation wiser than
the children of light" (Latin and English versions, " generation ").
There is no doubt of the classical use of the Greek word here spoken of,
in the sense both of a nation in all its periods, and also as describing
those of the same characteristics and peculiarities; in fact, in a sense far

all these things be fulfilled. Heaven and earth shall
pass away, but My words shall not pass away.
    But of that day and *that* hour knoweth no man, no,

less restricted than the ordinary one, of a generation of the average
lifetime of man.   But it is of great consequence to notice the use of it
in the LXX. version of the Scripture—so familiar to our Lord and to the
men of His time—in corroboration of the extension of His words to the
time of the second advent, as foretelling that the Jewish nation, as
a separate and distinct *race* (and perhaps also as retaining its
characteristic attitude of unbelief toward Christianity, namely, as a
" perverse, crooked, and untoward generation "), will continue " until
the times of the Gentiles are fulfilled," when brighter days are in
prospect for them, and, through them, for the Gentile world (Rom. xi.
12, 15, 25).   There is also another meaning of the word " generation "
even more strongly supported by Holy Scripture, and by the classical
usage of the word, in accordance with which some of the earliest writers
of Christianity have understood " generation " to mean " dispensation ; " thus implying that no further dispensation of religion will be
revealed to men, but that the Church of Christ will endure to the end
of time.   In this sense are Ps. xiv. 5, xxiv. 6, and Luke xvi. 8,
above referred to ; and if those characterized by a common characteristic
may be termed a generation, so also we may have the generation of
Christians, *i.e.* the Church of Christ.   We may therefore give our
Lord's meaning thus : " This generation shall not die (forty years shall
not elapse) before all that I have spoken of the doom of Jerusalem
shall be fulfilled ; this generation of people, this Jewish race, shall not
pass from earth as a separate people distinct and peculiar, until My
second advent ; this generation of My people, this Christian dispensation, shall not be closed, or superseded by any further revelation, until
I come again in My glory."
    94. *of that day and hour.*—The approximate time had been declared,
the signs which should herald it were detailed, enough had been said to
warn the watchful ; but the precise time, " the day and hour," was
not to be revealed, being one of those " times and seasons which the
Father hath put in His own power," and veiled from all else.   It was
for no man, however vigilant, and for no angel watcher to know this,
nor for the Son of Man, but for the Father only.   The exact time,
both of the destruction of Jerusalem, and, much more, of the final end,
are not revealed by God to man ; nor is the individual hour of the
death of each revealed, however numerous and marked be the warnings
of life.   Probably we may infer that, though *known*, neither of these
last eras are *fixed*, as we are bidden to pray that God's kingdom may
come ; and as its advent is said to be advanced or hindered by the
prayers, and faith, and diligences of the Church, or by her failure in
these, so is the date of death known, but perhaps not decided.   Within

not the angels which are in heaven, neither the Son, but

certain limits, a control of its term may be permitted to man, in his care or abuse of the rules of life. (See xx. 24.) We cannot know the point when God's will and decision become absolute; we do know that when, to His eye, "the hour is come, *immediately* He putteth in the sickle."

95. *neither the Son.*—This statement has perplexed many; and some heretics (especially the Arians), who have denied the Divinity of our Lord, have quoted it in support of their theories. (See xxv. *b.* 21.) But Christ came on earth as perfect man; as one who grew in stature, understanding, and knowledge, like other men. His Divinity did not take away from the perfection of His manhood, or supersede it. As man, and as prophet, He knew what God revealed to Him, and as God's Messenger, sent upon a special service, He could only do the works which God gave Him to do, and declare what God commissioned Him to speak. (See xvii. 19.) "Let common sense decide," says S. Hilary, "whether it is credible that He who is the cause of all things that be, and are to be, should be ignorant of any out of all these things. And can He be ignorant of that day which is the day of His own advent? His ignorance must be connected with the hiding of the treasures of wisdom which are in Him." To the same point speaks Bishop Latimer: "Neither did Christ Himself know it as He was man; but as He was God He knoweth all things: nothing can be hid from Him, as He saith Himself, 'The Father showeth Me all things;' therefore His knowledge is infinite, else He were not very God. But as concerning His manhood, He knew not that time; for He was a very natural man, sin excepted. He had perfect knowledge to do His Father's commission, to instruct us, to teach us the way to heaven; but it was not His commission to tell us the hour of that day. Therefore He knew not this day to tell us of it anything, as concerning when it should be." If Christ therefore spoke of any limit or measure of His power, He spoke of what is common to man. If He spoke of any limitation of what He might reveal, or what He might give to mankind (as in the somewhat similar statement in Matt. xx. 23, where He could only confer the dignities of His heavenly kingdom upon those for whom they were prepared of His Father), He spoke as God's true and faithful Messenger of the covenant, who did the will of God, and spoke only as God gave Him commandment. In these characters, being "inferior to the Father," He knew only what God gave Him to know; as Himself Divine, He knew all things, as He had created and ordained all things, being one with the Father. With the point of difficulty as to what belonged to Christ's perfect manhood, and to His perfect Godhead, we have nothing to do; we cannot understand it. But we must not, as many have done, try to escape from a difficulty by evading it,—by saying, for instance, that, as far as *we* are concerned, Christ did not know; or that He meant to say He might not tell to

the Father.   But as the days of Noe *were*, so shall also
the coming of the Son of man be.   For as in the days
that were before the flood they were eating and drinking,

us the time of the end.   The union of the two natures in Christ is a
mystery to us, who cannot even comprehend the union of the " reasonable soul and flesh " in ourselves.   Christ, we are assured, spoke the
exact and direct truth ; and we need not attempt to explain away His
words, to make them intelligible to ourselves, and to avoid appearing
to discredit His omniscience.   Canon Liddon (quoting SS. Irenæus,
Athanasius, Gregory Nazianzen, and Cyril of Alexandria) takes the
literal view, that, " as God, Christ did know the day of judgment, but
it was consistent with the law of self-humiliation prescribed by His
infinite love, that He should assume all the conditions of real humanity ;
and therefore, with the rest, a limitation of knowledge."   " At the
particular time of His speaking, the human soul of Christ was restricted
as to its range of knowledge in one particular direction."   (See also
Hooker, " Ecclesiastical Polity," v. 54, 7.)

96. *the days of Noe.*—In S. Luke's earlier record of some of the
predictions of our Lord (which He now gathers into one perfect prophecy), we find the destruction of Sodom also given as a type of the
wrath of the last day.   There are thus three great types placed before
us, in each of which judgment comes suddenly on those unprepared,
but not without warning : the Flood, the destruction of the cities of
the plain, and the destruction of Jerusalem.   S. Peter, writing before
that last era, speaks of the judgment of the angels who fell, of the
world of the Flood, and of the sinners of the cities of the plain, as
warnings to the world.

97. *eating and drinking.*—Mention is not made of their irreligious
lives, their sins and blasphemies, but only of their ordinary occupa-
tions.   The picture of those over whom heavy doom was impending is
one of great unconcern, of entire absorption in the usual routine of a
careless life.   They were not thinking of the warnings of 120 years
uttered by Noah as a " preacher of righteousness."   The progress of
the Ark was also a warning, seen or heard of amongst them.   But, for
all this, the end was absolutely sudden, because they were unprepared
for it.   It will be so at the end of the world.   When all the bustle of
life is going on as usual, all the business of life replete with care and
anxiety, with eagerness and provision ; when the world is full of life and
energy, and work and enterprise, the full tide of its progress will be stayed
by the advent of Christ.   Its suddenness will be awful to all ; but there
will be those who are not surprised, and those who are taken by surprise.   In the reference of this warning to the inhabitants of Jerusalem,
there was the same suddenness.   Our Lord's warning allowed for the
escape of the Christians, but to all others the gates were besieged, and
they were shut in within the doomed city ; and the end itself came
upon them as a snare—they were ensnared in their ruin.

marrying and giving in marriage, until the day that Noe entered into the ark, and knew not until the flood came, and took them all away ; so shall also the coming of the Son of man be.   Then shall two bé in the field ; the one shall be taken, and the other left.   Two *women shall be* grinding at the mill ; the one shall be taken, and the other left.

Watch therefore : for ye know not what hour your Lord doth come.   But know this, that if the good-

98. *the one shall be taken.*—This is a very remarkable statement. It shows that all will be engaged in the interests of their life, in which both good and bad are partners, bound by all the closest ties of a common calling, or of relationship. They will be engaged, one as the other, with their ordinary business ; but to Christ's eye there is a difference, and by Him there will be made a separation. The one will be taken by the angels to meet his Lord ; the other left to the terrible wrath of the judgment upon the wicked, and upon those who forget God. There is in these words especially, as in the other parts of this prophecy, a reference to our individual end ; for the vast multitude of those for whom the day of judgment is set will not be surprised by it, as not being then alive upon earth. But to all there is a day of Christ's coming : in the hour of our death He severs in the same way amongst us. Of those engaged in the same interests of life, or of the same family circle, each is, in his turn, taken, whilst others are left behind ; mortal sickness calls each more or less suddenly away in turn, and one is taken to Christ, another is left by Him. The end comes always with suddenness to those who are off their guard, though not perhaps with the extreme suddenness with which the world's life shall be stayed to those who are alive on earth at Christ's appearing. The passage has received, from some commentators, a millennial application.

99. *watch therefore.*—As the end will be so sudden, and the separation so unexpected and complete, the only hope of safety lies in watching. This is the point, the key-note, of the whole prophecy. Many signs and wonders are given, and the prospect of the end is unfolded ; the exact date only is withheld, that men may be always expecting Christ, and always ready. And here, too, the warning becomes a personal one ; it is no longer what shall befall Jerusalem, or what is the end of the world, which is made prominent, but our individual interest in the end. For as that end finds us, our condition will remain for ever ; and Christians have not to look to either of these great catastrophes, as necessarily closing our own probation, the one being past in ages long distant. But the hour of death closes our prospects as thoroughly as will the day of judgment those of the living, who hear the herald angel proclaim that time shall be no longer, and " Behold, the Bridegroom cometh ! "

man of the house had known in what watch the thief
would come, he would have watched, and would not have
suffered his house to be broken up. Therefore be ye
also ready : for in such an hour as ye think not the Son
of man cometh. Who then is a faithful and wise servant, whom his lord hath made ruler over his household,

100. *the goodman.*—An old English term equivalent to master of
the house. In this similitude it, of course, means the disciple of Christ.

101. *the thief.*—This is Christ ; but He here adopts the view that
an enemy might take of Him. As this man had suffered his house to
be broken through in his negligence, he did not take any right view of
the arrival of Christ, whose coming shattered all his hopes, and broke
in upon all his cherished and selfish purposes. There is something of
the same hostility manifested in the view of the slothful servant in
the parable of the talents, to whose mind his lord was simply an
" austere man." Whether regarded in this light, or as the thief in the
night, who robs those whom He surprises of their false security, our
Lord does not condescend to notice the injustice or indignity of this
view ; the answer in either case is, that, if He were what He is supposed to be, it was all the more important to provide against His
coming. " Be ye also ready," is still His charge. (See xx. 17, 22.)
Hilary gives a different view ; He takes " the thief " to mean the
devil ; and, therefore, that had the Christian known the hour and
occasion of temptation, he would have been on the watch, and guarded
his faith ; for his opportunity is when men are off their guard. This
sense is by no means untenable ; but the majority of writers take the
view above stated, which, indeed, best agrees with the context. A
parallel may be seen in our Lord's representation of Himself as the
good *Samaritan* (so the Fathers interpret the parable). The Jews held
Samaritans utterly reprobate.

102. *broken up.*—Gk. " digged through." Many houses in the
East are of mud, or of sun-dried bricks, and the way of forcible entry
would be to dig through the mass of earthwork. (See Job xxiv. 16.)

103. *who then.*—(See Luke xii. 41, 42.) The exhortation now turns
to all to whom authority is given in Christ's Church, especially to the
ministers and stewards of His mysteries. He asks, " Who is faithful
and wise ? " that each may examine his life, and answer accordingly.

104. *faithful and wise.*—" Faithful " to Christ's interests, to his duty,
and to souls entrusted to his guidance ; " wise " in heavenly wisdom,
prudence, discretion, in the knowledge of men, and of skill to influence
them ; forbearing and merciful in his views of character, for this, too,
is wisdom ; and wise in the fear of the Lord, which is " the beginning
of wisdom."

105. *his household.*—" Thy household the Church " (Collect for
22nd Sunday after Trinity).

to give them meat in due season? Blessed is that servant, whom his lord when he cometh shall find him so doing. Verily I say unto you, That he will make him ruler over all his goods. But and if that evil servant shall say in his heart, My lord delayeth his coming; and shall begin to smite his fellow-servants, and to eat and drink with the drunken; the lord of that servant

106. *meat.*—S. Luke has, "their portion of meat." One who "rightly divides the word of truth," and is wise in his discrimination of those entrusted to His care, will know how to give the portion, both in quality and in quantity, which is best for them. (See John xvi. 12; 1 Cor. iii. 1, 2; Heb. v. 12–14.) Although the Scriptures contain that truth which can save every soul, it is not wise to set the same aspect of truth before every mind upon every occasion; nor will each take the same view of Christ's Gospel. Circumstances, temper, position, the pressure of sorrow, or freedom from it, the consciousness of sin, and many another accident, combine to influence our view of truth. The Church of Rome is so conscious, and over-sensitive, of the danger of an indiscriminate study of Scripture, that she closes the holy book to the general reader, and gives forth authorized portions. But the "faithful and wise servant" will keep nothing back of all that God has spoken; but yet he will know when, and where, and how to bring forward the varied riches of Christ's righteousness. "Every scribe which is instructed unto the kingdom of heaven" (the Gospel of Christ) "bringeth forth out of his treasure things new and old" (Matt. xiii. 52).

107. *ruler.*—The same prospect of reward and distinction in the joy of their Lord, which is opened to the good and faithful servant in the parable of the talents. The word rendered "appoint Him," really means to establish. It conveys a permanent and irrevocable force—he has earned in time the reward of eternity.

108. *to smite.*—To abuse his lawful authority for purposes of oppression, as did the Pharisees; to persecute and destroy, instead of exercising the wisdom of discrimination and tolerance; to sit as a "lord over Christ's heritage," instead of ministering to the necessities and weakness of Christ's brethren. Enough had been displayed of this spirit of priestly domination in the Jewish Church. (See Ezek. xxxiv.)

109. *to eat and drink.*—The danger of luxury and gross indulgence is here expressed. It is impossible for those to rouse the spirit of piety and temperance in their people, who are associated in the excesses, not perhaps of a vicious life, but of self-indulgence, with those amongst whom they ought to show themselves "a pattern of good works," and whose certain duty it is to be cautious, lest even their good shall be evil spoken of.

shall come in a day when he looketh not for *him*, and in an hour that he is not aware of, and shall cut him asunder, and appoint *him* his portion with the hypocrites: there shall be weeping and gnashing of teeth.

Take ye heed, watch and pray: for ye know not when the time is. *For the Son of man is* as a man taking a far journey, who left his house, and gave authority to

110. *cut him asunder.*—A terrible and severe punishment under Eastern kings, elsewhere illustrated in Scripture. It represents the utter severance from all hope and prospect of happiness, from all privileges and opportunities of religion, and from the reward and life of the righteous servant; including a reference to the temporal severance of soul and body in death, in that sense judicial, as well as to future and final punishment.

111. *with the hypocrites.*—Those whom our Lord has above (see xiv.) branded with the most entire reprobation. The "evil servant" acts the part, and assumes the office and privileges, of a "faithful and wise servant," and caricatures his true character amongst those under his charge, thus giving a false representation of his Lord's service. Trapp says, "Hypocrites, then, are the freeholders of hell; other sinners are but as tenants and inmates to them."

112. *weeping,* etc.—See viii. 33.

113. *take ye heed.*—This passage from S. Mark seems a summary of the warning given in S. Matthew's words, and of the spirit of the parables of the ten virgins and of the talents, concisely stated, with, if anything, an extent of application. It is spoken to the Apostles, and to Christ's servants, their successors in every age. He addresses them in the supposition of their being faithful servants; for we must note that the master of the house here, who may come to them at any watch of the day or night, is the same who surprises the careless servant, who did not know in what watch he would come, and who looked on his lord as a thief in the night. (See notes 99, 101.)

114. *far journey.*—He went from earth to heaven, and left His household the Church in the hands of His Apostles, and their successors.

115. *authority.*—He left His authority in the Church collectively, to ordain rites and ceremonies, to bind and to loose in His name; and, to those "appointed to any office and ministration in the same," there is left personal authority for the execution of their duty within the rules and ordinances of His Church, and of their commission. He is present to ratify and confirm their words in His behalf. It is well that we should observe that Christ has left "*authority*" to His *servants*, and reverence their office for His sake; and that it is not an office or authority to be usurped, even from good motives, by any who are not "lawfully called, and sent to execute the same." (See App. XIV.)

his servants, and to every man his work, and commanded the porter to watch. Watch ye therefore : for ye know not when the master of the house cometh, at even, or at midnight, or at cockcrowing, or in the morn-

116. *his servants.*—The Apostles, and their successors, in the various orders of the ministry of His word and sacraments.

117. *to every man.*—To every individual member of His Church is work assigned in His behalf. The responsibility and reward of working for Him are not confined to those in authority; all may work for Him, as they do their life's duty in the world. For, as every one who comes into the world has a life's occupation assigned to him, together with his "daily bread" (that is, "all things needful for the soul and body"), by God's good gift; so is it with spiritual matters. Every one has his appointed work in Christ's kingdom; it comes within the conditions of his daily life, and is as thoroughly his proper duty as is any duty of his ordinary life—quite as much so as is the case with those whose duty of life lies altogether in the ministry of the Gospel ; indeed, there are cases where the ordinary workman may "receive a prophet's reward" (Matt. x. 41). The chief reason why we have life assigned to us at all, is that we might live as probationers for eternity in the midst of the experiences of the world. However subordinate the claim of religion may be upon our time to that of our life's calling, the interests of religion are paramount; and therefore our Lord reminds us that He has apportioned to every man his work.

118. *the porter.*—(See John x. 3.) This is no humble or unimportant official; He is one who gives admission into the Church of Christ, and who rouses the servants of Christ to their work. This is a post, in the service of Christ's ministry, of honour at the very least. Some commentators explain it to be S. Peter, to whom was committed the keys; and, more generally, S. Gregory understands it of the order of the clergy, to whose care the Church is committed ; but others of the ancient writers understood it of the Holy Spirit Himself, whose office it is to watch over, and guard, the Church during Christ's absence from earth, and to rouse it to newness of life and energy, and whose office at the entry of each one into the fold of Christ is so indispensably necessary, that, "except a man be born of water and of *the Spirit,* he cannot (even) *enter* into the kingdom of God." Man may confer the outward sign, but he cannot inspire the spiritual grace which is given simultaneously with the sign. Therefore it is no ordinary minister of Christ's Church who is "the porter."

119. *at even.*—(See xxvii. 14.) The "watches" here enumerated are those of the Roman sentinels, reaching from six in the evening to six in the morning ; these had become regular measures of time amongst the Jews. The watchers of the *night* are mentioned, as life itself is a night to those who are "children of the day" of eternity ;

ing : lest coming suddenly he find you sleeping.   And
what I say unto you I say unto all, Watch.

And take heed to yourselves, lest at any time your
hearts be overcharged with surfeiting, and drunkenness,
and cares of this life, and *so* that day come upon you
unawares.   For as a snare shall it come on all them
that dwell on the face of the whole earth.   Watch ye

life on earth being the night to which the glorious day of eternity
succeeds.   The watchers may represent the various periods of our age,
for the experience of all is that Christ comes at every period, from
infancy to extreme old age—as some of the Fathers explain those words,
" many shall come from the east " (when the sun of life is rising),
" and from the west " (when the sun is setting in the clouds of death).
And none can foresee the hour of his Lord's coming to himself, or can
over-estimate the importance of watching for Him.   The " watches "
may also represent the ages of the Church, and of time's progress in
this dispensation.

120. *sleeping.*—It is not stated that they were engaged in any
wicked courses, like the " evil servant ; " it is enough that they were
slumbering.   This charge will probably include far more than those
who fall under the condemnation of wilful sin ; it comprehends all
all who are excellent and praiseworthy in life and action (this any
heathen may be), but live without any reference to Christ's life—they
are asleep as to that inner life—and also those who are not abusing
their trust, but are simply negligent of it, and of their Lord's interest.
The slothful servant in the parable of the talents, is a *wicked* servant
because he is slothful.   " The wicked shall be turned into hell, and all
the people that *forget* God " (Ps. ix. 17).

121. *unto all.*—There is no minister of Christ's Gospel, and no
member of His Catholic Church, in any age of His dispensation, who is
not included in this warning.

122. *surfeiting . . . cares.*—" They did eat, they drank, they married wives, they were given in marriage . . . they bought, they sold,
they planted, they builded "—these are our Lord's summary of the vices
and distractions of life in the days which He speaks of as typical of
those of the Jewish state, of the close of life generally, and of the end
of the world especially (Luke xvii. 27, 28).

123. *as a snare.*—As a *hand-net* thrown unawares over birds resting
and slumbering on the ground. (See note 124.)   Such is the full force
of the Greek word.

124. *that dwell.*—Gk. " that sit."   The word denotes the rest and
security of those who are settled down unsuspicious of danger, against
which they take no precaution, being quite absorbed in the interests
to which they have postponed every higher aim and aspiration, and

therefore, and pray always, that ye may be accounted worthy to escape all these things that shall come to pass, and to stand before the Son of man.

XIX. *PARABLE OF THE TEN VIRGINS.*

S. Matt. xxv. 1–13.

Then shall the kingdom of heaven be likened unto ten virgins, which took their lamps, and went forth to meet

every hope of another life. They sit down to the enjoyment of their existence here, and will not think that it is not their rest, and that they are " dwelling " in the very extremity of peril.

125. *and to stand.*—These concluding words form the most stirring exhortation to vigilance of life, that even our Lord has spoken. The mention of the terrors of wrath so suddenly to be manifested, and so inevitable, which they who are found watching shall escape; their standing confessed and welcomed before the heavenly company, more bright and blessed than man's heart can conceive of, and in the presence of majesty so divine and so gracious as that of the Son of man " upon the throne of His glory; " and then, also, the conviction that they are by all—and especially by God Himself (Rev. iii. 4, 5)—" accounted worthy to stand " there, form altogether a succession of prospects so dazzling, that no thought of human ambition can find expression in comparison with " the hope set before us in the Gospel."

1. *then.*—This parable, and the next, are in continuation of the subject of our Lord's advent. The mention of " the kingdom of heaven " shows that He has ceased to refer at all to the fall of Jerusalem, but is speaking of the Gospel dispensation, and of the hour of death, and of the final judgment. When He comes in this way, " then shall the kingdom of heaven," the circumstances of the Christian dispensation, be seen to resemble the following parable.

2. *ten virgins.*—This term *virgins* implies that they possessed the true faith pure and undefiled; the sins of apostasy, of the profession of a false faith, of heresy, and of idolatry, are termed spiritual fornication, in Holy Scripture. The term *ten* expresses a Jewish notion of completeness. Our Lord uses the same number on several occasions; we read of the " ten pieces of silver," the " ten talents," the " ten servants," and " ten pounds." There are far more numerous illustrations of this favourite number in the Old Testament. Abraham summed up his pleading for the cities of the plain in the words, " Peradventure ten shall be found there; " on going to demand Rebekah for Isaac, Abraham's servant took ten camels with him, and the weight of the

the bridegroom. And five of them were wise, and five
were foolish. They that *were* foolish took their lamps,
and took no oil with them: but the wise took oil in their

bracelets was ten shekels of gold. It seems also to have been the
number for a propitiatory present. Jacob sent ten bulls and ten foals
as a present to Esau ; Joseph sent to his father ten asses, and ten she-
asses, laden with the good things of Egypt ; David took ten loaves with
him, and ten cheeses for the captain of his brother's company, when
he went down to the host assembled in the valley of Elah. This
number also entered into the measurement of holy things. The
curtains of the Tabernacle were ten ; the width of the sea of brass in
the Temple of Solomon was ten cubits from brim to brim ; there were
ten bases also, and ten lavers of brass. Amongst instruments of
music, we find the " instrument of ten strings," or the " ten-stringed
lute," frequently mentioned in the Book of Psalms. In fact, the
instances of the use of this number are so frequent, that it is difficult
not to notice its significance amongst Scripture writers. A reference
to a concordance to Holy Scripture, will give ample and varied
illustrations.

3. *their lamps.*—The outward expression of their faith; the use of
means of grace; whatever, in short, may seem to display the inward
spiritual grace.

4. *went forth,* etc.—The Vulgate and many of the Latin Fathers, read,
" to meet the bridegroom *and bride.*" Maldonatus argues in favour of
the reading; but it has very little support from Greek versions, and is
doubtless a corruption from the margin. The bride was not then with
Christ, the bride being the Church. They " went forth " from the
world that lieth in wickedness and ignorance, to meet Christ in the
actions of a life regulated by His rules and example.

5. *five were foolish.*—Gk. " *the five;*" *i.e.* the other five. These
were not absolutely wicked servants, living in open opposition to
Christ, utterly despising and rejecting His faith; they were, on the
contrary, professors of His religion, claiming its privileges, and assuming
to themselves its hopes and promises. But their folly consisted in their
neglect of the real spirit of His Gospel; they were content with their
formality. Some writers make the wise those who had faith, and also
the works of faith; the foolish, those who had faith without works, *i.e.*
a dead faith (James ii. 26).

6. *oil.*—The grace of the Holy Spirit, which alone can give life, and
true light, to the outward profession of religion.

7. *their vessels.*—The general meaning is, that they possessed and
used the means of replenishing their souls with the gift of a spiritual
life; and they were careful not only to profess the faith, but to lead
holy and useful lives in the practice of the works of faith. The expression itself belongs to the circumstances of the parable, and may

vessels with their lamps. While the bridegroom tarried, they all slumbered and slept.

not be too closely pressed. The parable itself gives an exact representation of customs observed at marriage festivals in the East; the bridegroom arrives with the bride, whom he is conducting to his own home. A traveller in India mentions his witnessing just such a procession as this arrive at the bridegroom's house at the dead of night. As it approached, the voices of criers proclaimed, to those who were waiting to meet it, the very terms of the parable, "Behold, the bridegroom cometh; go forth to meet him;" and he records his vivid realization of the exclusion of those who arrived too late, as the great doors were closed in the face of the crowd outside,—a daily occurrence at such festivals.

8. *tarried.*—Our Lord here shows that He might tarry beyond the time expected; this being one of many suggestions given by our Lord and His Apostles, that this would be the case with regard to the second advent.

9. *all slumbered and slept.*—The words are expressive. They denote the gradual and entire cessation of watchfulness; first the dozing, then the falling into deep sleep. The sentence itself has given rise to much criticism, as it is declared that *all* slept, both the wise and the foolish. Many of the ancient writers explain that the sleep of death is meant, which is common to all, but in the awakening from which there is so great a difference; others, that the virgins became more or less forgetful of their duty, until, when roused, it was too late for the foolish to be prepared, and the wise had only just time to make themselves ready. But there is nothing in the discourse of which this parable is a part, to show that our Lord anticipated that every disciple would fail in his duty. Such has never been the case in any age of Christianity past. Perhaps the most suitable explanation, and best supported, is that, during the interval of waiting upon earth, all are absorbed in the duties of life; for it is impossible that men can be entirely oblivious of their duties, even in the occupation of religion. But the difference amongst men is this, that, whilst the wise are fully engaged in their life's work, they are not forgetful therein of their Lord's paramount interests. They may not be thinking of Him or expecting Him on the instant, and so far may not be watching; but the moment the call is given, they are ready. They were living in a state of preparation, however momentarily unprepared. The attitude of their mind was preparation, their work an anticipation of a future account; and therefore they "slept," or rested, in calm and assured confidence in their Lord, with regard to the hour of His coming. The best illustration of this state, and the instant response to the call, is in the words of Solomon's song, so generally interpreted as conveying, spiritually, truths concerning the "mystical union which is betwixt Christ and His

And at midnight there was a cry made, Behold, the bridegroom cometh; go ye out to meet him. Then all those virgins arose, and trimmed their lamps. And the foolish said unto the wise, Give us of your oil; for our lamps are gone out. But the wise answered, saying,

Church:" "I sleep, but my heart waketh: it is the voice of my beloved that knocketh, saying, Open to me. . . . I rose up to open to my beloved" (Cant. v. 2–5). The foolish were so totally absorbed in the routine of their worldly occupation, that they had given no earnest thought to the spiritual requirements of the true faith which they professed with their lips. Like the "two men in one bed" (Luke xvii. 34), of whom one was taken from his sleep to everlasting life, the other left in death; so the wise, being ready, are taken in with their Lord, the foolish are left outside. If the *sleep* in this instance is interpreted of a common abstraction in the affairs of the world's business, it coincides with the above interpretation; if of death, then with that of the ancient writers.

10. *at midnight.*—There had been long delay; the night was far advanced when the long-expected summons broke their slumbers. There was a persuasion early current in the Church, that our Lord would return at midnight, at Easter time; and so the congregations on Easter Eve did not separate until the hour of midnight was past. Their service was a vigil in the true sense of the word.

11. *a cry.*—"The voice of the archangel, and the trump of God" (1 Thess. iv. 16); or perhaps the cry of watchers in the Church—for instance, of the "porter," to whom it was commanded to watch. (See xviii. 118.)

12. *go ye out.*—No longer in the duties of life (note 4), but in the hour of final account of the performance of those duties.

13. *trimmed their lamps.*—They hastily examined their state on the instant of the summons, which, it appears, a little preceded the arrival of the bridegroom. So there is generally some interval between the coming of death and its arrival, which we conclude from this parable to be almost useless as a season of repentance. In fact, if the interpretation of the ancient writers above mentioned is adopted, nothing could be more conclusive than this parable against trusting to a "death-bed repentance." There may be time to discover the worthlessness of a profession of faith without the works of faith, and to make a hurried and ineffectual attempt (with the help of those who minister the means of grace, and of those means themselves) to reverse, on the moment, the consequences of an ill-spent life. But the parable discourages all trust in such a venture—the doors of heaven open only to those who are ready.

14. *are gone out.*—Or, " are going out." They have glimmered through the season of their slumbers with a fitful and waning gleam

Not so, lest there be not enough for us and you : but go ye rather to them that sell, and buy for yourselves. And while they went to buy, the bridegroom came ; and they that were ready went in with him to the marriage : and the door was shut.   Afterward came also the other

of light, but now they are flickering to expire.   It is difficult to assert that there is no grace and no light in any life, until the end proves it ; but often the light which is going out, will expire in the moment when it should be raised to burn clearly.   There is not grace sufficient in the careless life to meet the crisis, and it dies.

15. *not enough.*—There was not too much for themselves, for the oil in their lamps was the oil of God's grace, and none of their own, further than they had made it theirs by diligent and prayerful use. For, with regard to the life of those who have lived best, our Lord bids them say, "We are unprofitable servants ; we have done that which was our duty to do."   Clearly, therefore, they could have no "merits of supererogation" to assign for the benefit of those who had not done their duty.   It is strange that the Romish doctrine concerning these merits should look to this passage for support ; for the sequel here shows the entire futility of dependence on such hope, for the "door was shut" against these virgins.   The words "not so," which precede, are not in the original ; which, though it shows the inability of the wise to comply, does not express their distinct refusal, which they are charitably reluctant to declare, whilst they advise their foolish companions to make the best of any hope there is at such a moment of supreme need.   This omission of refusal is expressive.

16. *go ye.*—Not spoken in unkindness or irony, but as the only advice possible at that moment of agony.   They might hope against hope that it would not prove too late.

17. *them that sell.*—God's commissioned agencies, the means of grace, His holy word, repentance, prayer, holy living ; and all these are, in a more direct sense, in the hands of "them that sell," the agents of His grace, His appointed ministers.   Dean Alford sees here an argument for "a set and appointed ministry ; and, moreover, for a paid ministry : for if they sell, they receive for the things sold."

18. *while they went.*—They were still engaged in the hurried and distracted inquiry, when the scene was closed by the arrival of the bridegroom.   So Christ comes suddenly at the last, and at once all probation ends, and all that is not done is too late to be done.

19. *ready.*—This is the sole qualification for admission ; and the lesson of the whole parable turns upon the readiness or unreadiness of the virgins.   If ready, they went in with the bridegroom to the marriage ; if not quite ready, the door was shut against their entrance, and it was not opened to their entreaty.

20. *afterward.*—Too late for admission, and certainly after a vain

virgins, saying, Lord, Lord, open to us. But He answered and said, Verily I say unto you, I know you not.

Watch therefore, for ye know neither the day nor the hour wherein the Son of man cometh.

XX. *PARABLE OF THE TALENTS.*

S. Matt. xxv. 14-30.

For *the kingdom of heaven is* as a man travelling into

inquiry amongst "those that sold," they threw themselves upon their Lord's mercy; but it is too late for the exercise of mercy. They cry "Lord, Lord," in the agony of their despair; but the rule of His kingdom is, "Not every one that saith unto Me, Lord, Lord, shall enter into the kingdom of heaven, but he that doeth the will of My Father which is in heaven." Alas! they have not done it, and the door of heaven is shut. Their fate is a most melancholy one, because they were not enemies of their Lord. They sat and slept amongst "the wise;" they were not evil-doers, nor hypocrites; they were only negligent. They felt, and pleaded, a certain interest in the festival from which they stood excluded, and they had no sympathy with those naturally outside; they were *nearly ready*, but not quite—they were only a little too late. Who shall say how much larger a class they represent than any class of open and notorious sinners? Probably, in our own experience, the negligent are more numerous than the sinners, —those usefully and honourably engrossed in the varied and important concerns of this life, being merely forgetful of the paramount interests of the spiritual life; not unconscious, however, of them, and ready to own them, often seized with a fitful anxiety about them. Such are more numerous than the sinners,—than those, namely, who are manifest infidels, profligate, or criminal.

21. *I know you not.*—I do not recognize you, and cannot acknowledge you. "The Lord knoweth them that are His," and them only.

22. *watch therefore.*—The lesson and application of the parable, and the *refrain* of the whole discourse. The arrival of our Lord may be delayed, but it is certain, and will be sudden. Only those who are ready can enter into His joy; the fate of those not ready is foreshown. The only hope, therefore, lies in watchfulness, in the exhibition of the Holy Spirit's grace, in the activity of a holy and earnest life.

23. *wherein,* etc.—These words are not found in the best MSS., and may therefore have crept in from the margin; they are immaterial to the point of the warning.

1. *the kingdom of heaven is.*—These words are not in the original, but are supplied by the translators. Some writers propose to supply

a far country, *who* called his own servants, and delivered

"the Son of man;" in which case it would be better to supply simply "He," so as to make the connection between those parables more distinct, as in the Vulgate, where any nominative to the verb is omitted; but this must, of course, depend on the retention of the words at the close of the last parable (see xix. 23)—which, however, the Vulgate omits—which alone can justify the insertion of a preface unusual in our Lord's parables. No doubt the words supplied by our translators are really the best, being the common preface, and as best explaining the case; for it is not "the Son of man," but the circumstances of "the kingdom of heaven," which afford resemblance in all its particulars. This parable is, in a manner, supplementary to that of the virgins. "It sets before us the *outward work* of Christians, as the ten virgins the *inward grace* from which Christian work springs. Here also we see the 'diversities of gifts;' there the 'same spirit' by which they all are sanctified." (*Howe.*)

2. *a man travelling.*—There is a very similar parable given by S. Luke (xix. 12–27), which has been, by some writers, very wrongly identified with this, but which should be carefully compared with it. The principal points of resemblance and difference may be briefly stated, without entering here into any particular comparison. In both the gift of God is represented by that which is generally current on earth, *money*: in the parable of the pounds we are shown how great an improvement may be made of any single gift; in that of the talents, the necessity of the faithful use of God's gifts, rather than of success in any separate instance. But the parable of the pounds was spoken to the multitudes around Christ, "because they thought that the kingdom of God was immediately about to appear," and its principal aim is to show the common gift of salvation offered by Christ to all His people, and the very different result of the faithful or careless use of it; he that is greatest and he that is least in the kingdom of heaven, differing most widely from each other in holiness and usefulness of life, and the greatest honour being assigned to him who has best improved the good gift which he shares with other men,—showing, in fact, the gradations of reward in heaven. (See xxv. *a.* 3.) In the present parable, which is spoken to the *disciples*, with direct reference to the second advent, we see special gifts of grace, of a varying amount, intrusted to individuals, and the use which they make of these gifts. Christ accepts them with equal honour, if they have been equally faithful with their several trusts. There is a groundwork common to both parables; and they afford one of those instances in which, during the Holy Week, our Lord gathers in, connects, and strengthens diverse threads of His teaching, and of His using again, and pointing afresh, parable, doctrine, and prophecy delivered earlier in His ministry.

3. *a far country.*—Christ was about to leave the world, and to go unto the Father. Some of the early writers interpreted this of the

unto them his goods.   And unto one he gave five talents, to another two, and to another one; to every man according to his several ability; and straightway took

incarnation of our Lord; but the majority agree that the long journey is from earth to heaven, rather than from heaven to earth.

4. *his own servants.*—This conveys much the same idea as the term "virgins;" they were professors of the true faith, and not the world at large.   (See xix. 2, 5.)

5. *talents.*—Every gift of grace, of position, of influence, of opportunity, which we can turn to account in the service of Christ, is a "talent."   These vary as the work He has for us to do varies.   Some are intrusted with the orders and influence of the Christian ministry, like those to whom the parable was first addressed; some with social rank and wealth; and some with remarkable gifts of spiritual grace. Our value as Christ's servants does not always depend on the value of these gifts, and therefore we may not assume that the post of one man is superior, or that of another inferior, in the view of Christ who assigned them; for there is an equal reward proposed for equally faithful service; and the higher reward does not necessarily belong to him who holds the highest post, but to him who is most faithful at his post.

6. *to every one.*—There is here none excepted either from work, or gift, or grace to live for Christ.   "Unto every one of us is given grace, according to the measure of the gift of Christ" (Eph. iv. 7).

7. *his several ability.*—This speaks of the natural capacity, and of the personal improvement of that which God has already assigned, and which offers a fitness for the greater or lesser talents entrusted to each.   Again we notice the fact that it is not the excellence of the gift of ability or disposition, that is, of natural endowment, as it also is not the value of the special work, which we can reckon on as of the highest consequence to the service of Christ; but the faithful improvement of that which Christ has, in the exercise of His wisdom, assigned to each, which really advances the cause of Christ.   Most great matters hinge on apparent trifles; most great achievements result from the skilful turning to account of some passing opportunity.   The vigilance of a sentinel may save an army from a calamity which no skill in generalship could have reversed; a faithful guide may point out that vantage ground which makes science and valour successful; and how often, in the world's history, has one in the narrow circle of a family, and in a woman's circumscribed and quiet sphere, trained some great mind for God, which, in the next generation, has roused all Christendom.   Success lies in the unity of faithful work on the part of all the members of the Body of Christ, and it is impossible to say that this or that member's office is the most important.   The grand and simple requirement is, "that a man be found faithful."

8. *straightway.*—This especially concerns those to whom the parable

his journey.　Then he that had received the five talents went and traded with the same, and made *them* other five talents.　And likewise he that *had received* two, he also gained other two.　But he that had received one went and digged in the earth, and hid his lord's money.

was more particularly spoken.　Soon after our Lord had endowed and informed His Apostles, He ascended into Heaven; but these gifts were entrusted to them primarily, with a residuary interest for all who followed them, either in the possession of office in the Church, or in the gift of salvation, and the influence and opportunity which it entails, which are universal, and which increase as the Church gains extension in the world.

9. *traded.*—He used his gifts, whether of power or influence, position or opportunity, to the best advantage, to make the most gain to the cause of Christ.　He carried these into the world's market, and into the occasions of daily life, and gained with them all that he could gain.

10. *received one.*—The case of the least endowed is mentioned as an instance of a life lost and reprobated, because it is not unnatural for those humbly endowed, and with circumscribed influence, and comparatively few opportunities, to think that what they do, or neglect to do, is of little consequence; and that, had they had the opportunities and advantages of other men, they also would have done good service. The truth made plain is, that God does not ask what we would have done with what we might have had, but what we have done with what we had.　And if "to the poor the Gospel is preached" in an especial sense, we may surely conclude, that those under the Gospel, who are endowed with few worldly gifts, and not placed in seemingly important posts, in Christ's field of labour on earth, have yet their especial opportunities and especial influence.　For this at least is commonly true, that those of humbler life have more intimate relationships amongst each other; theirs is a society of greater personal intimacy, being of one common social level, and working much together, than is the case with their more isolated brethren in the ranks above them; and therefore, perhaps, their Christian character and example are more immediately and extensively current, if more locally, than in any other class of life.　The man of one talent may be, like "the man of one idea," insuperable and successful within his own range; and his neglect of his Lord's service may therefore be quite as detrimental to Christ's influence, as that of those endowed with five talents, or with two.

11. *digged in the earth.*—Buried it in disuse, for it seemed to him not worth the risks of trade.　He was not an enemy, that he should put it to any hostile use, or destroy it, or lose it; he buried it in neglect.　Some explain that he buried all his opportunities and abilities in the concerns of the world, "in the earth," that is, in earthly adventure; but the very point of his offence seems to be that he did not use

After a long time the lord of those servants cometh, and reckoneth with them. And so he that had received five talents came and brought other five talents, saying, Lord, thou deliveredst unto me five talents : behold, I have gained beside them five talents more. His lord said unto him, Well done, *thou* good and faithful servant : thou hast been faithful over a few things, I will make thee ruler over many things : enter

it at all, in any way—that he utterly neglected it. His lord reproaches him as a *slothful* servant.

12. *after a long time.*—See xix. 8.

13. *thou deliveredst.*—This is the servant's humble acknowledgment of the source and origin of his success. It was because God had endowed him with the means, and strengthened him in all his works, that he had gained in the trading with his capital; and although he said, " *I* have gained," he said it was " *beside them*"—that is, in the use of God's gifts he had accomplished this end. S. Gregory has a striking application of the rendering of the accounts of these servants, in which he represents the various Apostles presenting the scenes of their labour to Christ : Peter, Judea ; Paul, the Gentile world ; Andrew, Achaia ; John, Asia ; Thomas, India ; and the servants of God generally declaring the results of their labour.

14. *good and faithful.*—It has been noticed that our Lord does not say *successful*, but *faithful.* The servant has been good, and just, and charitable in his occupancy of his trust towards his fellow-men ; he has done them good in the use of it; and he has been faithful to the interests of his Lord. But his success is not so much measured, as is his goodness and fidelity. The same words exactly are addressed to the servant who had only the trust of two talents, and had gained other two. Probably the gain of these two was quite as important to his Lord's interest as the five; and therefore He acknowledges the faithfulness, rather than the success. For the success of a minor trust is not rarely of greater ultimate consequence than one seemingly wider; the minor trust being, perhaps, the key to some great extension of the influences of Christ's kingdom. This is a strong argument in favour of the great importance of apparently circumscribed spheres of labour, and insignificant posts. (See notes 7, 10.)

15. *ruler over many things.*—He who has acted faithfully in a subordinate trust is worthy of being entrusted with power. He who knows how to obey has been in the best training for command, and his obedience has been tested with the " few things " of an earthly duty ; but eternity only can illustrate the scope of the " many things " beneath the sway of an immortal and glorified " ruler."

16. *enter thou.*—Several writers have noticed, and have variously

thou into the joy of thy lord. He also that had received two talents came and said, Lord, thou deliveredst unto me two talents : behold, I have gained two other talents beside them. His lord said unto him, Well done, good and faithful servant : thou hast been faithful over a few things, I will make thee ruler over many things : enter thou into the joy of thy lord. Then he which had received the one talent came, and said, Lord, I knew thee that thou art an hard man, reaping where thou hast not sown, and gathering where thou hast not strawed : and I was afraid, and went and hid thy talent

expressed, the great munificence of this award. It is not, "Let the joy of thy Lord enter into thee," though that might fill the cup of any servant's happiness to the overflowing; his capacity to enjoy is not the extent of the happiness before him; he is bidden, " Enter thou into the joy of thy Lord." To possess the infinity and variety of that ever-lasting joy is the very "fulness of joy;" and, if eternity can increase his capacity for enjoyment of it, as he knows and acquires more of his Lord's mind, in personal intercourse with Him, this "joy of his Lord " will still open to him without limitation, and without restriction. "It is but little we can receive here, some drops of joy that enter into *us ;* but there we shall enter into joy, as vessels put into a sea of happiness." (*Archbishop Leighton.*)

17. *I knew thee.*—This knowledge of his was a most unhappy one, for it was a false one. He knew really nothing of his Lord, for he saw Him only through the narrowness and fear of his own heart, and fancied Him "altogether such a one as himself," unjust, unfaithful, slothful, grasping; whereas "God is love." He had evidently taken as little pains to acquire a just view of His character, as he had to make a just use of his trust; and when he came face to face with his Lord, and knew Him rightly, he must have found that the very ground on which he professed to act, vanished from beneath him. His mistaken course of conduct was founded on a mistaken estimate—a far worse error than that of one who has taken a right view, and works hard and earnestly, but makes some mistake in the details of his work, or in the application of his powers.

18. *reaping,* etc.—Requiring a far larger return than is possible from a restricted trust and limited power.

19. *afraid.*—The "fearful " (Rev. xxi. 8) are excluded from the happiness of the heavenly city in the fore ranks of a sad catalogue of manifest sinners. This unworthy fear was the first symptom of dis-trust in Adam's case, and betrayed a lively consciousness that he had done wrong: "I heard Thy voice in the garden, and I was *afraid,* and

in the earth : lo, *there* thou hast *that is* thine.   His lord
answered and said unto him, *Thou* wicked and slothful
servant, thou knewest that I reap where I sowed not,
and gather where I have not strawed : thou oughtest
therefore to have put my money to the exchangers, and

I hid myself" (Gen. iii. 10).   In 1 John iv. 18, the same truth is
differently expressed, from the point of view of one who loves his Lord:
" There is no fear in love ; but perfect love casteth out fear: because
fear hath torment.   He that feareth is not made perfect in love."   The
right fear of God is reverence, which is compatible with the deepest
love.   (See the Collect for Second Sunday after Trinity : " Give us a
heart to love and dread Thee.")

20. *that is thine.*—He thus gives back that which he has not wasted,
abused, misspent, nor spent in the service of an enemy.   But yet it is
not his Lord's just due, there being no interest added for its use—no
exercise of the ability which measured it as his fit and proper trust ; this
is not accounted for and rendered.   He delivers up this hidden talent,
not without defiance and effrontery.

21. *wicked and slothful.*—" Wicked," for his want of fidelity ;
" slothful," for his utter negligence ;   therefore thoroughly worthless.
It is difficult to say what form of wickedness may not lie to the charge
of the slothful.   All the sins of neglect, and they are multiform, are his
personal sins ; and he gives effect also to the wickedness of more active-
minded sinners.   He is doubly opposed in character to his Lord, being
" wicked and slothful ; " whereas He is holy and unwearied in doing
good.   Besides, a man is wicked who will not do the good he is able to
do (James iv. 17) ; this man would not have been called *wicked*, had he
wanted power to do right.

22. *thou knewest.*—" Out of thine own mouth will I judge thee; thou
wicked servant" (Luke xix. 22).   His Lord does not condescend to
defend Himself against charges so baselessly brought against Him by
the slothful servant.   He accepts the character under which this man
says he *knows* Him, and proceeds to judge him upon his own ground.
Allowing that such was His character, how much enhanced was the
wickedness of the servant who dared to face Him in this defiant negligence ; for, if he feared to risk his talent in the usual ways of trade,
there were yet certain recognized means open to him, which entailed
no personal danger, and no loss of his capital, and which would certainly ensure some return for its use.   " The goodness of the Lord,
which was denied by him, remains unknown to the wicked servant."
(*Bengel.*)

23. *the exchangers.*—Who these were, it is difficult to say with particularity.   Many writers seem to confuse the difficulty by explaining
the system of banking and exchange.   Our Lord's direction in another

then at my coming I should have received mine own with usury.   Take therefore the talent from him, and give *it*

parable may perhaps avail us here, " Make to yourselves friends of the mammon of unrighteousness ; " for it is in the use of means and opportunities of earth, and even by using the aid of those who are not themselves willing servants of Christ's kingdom, that we must advance His cause.   Under His control, even the workers of wickedness fulfil His will.   A servant of His must know how to avail himself rightly of all means by which Christ's work may be performed.   Thus, "the exchangers " would be those who can advance the great cause, directly or indirectly, without being themselves heart and soul engaged in it. There are, however, two explanations which modern critics have offered : one, that " the exchangers " were men of stronger mind and power, on whom the timid and hesitating servant might depend for impulse and guidance.   The objection to this is, that this man was not likely to lean on any other for support ; there is no weakness of character attributed to him ; he is resolute enough, but his resolution is to do nothing.   The other explanation is, that " the exchangers " represent charitable and religious societies for exclusively Christian purposes, which so many combine to support who can offer no personal assistance in the cause adopted by them ; and there can be no doubt that the interpretation is a just one.   The point of failure seems to be, that the parable represents the circumstances of the Gospel in all ages, those previous to the formation of these societies, as well as the present ; and therefore we must enlarge this interpretation to include the Church agencies and machinery for charitable, educational, and religious purposes in every age, from the hour when the Apostles appointed the seven deacons to " serve tables," to distribute and apply the alms and offerings of the Church, to the present days of many societies.   Though the servants of Christ who support these public efforts for carrying on His work by the agency of other men (thus putting their Lord's gifts to the exchangers), are not directly and actually employed in the work, yet they cannot be said to be " wicked " or " slothful," unless their own personal lives are aimless, and inactive, and prayerless ; for much interest in Christ's cause, many prayers, and much self-denial may characterize those who so work by deputy.   The rule is a good one, and capable of general application, that those who can do no separate and independent work for Christ, may yet serve His cause usefully, by placing themselves, or their influence, under the direction of His Church.

24. *take therefore.*—Our Lord's work must be done—if not by him to whom it was originally entrusted, at least by some other, whose diligent use of his own opportunities has given him an acquired fitness for, and a readiness to apply, extra opportunities which come unexpectedly in his way.   There is no want of work to the willing work-

unto him which hath ten talents. For unto every one that hath shall be given, and he shall have abundance :

man, and if he does another man's work, he will not fail to receive the reward ; as is implied in our Lord's words, "Hold fast that thou hast, *that no man take thy crown*" (Rev. iii. 11).   The difficulty here appears to be, that this extra work is conferred at the time of the rendering of the account ; but the parable need not be too closely pressed in this respect. All men do not render their life's account at the same moment ; very often a useless, idle life cuts itself short by neglect of the powers and rules of life, which an active mind extends by improving and taking care of them.   Just as the great day is, within the limits imposed by God's knowledge and decision of its term, capable of being advanced or retarded by the prayers and diligence of Christ's Church, so is it with the term of natural life.   God *knows* the date of our death, but probably there are few cases in which its actual determination is not influenced by causes over which we have control.   God cannot be said to decree the accidents of life. He has nothing to do with the extravagance of those who waste their vital powers in some ruinous and vicious indulgence, or throw away life by rashness, folly, or neglect. He permits these accidents to terminate lives, whose extension, on the other hand, He would have permitted (within the limits assigned to man) under proper care and caution. It is likely enough, therefore, that the man of ten talents, who has used his life to the best in God's service, and for God's sake has rightly valued and tended it, may often survive to do the work which his intelligent and active life enables him promptly to discern and undertake ; and so to reap the rewards also, which are taken from one who has misused and wasted health, ability, and opportunity, and has, by extravagance of life, shortened it, as he has also buried its golden advantages.   We may thus assign to this parable, which occurs within our Lord's last prophetic discourse, the double reference which runs throughout it, to the account to be given at the day of death, as well as to that of the day of judgment. (See xviii. 94.)

25. *that hath ten.*—There is an obvious propriety in his receiving the extra charge, for he had so improved his own gifts that he can put them to the most immediate and varied service. He can therefore discern, and turn to good account, many an opportunity passing else to loss, within the precise limits of his charge.

26. *to every one that hath,* etc.—(See viii. 35 ; and App. VI.) The general rule is, that whosoever improves God's gifts shall find them grow and increase to him, with an increase also of opportunities of putting them to practical use—unexpected openings shall present themselves to his readiness ; but he who neglects what is given him, must entirely lose it.   He thus unfits himself for God's service, and he must so miss the crown of life eternal. Probably, in the eternal world, this

but from him that hath not shall be taken away even
that which he hath.   And cast ye the unprofitable
servant into outer darkness : there shall be weeping and
gnashing of teeth.

XXI.   *THE LAST JUDGMENT.*

S. Matt. xxv. 31-46.

When the Son of man shall come in His glory, and
all the holy angels with Him, then shall He sit upon the
throne of His glory : and before Him shall be gathered
all nations : and He shall separate them one from

rule will be absolute, in the ever-increasing happiness and fruitfulness
of the life everlasting : the more we have, the more we *shall* ever have.

27. *the unprofitable servant.*—In one sense all are unprofitable
servants—they have but done what is their bounden duty to do ; but
this is eminently "*the* unprofitable servant." He is too slothful to use
his talent, either for the advantage of men, or in the cause of Christ.
And his indolence is quite as serious an impediment to the advance of
that cause, as is the direct wickedness of another. He therefore shared
the doom of the evil servant, and of the hypocrite. (See xviii. 111.)
So Dives goes to torment for neglect of the duties of charity; and
those placed on Christ's left are so ranked because they did not
minister to Christ's poor brethren.

28. *weeping,* etc.—(See viii. 33.) There is an intensity of woe in
the continued repetition of these words of doom by the merciful
Saviour.

1. *in His glory.*—It is impossible to imagine a scene of so great
majesty as this, nor could man have conveyed such a description ;
both the revelation of the fact, and the language in which it is expressed, are Christ's own. The whole family in heaven and earth is
gathered here; the whole angel world, and the entire human race of
every generation of life, is here assembled.

2. *all nations.*—There are several interpretations of these words,
which most materially affect the whole of the passage. Some writers
contend that this is the judgment of the Christian world only; some,
the direct opposite, only the heathen world; and others, of the whole
of mankind. This last is the generally received opinion, and probably the true one. The separation of judgments which either of the
two former theories would entail, seems to have been the object in
view in proposing them ; for these opinions are held, on the one side,
by those who wish to support the notion that, as there is nothing

another, as a shepherd divideth *his* sheep from the goats : and He shall set the sheep on His right hand, but the goats on the left.

Then shall the King say unto them on His right hand, Come, ye blessed of My Father, inherit the kingdom prepared for you from the foundation of the world : for

particular said about the future condition of the heathen, so Christ does not speak here at all of their judgment; on the other hand, by those who wish to support the doctrine of a post-millenial judgment, in which the saints who share in that millenium are not concerned; the judgment of the saints, in this view, being spoken of in the parables preceding. The whole passage is capable of harmonious interpretation, if we understand it of the final judgment of the whole race of man, which has been spoken of in the two last parables under certain aspects, and indeed through the whole of the discourse (xviii.-xxi.) delivered by our Lord to His disciples on the Mount of Olives.

3. *the King.*—We must notice that He who was just now spoken of as the Son of man, and who again uses the words "blessed of *My Father*," is here declared "the King." The Son of man, who was rejected on earth, is thus the Messiah, and now sits on the throne of His glory as Judge. He has ceased to be the Prophet of truth to those in error, and the Priest to make atonement; He has taken to Himself the kingdom.

4. *inherit.*—Heaven is an inheritance prepared and reserved for these in accordance with God's gracious promise; it is the inheritance of all whom He has adopted as His sons, whom Christ has acknowledged as His brethren, as "heirs together with Christ." It is a happy welcome, to enter as *sons* into an hereditary possession, rather than merely as strangers upon a gift.

5. *the kingdom.*—A glorious and royal inheritance, the portion of the sons of the great King; a strong contrast to the place of utter woe, which is no *inheritance,* but a place of penal banishment. It is said to be "prepared for you," and the preparation included also those who have forfeited it; for God never decreed their sad lot, or " prepared" for them otherwise than in heaven. Theirs is a self-elected doom (see note 12). Hell was "prepared for the devil and his angels," not for them.

6. *from the foundation.*—Adam's sin interfered to bar man's entry to the kingdom, but "an entrance shall be ministered abundantly into the everlasting kingdom of our Lord and Saviour Jesus Christ" (2 Peter i. 11), to all who accept His salvation. The sentence of exclusion is reversed, and man receives his lost inheritance, with more than its former blessing (Eph. i. 4; Luke x. 20; 1 Peter i. 2 ; 2 Tim. ii. 19).

I was an hungered, and ye gave Me meat: I was thirsty, and ye gave Me drink: I was a stranger, and ye took Me in: naked, and ye clothed Me: I was sick, and ye visited Me: I was in prison, and ye came unto Me. Then shall the righteous answer Him, saying, Lord, when saw we Thee an hungered, and fed *Thee?* or thirsty, and gave *Thee* drink? When saw we Thee a stranger, and took *Thee* in? or naked, and clothed *Thee?* or when saw we Thee sick, or in prison, and came

7. *I was an hungered*, etc.—This is a very extraordinary and touching revelation of the reality of human sorrow and suffering. We read of Christ that, whilst on earth, "Himself took our infirmities and bore our sicknesses" (Isa. lxiii. 9; Matt. viii. 17); and thus He takes upon Himself the distresses of His servants, and is personified in them in their times of trouble. And so it is that the sick we relieve, the misery we sympathize with and alleviate, and the charity (the love and the gifts) we dispense in the Name and for the sake of Christ, are truly charity done to Him, whose sympathy is so much the more perfect, and whose love is the more full than ours that *Himself* is bearing their trials with them; and it is Himself who receives our services of Christian love, though to our eyes the case may be that of "the least of His brethren," least in worthiness, in station, and consideration. And perhaps we may go lower even, outside the Christian world, to those of the great human family in whose nature Christ lived on earth, and suffered; and it may be that, in the performance of acts of common humanity to these, for the sake of the common Father of all, and of the common Redeemer and Brother of our race, our Lord will acknowledge love to Himself.

8. *the righteous.*—Those on the right hand, to whom the welcome is given of inheritance in heaven, receive this title, which is so noble a one for men. The angels are pure, and spotless, and holy; but *righteousness* is not only of personal holiness, but of active personal deeds under the probation of trial. And these are accounted righteous, and pronounced righteous for their deeds of love (see 2 Cor. ix. 9); they receive the imputation of their Lord's bright character, for He is "the Lord our righteousness." "Thus the alchemy of Divine love and power has made righteous many of those of whom it was written, 'There is none righteous, no, not one.'"

9. *when saw we Thee*, etc.—Partly in their humility, partly in their ignorance of the exact value of service, they cannot take to themselves this credit; at best they had done it for His sake. But they could not discern Him in the poor and miserable recipients of their kindness; they had not imagined so great an honour, and so rich a return for their charity, as this.

unto Thee?   And the King shall answer and say unto
them, Verily I say unto you, Inasmuch as ye have done *it*
unto one of the least of these My brethren, ye have done
it unto Me.   Then shall He say also unto them on the
left hand, Depart from Me, ye cursed, into everlasting fire,

10. *ye cursed.*—S. Chrysostom and other writers have noticed that
our Lord does not add in this case the words, "of My Father."   The
righteous are blessed of Him, because God is the Author of salvation,
and His will is that "none shall perish, but that all should come to the
knowledge of the truth."   But those finally cursed, are cursed of themselves; by their own acts of wilfulness they involve themselves in the
awful doom with which God and Christ decline to associate their name.
It is a marked feature in their case that it is not the act of God.   (See
notes 5, 12; xvii. 16, 17.)

11. *fire.*—Notwithstanding all that has been written and surmised
by those who desire to do justice to their own conception of God's
mercy, at the expense (it must be feared) of His truth, we cannot but
believe that our Lord does not speak figuratively in these words; but
that the punishment of the wicked is a material punishment, not
merely a matter of disappointment, remorse, conscience, or any other
explanation of a supposed figurative doom.   If any passages are distinct
and clear, and apparently free from figure and metaphor, those are so
which describe the material punishment of the wicked.   We must
wait until we see God face to face, and know Him as we are known by
Him, to understand how one attribute and another of His absolutely
perfect Being, work together in harmony; how, for instance, One so
merciful and loving as to give up His own Son, can doom poor frail
and erring man, at his worst not wholly devoid of a better side of
character, to endless wrath.   It is far better to take Christ's words
literally, and to leave Him to clear and vindicate Himself (as He will
certainly do at the last), than to construct any theory, however tempting
and beautiful, of what God should be; and to deny, explain, or pronounce parabolical all that militates with our theory.   It is all very
well to ask, what no one can answer, "How can God be just and
merciful in condemning to eternal wrath those who have offended
through defective training, and evil associations, and want of good
influences? or, to take the worst possible sinner in this brief life, what
is his sin to his eternal punishment?"   There must be an infinite offence
in sin; as for sin the Son of God must die, and none other could atone.
It is better to leave the mysteries of God to Himself, to reveal at His
pleasure, and to hesitate to pronounce as unworthy of Him, impossible,
and incredible, that which His own words, literally understood,
repeatedly and plainly convey; and to accept His salvation, which is
impossible to none, that we may not come into the place of torment of
those who are cursed from His presence.

prepared for the devil and his angels : for I was an hungered, and ye gave Me no meat : I was thirsty, and ye gave Me no drink : I was a stranger, and ye took Me not in : naked, and ye clothed Me not : sick, and in prison, and ye visited Me not. Then shall they also answer Him, saying, Lord, when saw we Thee an hungered, or athirst, or a stranger, or naked, or sick, or in prison, and did not minister unto Thee ? Then shall He answer them, saying, Verily I say unto you, Inasmuch as ye did *it* not to one of the least of these, ye did *it* not to Me.

And these shall go away into everlasting punishment : but the righteous into life eternal.

12. *prepared for the devil.*—(See notes 5, 10.) The word " prepared " is again used, as in contrast with that above. Here is another of those significant statements in the award of final doom, which mark so distinctly that God and Christ refuse to associate themselves in the punishment of wicked men. Theirs was the Saviour of sinners, theirs was the mansion prepared by Christ, theirs was the inheritance of the kingdom ; for them was the book of life—for we read of no book of death, and no limitation of those who may inherit ; of none for whom no mansion was prepared, or for whom Christ did not die. And for man there is no proper place of punishment ; the only place is that " prepared for the devil and his angels ; " and those who refuse salvation, and their prepared inheritance, must go to a world for which they never were intended, and to a society for which they are of their own nature unfitted. For there can be no fit association between even the most wicked of men, and any evil spirit. Both the place of their punishment, and its inhabitants, will be utterly abhorrent to those whose rejection of their own proper destiny has brought them there. Neither can those into whose place of torment they are cast, regard with any fellowship of being, or with any feeling other than contempt and hatred, those who come amongst them thus. There never can be peace and association between the tempter and the tempted, the accuser and the condemned.

13. *when saw we Thee.*—They would defend their neglect by the profession that they had not discovered, what even the righteous could not see, Christ's personal presence amongst those He came to save. The fact remained that they had not done anything for Christ's sake, or for mercy's sake ; their lives had been utterly un-Christlike. It was not likely that they, in their selfishness and negligence, should discern what the righteous had not perceived in their devotion and humility.

14. *everlasting punishment . . . eternal life.*—" Punishment " is a

And in the day time He was teaching in the temple :
and at night He went out, and abode in the mount that

positive word, not merely one which implies negation of reward. (See
note 11.) There are few subjects on which more has been thought
and written, than on this final sentence of the world. We would fain
hope (and surely Christ is more merciful than the most merciful of
men) that there may be some explanation or extenuation of this
sentence : but it is useless to mystify the statement in order to escape
from its difficulties. We may find instances of the interpretation of
the original word here used, to signify an age, or some period of limitation, and may satisfy our minds that any other interpretation than
that is inconsistent with Christ's mercy. Arguments may be brought
(and they are strong ones) for putting aside the naked severity of
this sentence; but what do they give in exchange for our setting aside
what we would do anything not to believe? They only leave the
difficulty involved in greater perplexities. For (to pass over any
argument for, or against, the eternal sentence of wrath as proceeding
from God) we come in the end to the startling conclusion, that the
eternity of life and the eternity of death stand or fall together, so far
as we can reason ; the same original word is used in either case,
although there may be a distinction between "everlasting" and
"eternal" in our translation. This is confessedly one of the most
difficult subjects of revelation ; it is safest to take it in its literal sense
(for the parallel passages strongly support the literal sense), and to
leave God to clear up this mystery in the day when He makes all
mysteries of faith plain. It is surely wisest for those who have to
minister, as stewards of Christ's mysteries, to other men, to put forward
only the literal declaration, and to own the difficulty, and to leave its
solution to Him who stated it ; rather than to mislead and perplex
their hearers by propounding theories which they cannot reconcile
conclusively with God's word.

15. *in the day time*, etc.—This is a summary of Christ's occupation
during the past days of the Holy Week, in which He concluded His
public ministry ; it does not refer to any subsequent teaching. Just
as S. John, at the close of the portion of his Gospel devoted to Christ's
personal ministry, gives a summary of its aim, and speaks of its
apparent failure as foreseen by God, and provided for (see xvii.; S.
John xii. 37–50); so here S. Luke concludes this section of his Gospel
with a few words concerning Christ's residence and daily occupation
during this eventful week.

16. *at night*.—He went out to Bethany with His disciples ; but it
seems likely that a great portion of the nights of this week were not
spent actually at Bethany, where He was lodging, in the open court,
housetop, or perhaps in the open air (as the Greek of Matt. xxi. 17
may imply), but in the quiet and seclusion of the Mount of Olives,

is called the mount of Olives. And all the people came early in the morning to Him in the temple, for to hear Him.

𝔚𝔢𝔡𝔫𝔢𝔰𝔡𝔞𝔶 𝔦𝔫 𝔥𝔬𝔩𝔭 𝔚𝔢𝔢𝔨.

XXII. *CHRIST DECLARES HIS BETRAYAL. THE RULERS CONSPIRE AGAINST HIM. SATAN PREPARES JUDAS TO BETRAY HIM.*

S. Matt. xxvi. 1–5, 14–16; S. Mark xiv. 1, 2, 10, 11 ; S. Luke xxii. 1–6.

And it came to pass, when Jesus had finished all these

and in prayer; setting thus an example of the watchfulness He so strongly urged. We read here that He spent the hours of night in the Mount of Olives, and there the betrayer and his accomplices found Him. S. Luke says (xxii. 39) that, on the night of His betrayal, He went, *as He was wont*, to the Mount of Olives ; " and it appears from S. John (xviii. 2) that the traitor was sure of finding Him there : " Judas also, which betrayed Him, knew the place : for Jesus ofttimes resorted thither with His disciples." It is certainly more credible that Christ should throw off the strife and trials of the day, and strengthen Himself for the scenes before Him, in solemn communion with His Father in prayer, than that He should spend the whole time in any social intercourse, either with those He so highly esteemed at Bethany, or with His disciples; much less that He, whose words are instinct with warning and exhortation to vigilance, should retire simply to rest and sleep, at this crisis of His Messiahship, and of the the world's redemption. The example, therefore, of Christ, prescribes to His disciples retirement from life's pleasures, and communion with God, in preparation for our own last end; not abandonment of life's proper duties, but such retirement as may facilitate communion with Him who is our life.

1. *had finished.*—The Evangelist marks the conclusion of our Lord's public ministry and doctrine, and of the prophetic discourse which He delivered as He sat on the Mount of Olives, overlooking Jerusalem, on His return journey to Bethany at the close of that last and most eventful day of His ministry. There now commences a new portion of His earthly history, that of the Passover; the former portion comprehended His life as the true Teacher, this as the Redeemer.

sayings, He said unto His disciples, Ye know that after two days is *the feast of* the passover, and the Son of man is betrayed to be crucified.

Then assembled together the chief priests, and the scribes, and the elders of the people, unto the palace of the high priest, who was called Caiaphas, and consulted that they might take Jesus by subtilty, and kill *Him*.

2. *ye know.*—Our Lord had repeatedly declared that He would be delivered up to be crucified; the disciples were aware of His having said this, though they did not fully understand or receive the declaration.　He now mentions the exact time, and speaks to them with a knowledge of His betrayal, and of the conspiracy which was taking place at Jerusalem.　He speaks of the Passover in connection with this sacrifice of Himself, in order to mark the typical character of that festival, in the circumstances of His own offering up as the Lamb of God.

3. *after two days.*—He therefore speaks on the fourth day, or Wednesday in Holy Week; and these few words are all that are recorded of Himself on this day.　It appears to have been spent in retirement, at Bethany.　We cannot raise the veil which the Evangelists have, by common consent, dropped upon the occurrences of this day; but we see, in the few words spoken by our Lord, that His mind was occupied with the fulfilment of ancient prophecy in His Passion, and He had regard to the evil agencies at work for its accomplishment.

4. *the passover.*—See App. VIII. A.

5. *then assembled.*—On the same day, and probably whilst Christ was speaking of His betrayal to His disciples, and of His voluntary sacrifice, an important council of the rulers was gathered at the palace of the high priest, to consult on the best means of carrying out their design against Christ.　They had quite resolved on His death, and also that it must not be attempted openly and publicly, but by craft; for His reputation amongst the people was so much on the increase, as to endanger immediately their own influence.　The conclusion they were arriving at was, that it was better to let the festival of the Passover take place without any act of violence against Christ; for the city was thronged with Jews from the provinces, amongst whom were very many who were friendly to Christ's cause—many who were living monuments of His mercy.　The arrival of Judas, and his proposal, gave a new turn to their deliberations.　This consultation may not have been a formal and regular sitting of the Sanhedrim, being not held in the chamber Gazith; and doubtless such members as were favourable to Christ's cause were not present; but it was, nevertheless, fully attended.

But they said, Not on the feast *day*, lest there be an
uproar among the people : for they feared the people.
   Then entered Satan into Judas surnamed Iscariot,

6. *on the feast day.*—Or, "not during the feast." The word *day* is
not in the original, and their words are not so definite as our translation suggests. They postponed execution of their design during the
eight days of the feast; just as Herod postponed the execution of Peter
till after the Passover (Acts xii. 3, 4).

7. *an uproar.*—From Josephus we learn that tumults at the time
of the great Jewish feasts were not uncommon ; and that a guard of a
Roman legion was quartered in the cloisters of the Temple, to prevent
outbreak. On one occasion, a private soldier so misconducted himself
that a serious outbreak ensued, which resulted in the death of 20,000
of the people (" Antiq.," xx. 5, 3). The Roman governor, whose head-
quarters were at Cæsarea, appears to have come to Jerusalem at these
seasons, to be ready in case of emergency; and it was, doubtless, thus
that Pontius Pilate was at Jerusalem at the present time.

8. *then entered.*—The word "then" refers apparently to the account
of the anointing of our Lord, which immediately precedes in the narra-
tives of SS. Matthew and Mark, but which S. John decides to have
taken place at Bethany six days before the Passover (cf. Matt. xxvi.
6–11 ; Mark xiv. 3, 9 ; John xii. 1–8), and therefore four days previous
to this, namely, on the evening before the triumphal entry into Jerusalem. There is little reason to doubt the correctness of the generally
received explanation for its insertion here by SS. Matthew and Mark,
namely, to connect the treachery of Judas with the disappointment he
experienced in finding that the costly box and its contents, valued at
about £10 of English money, were not given into his hands ; and his
personal annoyance at the rebuke which Jesus then gave to his
covetousness. The sin of Jesus was of no sudden growth ; long before,
Jesus had spoken (John vi. 70, 71) of the ascendancy which Satan
was gaining over him. He had probably expected more than the
other disciples from the supposed earthly reign of our Lord at Jerusa-
salem ; for he expected unrestrained opportunity of indulging the
passion of avarice, now a master passion, which possessed his soul. He
must have felt keenly the loss of the prospect which our Lord's
triumphal entry had seemed to open. The entry of Satan's influence
into his soul would give him other views of this event, than would
have occupied him but a few days before; and he noticed, with an
apprehension quickened by his avaricious hopes, and not allayed by the
feeling of personal attachment common to the disciples, that the rulers
were maturing their plans; and that the end was a settled one, one
which our Lord Himself foresaw, and acquiesced in. He was now
determined to get what he could before the end came ; and was basely
content to realize, by the betrayal of our Lord, one-third of the sum of

being of the number of the twelve. And he went his
way, and communed with the chief priests and captains

which he had been disappointed in the "waste" of the ointment.
S. Luke states that this idea was the direct inspiration of Satan, to
whose influence he had laid himself open by his avarice and theft.
Lange thinks that the preliminaries of the betrayal were concluded
before the triumphal entry into Jerusalem, and that Judas thus came
twice before the chief priests, once to offer, and again to conclude the
bargain. He thus gives to the word " then " an immediate connection of
time, rather than merely of event. It has been suggested that Christ's
rebuke, and a jealous suspicion of His greater love for the other Apostles,
and the feeling that his character was seen through, drove Judas to
this act; others have supposed that he may have hoped to force our
Lord to declare Himself, and also that he did not think that He would
be taken, but would pass through His enemies' hands, as on other
occasions. Such thoughts may have mingled with those of treachery,
and aided self-deception. But it is clear they were not the leading
thoughts; the precautions he took lest Christ should escape (see **xxix.**
10) do really forbid our placing other than the worst construction on
his act. He now clearly realizes the non-establishment of a temporal
sovereignty; all his hopes were gone, and his master passion prompted
his securing what he could at any sacrifice.

9. *the twelve.*—It is sad to notice how, in our Lord's case, as well as
often in the experience of His disciples, His " foes were they of His
own household; " it was one of His chosen followers who gave the
opportunity of seizing Him, which the Jews had sought in vain. (See
Ps. xli. 9, lv. 12, 13.) We see here one of those remarkable instances
of the candour of the Evangelists, which are frequent in the narration
of our Lord's Passion. They never spare themselves, or pass over their
own infirmities or failures in duty; they never magnify themselves,
and their attachment and devotion to their Lord, or vaunt their appreciation of His mission, and of the spiritual nature of His kingdom. All
that they misconceived, and their errors, failures, and weaknesses, are
set down in exact, impartial truth. The only thing they suppress is
the name of a disciple, when to divulge it might give needless distress,
or might prove dangerous; as in the case of the remark of Judas at the
anointing of our Lord (cf. Matt. xxvi. 8; Mark xiv. 4; John xii. 4–6),
and of Peter's assault on Malchus (see **xxix.** 18). S. John, writing
many years later, is at liberty on these points.

10. *communed.*—It is a strange picture this, of the disciple of our
Lord, and the venerable rulers of the Jewish Church, being confederate
in villainy against Christ; but anything was possible to the avarice of
the one, and to the murderous, underhand malice of the others.

11. *captains.*—Not a Roman, but a Levitical guard. (See Acts iv.
1, v. 24.)

how he might betray Him unto them ; and said *unto
them*, What will ye give me, and I will deliver Him
unto you ? And when they heard *it*, they were glad,
and promised to give him money. And they covenanted
with him for thirty pieces of silver. And he promised,
and from that time he sought opportunity to betray Him
unto them in the absence of the multitude.

Thursday in Holy Week.

XXIII. *THE APOSTLES PREPARE THE
PASSOVER.*

S. Matt. xxvi. 17–19 ; S. Mark xiv. 12–16 ; S. Luke xxii. 7–13.

Then came the day of unleavened bread, when the

12. *they were glad.*—They had not hoped for such a chance ; they
were already deciding to postpone their measures until after the feast
(note 5), for the attempt against our Lord appeared hopeless of immediate success, to those who had so craven a fear of the people.

13. *covenanted.*—The original word in Matt. xxvi. 15, rather implies
that this sum was "*weighed out*," or paid ; but from the other Evangelists we gather that the actual payment did not take place at once.
They appear to have promised him the sum agreed on, but not to have
given it into his hands until the attempt had proved successful. The
fact that Judas agreed to receive, and did receive, a sum of money, forbids our believing that he was primarily actuated by any noble motive
whatever. (See note 8 ; and xxix. 10.)

14. *thirty pieces.*—The compensation price for the life of a slave
(Exod. xxi. 32 ; Zech. xi. 12, 13). The sum agreed on was equal to
about £3 15s. of English money. Farrar explains the offer of so small a
sum thus : "The elders chaffered with him after the fashion of their
race, as the narrative seems to imply. They might have represented
that, after all, his agency was unessential, that he might do them a
service which would be regarded as a small convenience ; but that they
could carry out their purpose, if they chose, without his aid."

15. *promised.*—Gk. "*agreed*" to these proposals and terms.

16. *the absence*, etc.—In this lay the hope of success, and the in-
ducement to the chief priests to make agreement with Judas. He was
to betray Christ to them in some moment of His retirement, and in
some wonted haunt of His private life with His disciples,—a matter
hopeless, except through the treachery of a companion. The words
may also be rendered "*without tumult*," as in Acts xxiv. 18.

passover must be killed. And He sent Peter and John,

1. *The day*, etc.—SS. Matthew and Mark have " the first day." The feast continued eight days. In Lev. xxiii. 5, 6 ; Num. xxviii. 16, 17, whilst the fourteenth day is named for the Passover, the fifteenth is named as " the feast of unleavened bread." It seems that the scrupulous Jews had reckoned a day earlier in later ages, perhaps in their anxiety to be thoroughly clear of all leaven at the feast ; but the expression has given rise to much comment, and it is easier to confess the difficulty, than to propose any satisfactory solution. From Matt. xxvi. 17, 19 ; Mark xiv. 12, 14 ; Luke xxii. 7, 11, 13, we should conclude that our Lord and His disciples observed the feast of the Passover on this day, and that it was the usual day for such observance. But from the passages, John xiii. 1, 29, xviii. 28, 39, xix. 14, we should infer that the next day (Friday) was the day of the Passover ; and that, therefore, it was not partaken of by the rest of the nation at the same time with our Lord and His disciples. (See xxx. *d*. 2.) There are many solutions proposed, none of which are quite satisfactory. The three which merit the most consideration are :— (i.) That our Lord and His disciples anticipated the day, and that they observed a feast which was not in all respects that of the Passover ; for the lamb could only be slain in the Temple, and the violation of the usual day would have been potent to the people. Hammond observes that, of that which our Lord took, it is nowhere said in the Gospels that it was *sacrificed* (*i.e.* killed as a sacrifice) ; not " I sacrifice," but " I keep " it, celebrate it, and " I eat " it. Another matter which points to the somewhat special character of this supper, is that Judas left the supper table—a matter which they all thought quite natural, and for some reason connected with the feast (evidently, therefore, not quite observed) ; whereas the law decreed that on the night of the Passover no one should " go forth from his house until the morning." Christ's remarks, " My time is at hand," and, " With desire I have desired to eat this Passover with you before I suffer," are further adduced to show the reason for the celebration of this supper before the usual day, as He could not afterwards partake of the feast. This explanation is in the main that of the earlier writers, of Justin Martyr, Irenæus, Tertullian, and Clement of Alexandria ; and it possesses the apparent probability, that Christ, according to this view, would suffer at the precise time appointed for the slaying of the typical Paschal lamb, which is the generally received opinion. (ii.) That our Lord observed the right day, but that the multitude of the nation did not do so. In this case He would have instituted His Holy Supper at the hour when the Passover should be celebrated ; thus fulfilling the type, but not offering Himself until a day later than the day of the Paschal feast. This view has received support by a dexterous manipulation of several passages of the Gospels ; but this savours too much of special pleading, and there is little further to be said in favour of it beyond conjecture. (iii.) That of several of

saying, Go and prepare us the passover, that we may

the ancient writers, that Christ observed the right day, but that the Jews were so busy plotting His death, that they forget to do so ; and that they were apparently so engaged all the night of His trial. But this is scarcely likely. The exact observance of the feast would surely be prior, in their opinion, to the killing of Christ upon any particular day—they had indeed almost resolved to wait until after the Passover (see xxii. 5); it is impossible that all the nation were so engaged ; besides, the remark in John xviii. 28 shows that those most implicated had not forgotten, but had every intention of keeping the Passover according to established custom. The first opinion entails the difficulty of our Lord's changing the day of the most sacred feast of the nation ; but against this we may notice the words " My time is at hand," as conveying a reason for His unusual act, and also the fact of His having changed (or His Apostles, with His authority) the greatest of all festivals, the world-wide sabbath, to the Lord's day—that festival being the right, not of the Jews only, but of the whole human race. And in no way could our Lord so fitly have superseded the festival of the Passover by the festival of His Supper, as by its inauguration at an observance of that feast. Whether, therefore, our Lord observed the Paschal supper, with all its rites, or merely a solemn supper in anticipation of that feast, His own death fulfilling it exactly at the right time, in all its points; or whether He did observe the right day, and the Jews the wrong day—is somewhat difficult of decision ; but the balance of opinion, especially of the ancient Church, is in favour of His having anticipated the day, and of His having suffered on the right day, at the exact time when the Paschal lamb was appointed to be slain. The difficulty, though apparent to us, must have been reconcilable in the apostolic ages, for it is not likely that S. John would have given any account of this supper inconsistent with that of His fellow-Evangelists, or with truth. Indeed, there would not be much difficulty, if (as Maldonatus supposes) we may understand that John speaks not of the Jews' Passover, but of that of Christ ; and Corn. à Lapide, in mentioning the view of Euthymius and the Greek writers, that Christ anticipated the day observed by the Jews, says they took S. John's words (ch. xiii. 1), which generally are argued as a difficulty, in proof of their view, " Before the feast of the Passover," that is, before the fourteenth day of the month, *i.e.* on the thirteenth. (See xxiv. *c.* 1.) There may be many minor, and apparently irreconcilable, difficulties to the mind of modern critics, where there were none to that of the earliest writers, and no recognized necessity for explanation ; and this appears to be one of them. How many are the difficulties which modern critics have detailed in the O. T., which the writers of the N. T., nay, our Lord Himself, passed over without question or remark, whilst quoting the books in which they occur as Scriptures of truth? Their object was not primarily that of criticism ;

eat.   And they said unto Him, Where wilt Thou that

but they surely would not have passed over anything as truth, which contained vital error. Their silence as to the apocryphal writings is sufficiently significant of this. It is natural that the keenness of criticism, never so profound as now, should detect many difficulties in the course of investigation of writings of great antiquity, which allude to customs locally well known, but of which the exact details are lost. It is interesting to read the arguments of disputants on both sides; and most happy is the thought that in no way is vital truth weakened, though it often receives incidental corroboration by any such encounter of learned minds.

2. *must be killed.*—Bishop Wordsworth observes that "the" Evangelists (Mark xiv. 12; Luke xxii. 7) distinguished between "to kill the Passover," and "to eat the Passover;" the Paschal lamb of each household was "*killed*" on the fourteenth in the Temple, but was "*eaten*" on the fifteenth in private houses, by their "several households." But this does not explain all the difficulties mentioned in note 1, since to eat the Passover in the evening of the fourteenth, our Lord's disciples must have killed the lamb before the conclusion of the thirteenth day. His remark is in coincidence with the command of Exod. xii. 6–8, that the Passover must be killed on the fourteenth day, and eaten on the same night, which would be after the fifteenth day had commenced, for the day was reckoned from sunset to sunset. The people, on the occasion of the Passover, were "all priests unto God;" each killed for himself the Paschal lamb; though the priests only appear to have made offering of the blood of the sacrificed victim.

3. *He sent.*—There is the same particularity in this mission, as in that for the colt on which Christ rode to Jerusalem, and the same provision regarding the circumstances of the mission. Christ foretold exactly which they should see, and directed how they should give His order to the goodman of the house. In the former case He directed them to say, "The Lord hath need of him;" here, "The Master saith." In one instance our Lord went to triumph; in the other, to die. But the disciples must have noticed in each case the same minute foreknowledge of all that was before Him, and the same determination to accomplish all. Amongst other reasons, there was no doubt this intention in our Lord's direction, to impress upon them that not the most trivial details of arrangement, much less the deep solemnities of this solemn and last journey to Jerusalem, were unexpected by Him, or contrary to His will. (See i. 6–8.)

4. *where wilt Thou.*—Our Lord had no place in Jerusalem, "the city of the great King" which knew Him as its Lord; to the last He "had not where to lay His head." No invitation appears to have been given to Him, though the Teacher on whom all eyes were fixed, during this festival week (see i. 59); or, if given, He had accepted none. But both our Lord, and the two disciples, knew that there were those who were

we prepare ?   And He said unto them, Behold, when ye
are entered into the city, there shall a man meet you,
bearing a pitcher of water; follow him into the house
where he entereth in.   And ye shall say to the goodman
of the house, The Master saith unto thee, My time is at

ready to receive Him ; and they only waited His direction whom to
address.

5. *a man meet you.*—A servant of the house. It is remarkable how
minute the direction is : Soon after their entering *within* the city, they
should *meet* this *man* (perhaps the easier distinguished as it was rather
a woman's office to bear water), bearing an *earthen pitcher* containing
water (probably that used afterwards to wash the disciples' feet) ; he
was returning from the well, and they were to turn round, and "*follow
him into the house* where he entereth in ; " they were to deliver their
message, which would at once be recognized by the *goodman* of the
house, and complied with ; and they would be shown a *large upper
room, furnished* (the word implies being provided with couches, and
tables, and carpets for the banquet) and *prepared* (or made ready).
(Mark xiv. 15.)   Some of the early writers give a mystical interpretation,
which is minutely worked out, that this indefinite house-owner is *every*
man ; the upper room, the human understanding, furnished with good
graces and purposes, and cleansed from malice and wickedness. Such
a house would be one in which Christ's presence would be welcome, and
where He would readily dwell. This interpretation would favour that
below, that this man, though well disposed and ready for Christianity,
was not yet fully a believer. They further suppose that the name may
not have been given, lest Judas should know the house, and bring the
Pharisees there before the time.

6. *the Master saith.*—It is not necessary that this man should be
considered as one of our Lord's disciples, because the rule was that all
dwellers in Jerusalem, who had spare accommodation, should receive
those who came up to the city from the provinces, at the great national
festivals. But from our Lord's specifying His designation amongst
His disciples, and making mention of the Apostles, and of His own
approaching end, it is highly probable that, if not now a believer,
he was, at least, an inquirer into the faith. Theophylact does not
consider Him to have been a disciple, and points out how Christ, in
this instance, as also in that of the bringing of the ass and colt on
which He rode to Jerusalem, could incline the hearts of men, and so
could have avoided His Passion. But we must notice our Lord's
official designation of Himself, and the personal nature of His message,
" The Master saith *unto thee ; *" the reference to the end of His career, and
the fact that this man did not dispute the observance of the Passover
on this day, instead of on the right day. There is a strong tradition,
of very early origin, which states that this was the house of " John

hand; I will keep the passover at thy house with **My** disciples; where is the guestchamber? And he will shew you a large upper room furnished *and* prepared: there make ready for us.

And His disciples went forth, and came into the city, and found as He had said unto them: and they made ready the passover.

XXIV. *CHRIST'S LAST PASSOVER.*

S. Matt. xxvi. 20–29; S. Mark xiv. 17–25; S. Luke xxii. 14–30;
S. John xiii., xiv.

(*a*.) *The Supper.*

S. Matt. xxvi. 20; S. Mark xiv. 17; S. Luke xxii. 14–18.

And in the evening He cometh with the twelve.　And

whose surname was Mark " (Acts xii. 12), afterwards a house where the Apostles were accustomed to assemble. This is neither impossible nor unlikely. John Mark was early of note amongst the disciples, and this is not the only tradition which attaches to him at this time. (See xxix. 29.) He appears to have been not a declared believer, though most friendly disposed towards Christ, who knew his heart, and who also may have selected his house as that of a friend; though had he been at the moment a professed disciple, He would doubtless have designated him by name—privately, if it was necessary to hide it from Judas (see note 5)—to the two who went to bear Christ's message to him. His not being a declared disciple would account for his not being present at the Last Supper; his being a friend, for his ready attention to the behests of Christ. There is no proof of the truth of the traditions above referred to, but they are most interesting, and valuable for their antiquity. The " Speaker's Commentary " suggests that Christ had previously, and without the disciples being aware of it, made arrangement with this man; but this does not seem very probable, or necessary.

7. *large upper room.*—Farrar thinks this may have been the same where our Lord, when risen, first showed Himself to His disciples, and where the Holy Ghost was first given; but for this there is nothing but conjecture, possibility, convenience, and our not being aware of there being any other room where the disciples could meet.

1. *in the evening.*—Few would, perhaps, recognize Him in the twilight, and He may have waited for the hour when He would attract less observation and danger. The Greek of S. Matthew gives, " *In the*

when the hour was come, He sat down, and the twelve
apostles with Him.

course of the evening He sat down with the twelve." The whole
narrative of His Passion shows that, whilst He did not shun, He did
not court, the action of His enemies.

2. *the hour.*—Probably the legal hour for the Paschal feast.

3. *sat down.*—Whitby notices that "it was ordered that the children
of Israel should eat the Passover standing (Exod. xii. 11); but this
posture was afterwards exchanged for that of reclining, in commemo-
ration of their rest in Canaan."

4. *the twelve apostles.*—This was the last occasion on which the
twelve assembled with our Lord; from this supper the traitor Judas
went away to his evil work. It has been the subject of much debate
at what period of the Last Supper he went out from them. Many of
the earliest writers say he was present at the Lord's Supper; and their
opinion, with the possibility of there being some tradition to guide
them, is of much weight. But yet there is nothing like unanimous
consent on this point; and those who mention the presence of the
traitor at the institution of the Lord's Supper, speak of it somewhat
incidentally, by way of warning against partaking with evil purpose,
and apparently taking it for granted that he was present, rather than
alleging it as an ascertained fact; whilst many of the modern critics
incline strongly to the opposite opinion. In the absence of any real
evidence upon the point, we feel disposed to adopt this latter view,
which does not want its advocates amongst the Fathers, and which
appears to be more in accordance with the harmony of events at this
crisis. Following S. Luke's account, we should conclude that Judas
was present, and probably this account has been the foundation of that
opinion; but S. Luke appears to give the institution of the Lord's
Supper immediately after the presentation of the first cup (note 9),
as if to show the abolition of the Paschal feast and the institution of
the Lord's Supper in their closest connection. S. Luke appears to
desert his usual sequence of facts, in order to give us the two suppers
in this their bearing on each other; just as S. Matthew gives the
anointing at Bethany four days after its actual occurrence, in order to
introduce the crime of Judas. (See xxii. 8.) All the Evangelists
thus occasionally give a sequence of result, rather than of actual event.
From the comparison of S. Matthew (xxvi. 21–25), and S. Mark
(xiv. 18–21), with S. John (xiii. 21–38), we should incline to the view
that Judas had gone out before the institution of the Lord's Supper;
but that he sat down to the Last Supper with them, and that our Lord
washed his feet amongst the rest; and then that he heard our Lord
denounce the treachery of the traitor in their number without naming
him, thus giving to him two last and powerful appeals to any better
feelings which might remain subject to holy influence. The "dish"

And He saith unto them, With desire I have desired to eat this passover with you before I suffer : for I say unto you, I will not any more eat thereof, until it shall be fulfilled in the kingdom of God. And He took the

and the "sop" of which Judas partook must have been part of food of the Last Supper, not of the Lord's Supper. (On the argument from the English Communion Service, see **xxiv.** *d.* 15.)

5. *with desire*, etc.—An Hebraism for, "I have most earnestly desired." This was His last occasion of eating with them, and one of infinite solemnity ; for it was the last Feast of the Passover, in which all the types of the Passover were fulfilled and exchanged for reality, in the circumstances of His death ; and at which was instituted the new supper, a more perfect type of the supper of the saints in heaven. Our Lord thus united all the memories of the past ages of deliverance and expectation, with the memories peculiar to His own sacrifice of Himself for the sins of the world, in the prospect of their joyful renewal in the kingdom of His glory. To the minds of His Apostles these great thoughts would be hallowed by the touching personal recollections of that last meal with Him upon earth before His Passion. The Supper which would be associated with so many great and holy thoughts, was the object of His earnest desire. (App. VIII. A.)

6. *I will not*, etc.—The early writers understand that Christ would no more celebrate the Mosaic Passover, until the type was fulfilled in the reality of the kingdom of God, that is, the Church after His resurrection.   After the resurrection He again ate and drank with His disciples (Acts x. 41); though "not for need, but to manifest His true Body." (Ælfric.)

7. *the kingdom of God.*—In the midst of the sorrows and imminent troubles of the hour, "the kingdom " is still a clear and bright prospect before our Lord ; not the less assured that there must be, in His case, suffering before triumph. Nor does He represent it as that whose attainment is in the least degree doubtful ; the dark hours of contest and suffering are not hours in which the result is at hazard, as victory may be lost or won in any earthly contest. And this confidence of His in the certainty and glory of His kingdom seems always to catch the thoughts of the disciples, who at present rightly understood neither the magnitude of the crisis, nor the true nature of His kingdom ; they never can quite give up their expectation of a temporal sovereignty.

8. *He took.*—The original word implies that He Himself partook of it, as the master of the house usually did first at the Feast of the Passover.   When "He *took* the cup " in the Lord's Supper, the word equally expresses the fact that He did not, in that case, partake of it personally. In this case He uses the same word " *take* " to the disciples, but the order to *partake* follows. Perhaps the exact order of this act may be subsequent to His sitting down again after the washing of the disciples' feet.

cup, and gave thanks, and said, Take this, and divide *it* among yourselves : for I say unto you, I will not drink of the fruit of the vine until the kingdom of God shall come.

(*b*.) *The Strife for Precedence.*

S. Luke xxii. 24–30.

And there was also a strife among them, which of

9. *the cup.*—Gk. "*a* cup." The definite article is not expressed here, as in the instance in Luke xxii. 20, which is distinguished as "the cup after supper." This distinction is very evident and marked—the latter being "*the* cup" of the Lord's Supper; this being "*a* cup" of the Paschal feast, namely, the first cup of thanksgiving. (See xxiv. *e*. 11 ; App. VIII. A.)

10. *I will not drink.*—(See note 6.) As, after eating of the Passover with them, our Lord said, "I will not any more eat thereof;" so here, after first partaking of the cup of thanksgiving which He delivered to them in the usual order of the feast, He declares, "I will not drink of the fruit of the vine" (the type now in this act being fulfilled) "until the kingdom of God shall come;" and therein this type, and also that memorial Supper of the sacrifice of the death of Christ, the true Paschal Lamb, shall find their perfect fulfilment. Some of the early writers understand this of the external ordinances of religion also : that Christ would not again partake of the ceremonial of Temple or synagogue worship amongst men ; or the rites belonging to these, foremost of which is this ceremonial of the Paschal supper. The former, however, is the more obvious and simple interpretation.

1. *a strife.*—There has been much question as to the order in which this took place ; by some writers it is placed after the institution of the Lord's Supper, and in some sort of connection with the question as to who was the traitor, in the order assigned to it by S. Luke, who alone mentions it. He does not, however, seem to be narrating events in their exact order (see xxiv. *a*. 4); and the original words, "there *was* a strife," seem rather to imply that there had been lately such a thing, than that it was a matter of the present moment. It seems best to place it here, in accordance with the views of the majority of critics. The words, "I am among you as he that serveth," which are pressed to show a reference to the washing of the feet of the disciples, by those who assign to this "strife" a place later in the evening, and which certainly may bear that reference, need not be so interpreted, as on the occasion of a similar dispute amongst the twelve, our Lord had pointed His reproof in somewhat similar terms. (See Matt. xx. 28.) There is a much greater significance in our Lord's lesson of humility

them should be accounted the greatest.　And He said unto them, The kings of the Gentiles exercise lordship over them ; and they that exercise lordship upon them are called benefactors.　But ye *shall* not *be* so : but he

which follows, the washing of the disciples' feet, if the strife for precedence did occur thus early.　Bishop Ellicott places it as they were taking their seats at the supper table, and says that the strife was " perhaps to occupy places nearest to One to whom every hour was now deepening their love and devotion ; " but the Evangelist's narrative seems to ascribe it to an inferior principal motive ; and would our Lord have reproved a strife of love by inculcating the necessity for *humility* ?

2. *the greatest.*—If, with Bishop Ellicott, we see one reason for this strife in a loving desire for " chief rooms " at so high a solemnity as the Last Supper, there appeared a stronger ground for it in the mention, in our Lord's words just spoken, that He would eat and drink no more with them *before the kingdom of God should come.* (See xxiv. a. 6.)　A contest of a similar nature had taken place on more than one occasion (see Luke ix. 46–48 ; Matt. xx. 20–28) ; and it is a coincidence that, in each of these instances, as in the present one, the strife arose after our Lord had referred to His crucifixion and sufferings.　They evidently connected the advent of the kingdom with the termination of the present life of preaching and trial, though they were slow to perceive the nature of that kingdom of which He spoke, and did not realise the fact that He must die.

3. *the kings of the Gentiles.*—(See Matt. xx. 25.)　This, and our Lord's reference to His own service and ministration, form another illustration of our Lord's iteration and resetting of the lessons of His previous teaching, during the last week of His ministry.

4. *them.*—The Gentiles.

5. *benefactors.*—Several kings and princes of the old heathen world affected the title " Euergetes ; " but the principle was a common one. The strife, in earthly kingdoms, was for pre-eminence ; and no sooner did a man succeed in obtaining royal or princely power, than he used it to rule with a strong hand over those whom he made his subjects, and the titles " father of the people," " friend of the poor," " husband of the state," and " benefactor," were substituted for the more truthful brand of tyrant, or oppressor.　Such a character must be avoided by those " great in the kingdom of heaven ; " nor might the reality of oppression be cloked by any such euphemisms as those named, in the kingdom of Christ. Aristotle, quoted often, says tersely, " They made them kings who had been their benefactors."　And so, probably, the earliest and best sovereigns have been often fathers and friends, rather than oppressors, of their race ; and those who had need to grace a bad title, afterwards affected such names, which flattery was too ready to ascribe to them.

that is greatest among you, let him be as the younger;
and he that is chief, as he that doth serve. For whether
is greater, he that sitteth at meat, or he that serveth?
is not he that sitteth at meat? but I am among you as
he that serveth. Ye are they which have continued
with Me in My temptations. And I appoint unto you a

6. *among you.*—The example of Christ illustrated the lessons of
humility which He taught; but, apart from this, it is clear that the
truest servant of God upon earth, must be he who could do truest
service to God's children on earth. By kindness and humility, he
may open and win every heart; but by assumption and pride, every
heart must be closed against him. Such influence, amongst men, as
results from fear, is the very opposite of the influence of Him who is
love. The one is the principle of the kingdom of God; the other, that
of the kingdom of this world.

7. *chief.*—Gk. "of the first rank." The Apostles, then the bishops;
for thus the ancient writers unite in interpreting Heb. xiii. 17, where
the same word is used. (*Elsley.*) It is quite possible that our Lord's
words should bear this extension; and that, in fact, it was really based
upon His words.

8. *he that serveth.*—These words (see note 1) form a principal argument for the later position of this paragraph; if it is placed *after* the
washing of the disciples' feet, the reference here, of course, is very
distinct and evident. But, considering that they occurred at the Last
Supper, and that they are certainly the resetting of His former charge
(note 3), there is surely ample explanation of them, without its being
necessary to say that they refer (except by anticipation) to that act
of humility. If this reference is held to be true, we should have to
preface the account in John xiii. 1–7, by the introductory statement
in Luke xxii. 24; and then subjoin Luke xxii. 25–30, after the
passage from S. John, as giving a further point to this lesson of
humility. The argument, however, seems rather forced; it is better
to suppose the washing was an enforcement of this lesson.

9. *continued.*—The word suggests a sad memory of some who had
gone away, and "walked no more with Him;" of many who had been
" offended " in Him; of those who had " put their hand to the plough,
and looked back " from the kingdom of heaven.

10. *My temptations.*—All the trials, strife, provocations, "contradiction of sinners against Himself," and privations of Christ's earthly
career. They had borne up through disappointment and deferred
expectation, and were faithful to the end. Though, after the temptation in the wilderness, Satan left Him " for a season," yet were His
" temptations " continuous.

11. *appoint.*—The original word is strong and formal; it implies,
if not a covenant gift, at least an authoritative power to convey the
enjoyment of what is appointed.

kingdom, as My Father hath appointed unto Me; that ye may eat and drink at My table in My kingdom, and sit on thrones judging the twelve tribes of Israel.

(*c.*) *Christ washes the Disciples' Feet.*

S. John xiii. 1-20.

Now before the feast of the passover, when Jesus knew that His hour was come that He should depart out of this world unto the Father, having loved His own which were in the world, He loved them unto the end.

12. *a kingdom.*—Whitby considers that this refers to the government of the Apostles, in Christ's kingdom on earth. In this case the "thrones" further promised, would be the future reward of their conscientious discharge of this earthly viceroyalty.

13. *on thrones.*—It has been noticed that our Lord does not, as in Matt. xix. 28, say "*twelve* thrones," for the traitor was among them whose throne was to be filled by another; though, even then, the promise may have borne to him a special meaning,—would he but repent, there was in Christ's kingdom all that a right ambition could desire, of power, and honour, and reward. There is here, again, an instance of the fact spoken of in note 3.

1. *before the feast.*—*i.e.* just before; a formal announcement of this significant action of humility and love. Some writers (see xxiii. 1) understand this to imply the day before the usual day of the Passover. Tholuck's explanation of the difficulty there alluded to, may be thus stated: "Before the feast of the Passover," should be understood as, "before the Passover properly so called," which really commenced twenty-four hours later, on the 15th Nisan. In John xix., *vv.* 14 and 31 thus admit of explanation, since the "preparation of the Passover" is the day before the Passover proper; and in *v.* 31 that sabbath is called a "high day," because the first day of the Passover fell on it; which, just as much as the last, was regarded as a great day. Thus, in John xviii. 28, "the Passover" would not be the Paschal lamb, but the other sacrifices and observances of the feast; perhaps specially the Chagigah, peace-offerings.

2. *He loved them.*—The approach of death, and the entering into His glory, did not alter His regard for them; nay, He selected this very crisis for displaying to them the most convincing proofs of His devotion and love. Before sitting down with them to this feast, Luther says, "There were high thoughts which might have so withdrawn Him

And supper being ended, the devil having now put into the heart of Judas Iscariot, Simon's *son*, to betray Him; Jesus knowing that the Father had given all

from the world, as to have left no room in His mind even for His disciples."

3. *supper being ended.*—This is an inaccurate rendering, and is unfortunate in giving an impression exactly the reverse of what is correct; it should be, "supper being prepared," or ready.

4. *the devil*, etc.—S. John marks the origin of this act, it was the inspiration of Satan; but the evil seed found congenial soil in the debased heart of Judas, which was already prepared to receive, and to mature, such wickedness; and no appeal of our Lord's mercy could now win him from it. It is worth noticing, in this distinct instance, the real history of every evil act done against Christ's cause upon earth; it is of the *suggestion* of Satan, but it is the *act* of one of those for whose redemption the Saviour gave His life's blood. Satan could not accomplish his purpose by his own means; it was out of the range of power permitted to him, as an evil spirit, to interfere personally in the betrayal of Christ; but he could do it through Judas. So also it was beyond his power to compass the death of Christ; but he made use of the rulers, in whose case we find the same declaration of Satanic influence, as urging their deeds of murder, and false witness, and mockery of injustice. Our Lord says, "Ye are of your father the devil, and the lusts of your father it is your will to do. He was a murderer from the beginning, and abode not in the truth, because there is no truth in him" (John viii. 44). It is so in every act of sin, and of successful wrong; the devil may inspire it, man only can execute it.

5. *Jesus knowing*, etc.—The whole paragraph bespeaks our closest attention to the act that follows, in all its several particulars, and to their deep spiritual significance. We are not to suppose it a mere practical lesson of humility, tinged with the sorrow, and regret, and affection of this parting hour; and referring only to the strife among the disciples on this particular occasion. There was in it the most thorough deliberation; and it was fraught with consequences of far deeper and more general moment. The victory of Christ lay through humility, and the success of His Gospel in the world must certainly be impeded, and thwarted, by pride and contention for worldly eminence, amongst those set in charge with the publication of it. The same mind essentially must be in them which was also in Him. And, therefore, though fully aware of the treachery of Judas, who had sold his life; aware also that God had given into His hands all power on earth and in heaven, the traitor and all enemies, and far more, the salvation of all believers being within the exercise of that power; feeling, never more than in this hour of trial, the truth of His eternal Sonship with the Father, of His mission direct from God, and of the approaching

things into His hands, and that He was come from God, and went to God; He riseth from supper, and laid aside His garments; and took a towel, and girded Himself. After that He poureth water into a bason, and began to wash the disciples' feet, and to wipe *them* with the towel wherewith He was girded. Then cometh He to Simon Peter: and Peter saith unto Him, Lord, dost Thou wash

glory of His ascension; He, the Lord of all power and might, rose up, and assumed the form of a servant, and performed the most menial of services for these twelve men, representatives of the race He came to redeem, one of whom was His betrayer, none of whom were perfect in their devotion to Him. It was an act almost unintelligible to those who witnessed it; but its spiritual significance was worthy of One so conscious of His high estate, and yet so lowly. It was an ever-memorable lesson of the victory of true humility and love, over the false pride of men. The spirit which stirred in the Apostles must be fatal to their mission to the world; the spirit in Him was that of "the victory which overcometh the world."

6. *He riseth.*—There was now no host to receive them as guests, and there was no servant amongst them; one, therefore, must assume the part of the host, and provide for the customary washing of feet; one must perform the act of a servant. They all strove to avoid this. All were desiring priority of place; none would condescend so far. Our Lord, therefore, took upon Himself the form of a servant, and also discharged the service of a host; and, though He had the full knowledge that He was the Lord of all, He set them this example of humility, before He received them at His table as His guests. He left them reclining at the table, and, putting aside His upper garments, He girded Himself like a servant; poured the water (see xxiii. 5), as a servant should do, into the basin, and went behind the Apostles as they lay, washed their feet, and wiped them with the towel. The details are as carefully and deliberately mentioned, as our Lord's consciousness of His pre-eminence, and of their inferiority, are noted in the preceding paragraph, "He was amongst them as he that serveth." S. John here shows his usual care in impressing on us the *Divinity* of Christ (the key-note of his Gospel), whilst speaking of His special condescension.

7. *Simon Peter.*—Whether Peter was, as some suppose, the first in order to whom our Lord came, or, as some think, with more reason, not the first; our Lord's proceeding had evoked no remark until He came to the feet of Peter. Astonishment at so unusual and singular a service, and the knowledge that so much ever underlay the actions of their Master, kept them silent, though wonderstruck. But when He came to Peter, his prompt and fiery spirit resented the apparent

my feet ? Jesus answered and said unto him, What I
do thou knowest not now ; but thou shalt know hereafter. Peter saith unto Him, Thou shalt never wash
my feet. Jesus answered him, If I wash thee not, thou
hast no part with Me. Simon Peter saith unto Him,
Lord, not my feet only, but also *my* hands and *my* head.
Jesus saith unto him, He that is washed needeth not

degradation of His Lord ; and very probably some of that humility,
and perception of our Lord's Divinity, now moved him, as it did on
other occasions, and he deprecated this submission of the Lord's proper
dignity in his case. "Lord, dost Thou wash my feet !" In each separate
word there is emphasis.

8. *thou knowest not now.*—Peter should have given his Lord credit
for having wise and right views, even in an act which he could not
comprehend. It is sad to make so serious a mistake, and to run the
risk of losing so important a blessing, through the intemperance of his
own zeal. Our Lord's answer is a reproof to all such mistaken
fervour, and to all those who arraign the wisdom and propriety of
God's doings, at the bar of their own discretion : another witness to
the representative nature, and deep spiritual significance, of this incident.

9. *hereafter.*—Presently, afterwards ; as soon as our Lord had
finished His self-imposed task, He gave an explanation of it. But the
promise, " Thou shalt know hereafter," will be verified in the experience
of every one of those who read Christ's unknown mercies of their past
life, in the light of His explanation of them in the world of glory.

10. *never.*—Gk. "never for ever." S. Peter was still under the
vehement influence of his own sentiments, and beyond the call to right
consideration of our Lord's ways. He therefore speaks in words which
at once recall him to himself, though only to desire, with opposite
impetuosity, the service which he had refused ; and that still, not as
our Lord would render it, but in a measure unnecessary and beyond
reason. His impetuosity again led him into an error, nearly as great
as that former one. (See note 7.)

11. *he that is washed,* etc.—Gk. " that has been washed." There is
a distinction in the original which is important, but which is not
preserved in the translation. The passage may be more exactly expressed thus, "He that has been *bathed* needeth not save to *wash* his
feet." One who has bathed may be defiled, as he treads the roads of
life ; and even on an honest errand (S. Bernard warns us) we collect
dust ; but that affects his *feet* only—when they are washed he is clean
as before. The spiritual lesson conveyed thus is very special. He
who has been bathed in the "laver of regeneration" (Titus iii. 5), the
" one baptism for the remission of sins," need not repeat that washing,

save to wash his feet, but is clean every whit: and ye

and may not; but the defilements of every day, contracted as men walk the path of life, the daily sins, must be daily forgiven, and daily cleansed. If this is not so, though washed from all original sin, yet we have no part with Christ. Peter, in his ardour, made two mistakes: first, he would have refused this daily cleansing; and next, he would have undervalued the perpetual efficacy of the "washing of regeneration," and required that to be repeated which is once and for ever. These are fundamental errors, most serious in the case of an Apostle. And such errors are not his alone. There are those who, overlooking our Lord's correction of Peter's misconceptions, would rest contented with what they term their conversion, thinking that, once cleansed, they must be for ever and absolutely clean. There are those also who altogether undervalue the efficacy of their regeneration in baptism; placing all their reliance on acts of subsequent penitence, forgiveness, restoration; not considering that every exercise of the grace of repentance is the consequence of the effective working of that Holy Spirit who was given to them in baptism, and that all forgiveness is the performance of God's part of the baptismal covenant "for the remission of sins;" and that it is not because of any subsequent conversion or spiritual gift, that they can approach nearer to God, but because of the effective working of the original gift, hitherto perhaps dormant. It is, in fact, as the Apostle says, "because ye *are* sons" (by adoption in baptism) "God hath sent forth the Spirit of His Son into your hearts." How very significant, then, and of what universal application, are the lessons which centre in this action of our Lord! Besser, and others, quote words of S. Augustine which are aptly illustrative of what is above stated: "In holy baptism one is wholly washed; but afterwards, by living amongst the things of the world, we tread the ground with our feet. Human feelings and emotions, without which we cannot live in this mortal state, are, as it were, the feet which gather up the dust of this earth; and thereby we become so polluted that, 'if we say that we have no sin, we deceive ourselves, and the truth is not in us.' Hence daily our feet are washed by Him who is our Advocate with the Father, and who intercedes for us: and daily we confess that we have this feet-washing when we pray, 'Forgive us our trespasses, as we forgive them that trespass against us.' And when we make this confession, then He, who washed the disciples' feet, 'is faithful and just to forgive us our sins, and to cleanse us from all unrighteousness.'" Bishop Jeremy Taylor explains the passage of the "purging away the guilt contracted in our passage from the font to the altar:" "The Sacrament of the Lord's Supper (just about to be instituted) was certainly designed to supply a constant source of cleansing, or renovation" (see II. vii. 9), "so that our sinful bodies may be made clean by His body, and our souls washed through His most precious blood." Thus, the two Sacraments ordained by Christ Himself, offer—the one, a

are clean, but not all. For He knew who should betray Him ; therefore said He, Ye are not all clean.

So after He had washed their feet, and had taken His garments, and was set down again, He said unto them, Know ye what I have done to you? Ye call Me Master and Lord: and ye say well; for *so* I am. If I then, *your* Lord and Master, have washed your feet ; ye also ought to wash one another's feet. For I have given

regeneration from original sin; the other, a constant cleansing from daily sin, and a constant supply of necessary grace : the last follows and supplements the virtue of the first. S. Augustine gathers from this passage the fact that the disciples were themselves baptized, either with John's baptism, or, more likely, with that of Christ; for, as Christ baptized by their ministration, He must have done so by those who were themselves baptized.

12. *not all clean.*—In the instance of the traitor Judas, not only was the original baptism inefficacious, but this washing also was lost upon him. The application of all means of Christ's grace are ineffectual to those once in a state of salvation, if there is no repentance, faith, obedience, love, humility, in the heart of those who are partakers of them. Again the rule is general.

13. *so after*, etc.—There is again the same deliberation pourtrayed with minute care, as if every incident was intended to be earnestly regarded by all readers. Our Lord also calls the attention of the twelve, by questioning them in a manner unusual to Him.

14. *so I am.*—Our Lord here expresses the special consciousness, with reference to this occasion, of all that He was beyond what He seemed to be, which S. John so carefully marks. (See notes 5, 6.) Our Lord's meaning, in the title which He here claims, is in the fullest sense of Divinity ; the disciples probably did not fully so understand the title until afterwards. (See P. II. vi. 11.) Dr. Donne remarks, "To call Him Lord is to contemplate His kingdom of power, to feel His kingdom of grace, to wish His kingdom of glory."

15. *ye ought also*, etc.—A charge so solemnly given, at such an hour, and so carefully emphasized, must be considered binding in a more than ordinarily degree ; and yet, neither in the early ages, nor in any subsequent age, has there been any general compliance with the letter of the command. Circumstances of climate, and of social custom, would render this, for the most part, an impossibility. Origen notices this washing as " merely a matter of custom, and the custom is now generally dropped." Indeed, we might as well say that those who wished to do as they would be done by, should act the parable of the good Samaritan, or any other which teaches general duty. The washing of the feet of beggars, in the Romish communion, by princes of the

you an example, that ye should do as I have done to you. Verily, verily, I say unto you, The servant is not greater than his lord; neither he that is sent greater than He that sent him. If ye know these things, happy are ye if ye do them. I speak not of you all : I know whom I have chosen : but that the scripture may be

Church, and other princes, is merely the enacting of the *figure* in which our Lord conveyed this lesson of humility. We must therefore look to the spirit of the act; and know that humility, and the readiness to serve the highest interests of those for whom Christ died, at the cost even of our own personal dignity, the deep anxiety to cleanse, and purify, and strengthen them amidst the defilements of their life in the world, are objects to be borne in mind by Christ's servants, with all particularity. " I have given you an example, that ye should do as I have done to you." The lesson is one of the necessity of putting into action what we know of Christ; not of speaking only, but of doing as He has done. " Let us confess our faults one to another; forgive one another's faults; pray for one another's faults. In this way, we shall wash one another's feet." (*Augustine.*)

16. *is not greater.*—And therefore there can be no degradation in your following the example of your Lord.

17. *he that is sent.*—Gk. " the Apostle ; " a clearer rendering in this instance.

18. *if ye know these things.*—Now comes the practical application. This incident, introduced with so great solemnity by the Apostle who narrates it, stamped by our Lord's earnest and striking manner as a lesson most valuable and notable, teaches the all-sufficiency of the " washing of regeneration ; " the absolute necessity of the daily cleansing from all daily sins ; the deep importance of humility on the part of those who would win the world, which labours under the curse of pride, to the humility of Christ ; the divine excellence of love, that charity which " never faileth ; " the blessedness of ministration in these matters of one with another. For now the whole is concluded with our Lord's blessing, not on those who *know*, but on those who *do* what He has taught. This knowledge is amongst the profoundest truths of our religion. But knowledge cannot save the soul, our soul, or that of others ; but—" blessed are ye if ye *do* as I have done to you."

19. *chosen*, etc.—These words are important : if incorrectly received, they may give support to that doctrine of the election of some, and of the exclusion of others, which is so dangerous. If we read them in connection with those of John vi. 70, " Have I not chosen you, and one of you is a devil ? " we see that they were all chosen, but one was falling from his high estate, notwithstanding such election. The real meaning is, " I am fully acquainted with the qualities, tempers,

fulfilled, **He that eateth bread with Me hath lifted up his heel against Me.** Now I tell you before it come, that, when it is come to pass, ye may believe that I am *He.* Verily, verily, I say unto you, He that receiveth whomsoever I send receiveth Me; and he that receiveth Me receiveth Him that sent Me.

infirmities of those whom I have chosen; I know them well, and what is in them; and one of these, who eats bread with Me, has betrayed My cause and My person."

20. *that the Scripture.*—(See i. 14.) Not, "this is done in order to fulfil that which is written;" but, "all this which is taking place has been foreseen and foreshown, and is therefore as God wills it should be." (See xvii. 1, 5.)

21. *lifted up his heel.*—Heb. "magnified." He has endeavoured to trample on Me in a proud and vaunting manner, when I was prostrate; or, as Dean Burgon applies the phrase, of a wrestler, tripping up his adversary treacherously to procure his fall, and thus a "*supplanter.*"

22. *I tell you.*—Our Lord carefully impresses upon the disciples His perfect acquaintance with what is about to happen, and its being in accordance not only with the prophecies of Scripture, but with the permission of God, and with His own acquiescence. He declares that there is a traitor amongst His own most intimate associates; soon He more particularly dwells on this (xxiv. *d.*), and He imparts to them this, His foreknowledge, in order that their faith may not fail in the hour of its trial. For, however awful and menacing the power which may be used against Him, they must remember that He knew it all, and might certainly have avoided it, had it not been exerted against Him within the limits ordained of God, and sanctioned by Himself. And therefore, when all shall happen to Him as He foretells it, they must believe that the rejected, and even crucified, Son of man is the true Messiah that should come. This declaration is a key to the design of all prophecy, that, on its fulfilment, we should believe the omniscience and truth of our God.

23. *he that receiveth.*—The connection of these words with the preceding incident is, at first sight, somewhat difficult; but our Lord may have thought it necessary to reassure them in the practice of self-denial and humility, that, lowly as they came before the world, they brought His presence with them; and that, therefore, the servant's word should be ratified by the Master. Whoever accepted them and their message, accepted Himself and His Gospel, and God who sent Him. That, therefore, the humility of their lives would be productive of higher glory, than any self-assertion, or proud bearing, would entail. He thus also shows that the fall, and disgrace, of one of them, did not detract from the dignity, and spiritual eminence, of those who heralded His cause after the example of His own lowliness and love.

(*d.*) *Christ foreshows His Betrayal.*

S. Matt. xxvi. 21–25 ; S. Mark xiv. 18–21 ; S. Luke xxi. 21–23 ; S. John xiii. 21–38.

When Jesus had thus said, He was troubled in spirit, and testified, and said, Verily, verily, I say unto you, that one of you which eateth with Me shall betray Me. Then the disciples looked one on another, doubting of whom He spake. And they began to be sorrowful, and to say unto Him one by one, Lord, *Is* it I? and another *said*, Is it I? And He answered and said unto them, *It is* one of the twelve, that dippeth with Me in the dish. The Son of man indeed goeth, as it is written of Him:

1. *troubled.*—(See xvi. 15). There are several occasions on which the wave of sorrow for human misery, faithlessness, and sin, seems to have rolled over the spirit of the Saviour. (See Luke xii. 50, xix. 41; John xi. 33–38, xii. 27; Matthew xxvi. 38, 39.) Here He mourns over the lost soul of one of the chosen twelve, and for his dark treachery, and for the failure of every hope of winning him from his evil purpose. S. Luke (xxii. 21) preserves the abruptness with which He spoke, under overwhelming pressure of grief, and sense of treachery: "But, behold, the hand of him that betrayeth Me is with Me on the table."

2. *testified.*—He spoke with unusual and emphatic earnestness. The word is one of frequent use, and always bears a solemn and formal sense.

3. *Lord, is it I?*—They were conscious, all but one, that they had entertained no such base intention; but they had humility enough to fear it possible, since their Lord, in His unerring knowledge of what was in man, declared so solemnly that such should be the case. This self-distrust, and humility, of the disciples, must be remembered in their favour, when we have so soon to consider their fall, and desertion of their Master.

4. *that dippeth with Me.*—This is an enhancement of the declaration, that the betrayer was one of the twelve: "Yes (our Lord says), it is one of those who have *eaten* with Me"—a bond most sacred in the customs of Eastern people. Amongst the tribes who, at this day, roam over the desolate districts of Palestine and Syria, any traveller is generally safe from harm from any with whom he has eaten bread and salt.

5. *goeth,* etc.—Goeth to His death, as God has foreordained. It was truly determined that Christ should be delivered up to die, not that Judas was forced by God to be the guilty means. Though it was so

but woe to that man by whom the Son of man is betrayed! good were it for that man if he had never been born. Then Judas, which betrayed him, answered and said, Master, is it I? He said unto him, Thou hast said. And they began to enquire among themselves, which of them it was that should do this thing.

foreseen, the *act* of betrayal was entirely his own. The devil found him a willing agent, and ready; he rejected the mercy and long-suffering, and despised the warnings, of Christ; and so God gave him up, and permitted him to be hurried away, in the career of wickedness. As Christ went voluntarily to His death, and not of necessity; so there was no Divine compulsion upon Judas to act as he did. "For, as respects the end for which he was designed, it would have been better for him to have been born, if he had not been the betrayer; for God created him for good works: but after such dreadful wickedness, it would have been better for him never to have been born." (*Theophylact.*)

6. *good were it.*—This is a very strong argument for the eternity of punishment; for if there could be any time when the sin of Judas could be forgiven, and he admitted to future and eternal happiness, so strong an expression could scarcely have been used. We need not suppose that the chief and hopeless feature, in the sin of Judas, was that it was done against Christ; for He especially declared that there was pardon for all sin against Himself. (Matt. xii. 32.) But the case of one who sinned against " the covenant of salt; " who was so completely under the influence of a master passion, that he sold his Lord for so paltry a sum as the price of a slave; whose master passion was the sin of " covetousness, which is idolatry," and who knew that he was doing his best to mar the redemption of the world, in the line to which his forefathers had looked since the days of Abraham; who would ruin that redemption of mankind for his own avarice's sake, was a villain beyond all that have ever disgraced the form of man. There could be no pardon for such guilt; however beyond all expression, it was enhanced by the fact that he, with his fellow-Apostles, had said of the Lord he betrayed, by their spokesman, Peter, " Thou art the Christ, the Son of the living God." However deserved, it is an awful doom, to be the only one whose sentence of condemnation has been pronounced before the great day.

7. *thou hast said.*—You say truly, you are the betrayer. No doubt, our Lord so said this that it passed unnoticed by the rest of the Apostles, for they did not connect Judas with this crime, even when he left the supper-room. Tradition asserts, with probability of truth, that Judas occupied the place nearest Christ, on His left; and so a whisper might convey this answer. It is strange to find Judas so daringly asking this question; he could scarcely hope that, after so many, *to him,* intelligible declarations, his treachery should be unknown

Now there was leaning on Jesus' bosom one of His

to Christ. Whether in fear, or desire to avert suspicion, or to test if Christ did really know the secret of his own guilty conscience, he so questioned, it is impossible to say; but it appears as if he knew Christ would not denounce him; and so he dared everything, in the audacity of a heart thoroughly hardened. Maldonatus, Stier, and others, notice the difference in the words "*Lord*" used by the eleven, and "Master" (Rabbi) by Judas; they uttered, in most humble submission, the name " Lord," which was the answer to their own question: that word does not pass the traitor's lips, but instead of it he uses the cold and ceremonious "Rabbi"—a difference which is hardly accidental. Bishop Goodwin, to the same effect, says, " It has been observed that Judas is never recorded to have called Christ by the name of *Lord ;* both on this occasion, and in the garden, the title is *Rabbi ;* possibly we should do wrong in assigning any special importance to the circumstance, but the words of S. Paul seem naturally to come to mind, ' No man can say that Jesus is *the Lord*, but by the Holy Ghost.' "

8. *among themselves.*—The sorrow which lay upon them was so painful that they could not bear it, and began to inquire of each other what any one had done towards so awful a sin. It is surely a remarkable evidence of the result of our Lord's teaching, and of His spirit within them, that, though at this season of trial they failed in several particulars of action, yet there was not one of them capable of suspecting another, more than himself, of this crime, at which they all shuddered ; nor did any fix on Judas, although he had given more than one token of the influence of his ruling passion, and its strength in severing him from them in aim and spirit. It would be difficult to find any twelve men equally humble-minded, guileless, and graced with that spirit of charity which "thinketh no evil" of another ; if we did find them, we should certainly recognize in them the mind of Christ, and " take knowledge of them that they had been with Jesus." S. John says, " They looked one on another " (none of them specially on Judas), as if each felt *himself* might be the one spoken of.

9. *leaning.*—The Jews reclined at table, leaning on the left arm. John, therefore, must have been on the right hand of Jesus; by leaning closer to Him, he would be able to address our Lord, and to hear His reply, unperceived by the rest. (See note 7.) S. Chrysostom thinks that Peter desired to know this, not out of curiosity, or in grief, or indignation, but in order that he might prevent it, if he knew the traitor. (See note 18.)

10. *on Jesus' bosom.*—This position was one which was expressive of favour and love. Christ speaks of Himself as "the only begotten Son, which is in the bosom of the Father," and therefore able to "declare Him " to the world (John i. 18). He also spoke of Lazarus as "carried by the angels into Abraham's bosom." The ancient

disciples whom Jesus loved. Simon Peter therefore beckoned to him, that he should ask who it should be of whom He spake. He then lying on Jesus' breast saith unto Him, Lord, who is it? Jesus answered, He it is, to whom I shall give a sop, when I have dipped *it*. And when He had dipped the sop, He gave *it* to Judas Iscariot,

writers have, therefore, noticed that this was more than man's intimacy with man; and that, to the communion thus permitted to him by Christ, is owing the deep spirituality of his Gospel, Epistles, and Revelation. Far less admirable is the explanation of Bishop Sanderson, which has been adopted by some: "Our Lord showed a more affectionate regard to S. John, than to any other of His disciples, for no other known reason, so much as for this, that he was near of kin to Him; His own mother's sister's son, as is generally supposed." (See xxxi. 23.) This reason, too, seems only based upon supposition, or a doubtful tradition; and it is decidedly in contradiction of our Lord's own declaration, that ties of earthly relationship were inferior, in His estimation, to that of co-operation with Himself in doing the will of God. (See Mark iii. 32, 35.) There were also others of the disciples of kin to our Lord; this, therefore, does not satisfactorily account for the intimacy allowed to S. John.

11. *lying on Jesus' breast.*—Different words, in the original, from those above rendered "*leaning, bosom:*" there is implied the throwing himself backward, from the former to a somewhat closer and higher position. Then S. John would bring his face nearer to that of Christ, and so question Him privately. The gesture, though natural and easy, was one of affection and intimacy. (See S. John's reference to this in John xxi. 20.)

12. *Jesus answered.*—Privately, and apart from S. John, who thus alone knew the traitor. Whether he at once divulged this to Peter, is not said; probably the horror of realizing the fact that his fellow-disciple Judas was so dark a traitor, occupied his mind for the few minutes until Judas went out.

13. *the sop.*—This act would not in itself excite attention. It was not an unusual act at any feast; but yet it denotes a special kindness, and we may suppose that S. John now witnessed the last appeal made by Christ to Judas, to whom He had shown His full knowledge of his intended treachery. The sop, thus given, may have been equivalent to a special offer of pardon, and a tender appeal to the fallen Apostle's recollection of many acts of mercy and kindness during their long intimacy. It is an appeal to the Eastern custom of eating bread with one; and is a covenant, on the part of him that offers, and of him that eats, that no treachery is intended. (See the aggravation of the act of treachery shown in Ps. xli. 9.)

the son of Simon.　And after the sop Satan entered into him.　Then said Jesus unto him, That thou doest, do

14. *the son of Simon.*—Who this Simon was, whose sad distinction it is to be recorded as the father of the traitor, wherever the Gospel is preached, is not known.　It is probable that he was a native of Kerioth, or Carioth, a town in the south of Judæa.　The name "Iscariot" would thus be a local, rather than a personal, appellation. It is applied to Simon, in John vi. 71 ; that reading of the original Greek being probably correct, which attaches the word " Iscariot " to Simon, not to Judas ("Judas, the son of Simon Iscariot").　In John xiii. 2, and in the present instance (*v.* 26), MSS. of value give the reading " Judas, the son of Simon Iscariot."　In John xii. 4, the reading adopted by Dean Alford gives simply, ' Then saith Iscariot, one of His disciples," etc. ;　where the Gk. article prefixed to Iscariot, would give the sense of, " the native of Kerioth."　In Keble's " Lyra Innocentium " (Cradle Songs, No. 13), there are beautiful thoughts grounded on the " Infancy of Judas."

15. *Satan entered into him.*—" Observe that at first Satan did not enter into Judas, but only put it into his heart to betray his Master ; but after the event he entered into him.　Let us beware that Satan thrust not any of his flaming darts into our heart; for if he do, then he watches till he gets an entrance there himself." (*Origen.*)　It is evident that Judas set his heart against this offer from his Lord, and was then given up, as reprobate, to his appropriate service, as a minister of God's wrath fitted to destruction.　The expression here is very different from that of John xiii. 2, " The devil having *put it into the heart* of Judas to betray Him."　That expresses powerful temptation only ; this, absolute mastery and possession of his being ; but it is noticeable, again, how different this is from any cause of demoniacal possession mentioned in the N. T., where Satan seemed to have assumed a power over the bodies of men.　Judas gave himself up (his free will and conscious preference were yielded) as the agent of Satan for this sinful service ; and the demoniacal possession is, in such a case, of the spirit, not simply of the body, of the possessed.　This " sop " need not be confounded with any sacramental element—it was a portion of the Paschal supper only.　In one of the exhortations to the Communion Service of the Church of England, a sacramental character is attributed to this incident ; warning being given that Christ's people do not receive the Lord's Supper as Judas received the sop, in disdainful rejection of the dying plea urged by the Saviour to win them to the right.　But it is not necessary to affirm (though certainly the opinion may be held) that the Church of England thus maintains the presence of Judas at the institution of the Lord's Supper ; the parallel of warning is sufficiently just, without supposing his presence on that occasion.　His presence at the institution of the Lord's Supper is,

quickly.   Now no man at the table knew for what intent He spake this unto him.   For some *of them* thought, because Judas had the bag, that Jesus had said unto him, Buy *those things* that we have need of against the feast ; or, that he should give something to the poor.   He

however, assumed by S. Augustine and others of the early writers, though not unanimously ; it is rejected by S. Hilary, and by the majority of those of note of modern date.   (See xxiv. *a.* 4.)

16. *then said Jesus.*—" *Then,*" when His Spirit perceived that Judas had cast away His offer, and was resolved and God-forsaken.   Christ could no longer tolerate his presence, and the restraint which it imposed on his utterance.   He had much to say to those who were true of heart, and little time to say it ; and there was no longer hope of gaining Judas.

17. *do quickly.*—So said our Lord to the Pharisees, " Fill ye up, then, the measure of your iniquity " (Matt. xxiii. 32).   It was the judicial sentence, which was spoken to these and other agents of wrath ; to Pharaoh, when *God hardened* his heart (Exod. x. 20) ; to Balaam, when God said, " Go with the men " (Num. xxii. 35) ; to Saul, when " the Spirit of the Lord departed from him, and an evil spirit from God troubled him " (1 Sam xvi. 14).   The truth noted by S. Augustine is a profound truth, forcibly expressed : " God makes an agent of what is evil, but is not the Author of evil."

18. *no man . . . knew.*—Though S. John, at least, now knew Judas for the traitor, he did not apprehend immediate action, and therefore had no suspicion of the meaning of our Lord's words.   None of the rest had any idea of their true import ; had this been evident, some of them must have endeavoured to prevent his action.   " Had Christ made him known, perhaps Peter would have killed him." (*Chrysostom.*) Judas had been a very clever dissimulator, and they were very far from supposing him other than he seemed, a careful and diligent dispenser of their common fund.

19. *the feast.*—Either the period of the feast, which extended over eight days ; or, it might mean, for that very feast which they were celebrating.   It may have appeared that Judas went in haste to get something which had been forgotten, and which would be immediately wanted ; hence the significance, to the minds of the disciples, of the words, " That thou doest, do quickly."   For anything later there would have been no need to hurry—the next day would have afforded time enough.   A fair argument is founded on this interpretation of the act of Judas in favour of this feast being an anticipation of the real Passover, as kept by the nation.   Not only might no one go out of the house until the morning ; but, if he did go out, there would be no place open, where he could buy things needed for the feast.   (See xxiii. 1.)

20. *the poor.*—This was evidently our Lord's principle and practice.

then having received the sop went immediately out : and it was night.

Therefore, when he was gone out, Jesus said, Now is

Though He "had not where to lay His head," and the very necessities of daily life were frequently "ministered to Him of their substance" by holy disciples (Luke viii. 2, 3), yet the service of the poor was a constant charge. We see in this a reason for the plausible, but hypocritical, suggestion of Judas (John xii. 5, 6), and for the primary importance so early attached by the Apostles to the Church's duty of almsgiving (Gal. ii. 10). How very forcible, to the minds of the disciples, conscious of the blessing of alms received from the hands of Christ Himself, must have been the words of the Lord Jesus, " It is more blessed to give than to receive." And yet, as occurring at the moment, "these are conjectures which are very improbable in themselves, for what could be purchased so late at night, at such a high festival season ; or what distribution of alms was possible at such an hour ? We can see how far the rest were from suspecting such evil as was familiar to the mind of Judas, and how readily the idea occurred that some want of theirs, or some act of mercy, was the occasion of the departure of Judas." (See note 8.) We must not omit to notice here the lesson to the *poor* of giving alms to the poor (as the widow's mite teaches them to give offertory to God); the reason for S. Paul's injunction to the day labourer, in Eph. iv. 28, is, "that he may have to give to him that needeth."

21. *immediately.*—The man so full of the presence of the devil, could no longer bear to remain in the presence of Christ; but he now " went out " for evermore from the blessed company and the grace of Christ.

22. *it was night.*—Many commentators, both in ancient and modern times, have noticed this expression as used here. Some of the former have pointed out the significance of this hour, in coincidence with the more than darkness of night in the heart of Judas ; amongst the latter, none have spoken more suggestively than Dean Alford, "I quite feel that there is something awful in this termination, 'It was night.'"

23. *when he was gone out.*—There is an immediate sense of relief apparent in our Lord's mind ; He ceased to be troubled and oppressed, as He was when the "hand of him that betrayed Him was present with Him at the table." But not this only. The one being lost absorbed the anxiety of the Saviour, until his case became quite hopeless, and " he went out." And, further the departure of Judas ushers in the Passion, and its grand consequences, which were the prelude to the manifestation of His glory in His resurrection and ascension. The departure of the wicked, in like manner, is a prelude to the future manifestation of Christ's glory, in which only those who are clean in His sight will be present with Him. The last discourse of our Lord to His disciples

the Son of man glorified, and God is glorified in Him. If God be glorified in Him, God shall also glorify Him in Himself, and shall straightway glorify Him. Little children, yet a little while I am with you. Ye shall seek

actually commences here. It is broken off by the institution of the Lord's Supper, the foretelling of Peter's fall, and the walk to Gethsemane; but the thread is regularly resumed at every interruption.

24. *the Son of man.*—This designation is specially significant here. Our Lord's mind forecasts the victory which shall follow His Passion and death, and the glory which, in human form, as the Son of man, He shall win to Himself, and for the race of which He is the representative. Many a time had God's justice and law been broken and outraged, and His mercy despised, by man; but now, in Christ, God is glorified in man, in His humility, and obedience, and faith, and in His victory, and in bringing mankind to His kingdom. He is glorified in the martyrdom (in life or in death) of every witness to the truth, and in his victory through Christ. For God had given His only Son to work out the salvation of mankind, and the accomplishment of the mission redounded to the glory of God, whose attributes of justice, holiness, and love, were now illustrated before the whole universe of His creation.

25. *if.*—*i.e.* since, because.

26. *in Himself.*—He will receive Him into heaven, and place Him upon His throne of universal dominion; all powers in heaven, and in earth, and throughout God's creation, being made subject to Him; and so Christ will be glorified in Himself, *i.e.* with His own proper glory. The sentence is somewhat difficult; but several of the ancient writers have thus referred "Himself" to Christ, giving the sense that God will bring into prominence the Divinity into which Christ's manhood is taken. Thus S. Augustine: "The glorifying of the Son of man is the glorifying of God in Him; if God is glorified in Him (for He came not to do His own will, but the will of Him that sent Him), God shall also glorify Him in Himself, so that the human nature which was assumed by the eternal Word shall also be endued with eternity."

27. *straightway.*—Forthwith; the time is immediately at hand. "He predicts His own resurrection, which was to follow immediately; not at the end of the world like ours." (*Augustine.*)

28. *little children.*—This is the sole instance of the use of the original word by our Lord to His disciples. This term has attracted attention in all ages, as expressive of affectionate tenderness, which the approach of the last scenes of trial only serve to enhance and elicit. "Little children, He says, for their souls were yet in infancy." (*Origen.*)

29. *yet a little while.*—There was but an hour or two of this last and intimate intercourse, whilst He was yet with them in bodily presence;

Me : and as I said unto the Jews, Whither I go, ye cannot
come; so now I say to you. A new commandment I
give unto you, That ye love one another; as I have
loved you, that ye also love one another. By this shall
all *men* know that ye are My disciples, if ye have love
one to another.

Simon Peter said unto Him, Lord, whither goest

and then, within a few days, He would ascend up from earth to
heaven.

30. *ye shall seek Me.*—Often would they earnestly long for His
presence, and counsel, in after days of trial and depondency ; when
they were in the terrors of the baptism wherewith He was baptized,
and had not so clear a forecast of victory as He.

31. *unto the Jews.*—(John vii. 34, and viii. 21.) They could not follow
Him then, but should follow Him afterwards. But to the Jews the
sentence was indeed a sore one. They would awake to a consciousness
of His true character and office, and they should seek Him ; they should
run eagerly after false Christs ; and, for disbelief in the true Messiah,
they should die in their sins.

32. *a new commandment.*—Not absolutely new in itself, for the law
of Moses commanded that man should love his neighbour as himself ;
but (as the original word suggests) new, or fresh, in its application.
For it was not to be after a man's own personal and imperfect model,
that he was to love his neighbour ; but now, after the example and
standard of Christ, and for His sake in whom human nature centres,
and is sanctified, which is a new motive to the old commandment. It
refers not to the world as such, but to Christians, and is Christ's command to them, as brethren, and as members of His Body, to be
observed for His sake. Tholuck calls it, "a new manifestation of
love."

33. *all men.*—*i.e.* all mankind. Amongst Christians it shall be
the distinguishing features of brotherhood ; and before the world at
large, it should be the marked characteristic of Christ's people. Our
Lord's declaration was soon and thoroughly fulfilled ; witness the
oft-quoted testimony of the heathen, "See how these Christians love
one another."

34. *whither.*—They did not fully realize the meaning of His death,
and its consequences. They saw that something lay beyond it ; but
what, they could not understand. They seem to have had some idea
that the conclusion of this life of proclamation of the Gospel, and of
miraculous evidence in support of it, would be the inauguration of that
kingdom on which their hopes were bent. Perhaps Satan (who would
repeat our fall through pride) suggested to them, as he did to Eve,
that this death was but the act of termination of an inferior, the

thou? Jesus answered him, Whither I go, thou canst
not follow Me now; but thou shalt follow Me afterwards.
Peter said unto Him, Lord, why cannot I follow Thee
now? I will lay down my life for Thy sake. Jesus
answered him, Wilt thou lay down thy life for My sake?
Verily, verily, I say unto thee, The cock shall not crow,
till thou hast denied Me thrice.

(e.) *The Institution of the Lord's Supper.*

S. Matt. xxvi. 26–29; S. Mark xiv. 22–25; S. Luke xviii. 19, 20;
[1 Cor. xi. 24, 25.]

And as they were eating, Jesus took bread, and gave

commencement of a superior life; and whispered to them, "He shall
not surely *die.*"

35. *not now.*—A happy modification of the mournful words, "Whither
I go, ye cannot come." The passage may suggest the recognition, and
companionship, of those who follow the departed to the world beyond
the grave; we follow them, as we follow Christ, to be with them in His
presence.

36. *my life.*—Peter, as ardent now as when our Lord had washed
his feet, would dare death for Christ, and go with Him wherever
beyond death He was going. Devotion could not go further, in itself,
than this. But, alas! it was the blind devotion of an enthusiast, who
spoke in ignorance of what he undertook, and in ignorance, too, of his
own powers. It was very near akin to presumption, to promise to die
for a cause which he did not rightly estimate. But so valuable was
zeal like that of Peter, prompt and unselfish in its right application,
that he must now learn (and others through his sad experience) that
they must count the cost, and know themselves, before they can take
up the cross, and demand the baptism of Christ's sufferings.

37. *till thou hast denied Me.*—Within the compass of the same
night in which you promise so much, you shall refuse to share My
peril; and not once only, but three times severally and emphatically
deny that you know Me, to whom you now offer your life's sacrifice.
(See xxvii. 16.)

1. *as they were eating.*—The three first Evangelists, and S. Paul
(whose independent account of this holy mystery, " received of the
Lord," and not from the Apostles, must be read with theirs), emphasize
the fact that the Lord's Supper was instituted at the last celebration of
the Paschal supper. The bread and the wine were, therefore, those

thanks, and blessed *it*, and brake *it*, and gave *it* to the

of that festival. The analogy (see App. VIII. A.) between the two festivals is direct; the type is fulfilled, and therefore superseded by the reality.   The "Lamb of God" takes the place of the Paschal lamb; the unleavened bread, and the cup of thanksgiving, have done their part in anticipation of that which is now set forth.   Thus Christ Himself celebrated the last Paschal supper, and, as He was doing so, He gave that ordinance in its stead which shall last for ever.   We must not press the hour of the original institution to countenance what the voice and practice of the ancient Church reprobates, namely, evening celebrations. Whatever may be urged in favour of these, amongst classes of persons professedly unable to be present at an earlier service than that of the evening hours, it is likely that very few of these could not attend an early celebration. Those fatigued by the work or troubles of the day, are not generally able to prepare themselves properly for so late a celebration; and, doubtless, a little care and management, a little pre-arrangement with those on whom their leisure depends, would enable them to attend at the early hour, or after morning·service. And it is certain that the exceptional cases are few, if indeed there are any such, where it is *impossible* to communicate otherwise than at night. We hear, indeed, of the large numbers gathered at such celebrations; but it must be owned that, as a rule, the supply creates the demand, rather than the demand necessitates the supply of such ministrations. Christ did not, as was the case with the Passover, appoint any set time or frequency for the celebration of His Supper (in the Acts of the Apostles we find traces of a weekly, if not indeed more frequent, celebration); but the words of S. Paul (1 Cor. xi. 26), whilst they leave the frequency of the act of communion to the conscience and love of Christians, give the most forcible and encouraging argument for a frequent and regular observance of our Lord's dying command, in accordance with the times and seasons prescribed by His Church. (See App. VIII. B.)

2. *bread . . . the cup.*—Gk. "*the* bread." (See viii. 10, 11.) These elements are the outward part or sign, in this Sacrament, of the presence of the inward part or thing signified. They were typified earlier than in the Paschal feast. Clement of Alexandria points to the priesthood of Christ, and His consecration of these elements, in the person of Melchisedec, "who was King of Salem, and priest of the most high God, and gave bread and wine, consecrated food, as a type of the Eucharist." The bread and the wine are natural food, but after consecration they are not simply this. They do not, indeed, become changed as to their substance, nor is any other substance, than that which is theirs originally and naturally, present with them. The "consecration changes the name and use of the bread and wine, but not their substance;" they become "the sign and sacrament of an holy thing," capable, by Christ's word and the Holy Spirit's agency, of conveying,

disciples, and said, Take, eat; this is My Body which is

to the faithful communicant, the Body and Blood of his Lord, "which are verily and indeed taken and received by him in the Lord's Supper." But "we do not," says Justin Martyr, one of the earliest of the ancient writers, "receive these things as a common bread, or as a common cup; but, as through the word of God, Jesus our Saviour, becoming incarnate, took flesh and blood for our salvation, so are we taught that the food over which thanksgiving has been made, through the prayer of that word which came from Him (by which food our blood and flesh are nourished by its conversion into them), is the Body and Blood of that Jesus who was made flesh." So Irenæus: "The bread from the earth, receiving the invocation of God, is no longer common bread, but the Eucharist, consisting of two things, an earthly and an heavenly." Very much has been written, in every age, on the change of the elements; and difference of opinion with regard to this, the chiefest and central act of Christian worship, is a difference which causes distinct separation; thereby "many are offended." There is also a great and culpable want of definite impression on this subject within our communion; the notion of the real presence of Christ in this Sacrament being, to some minds, almost equivalent to the doctrine of the Romanist, or of the Lutheran; whilst, to others, their dread of acknowledging *any* real presence, inclines them to look on the bread and wine without that reverence with which Christ's ordinance invests them, and as merely memorial and spiritual. And their neglect of the Holy Communion is a lamentable, but natural, consequence of their defective views. Their error approaches that of him who abuses this Sacrament, though from a different point of view—it comes of "not discerning the Lord's Body." (See App. VIII. B.) The Catholic truth is, that, whilst we receive the bread and wine in a natural way, we receive the Body and Blood of Christ in a spiritual way, through faith. The Body of Christ is now a spiritual body, and His presence is a real spiritual presence. It is really and spiritually imparted and received; it is not bodily food for the body; but Christ's Body is a spiritual body, and the food of our spiritual life, the food of the spirit. "Yet what these elements are in themselves it skilleth not. It is enough, to me which take them, they are the Body and Blood of Christ. His promise in witness hereof sufficeth. His word He knoweth which way to accomplish." (*Hooker.*) Wise, too, are the words of Thomas à Kempis: "Thou oughtest to beware of curious and unprofitable searching into this most profound Sacrament, if thou wilt not be plunged into the depth of doubt. Many have lost their devotion whilst they sought to search into things too high. Faith is required at thy hands, and a sincere life; not height of understanding, or deep inquiry into the mysteries of God. Submit thyself unto God, and humble thy sense to faith, and the light of knowledge shall be given thee, in such degree as shall be profitable and necessary

given for you: this do in remembrance of Me.   And He

for thee." The language of our Church, in her Homily, is very far from looking upon the Lord's Supper merely as memorial, or upon the elements as merely figures: "Thus much we must be sure to hold, that in the Supper of the Lord there is no vain ceremony or bare sign, but the communion of the Body and Blood of our Lord in a marvellous incorporation, which, by the Holy Ghost, is wrought in the souls of the faithful."   And S. Chrysostom distinguishes clearly the thing signified from the sign: "Nothing merely sensible hath Christ delivered to us, but hath conveyed what is spiritual in things sensible. If thou hadst been without a body, bodiless gifts would have been bestowed upon thee.   But since the soul is combined with the body, in things sensible He bestoweth spiritual gifts."   The words of Archbishop Cranmer are also notable: "Inwardly we eat Christ's Body, and outwardly we eat the Sacrament; so one thing is done outwardly, another inwardly: like as in baptism, the external element whereby the body is washed, is one; and the internal thing whereby the soul is cleansed, is another."   Similarly also Ælfric.

3. *gave thanks.*—Hence the name "Eucharist," or "the giving of thanks." That our Lord gave thanks, was an expression of His willingness to suffer and to die for us; we give thanks for that willingness and death for us, and that He has thought us worthy to be united with Himself in the same readiness to bear our cross, and to do God's will to the "death unto sin." And, in the expression of our thanks for His "inestimable gift" of Himself for us, and (in this Sacrament) to us, we may fitly include thanksgiving for every separate mercy which we would desire to commemorate; for, in a general thanksgiving to God for the chief of all gifts and mercies, we may specially comprehend all minor gifts and mercies of which we are, at any given time, sensible.

4. *blessed it.*—This includes the act of consecrating these common elements of food, to the especial purpose which Christ designed them to serve.   Without consecration, those elements would remain as they naturally are; no more fitted or gifted to convey the presence of Christ, than any other bread and wine.   But the act of consecration is not the only necessity to that end; there must be the operation of the Holy Spirit also; and, further than this, faith is necessary in the spirit of the communicant to the reception of spiritual food.   Without faith, they who receive are not partakers of Christ; nor do they receive the Body and Blood of Christ, as do the faithful in the Lord's Supper.   But yet they do not come in contact with His presence in this Sacrament with impunity; but, "to their condemnation, do eat and drink the sign and sacrament of so great a thing."   They profane the most sublime of holy mysteries to which they have access upon earth.

5. *brake it.*—His doing this was another sign that He voluntarily suffered Himself to be marred, and wounded, and "bruised for our transgressions."   The term, "the breaking of bread," is used in the

took the cup after supper, and gave thanks, and gave it

Acts of the Apostles to express this solemn Sacrament. The bread
which Christ broke was one of the ordinary Paschal loaves, of which
all were thus partakers. It may be pressing words too closely to say
that any wafer bread, which is separate and complete, and not a frag-
ment, is discouraged by this term; but yet the many fragments of a
common loaf, as generally used in the English Church, or of one large
wafer, certainly appear to be more in accordance with this first example.
The Eucharist could scarcely have been designated "the breaking of
bread," had the bread consisted of numerous independent wafers, even
though made from a common mass of meal. The words attributed to
Ignatius (to the Philadelphians, iv. Longer Ep.) are noteworthy: "There
is one flesh of the Lord Jesus Christ; and His blood which is shed for
us is one : one loaf also is broken to all (communicants), and one cup
is distributed amongst them all."

6. *gave it.*—Again expressive of His voluntary act, who thus imparts
Himself to the faithful communicant. Bishop Latimer gives the following distinction as to what He gave : " He gave not His Body to be
received with the mouth ; but He gave the Sacrament of His Body to
be received with the mouth : He gave the Sacrament to the mouth, His
Body to the mind," that is, spiritual food to the spirit. (See notes 1, 2.)

7. *to them.*—There is a strong presumption that He did not Himself
partake, either of the bread, or of the wine now consecrated. The body
was His own. To receive it the disciples must partake of it; but it is
not probable that He would also do so.

8. *this is My Body . . . this is My Blood.*—These have indeed been
words of controversy in all ages; the point lies in the term "*is.*" The
verb itself was probably not expressed, if our Lord spoke in the Syro-
Chaldee; it is expressed, however, in the Greek of the Gospels, and is
exactly rendered in our version. Some take it quite literally; others
declare it is equivalent to the term "represents." The soundest critics
do not exactly hold with either. The bread and the wine may, to our
sight, *represent* Christ's Body (*present* would be a more accurate term),
but they do more than "represent" it; they are the visible means of
conveying the spiritual reality, a visible sign and pledge to assure us
of the presence of what we cannot see. For the Sacrament is not representative only, but real. It is, on the other hand, impossible that the
disciples could have understood the words simply as literal; for they
saw Christ's Body before them, and must therefore have understood
them in a mystical and spiritual, rather than a purely literal and
material sense. The truth must lie between the two; but we cannot
exactly define the line of separation between the material and spiritual.
The tendency of our age is to demand the definition of mysteries; the
demand of the religion of Christ is *faith* in the mysteries of the Spirit,
which may only be spiritually discerned. There can be no doubt of
the presence of Christ in the Sacrament, and that His Body and Blood

to them, saying, Drink ye all of it ; for this is My blood

are "verily and indeed taken and received *by the faithful* in the Lord's Supper," though by the faithful only. (See note 4.)　"By the declaration of our Lord," says S. Hilary, "and by our faith, it is truly flesh and blood ; and the receiving of these, and drinking of these, cause that we should be in Christ, and Christ in us." The testimony of the early Fathers is clearly and distinctly in favour of a real, though mystical and spiritual, presence of Christ. To give one instance, of the earliest. Ignatius (to the Smyrneans, Shorter Ep.) says, "They (certain heretics) abstain from the Eucharist, and from prayer, because they confess not the Eucharist to be the flesh of our Saviour Jesus Christ, which suffered for our sins, and which the Father, of His goodness, raised up again." Nor do they (fairly read, and interpreted by their own collective statements and contexts) betray us either into the errors of transubstantiation, or of consubstantiation ; against a mere memorial rite they are most decided. To multiply quotations would be to endeavour to bring into the compass of a single note what demands a special treatise. It is therefore impossible to enter on the field of controversy. The doctrine, so far as it is *defined* by the Church of England, may be fitly expressed in the words of Hooker (who has in nothing more merited his designation of "judicious," than in his treatment of this subject) : "It is on all sides plainly confessed, first, that this Sacrament is a true and real participation of Christ, who thereby imparteth Himself, even His whole entire person, as a mystical Head unto every soul that receiveth Him ; and that every such receiver doth hereby incorporate, or unite, himself unto Christ as a mystical member of Him, yea, of them also whom He acknowledgeth to be His own. Secondly, that to whom the person of Christ is thus communicated, to them He giveth, by the same Sacrament, His Holy Spirit, to sanctify them, as it sanctifieth Him which is their Head. Thirdly, that what merit, force, or virtue soever there is in His sacrificed Body and Blood, we fully and wholly have it by this Sacrament. Fourthly, that the effect thereof is in us a real transmutation of our souls and bodies from sin to righteousness, from death and corruption to immortality and life. Fifthly, that because the Sacrament, being of itself but a corruptible and earthly creature, must needs be thought an unlikely instrument to work so admirable effects in man, we are therefore to rest ourselves altogether upon the strength of His glorious power, who is able, and will bring to pass that the bread and cup which He giveth us shall be truly the thing which He promiseth." "The real presence of Christ's most blessed Body and Blood is not, therefore, to be sought for in the Sacrament, but in the worthy receiver of the Sacrament." Without the operation of the Holy Spirit, and without the faith of the communicant, there is but "the sign and sacrament of so great a thing." (See note 4. See also App. VIII. B.)

9. *do this.*—The original word bears a solemn, formal, and technical

of the new testament, which is shed for many for the remission of sins.

sense; it implies both the *offering* of a sacrifice, and the *observance* of a religious rite, solemnity, sacrifice. The Apostles could not fail to perceive a significance in the word itself; it confers perpetuity in the ordinance, through the hands of Christ's ministers. Let us give the term its fair technical force; we shall not then fall into the error of attaching less value than is due, to its rightful celebration by lawfully ordained ministers; and, on the other hand, S. Paul's words will preserve us from using the word merely in its stricter sense of sacrificing: " As oft as ye eat this bread, and drink this cup, ye do *show* (*forth*) the Lord's death till He come" (1 Cor. xi. 26). We do not now renew the sacrifice once offered whilst we *celebrate* (S. Paul's term) the ordinance of Christ's death. (See App. VIII. B.)

10. *in remembrance.*—Gk. may mean "for My memorial," both to men, and before God, with whom we thus plead the sacrifice of Christ. The main sense, however, appears (from S. Paul's words above quoted) to be, "your memorial of Me," *i.e.* the memorial made by us before the world, the "*celebration*" of the Lord's death. Thus, the memorial is in order that we may remember and proclaim Christ, rather than as showing that we do not remember Him. These passages do not fairly bear the construction sometimes put upon them, that the Eucharist is a memorial rite, only or primarily. Dr. Plumtre notices the use of the same word in the LXX., concerning the shew-bread in Lev. xxiv. 7, and says, "The word has thus acquired the associations connected with a religious memorial, and might be applied to a sacrifice, though it did not in itself involve the idea of sacrificing. The fact that our Lord and His disciples had been eating of a sacrifice, which was also a memorial, gives a special force to the word thus used."

11. *after supper.*—These words (from S. Luke's account) may merely distinguish between the former cup (see xxiv. *a.* 9), and this now adopted to the institution of the Lord's Supper; or, as many writers think, they may mark an interval between the giving of the bread and the wine, and that probably part of His discourse may have intervened. But this is not expressed in the accounts of SS. Matthew and Mark, though that of S. Paul seems to support S. Luke. There has, however, never been any doubt as to the fact that our Lord so connected the giving of the bread, and of the wine, that the sacrifice of His Body and Blood was represented as one complete sacrifice; and the probability is very strong in favour of the former view. The "Speaker's Commentary" (alluding to 1 Cor. x. 16) considers this to be the third cup of the Paschal feast, usually taken after eating the lamb, and known as the " cup of blessing."

12. *drink ye all.*—It is impossible not to feel the force of this injunction against such presumption as that of Rome, which refuses the

But I say unto you, I will not drink henceforth of this

cup to the laity. As, "without shedding of blood, there is no remission" of sins; so, naturally, the obvious right of all Christians is participation in that which conveys specially *the Blood* of Christ. S. Mark gives emphasis to this command; he adds, "and they all drank of it." There is nothing which fairly can imply (though the *words* may be strained for the argument) that *they* all, and not all those to whom they ministered, were to partake of the cup. This institution was a general Sacrament for all ages, and for the whole Church, not merely for the clergy; though none were present at its institution, but those to whom was committed the ministration of the Word and Sacraments, of both together, and who were specially charged to set them forth.

13. *My Blood.*—(See note 8.) It is sad to think how much is lost of the virtue of this Sacrament, which we must rightly receive by faith, to those who dispute and define concerning the change in the elements, and *how* they embody the sacred reality which they signify and convey. The words of Hooker are sound, and reverent, and true: "I wish that men would give themselves to meditate with silence *what we have* by the Sacrament, and less to dispute of the *manner how.* If any man suppose this were too great stupidity and dullness, let us see whether the Apostles of our Lord themselves have not done the like." "This heavenly food is given for the satisfying of our empty souls, and not for the exercising of our curious and subtle wits." A very ancient writer (Hippolytus) speaks to the same point, and may well counsel those who require faith to appreciate, rather than intellect to fathom, the nature of this holy mystery: "To those who want understanding, *i.e.* to those who do not yet possess the power of the Holy Ghost, she (Wisdom) saith, 'Come, eat of my bread, and drink of the wine which I have mingled;' *i.e.* the Divine Flesh, and the precious Blood, which He hath given us to eat and drink for the remission of sins." How strange to Jews must have been this command! They were forbidden, either in sacrifice, or at any time, to eat "the blood which is the life thereof." Christ's innovation of the old world rule was, therefore, the more striking.

14. *new testament.*—Or "*covenant.*" The shedding of blood was necessary to the ratification of a covenant. The body of the sacrifice was offered up, and then divided amongst those who sacrificed and offered it; but the covenant was further sprinkled with the blood of the victim. The Christian covenant, therefore, the "new testament," is fully ratified in the Blood of Christ. Some MSS. of repute omit the word "*new.*"

15. *for many.*—There is a full consent of scholars to this word "many" being equivalent to "all;" and to its being so used by the writers of the New Testament Scriptures. The doctrine of redemption by Christ, is the doctrine of an universal redemption of the human race, as offered to every man and wrought for all; though it is not, alas!

fruit of the vine, until that day when I drink it new with you in My Father's kingdom.

XXV. *THE FAREWELL DISCOURSES.*

S. John xiv.—xvi.

(a.) *Christ consoles His Disciples.　Faith and Prayer.*

S. John xiv. 1-14.

Let not your heart be troubled: ye believe in God,

accepted by all.　Any limitation of meaning, therefore, in such terms as "many," and other equivalent expressions, must be sought on the side of man, not from the view of Christ, or of God, who "willeth that all men should be saved." (See Dan. xii. 2; Matt. xx. 28.)

16. *remission of sins.*—It should not be overlooked, in our receiving of the Holy Communion, that we do not only offer the "sacrifice of thanksgiving," but also express our faith in the remission of sins; so putting forth our plea for forgiveness of all that is past, through the merits of Christ's death.

17. *I will not drink.* (See xxiv. *a.* 6–10.)　It seems that our Lord here repeats the words which He uttered on the occasion of giving the first cup before supper.　Of the first cup He probably partook, but not of this latter. (See note 7.)

1. *troubled.*—At His leaving them, and in such circumstances of apparent tribulation, and in prospect of His betrayal, and denial amongst themselves.

2. *ye believe,* etc.—The A. V. seems to follow the Latin in its rendering here; but it is generally agreed that there should be no change of moods here; and there are two ways of reading the verse, both well supported.　The first places both verbs in the indicative mood, "Ye believe in God, ye believe also in Me;" but against this there lies the valid objection, that Christ is exhorting His disciples, both to faith in the Father, and in Himself also.　The other reads, imperatively, "Believe in God, believe also in Me."　The Syriac and Arabic versions both render the passage in this way; and this sense is in accordance with the terms of the passage, in which our Lord shows faith in God, and in Himself, to be the real source of comfort, both in this trial, which was imminent, and in all those that should come upon His Church, and upon individual members of it.　If they had such faith, then there was great comfort in the ready access to the Father through the Son by prayer, in every perplexity and trouble.

believe also in Me. In My Father's house are many mansions: if *it were* not *so*, I would have told you. I

3. *many mansions.*—The word expresses a permanent dwelling. The kingdom of the inheritance of Christ's people was "prepared for them from the foundation of the world;" but there is now a personal and particular interest in the mission of Christ in human form, to prepare for the redeemed race of man. That the mansions are *many*, is equivalent to saying that there is his eternal home prepared for each, to the exclusion of none but those who bar entrance against themselves. (See xxiv. *e*. 15.) Many of the early writers, however, see in the words "many mansions," intimation that they will be *many* in degrees of dignity and excellence; that they will differ, "as one star differeth from another star in glory," according to the tenor of their life on earth, and their identity with the mind of Christ. And this appears to be a just criticism. Christ's words at this time are surcharged with deep meaning, and may well convey more than the bare intimation, that there is room for all, and a home for each in heaven. It is in accordance with the teaching of Holy Scripture, expressed in many passages, to hold that, though all will be perfectly happy in heaven, the measure and capacity of each, with regard to its enjoyment, will differ, as differ the capacity and excellence of men on earth. Two cups (to give a plain illustration) may be perfectly full, and yet the capacity of one may infinitely exceed that of another; their uses and intrinsic value may also differ, each being perfectly suited for its special service. The first intimation of the kingdom of Christ was given to the Apostles; and at once a distinction is expressed in their favour above all others. Dare any assert that his " mansion " will be as theirs,—theirs, who continued with Christ in His early tribulation; and through whose word, written for our learning, all subsequent ages have believed in Christ? Twelve thrones of pre-eminent glory are set for these master builders of the Catholic Church. We know, also, that there is within the glory of Christ's kingdom, a "right hand " and a " left hand," where seats shall be assigned by Christ to those for whom they are prepared of His Father.   It would be impossible to suppose that, when Christ said to the penitent malefactor, " To-day shalt thou be with Me in paradise," He promised him less than a perfect happiness. But who could suppose that the happiness awaiting the proto-martyr Stephen, or S. Paul, at the end of his life of labour, crowned with martyrdom, was identically the same with that of the penitent thief, who certainly believed when the opportunity of salvation presented itself to him; but who could look back on no useful and honourable career in Christ's service, no experience of trouble, of prayer, of faith, of support in communion with Christ; and to whose preaching, or writing, none could owe their soul's salvation, for his career on earth was already closed when the offer of salvation dawned upon him ?

go to prepare a place for you. And if I go and prepare a place for you, I will come again, and receive you unto Myself; that where I am, *there* ye may be also. And whither I go ye know, and the way ye know. Thomas

Again, we may conceive of a faith and love so true, of a realization of the mind of Christ so clear, even in the case of one of but few opportunities, and of early age; that, in its rare devotion, it might surpass the excellence of one of vast and practical powers of work, and of great success, but of duller apprehension of the Saviour's spirit; and such a one would probably stand nearer to Christ, than many another in the kingdom of His glory. Here is no difficulty in understanding some of the reasons why, though all may be perfectly happy, according to their nature and capacity, and their conception of happiness, there may be, in the kingdom of Christ, " many mansions," many gradations of happiness and glory. All labourers in Christ's vineyard will receive, every man, the *penny*, the common reward of perfect and eternal happiness in Christ; but how varied will be the recollections, how different the experience of service with Christ, to be remembered in heaven! " The penny was the same for all; for life eternal, which this penny signifies, is of the same duration to all. But there may be many mansions, many degrees of dignity in that life, corresponding to people's deserts." (*Augustine.*) " The many mansions agree with the one penny, because, though one may rejoice more than another, yet all rejoice with one and the same joy, arising from the vision of their Maker." (*Gregory.*)

4. *I will come again.*—It was a special consolation, in Christ's departure, that He had not merely finished His career in victory, and fled the scenes of strife, to rest and await their arrival. He was leaving earth, as He had come to earth, on a special mission in man's behalf; He was going to prepare a place for His redeemed. And now, in this promise of His advent, all the promises of His Gospel, all the hopes of His people, are made to centre. He will come again, when all work of His, in our behalf, in heaven is finished, to stamp the value of loving labour done in His behalf on earth, to judge all nations, and to welcome His people to the kingdom which He has prepared for them.

5. *ye know.*—After so many intimations of His purpose, it was only remarkable that they should not have some comprehension of it; and yet it could only have been a general comprehension, for He proceeds to declare it to them. Thomas, who was slow to understand things spiritual, and whose bent of mind inclined rather to things practical, than to the mysteries of faith, demurs to what our Lord seemed to take for granted of them. They did not know whither He went, and therefore they could not know the way. The spirit of Thomas, though not of the brightest faith, is of very great value in the Church of Christ. It is not right to class him amongst the incredulous, or doubters. To his remark, on this occasion, we owe the very distinct and clear

saith unto Him, Lord, we know not whither Thou goest; and how can we know the way? Jesus saith unto him, I am the way, the truth, and the life: no man cometh unto the Father, but by Me. If ye had known Me, ye should have known My Father also: and from hence-

enunciation, which Christ gave, of His being Himself that which all seek, "the way, the truth, and the life," and the sole Mediator between God and man, to the exclusion of all others, whom superstition and error have summoned to displace Him. On another occasion (see P. II. iv. 20, 21, v. 5, 7–9), we owe to his hesitation to accept doctrine without proof, that evidence of the resurrection of our Lord, which renders it impossible for after ages to say that Christ presented the phantom, not the substance, of His body to the disciples, after He rose again. Our Lord accepted the honest scruples of Thomas; and though, at the same time, He declared more blessed the spirit which could believe without sight or proof, He does not condemn that caution which has resulted in the strengthening of so many minds. The religion of Christ can stand the test of practical common sense; it is never opposed to it, and therefore such a spirit will find its place and satisfaction within Christ's fold. But it is not a disposition of the highest spirituality. It demands proof and sight; it partakes of the infirmities of human nature, against which Christ's Gospel appeals, in its training mankind, by faith, to attain to the excellence of spirituality. Dean Burgon explains that Thomas thought that, if he knew whither Christ was going, he would know the way; whereas Christ shows him that "the way is not to be discovered by knowing the 'whither,' but the 'whither' by knowing the Way."

6. *I am the way*, etc.—"Without the way, there is no going; without the truth, there is no knowing; without the life, there is no living. I AM the way which thou oughtest to follow; the truth which thou oughtest to trust; the life which thou oughtest to hope for. I AM the way inviolable, the truth infallible, the life that cannot end. If thou remain in My way, thou shalt know the truth, and thou shalt lay hold on eternal life." (*Thomas à Kempis.*) "He does not mislead us, who is the Way; nor allure us by false promises, who is the Truth; nor leave us in the horror of death, who is the Life." (*S. Hilary.*)

> "Thou art my Way; I wander if Thou fly;
> Thou art my Light; if hid, how blind am I!
> Thou art my Life; if Thou withdraw, I die."   (*Quarles.*)

7. *from henceforth.*—If they had rightly known the Son, in His character and work as a Divine Saviour, they would have seen the Divinity of the Father manifested in the redeeming love of Him who was one with the Father; for the Son alone can reveal the Father (Matt. xi. 27). But, now that He was immediately about to be

forth ye know Him, and have seen Him. Philip saith
unto Him, Lord, shew us the Father, and it sufficeth us.
Jesus saith unto Him, Have I been so long time with
you, and yet hast thou not known Me, Philip? he that
hath seen Me hath seen the Father: and how sayest
thou *then*, Shew us the Father? Believest thou not
that I am in the Father, and the Father in Me? the
words that I speak unto you I speak not of Myself, but

glorified, they would understand what they had hitherto failed clearly
to perceive. This seems to be the only way in which man can now
see "Him who is invisible," whom "no man hath seen, nor can see,"
namely, in the Person Christ.

8. *Philip saith.*—Philip would fain have such a vision of God, as had
been granted to Moses, or to Elijah; he would see the glory of God in
fire and majesty; if he could have such a vision of "the excellent
glory," his faith would be established for ever. Our Lord's reply is a
revelation of a very different nature; half reproachfully, He speaks of
the time He had spent amongst them—of the manifestation of Deity,
not in the glory of "the ministration of condemnation," as under the
law, but in the more exceeding glory of "the ministration of
righteousness" (2 Cor. iii. 8). It was not easy, perhaps, for men to see,
in the gentleness, humility, and self-denial of the Saviour, the glory
of the eternal Father; but yet His miracles had been the works of
God, His words such as "never man spake." And when the disciples
were endued with power from on high, then they could see in "Christ
the power of God, and the wisdom of God;" that Christ was "the
brightness of His glory, and the express image of His Person; and
that in Him dwelleth all the fullness of the Godhead bodily;" and
that "God was, in Christ, reconciling the world unto Himself." For,
as Irenæus says, "the Son is that which is visible of the Father; the
Father, that which is invisible of the Son." The beloved disciple had
learnt the truth, when he wrote, "We beheld His glory, the glory as of
the only begotten of the Father." J. Williams quotes a suggestion of
S. Chrysostom, that Philip had known Christ in Galilee, before he was
called to be an Apostle, which supposes a longer acquaintance than
others had had with Him.

9. *words.*—The words of Christ were not merely His human words;
they were the terms of God's commission to man by Him, and they
breathed Divinity. He "spake as never man spake," and "His word
was with power." Mighty works were done at His word; the word and
the work with Him were one (Ps. clxviii. 5). His words had power
to heal the sick, to comfort the broken-hearted, to speak forgiveness
and peace; and they were "spirit," and they were "life." Such words
and works were evidence of Deity. Well might He challenge man's

the Father that dwelleth in Me, He doeth the works. Believe Me that I *am* in the Father, and the Father in Me : or else believe Me for the very works' sake. Verily, verily, I say unto you, He that believeth on Me, the works that I do shall he do also : and greater works than these shall he do; because I go unto My Father. And whatsoever ye shall ask in My Name, that will I do, that the Father may be glorified in the Son. If ye shall ask anything in My Name, I will do *it*.

belief on the evidence of these. "He first demands belief in His words; but, failing this, men must at least believe Him for the works' sake, by which the Father is manifested in Him ; and, so believing, they must in the end credit His words." "Why does He pass from words to works ? Why does He not say, as we might have expected, He speaketh the words ? Because He means to apply what He says, both to His doctrine, and to His miracles; or, because His words are themselves works." (*Chrysostom.*)

10. *greater works.*—Not works in themselves greater than the works of God in Christ; but in Christ's Name, and in His power, the Apostles did perform spiritual works of a wider range, productive of greater and more general results, than He had wrought amongst " the lost sheep of the house of Israel," who restrained Him by their unbelief. He is still speaking of words and works together; the word, by the Apostles in Christ's Name, working the conversion of the world, and effective of the work of righteousness in each individual convert. And far larger were the numbers of the converts on the preaching of the Apostles, than when Christ delivered the Gospel. They evangelized the world, a result which Christ anticipated in prayer : " Neither pray I for these alone, but for them also which shall believe on Me through their word." The miracles of Christ were in themselves, in a sense, incomplete; their result was not attained during His administration. They were wrought, and regarded, as signs of His power to effect far greater and spiritual things; and these things He effected by the power with which He commissioned the Apostles, after His resurrection. The means is subordinate to the result—the seed-time to the harvest, the miracle to the inspiration of faith and love, the body to the spirit. The " greater works " wrought by the Apostles, were the direct results of that ampler commission given by Christ to them, when He had gone to the Father, to receive at His hands investiture of the kingdom and glory which He had won. And thus, in the spread of His Gospel, by the agency of the Apostles, after His ascension into heaven, the Father would still be glorified on earth in the Son, whose mission of redemption gathered increasing numbers of Christians to the kingdom of heaven.

11. *I will do it.*—Christ had referred to the Father as doing every-

(*b*.) *The Promise of the Comforter.*

S. John xiv. 15–31.

If ye love Me, keep My commandments. And I will pray the Father, and He shall give you another Comforter, that He may abide with you for ever; *even*

thing previous to His own glorification; now He speaks of Himself as the source of power and gift. He appoints that prayers and supplication shall be addressed to heaven in His Name, as that which should prevail. In no other name could men be accepted with God, than in that of the Son of God. And in the bestowal of gifts of grace by Him, in answer to prayer made in His Name, God the Father would be glorified. He then repeats, more clearly, and with wider scope and removal of limitation, the promise, "If ye ask *anything* in My Name, I will do it." On the strength of this command and promise, we now address God "through Jesus Christ our Lord." But the *Spirit* of Christ must be in the heart, as the *Name* of Christ upon the lips, of those that ask. The words "in My Name" have, further, the sense of *in My cause*; for that must be the first subject of our prayers, the first thing that we seek.

1. *if ye love Me.*—Our Lord had just given promise of an unlimited answer to prayer; He now demands something from His people, obedience; and He puts this as the test of their love to Himself, not as the condition of His gift to them. Those who gain their requests in the Name of Christ, and so experience His love to them, best show their love to Him by keeping His commands. This is the devotion which Christ requires; it is very different from mere profession, or from any external adherence, or compliance with the routine of Christian practice. He requires a ready obedience to Himself, but it must spring from the principle of love in the heart. Right obedience is the fruit of love. He will not have slaves, or servants; He will have "friends," and "brethren." God will have "sons" in Christ.

2. *I will pray.*—The word should not be "pray," but "request." It is a different word from that used of *man's* prayer to God. It expresses the familiarity enjoyed by Christ, both as the Son of God, and as sitting at His right hand in His glorified humanity. (See xxvi. 25, 45.)

3. *another Comforter.*—Christ Himself being one also. The word "Comforter" (Gk. "Paraclete") implies one called in to help; as the Holy Ghost was summoned from heaven by Christ, to abide in His Church on earth, to sanctify and illumine it, to inspire it with sound judgment, and to make manifest the truth of Christ—for the sense of Teacher is included also. (See John xvi. 13.) It also implies an Advocate (as the same word is rendered in 1 John ii. 1), "who maketh

the Spirit of truth; whom the world cannot receive, because it seeth Him not, neither knoweth Him: but ye know Him; for He dwelleth with you, and shall be in you.

I will not leave you comfortless: I will come to you. Yet a little while, and the world seeth Me no more; but

intercession for us" (Rom. viii. 26), maintains our cause in the world, both against evil, and with God; who is our Patron, pleading and managing our cause, and giving us counsel and inspiration of the right, and strength to keep it. In a third sense, He is a Comforter, as inspiring consolation; but not merely the consolation which one man may offer another, with kind words, and good advice, and sympathy, but that which is accompanied with power and strength (His power, strength in us). It is infirmity which requires consolation; He is the Spirit of might and strength who offers it, in supplying that which we have not in ourselves. It is, indeed, difficult to say what the comprehensive term *Paraclete* will not convey. This passage, and one or two others in our Lord's discourses at this time, convey the great doctrine of the Trinity in the Godhead. The Holy Ghost is sent by the Father, at the instance of the Son; each Person is shown distinct in office, in individuality, and each Divine. It is most worthy our notice how evident this truth is, throughout the last discourse of our Lord. Nowhere else can we gather so clearly, the separate office of the several Persons of the Divine Trinity in effecting our salvation, their unity of purpose and will, and their Divinity. Nowhere else can we see so clearly the greatness of God's love, and the mightiness of the work of our salvation.

4. *abide.*—This Comforter would not be separated from them (as Christ would now be) by death, or departure from the world; His presence would know no break.

5. *seeth Him not.*—The world, the worldly minded, fail to perceive the work and office of the Holy Ghost; they do not recognize His presence, and cannot judge of the nature or importance of spiritual influences, which are spiritually discerned. (See 1 Cor. ii. 14.) But He should be their indwelling Spirit, and they should recognize His presence by His working in their hearts.

6. *comfortless.*—Gk. "orphans." When Christ is removed from them, they shall not mourn, as those who are bereaved of their mainstay; the Spirit of Christ shall rest upon them, and Christ Himself shall be present with them, when gathered together in His Name, and when thinking on His word (Matt. iii. 16); and He shall return again, to receive them to Himself. This separation and removal of Christ are, therefore, anything but eternal.

7. *the world,* etc.—As Christ had said to the Jews, they should not

ye see Me : because I live, ye shall live also. At that day ye shall know that I *am* in My Father, and ye in Me, and I in you. He that hath My commandments, and keepeth them, he it is that loveth Me : and he that loveth Me shall be loved of My Father, and I will love him, and will manifest Myself to him. Judas saith unto

henceforth see Him; so He did not show Himself to all the people, to all the world, after His resurrection—for they did not perceive the truth for which He lived, and died, and rose again; but to witnesses ordained of God, sufficient for the satisfying of every reasonable doubt of His real presence amongst them. But His public ministry on earth was ended; His commission to the world rested in the person of His Apostles. With regard to the disciples, the sense of the passage is this: Ye shall see Me die, and so shall ye die; but as certainly as I live again, so shall ye live also.

8. *ye shall know.*—They now asked questions regarding the manifestation of God, and how and when Christ should manifest Himself to the world. But all these anxieties should be set at rest for ever, in the day when the gift of the Holy Ghost should be given to them. The mystery should then be revealed to them, that Christ was in God, and His people and Himself in living communion, one, as Christ and God are one. (See John xvii. 21, 23.) The words may also include the earlier promise, that, on Christ's return from the grave in power, they should know that He was One in power with the Father; but those who would receive that illumination, must not sever themselves from Christ, by neglect of His commandments. S. Augustine refers this knowledge of Christ to a later date, that of sight in heaven.

9. *that loveth Me.*—"He that hath them in mind, and keepeth them in life; he that hath them in words, and keepeth them in works; he that hath them by hearing, and keepeth them by doing; he that hath them by doing, and keepeth them by persevering,—he it is that loveth Me. Love must be shown by works, or it is a mere barren name." (*Augustine.*) Especially so of His command, "Do this in remembrance of Me." If *there* it is the communicant who loves and obeys, what is the position of one who refuses to obey ?

10. *manifest Myself.*—Spiritually, but assuredly. To the doing of Christ's will, much is promised. Whilst men are disputing about creed, and doctrine, and mystery, "he that *doeth God's will* shall *know* of the doctrine." Whilst volumes are being written, and acute minds are engaged in controversy, on the subject of Christ's presence in His Church, and in His Sacraments, and whilst many are professing loudly their love to Christ, he that *doeth His will* shall be *loved* of Him, and to him will He *manifest* Himself. These shall see Him; and He will dwell in them, and be one with them, as He is one with the Father. "As the reward of faith, they shall have sight. Now

Him, not Iscariot, Lord, how is it that Thou wilt
manifest Thyself unto us, and not unto the world? Jesus
answered and said unto him, If a man love Me, he will

He only loves us so that we believe; then He will love us so that we
shall see.   And whereas we love now by believing that which we
shall see, then we shall love by seeing that which we have believed."
(*Augustine.*)

11. *Judas . . . not Iscariot.*—This was the brother of James, and
writer of the Epistle which bears his name; he bore also the name
of Thaddæus, or Lebbæus. (Cf. Luke vi. 16; Jude 1; Matt. x. 3.)

12. *how is it?*—Gk. " what has come to pass?" what change has
transpired?   Jude could not understand how it could be consistent
with prophecy, and with the office of the Messiah, that He should be
manifested only to them; that He should not rather seek the most
public and formal opportunity of declaring Himself to the world.

13. *Jesus answered.*—Christ's reply to the question of Jude is
distinct: Those who love Christ will keep His word; to those only,
who keep His word, shall there be an inward and spiritual manifestation of His presence, which the world cannot appreciate.   Love
and obedience are the grand requisites to this blessing.   The three
objections proposed by the disciples, Thomas, Philip, and Jude, have
represented the difficulties of many in after ages.   It would be well
if those who entertain such difficulties, would come as honestly to
our Lord for their solution.   There are ever those, like Thomas, to
whose practical mind that which appeals to faith, and to the spiritual
life, is hard of realization.   They understand what they can see, and
handle, and demonstrate, of the word of life; but that which is not
seen, and eternal, is out of their grasp.   To such there is one answer.
These things can only be seen through Christ; no man cometh to the
Father, but by Him, the Way, the Truth, and the Life.   There are
those, like Philip, who would have some special and remarkable sign
given to them, and regard such signs as are instinct with the majesty
and terror of the Lord, rather than those which come with the gentle
influence of the Spirit, and the " still, small voice" of His motion.
To such are proposed the prayerful study of the words and work of
Christ; seeing Him in these, they behold God in Him, and shall live.
And there are many also, like Jude, who cannot separate the promise
which the Gospel has of this world, from that which is of the world
to come; their visions of Christ's example are mixed up with much
that is of earth; the notion of a personal and spiritual manifestation
of Christ is more difficult than that of His manifestation in power
before the world.   To them the kingdom of God shall come " with
observation."   The answer of Christ to each Apostle, is designed to
meet the difficulties and doubts of many minds.   It would be well,
indeed, if those who entertain them, would weigh them with the

keep My words: and My Father will love him, and We will come unto him, and make Our abode with him. He that loveth Me not keepeth not My sayings: and the word which ye hear is not Mine, but the Father's which sent Me.

These things have I spoken unto you, being *yet* present with you. But the Comforter, *which is* the Holy Ghost,

answers here given by Christ, which He will also give individually to themselves, in answer to earnest prayer; bearing in mind S. John's monition and promise, "These things are written that ye might have life."

14. *will love him.*—It has already been said that the Holy Spirit would abide with us for ever; we have, therefore, the promise of the abiding presence of the Holy Trinity. God's love to man was manifested in the gift of His Son. But this is an especial love; not merely for sinners, who might be saved by it, but for those who are saved by Christ. So God is near all His creatures—"in Him we live and move and have our being;" but in an especial sense He dwells "with him also that is of an humble and contrite spirit," in whom is the Spirit of Christ. And His sanctifying presence there will be permanent, as in a dwelling-place. Tittmann alludes to another interpretation, as being worthy of notice, and spiritually true: "We (I and my faithful servant) will come unto the Father, and make our abode with Him, in the mansions prepared in heaven; 'where I am, there shall ye be also.'" The former is, however, the more obvious, and generally received interpretation.

15. *My sayings.*—Our translation marks a difference here, between the man who keeps Christ's *words*, and him who "keepeth not My *sayings*;" but not so distinctly as the original expresses it. The same term is used in each instance; but in the singular number in the former, in the plural in the latter case—"he will keep My *word*;" "keepeth not My *words*." He who loves Christ, keeps all His sayings in their entirety, as the word of Christ; he who loves Him not, disregards them singly and separately, in every case. It is the sign of his want of love, that he rejects every word of Christ. He rejects the Father also, for the word of Christ is the word of God, "who in these last days hath spoken to us by His Son;" the word of Christ is not His merely, but the word of the Father which sent Him.

16. *present with you.*—Truth declared by Christ orally was not thoroughly understood, and therefore not remembered by the disciples. But it was the office of the Holy Spirit to recall, and re-present to their minds, and to open their minds to receive, and understand, what Christ had spoken to them, whilst still present with them. He did not deliver to them new truths, but restored to them those which Christ Himself had delivered, but which, in their want of right in-

Whom the Father will send in My Name, He shall teach
you all things, and bring all things to your remembrance,
whatsoever I have said unto you.　Peace I leave with
you, My peace I give unto you: not as the world giveth,
give I unto you.　Let not your heart be troubled, neither
let it be afraid.　Ye have heard how I said unto you, I
go away, and come *again* unto you.　If ye loved Me, ye

telligence, they had let slip.　This was a remarkable gift.　It was not
merely a power of memory, or a gift of understanding, or a fresh
inspiration; it was the union of these, "with a right judgment in all
things."

17. *in My Name.*—On Christ's behalf, and as His representative.
In John xvi. 7, Christ says, "*I* will send Him;" here, *the Father* sends
Him.　We see, therefore, that He "proceedeth from the Father and the
Son." (See xxv. *d.* 12.)　But there is also the meaning that the Holy
Ghost will be sent in answer to prayer in the Son's Name; for Christ
promised, with regard to prayer, that our "Heavenly Father will give
the Holy Spirit to them that ask Him."　To us, therefore, who are
deprived of Christ's presence by His removal from amongst us into
heaven, He will give the presence of the Comforter, if we plead His
promise in His Name.

18. *teach you.*—This is the promise of spiritual illumination.　The
Holy Spirit will unfold the true spiritual meaning of Christ's kingdom,
and of all things connected with it, and of all doctrine delivered by
Christ; how best to set forth the riches of His glory before the world;
how to bear themselves, in word and life, amongst men.　And, with
these, He would recall to their memory all that Christ Himself had
spoken to them.　(See note 16.)　"Unless the Spirit be present to the
mind of the hearer, the word of the teacher is vain; for, unless there be
a Teacher within, the tongue of the teacher outside will labour in vain.
Nay, the Maker Himself does not speak for the instruction of man,
unless the Spirit, by His motion, speaks at the same time." (*Gregory.*)

19. *not as the world giveth.*—The world can give a kind and courteous salutation, such a greeting as is common to all civilized nations;
it can produce kindly and peaceable feelings; but these are not permanent, and have little solid value.　The peace which Christ be-
queaths, is that "peace which passeth knowledge," which is "shed
abroad in the heart of him that believeth," by the Spirit of God.　And
His peace can render a man superior to the evil of the world, for his
heart and hope are in heaven; it can give a man peace at the last, in
the hour of death, in the day of judgment, in the kingdom of heaven.

20. *troubled.*—(See xxv. *a.* 1.)　Christ had shown His departure to
be for their interest; He now declares it to be for His interest also;
and, therefore, on no account a source of trouble and fear to them.

would rejoice, because I said, I go unto the Father : for
My Father is greater than I. And now I have told you
before it come to pass, that, when it is come to pass, ye
might believe. Hereafter I will not talk much with you :
for the prince of this world cometh, and hath nothing in

21. *greater than I.*—Instead of mourning for Christ's departure, they
should rightly rejoice, for His sake and their own ; for, being " inferior
to the Father as touching His manhood," and as " He that is sent "
may be, within that commission, less than " the Father who sent
Him," the Son of man, on His removal to heaven, would be glorified ;
as if He said, " The glory wherewith My Father is eternally invested,
is greater than that which this human nature and life of Mine is
capable of." (*Bishop Hall.*) They too would be glorified in Him, who
bore their nature, and who, as man, would have ascended into heaven.
Many writers notice that, though One in power, and equal as touching
their Godhead, Christ is the second Person in the Holy Trinity, " God
of God," and the Father, in the order of Persons, is greater than the Son ;
but on such a mystery as this, He only can speak with authority, who
declares Himself " One with the Father." But Christ here speaks of
His present state, as the suffering Redeemer, and as far below that
which will grace Him as the glorified Redeemer, when He would be
exalted to His proper place at God's right hand, " as the King of
glory." This verse was used as a principal argument by the Arians ;
but they misapprehended and misapplied it. Heresy always rests on
the misapprehension and misapplication of Scripture truth. As well
might they contend that Christ was inferior to His earthly parents,
when, as a child, He was subject to them. (See xviii. 95.)

22. *ye might believe.*—This is a summary of the intention of all
prophecy, to be a witness, on its fulfilment, of the eternal foreknowledge and truth of God. If the disciples had present faith in Christ,
they would find every word of His verified, and the exercise of miraculous power could give no greater testimony to His Divinity. The
word of prophecy is, in comparison with all testimony, " the more sure
word of prophecy." If, therefore, they were now sorrowful under the
aspect of His humiliation, and of His apparent inferiority to the Father,
with whom He claimed equality, they would, on His resurrection and
ascension, have proof that He spoke truth of which He had Divine
foreknowledge, and they would be confirmed, not offended, in their
belief in His doctrine.

23. *hereafter.*—Before He suffered. He did, however, speak to them
for a little longer in the discourse which S. John records.

24. *the prince of this world.*—Satan, who had " departed from Him
for a season " (Luke iv. 13), now returns to the last conflict ; and Christ
is aware of his onset. Personally, and by the agency of evil men, he
came to do all that desperation could prompt, to thwart the merciful

Me. But that the world may know that I love the
Father; and as the Father gave Me commandment, even
so I do.

Arise, let us go hence.

(*c.*) *The True Vine.*

S. John xv. 1–17.

I am the true vine, and My Father is the husbandman.

purpose of the Saviour. Our Lord designates him according to his
usurpation, and as distinguished from His own true right.

25. *hath nothing.*—There is no vantage point in Christ; no sin, no
infirmity, no evil habit or propensity; there is no hesitation, no want
of obedience to God, or of devotion to man. There was truly *nothing*
in Christ to which the spirit of evil could attach himself; and, therefore, "no weapon formed against Him could prosper."

26. *so I do.*—Christ goes forth, conscious and willing, to this struggle,
and to His death. He sets before the world the proof and example of
His love to God, and of entire obedience to His will; that all who
profess His Name should do as He has done—take up their cross, and
follow Him willingly and obediently, that the world may see and
know the truth of their discipleship, in its resemblance to that which
is recognized as the devotion of Christ.

27. *arise.*—It is sometimes thought that Christ now left the Supper-
room, and that S. John xv.–xvii. were spoken on the road to Gethsemane. But there is a great apparent difficulty in our Lord's de-
livering, before twelve men, during the darkness of a night walk, the
carefully spoken address which follows. How could so many hearers
so group themselves, as to hear intelligently all He said, as they walked
forward together? That they did so hear, we see from John xvi. 17–19,
29–31. The words certainly mark a transition. Perhaps it is enough,
however, to suppose, with many writers, that the Last Supper was now
concluded, and that they rose up from the table to depart; but that,
before they left the house, Christ spoke the words that follow, and
then knelt down to pray for them in the wonderful words of John xvii.;
which, again, we can with difficulty suppose Him to have done by the
roadside, or as they walked. So many thousands were at Jerusalem
at this time, crowding the city and its precincts, that there would have
been every probability of interruption, had any recognized the accents
of prayer, or teaching. He seems carefully to have avoided public
attention on this especial day; and, during the prayer of His agony,
He even withdrew from the disciples, leaving them posted in two

Every branch in Me that beareth not fruit He taketh

detachments, to make privacy certain. The words may include the sense, "Arise, let us go hence to that appointed work which I have undertaken voluntarily." The ancient writers connect it in this way with the verse preceding.

1. *the true vine.*—Israel had been of old the vine of God; now Christ declares Himself to be the real and perfect Vine, original and *architypal. (Alford).* This is not a parable; S. John does not give our Lord's parables, properly so called; but it is a similitude, like that of the good Shepherd. Many reasons have been supposed for the choice of this figure. Some say that our Lord spoke it as He passed through vineyards, or as He passed by the Temple, where there was a vine of costly beauty, wrought by Herod's order; but see xxv. *b.* 27. Others think that a vine may have been trained to the wall of the house where the Last Supper took place. Others, again, that the institution of the Lord's Supper gave occasion for this discourse, our Lord representing Himself here as the "true Vine," as He had before (John vi. 32, 33, 41) declared Himself as the "true Bread;" thus hallowing the sacramental type of Himself in either kind. This is the only one of these suppositions which appears worth a second thought. But why should it be necessary to find an accidental reason for our Lord's use here of a figure so suitable for expressing His intimate union with His people, and which had been already prominently and commonly used in those ancient Scriptures, upon which it was His wont to throw the light of fulfilment and illustration? The vine was the Church of God; Christ would now found a true Church, of which He was Himself the living Head and Source; and, therefore, He was the true Vine. Israel ceased to be the vine of God; it was a degenerate Church. As the true Vine, Christ naturally gives us of the fruit of the Vine; as He is " the true Bread from heaven," He naturally gives to us of that true Bread of life; and thus it is that, under either form, He gives *Himself* in the Lord's Supper. The union expressed under this figure, is the closest of all revealed to us by our Lord. The good Shepherd and the sheep are in a close relationship to each other, but they are not of the same nature, in any sense; there could be no personal sympathy between them. But the Vine and the branches are of the same nature, as Christ took on Himself the nature of His people. The ancient writers are careful to notice that it was as *man*, not as God, that our Lord thus represents Himself to us. It is the taking of mankind into Himself as man, that is conveyed in this figure. As to the universality and comprehensiveness of this Vine, in its spreading branches, see Ps. lxxx. 9–11.

2. *the husbandman.*—The original word implies a master-worker, and employer of labour; here His rights are those of a Creator, as well as of one possessed of absolute power to enforce His will, and of infinite

away: and every *branch* that beareth fruit, He purgeth it, that it may bring forth more fruit. Now ye are clean through the word which I have spoken unto you. Abide in Me, and I in you. As the branch cannot bear fruit of itself, except it abide in the vine; no more can ye,

goodness to exercise it beneficially. He tends and trains the branches, and prunes them, that they may arrive at the highest perfection; the bad He removes, lest they should injure the vitality of others. The Arians pointed to this figure, as supporting their doctrine of Christ not being God, of the same nature as the Father. But, as has been said, the Vine is Christ, as to *human* nature.

3. *purgeth.*—Or, "*cleanseth;*" for there is a connection between the words "*purgeth*" and "*clean*" in the original, which should be shown. We see how this cleansing is effected; it is by the gentle influence of the word which Christ has spoken, primarily, as well as by the sterner method of pruning—by the kindly exercise of God's Holy Spirit, as well as by the discipline of suffering and trial. The ancient writers give, as the first instance of this action, the purging of the hearts of the disciples from too earthly a conception of, and love for, Christ, and from their fear of the Jews, by the influence of the Spirit on the day of Pentecost; and thenceforward their greater faithfulness in Christ's service.

4. *now ye are clean.*—Gk. "ye are already clean." It needs, therefore, only to maintain that which Christ has effected.

5. *through the word.*—The language of S. Paul (Eph. v. 26) attributes the same cleansing efficacy to the word of Christ, "who loved the Church, and gave Himself for it, that He might sanctify and cleanse it with the washing of water by the word." Christ had lately washed their feet; but in this case, and even in baptism itself, the cleansing of the water would be nothing, without that of the word.

6. *abide in Me,* etc.—Christ speaks of that which is possible to us. Though He may withdraw Himself from us, He will not do so of His own free will. The severance, if it is made, will be made on our side, and by ourselves. And so our Lord warns us, that we may be careful and mindful to abide in Him, that He may be able, within the limits of His saving grace, to abide in us. The verb here is imperative in both clauses: "Abide in Me, let Me abide in you."

7. *no more can ye.*—The force of this figure is indisputable. Without our union is maintained, we may appear to be outwardly correct in life and profession; but that spiritual life which can overcome the power of the "second death," cannot exist out of communion with Christ. The application of the figure of the vine throughout the chapter, is to Christians generally; but we must not overlook its primary application to the Apostles, as now commissioned to promulgate the Gospel in the world (John xv. 16). Their life, efficiency, and power depended on their

except ye abide in Me. I am the vine, ye *are* the branches: he that abideth in Me, and I in him, the same bringeth forth much fruit; for without Me ye can do nothing. If a man abide not in Me, he is cast forth as a branch, and is withered; and *men* gather them, and cast *them* into the fire, and they are burned. If ye abide in Me, and My words abide in you, ye shall ask what ye will, and it shall be done unto you. Herein

union with Christ. Hence we see the great danger and evil of schism; not the less real, because variety of form, and custom, and the toleration of charity, make us familiar with it.

8. *without Me.*—Without, in the sense of *outside of*. Apart from me, severed from me, it is impossible either to think, or to do, such things as be rightful.

9. *are burned.*—Gk. "they burn." The original is suggestive of that continued punishment of eternal death (see xxi. 11, 14): *they burn*, but they are not consumed. This is the climax of their sad lot. They grow careless of the graces and fruits of a spiritual life; they bear no fruit. Thus, they sever that union with Christ, which is an indispensable condition of life, and so are cast out as unfruitful branches. They necessarily are withered, for they are cut off from the source of life. " *They* " (the angel ministers of God's wrath, not "*men*") gather them from amidst the duties they have neglected, the opportunities they have missed, the privileges they have desecrated; they remove from the midst of the living, the impediment of these dead branches, and cast them into the "fire which is not quenched," and there "they burn." The point of the whole discourse is the vital necessity of union with Christ, the loss of which entails these fatal and most terrible consequences. (See Ezek. xv. 4, 5.)

10. *ye shall ask.*—We now see the main reason for that success in prayer, which Christ had elsewhere repeatedly promised. In union with Christ, our requests are urged with His force; they must necessarily be things agreeable to His will. He says not, " I will pray the Father for you," because this union includes union with the Father. "The Father Himself loveth you," is a natural consequence. The true success of prayer, therefore, depends upon our communion with Christ. The promise of Christ's answer to prayer, must have been a great and special promise, and brought hope to the Apostles in many of the experiences of the ministry; for the answer to prayer was, in itself, evidence of their unity with Christ. (See App. V.)

11. *what ye will.*—Still as those in union with Christ; for there is of necessity a limit to our requests, who "know not what we should pray for as we ought." But, "if we ask anything according to God's will, He heareth us" (1 John v. 14). God's will often crosses ours, for

is My Father glorified, that ye bear much fruit; so shall
ye be My disciples. As the Father hath loved Me, so

we know not the consequences which His literal grant would entail.
He does. Our petitions have often an evil tendency, therefore they are
postponed. They are not refused; no prayer fails; but He substitutes
often another, and better, thing for what we ask in the error of ignorance.
We have not asked for the grant substituted for our desire, and therefore
we do not discern that it is an answer to our prayer. There are, therefore, many prayers offered by us, which we do not *see* to be answered,
because they are not *directly* answered. Infinite wisdom and goodness
thus arranges for us; but out of this there grows trial of our faith in
prayer. There would be no exercise of faith in our prayers, if they were
invariably granted in the terms of our request. Prayer would then be
an independent miraculous power, instead of being gifted to work
miracles in faith. There is one other design in the withholding, or
delay, of answer to prayer. It is that we may persevere, and not be
content to ask once and faintly; but that we may take heaven by
force, as it were, by our earnestness and perseverance in prayer (Matt.
xi. 12). We must ask in patience, faith, wisdom, and *nothing wavering*
(James i. 5-8). How great a scope is open to our prayers in the
words, " What ye will 1 " Within the limits and conditions defined
to us, there is nothing excluded which Christ's wisdom and love could
desire for us.

12. *herein.*—The promise here given is a general one; but the
context of the passage gives it a primary and special reference, to
our prayer for the strength and graces of spiritual life. There can be
nothing, which we ask with reference to the true development of such life,
which is contrary to the will of God. The answer to such prayers, in
union with Christ, must be the quickening of our spiritual life; and
the result, fruitfulness in good works. In these God is glorified, as
He is also in the life of Christ, which is thus reflected in us. In
the special reference to the Apostles, our Lord here sets before them the
great object of His own ministry, as that also of *their* commission,
the seeking the glory of the Father.

13. *glorified.*—Nothing could stamp a more supreme value on the
works which are possible to us in the grand career of a Christian life,
than that God Almighty, the Creator and Sustainer of the universe,
permits an increase of His own eternal glory, through our ministrations
in the service of Christ.

14. *My disciples.*—This shall be the proof of discipleship. The
disciple is a follower of that which he has learnt of his Lord and
Master. Before the world, also, this shall be his distinction, that his
life is spent in the exercise in the same works of mercy in which
his Lord delighted to walk.

15. *as the Father.*—There is extraordinary force in the declarations

have I loved you : continue ye in My love. If ye keep My commandments, ye shall abide in My love; even as I have kept My Father's commandments, and abide in His love.

These things have I spoken unto you, that My joy might remain in you, and *that* your joy might be full. This is My commandment, That ye love one another, as I have loved you. Greater love hath no man than this, than a man lay down his life for his friends. Ye are My

of our Lord, in this last discourse. He surely could say nothing more expressive of His love to man, than that it was like that of the eternal Father for Himself. He adds, "Continue ye" (or *abide*—the original word is a repetition of that used before) "in My love;" the severance from it being on man's side. (See note 6.)

16. *if ye keep.*—Christ lays repeated emphasis on what man can do. He makes the keeping of His commandments the proof of our love to Him (John xiv. 15); and, at the same time, the certain way to retain His love. And, again, comparison is drawn with the love of the Father to Himself, and to His own life of obedience to His Father's will. But unless His love remains in us, we cannot keep His commandments, for without Him we can do nothing; and, without our love is in Him, we shall not love His commandments. This love is, therefore, a test of union with Him. Hence also, "the first and great commandment," comprising obedience to all the rest, is love to God.

17. *My joy.*—My own proper joy; the joy of perfect happiness in union with the Father. This source of satisfaction shall be yours also, in the same union; and no man shall take from you that which God confers. It conveys to you the joy that you really abide in Me.

18. *full.*—Perfect.

19. *My commandment.*—Christ's commandment is one, and it is simple; but it includes everything that a code could enforce. If His people possess the principle of love, as an active and living principle, they need no further law; none other is known in heaven, Christ's own kingdom, nor elsewhere, where He reigns supreme. His commandment is at once most touchingly enforced, and is vested with the utmost expansion, in the words, "As I have loved you."

20. *greater love.*—S. Paul (Rom. v. 6–8) gives another turn to the argument, which our Lord, in His tenderness to His disciples, did not, at this moment, press. Christ argues that none could show a fuller proof of love and devotion, than his laying down his life for his *friend*. S. Paul does not hesitate to remind us that Christ, the Son of God, did this for those who were as yet His *enemies*, and who were, by this act of surpassing devotion, to be made His friends : " Christ died for the ungodly," the doomed.

friends, if ye do whatsoever I command you.　Henceforth
I call you not servants ; for the servant knoweth not
what his lord doeth : but I have called you friends ; for
all things that I have heard of My Father I have made
known unto you.　Ye have not chosen Me, but I have
chosen you, and ordained you, that ye should go and bring
forth fruit, and *that* your fruit should remain : that whatsoever ye shall ask of the Father in My Name, He may

21. *if ye do.*—The consequence of obeying Christ's commands is so
important, that He may well say, those are His friends who do them.
For He has already declared that keeping His commandments is the
proof of love to Him, and the way to remain in the unity of His love,
and in that of the Father; and is the very same in which He had
Himself continued in the Father's love (John xiv. 15, 21, 23, xv. 10).

22. *I have made known.*—They did not now fully realize the depths
of Christ's revelation to them of things of spiritual meaning.　But
He had already said that the Holy Ghost would show this to them, in
making clear the full tenor of Christ's communications ; and then they
would also see how gracious was the assurance, and how high the
distinction, that they were friends of His.

23. *not chosen Me.*—Christ would repress any rising of pride, a sin
ever most dangerous to His cause.　In the affairs of the world, men
may choose their leader, and may plume themselves on their sagacity,
and on the support they give to him.　The disciples of the Jewish
Rabbis chose their own teacher, and prided themselves on their following him.　But, in the kingdom of Christ, those who are His subjects,
servants, disciples, friends, have been chosen by Him; from Himself,
the Fountain of life, springs all that is good, and all honour.　The
ancient writers connect this passage also with the figure of the vine.
The Apostles were chosen as leading shoots, to bring forth the fruitfulness of the vine; they had not so destined themselves, but were
elected by the great Husbandman to this work.

24. *ordained you.*—It is My appointment and design for you.

25. *go.*—Go forth, to your work; and that work is the evangelization of the world.

26. *should remain.*—With regard to yourselves, it shall be continuous; the constant effort of your life shall be maintained in union
with My life.　With regard to the interests of My kingdom, it shall
remain, undestroyed throughout all ages, in the Church, which shall
be founded in your labours, and which shall for ever flourish and
expand.　"It is an everlasting kingdom," "a kingdom which shall
never be destroyed."　(Dan. ii. 44, vii. 27.)

27. *ye shall ask.*—The result of being Christ's friends, and chosen
by Him, is, that God cannot but hearken to our prayers.　The prayer

give it you.   These things I command you, that ye love one another.

(*d.*) *Persecution by the World.   Perpetuity of the Witness of Christ.*

S. John xv. 18—xvi. 4.

If the world hate you, ye know that it hated Me before it hated you.   If ye were of the world, the world would

here spoken of is, primarily, that for the increase of spiritual life, and for the advance of the interests of Christ's spiritual kingdom. (See note 12.)   It is noticeable that fruitfulness, or success in God's cause, is here connected with prayer; a prayerful life must, therefore, be a spiritually successful life.   (App. V.)

28. *in My Name.*—This is more fully spoken of a little later in this discourse (John xvi. 23, 24).   It is henceforth the acceptable way of access to God in prayer; every prayer in Christ's Name being united with the impress of His advocacy and merits.

29. *these things.*—Christ closes this subject with an emphatic repetition of His one and great command.   But not only so.   He is speaking of their commission as Apostles; and they must bear towards each other, and to Christians, that love which Christ has towards them.   It will be the secret of strength and success.   They cannot go forth as leading branches of the true Vine, to bear permanent fruit, unless they possess that intimate bond of union, which binds them to Christ, and to His people.   This verse marks a transition; and is the link between what precedes, and the effect and experience of their mission, which now follows.   Unity is essential to success on the part of those who proclaim the Gospel; unity of doctrine, harmony of action and sentiment, in union with Christ.

1. *if the world.*—The brotherly love of the community of Christ is the true antidote to the enmity of the world.   Those who best fulfil their Lord's great command, will be best prepared to encounter that hatred.   The connection with the last section is close and evident.   As to the antagonism of the world, it could be no surprise to Christ's disciples; it has been already sufficiently foreshown in His own experience.   They well knew that He had fared worse upon earth, than the brute creation of His hand; "He had not where to lay His head," in the world which He made, and which He visited to redeem.   We notice here that, in the language of Christ, those who were once the chosen people of God, are placed in the fore ranks of " the world," being arrayed against God.

love his own : but because ye are not of the world, but
I have chosen you out of the world, therefore the world
hateth you. Remember the word that I said unto you,
The servant is not greater than his lord. If they have
persecuted Me, they will also persecute you ; if they
have kept My saying, they will keep yours also. But
all these things will they do unto you for My Name's
sake, because they know not Him that sent Me. If I
had not come and spoken unto them, they had not had

2. *the world hateth you.*—A sad and painful thing it would be, to be
shut out from the joyousness of the world, to find trouble and sorrow
in their contact with it, to see anger and hatred in every face, and to
feel like outcasts from their kind. But yet, in this same experience,
there is the assurance of their being in the right, and of being held in
honour by a far larger, and more noble, " cloud of witnesses," who once
maintained such witness as theirs for the truth of Christ, and of angel
spectators, unseen, but sympathizing ; of being in honour also with
God. For the world hateth the disciple, because he is as his Master ;
they persecute him, and disregard his saying and his mission, because
he is a follower and preacher of his Lord.

3. *remember.*—(See Matt. x. 24.) This is one of those sayings of
our Lord, which have their verification in various aspects ; and which,
therefore, appear to be rules of His kingdom of grace. (See App. VI.)

4. *My Name's sake.*—No form of religion, or of superstition, however
gross, has excited the same energy in opposition, as has been aroused
against Christianity ; and not from any charge that has been substantiated against it, for wrong or injury done to any man. Were it so,
it would at least have received the toleration accorded to a superstition. But what our Lord says here, has been exactly verified in the
history of His faith. It is neither for distinctive doctrine, or ceremony,
but *for His Name's sake*, that Christians have suffered reproach and
loss ; and that, because His Name is the watchword of antagonism
against all wrong, moral and social ; against all error, religious and
political ; and against every form of oppression, whether of physical,
moral, or spiritual power. It is the light disclosing the darkness of
evil, of ignorance, and superstition ; and, therefore, all the force of evil
is centred in opposition to the good cause of God. The world knows
not, and owns not, the Father, nor Him whom He has sent to be the
Saviour of the world. Naturally, it disowns the messengers of His
mercy ; but its frown is its recognition that they are, in truth and
success, His.

5. *come and spoken.*—Our Lord *came* to them from heaven, to live
amongst them, and to die for them. He did not send any less
interested than Himself ; He came in person, vested with a commission

sin ; but now have they no cloke for their sin. He that hateth Me hateth My Father also. If I had not done among them the works which none other man did, they had not had sin : but now they have both seen and hated both Me and My Father. But *this cometh to pass,*

and power superior to that of Moses, or of any prophet of old. He *spoke* to them as man never could speak, with personal authority and power, for "His word was with power." He did amongst them "*the works* which none other did," or could do, whether angel or man, in proof of His Divine mission. He gave thus a threefold witness, by presence, by word, and by miracle ; and it left those who rejected Him without excuse, or "cloke for their sin," without protest for their opposition.

6. *not had sin.*—Not the supreme and crowning sin, of rejecting the Divine atonement for sins.

7. *My Father also.*—Christ was the express image of the Father's Person ; He was the Son of God, equal to the Father as touching His Godhead. He came to the world as the Son of the Divine Father, charged with His terms of reconciliation and atonement ; and, therefore, he that hateth and rejecteth the Son, hateth and rejecteth the Father also. It is impossible to hate the Son, and love the Father ; for "every one that loveth Him that begot, loveth Him also that is begotten of Him"—a sentence true primarily of Christ, and then of His brethren (1 John v. 1).

8. *both seen and hated.*—There are two meanings here : they both saw the works of Divinity, and also hated both Christ who did them, and the Father who commissioned Him to work them. But the full and awful truth is, that they both saw the Godhead of Christ, and hated both the Son and the Father ; for it was the worst feature in their sin, that they did see and recognize both the Father and the Son, in the Person of Jesus Christ. It was impossible that men so studious and intelligent of Holy Scripture, should be deaf to the voice of the prophets, as fulfilled in Him, and blind to the evidence of Divinity which shone forth in His miracles and words ; except upon the principle set forth by the prophet, and remarked by our Lord and His Apostles, that they closed both their eyes and their ears, "lest they should see with their eyes, and hear with their ears, and should understand." They saw and knew what they did, so far as they would allow themselves to see and know. Where they knew not what they did, they knew it not in the ignorance of those who refused to know. (See xxxi. 5.) "There are some in the Church who not only do not what is good, but even persecute it, and hate in others what they neglect to do themselves. The sin of these men is not that of infirmity, or ignorance, but deliberate, wilful sin." (*Gregory.*) "They sit in the seat of the scornful" Jews.

that the word might be fulfilled that is written in their law, **They hated Me without a cause.**

But when the Comforter is come, Whom I will send unto you from the Father, *even* the Spirit of truth, which proceedeth from the Father, He shall testify of Me : and

9. *their law.*—These words are found in Pss. xxxv. 19, lxix. 4, both interpreted of the Messiah. The voice of the Scriptures, which they professed to reverence, thus again witnesses against them.

10. *but when.*—The opposition, and persecution, and hatred which were general against Christ, should never prevail against Him. The witness which His presence upon earth, His living word, and His Divine works had inaugurated (note 5), would be sustained, on His departure, by the Spirit of truth, and also by Christ's chosen witnesses, the Apostles ; thus it could never droop, or die. He who foretold the opposition His Name should encounter, thus strengthened the faith of His servants, by the prediction of their successful and victorious maintenance of His cause, with the aid of His Holy Spirit.

11. *the Comforter.*—In the words of this sentence, we notice a clear statement of the doctrine, of the trinity of Persons in the Godhead: the Comforter is sent from the Father by the Son. (See xxv. *b.* 3.)

12. *which proceedeth.*—This verse has excited comment in every age, as giving distinct evidence on the doctrine which divides the great Churches of the East and West. Christ, here and before, had declared that *He would send* the Holy Spirit ; He now adds (lest the words should convey less than their due force to the hearers' minds) that the Holy Spirit was essentially Divine, that He "*proceedeth from the Father.*" Whether too much stress has been laid, or not, upon the evidence of this particular verse, the doctrine itself is a vitally important one. There can be no doubt of its truth ; so repeatedly is the Holy Spirit called "the Spirit of Christ," as well as "the Spirit of God," that there can be no question concerning the equal procession, on this point. Again His mission is equally declared to be from the Father, and also from the Son ; in this case, also, there is an equal procession. The difference turns on the fact that, whilst the Holy Spirit is here said, in exact terms, to proceed from the Father, there is no similarly distinct declaration that He proceeds from the Son. The doctrine on this point is from inference, but an inference so irresistible as to amount to absolute certainty. (See xxv. *b.* 17.) In this instance Christ is evidently desirous of pressing upon the disciples, and on His Church through them, the unity of His witness with that of the Father and the Son ; hence (it may be partly to illustrate this truth of unity) our Lord emphatically declares that the Spirit of truth proceedeth from the Father, as He had before, with emphasis, declared that He would be sent, or given, by Himself. Thus understood, the passage does not support the error, that the procession of the Holy Ghost was

ye also shall bear witness, because ye have been with Me from the beginning.

These things have I spoken unto you, that ye should not be offended. They shall put you out of the synagogues : yea, the time cometh, that whosoever killeth

from the Father, and not also from the Son ("*filiogue*"). It rather anticipates any error, in supposing that He was sent by the Son alone, and not equally by the Father. But the probability is (and it is a sad reflection, though perhaps bearing the germ of future reconciliation), that the error is not so much one of difference in vital doctrine, as in the terms of expression of the true faith. The creed of the Church was settled without the separate mention of the procession of the Holy Spirit from the Son; the word "*filiogue*" was added by the Western Church in times of debate and strife, upon the point of doctrine being raised, and without the authority of a general council. And, therefore, the rivalry which existed between the East and West, found expression in this question; and violence and excommunication, on either side, produced a division which has never been healed. Bishop Harold Browne thus concisely states the case : " The Council of Constantinople (A.D. 381) had inserted in the creed of the Council of Nice (A.D. 325) the words ' proceeding from the Father ;' and the Council of Ephesus (A.D. 431) had decreed that no addition should be made to that creed thenceforth. Accordingly, the Greek Fathers uniformly declared their belief in the procession of the Holy Ghost from the Father ; the Latin Fathers, on the other hand, having regard to those passages which speak of the Spirit of Christ, and of the Spirit as sent by the Son, continually spoke of the Holy Ghost as proceeding from the Father and the Son. The Greek Fathers, indeed, were willing to use language approximating to the words of the Latin Fathers, but shrank from directly asserting the procession from the Son. Thus, they spoke of the Holy Ghost as ' the Spirit of Christ, proceeding from the Father, and receiving of the Son.' And it has been inferred that many of the earlier Greek writers held, as did the Latins, a real procession both from the Father and the Son, although they were not willing to express themselves otherwise than in the words of the creed."

13. *from the beginning.*—This was a qualification on the part of those who immediately succeeded Christ, and one which would gain them credit, as authentic witnesses to His cause. (See Luke i. 2; Acts i. 21, 22, v. 32; 1 John i. 1, 2.)

14. *offended.*—That you may not falter through despondency, on seeing the cause you advocate " everywhere spoken against," and yourselves everywhere opposed, and even the witness of the Spirit in your day only partially successful against the powers of evil. I have forewarned you of the event, and given these assurances of faith.

15. *the synagogues.*—This excommunication was a terrible act of

you will think that he doeth God service. And these
things will they do unto you, because they have not
known the Father, nor Me. But these things have I
told you, that when the time shall come, ye may remember that I told you of them. And these things I
said not unto you at the beginning, because I was with
you.

vengeance. It separated the outcast from the worship of his forefathers, and from their visible Church, to the Christian Jew still an
object of devout veneration. It severed him also from the society of
his dearest and nearest relations, who were debarred from associating
with him, in the most ordinary occasions of daily life. There has been
no system of outlawry so terrible, as that which has issued in the name
of religion.

16. *killeth you.*—As Saul thought he ought to persecute the Church
of Christ to the death; and as others of his nation persecuted him,
when he became an Apostle of Jesus Christ.

17. *service.*—(See Rom. viii. 36.) The original word is a technical
term; it often means a religious sacrifice. This meaning may be
pressed too far; but yet it must have often been verified in this sense,
when the heathen offered the life of a Christian martyr, to propitiate
his angry deities; and later, within the pale of Christianity, when it
became no uncommon thing for the blood of heresy to be poured out
before God, upon the altars of orthodoxy, by rival religious factions.
And, in a far nobler sense, mistaken zeal may have often sacrificed
earthly happiness, and the tenderest ties of kindred and friendship, in
the thought that the giving up of those in error, was a sacrifice acceptable to the God of truth.

18. *these things.*—It was from no wish to depress the minds of His
few faithful servants, at this most saddening crisis, that Christ spoke
such words of gloom. For, when the time came for their verification,
no comfort could be greater than the recollection that Christ had foretold all; and, therefore, He must be the true God, and they, His servants, must be right, though alone against the voice of unanimous
opposition. And these words of Christ would come to mind, hallowed
with all the interest of this last occasion of His life, and brightened
with the glory into which He had emerged from His agony. There
was no need to have saddened them with all this before. Whilst He
was with them, the main anger of the Jews was concentrated against
Himself; and, whenever it pressed them, He was there to comfort
them. It was only when He was gone, that its fury burst upon them.
And, with regard to the persecution of the Gentiles, that had been, as
yet, warded off by His order, "Go not into the way of the Gentiles."
Now, however, they must know the truth of their own position, and
be prepared for general opposition.

(*e.*) *The Departure of Christ. The Advent of the Spirit of Truth.*

S. John xvi. 5–33.

But now I go My way to Him that sent Me; and none of you asketh Me, Whither goest Thou? But because I have said these things unto you, sorrow hath filled your heart. Nevertheless, I tell you the truth; It is expedient for you that I go away: for if I go not away, the Com-

1. *now I go.*—Our Lord had spoken of this before, but now He announces it as immediately to take place. This declaration introduces a new division of the last discourse.

2. *asketh Me.*—They had asked the question before in so many words (John xiii. 36, xiv. 5), but without any definite idea what they were saying. Now they did more properly realize it, and yet none asked the obvious question of those personally interested, "Where goest Thou? Tell us of those scenes of glory which you are about to revisit; of your happiness there; of your present mission and its object; of the interest which we have in your future condition; of those many mansions which you will prepare for us."

3. *these things.*—Concerning My departure, and the approaching triumph of evil, and your prospect of trial and sorrow upon earth.

4. *filled your heart.*—So filled it, as to leave no place or thought for brighter and more stirring interests, for wider and grander views.

5. *nevertheless.*—Though you ask it not, yet will I tell you what is the real truth; it may at the first astonish and trouble you, but you will presently appreciate it.

6. *expedient for you.*—He had already said that, for His sake, they ought to rejoice because He was going to the Father; but, apart from any thought of His interest, it was for their own true advantage that He should go away. The coming of the Comforter, far more important to them than His own continued presence, depended on His departure and glorification. (See John vii. 39.) The main reason, no doubt, was this: that their spiritual nature would never rise to the true conception of His life and character, whilst He remained with them, present in the flesh, as man with man. "It was necessary, therefore, that the form of the servant should be removed from their eyes; for, so long as they looked upon that, they thought that Christ was no more than what they saw Him to be." (*Augustine.*) And, therefore, after an interval of training, and of cleansing the mind from thoughts of Him as they had known Him before, and of raising their hopes to the kingdom of His ascension, and thus from the sole belief in what was visible, to some conception by faith of the invisible and spiritual life

forter will not come unto you; but if I depart, I will send Him unto you. And when He is come, He will reprove the world of sin, and of righteousness, and of

of Christ, the Holy Spirit came upon them, henceforth to dwell in the Church of Christ, until the end of time. And other reasons there were, of less moment, but which combined to make the absence of Christ's person indispensable to the life of the Church. Already they had contended about the places of honour in His kingdom; and what a scene of strife may be imagined, as Christianity spread through the nations, when all were pressing to that city where Christ was sitting enthroned (for, in His human nature, He could be present only in one place), to the suspension of all the interests and duties of life—of those daily duties on which depend, under God's providence, supply of daily bread, the necessities of life, the activity of commerce. Christ must feed and clothe the multitudes, as did Moses in the wilderness, if He were to remain enthroned in the land of Judæa, under the present conditions of human life. And who could fill His present office of Mediator at the throne of God, were He personally present amongst men? However, therefore, we may think it desirable that we could lay our wants at the feet of Christ, present as of old upon earth, a moment's reflection will show us obvious reasons (others are known to His wisdom) for the higher efficiency of His present service in our behalf. How expedient, therefore, that He should go to the Father, to plead there for us, in our nature; and that His Holy Spirit, omnipresent and spiritual in His activity, should represent Him upon earth, sanctifying us, quickening our spiritual life, and making us fit for the spiritual "inheritance of the saints in light."

7. *reprove.*—The margin of the A. V. gives a far preferable rendering, "*convince.*" The Law gave the knowledge of prohibited sins, and of general sinfulness in man; but the effect of His presence in the world, and of His spiritual influence, will be to work in the world conviction of its own sin, especially of that supreme sin which includes all *acts* of sin—the unbelief in Christ; of the righteousness of Christ; and, more, of His being the only righteousness in which man can appear before God, for "He was manifested to take away our sin." This includes the idea of justification by His death; for the conclusion of His work, being His departure to the Father from human sight, is mentioned as that in which this conviction of His righteousness is centred (see John viii. 28); and it includes also the exhibition, in the death of Christ, of the righteousness of God, who required the death of Christ, as representing the sinner. And, lastly, He is to work conviction of the truth of God's judgment, of the final judgment, as the supreme end; but not of it only, but of His definite decision in all cases of human action, and of separation of the good from the bad. For, as judgment has been given against the usurper prince of this world, so

judgment: of sin, because they believe not on Me; of righteousness, because I go to My Father, and ye see Me no more; of judgment, because the prince of this world is judged.

I have yet many things to say unto you, but ye

will it pass against man, who submits to his evil influence. It will be victorious before the world, over every form and aspect of evil and wrong, as it has been over the author of all these; everything subordinate being included in the mention of the principal. This judgment took immediate effect in Judæa, where the opposition raised against the Gospel of Christ, under the leadership of "the prince of this world," resulted in the speedy destruction of the Jewish Church and national existence. And so have various forms of his power in the world been broken by the advent of Christianity; they fell upon Christ, and were broken in pieces. (See vii. 38.) The connection of the three clauses is immediate; for whosoever will not receive the Spirit's conviction of sin, and of the righteousness which is by faith in Jesus Christ the righteous, must inevitably be included in the condemnation which has been passed upon the prince of this world. To him who will receive it, this condemnation is the earnest of victory won, of deliverance completed; for certainly we are warned of judgment, in order that mercy may be shown to us. (See xvi. 26.)

8. *ye see Me no more.*—An appeal to faith. The whole statement is to the effect that the Holy Spirit convinces those who believe, that the only righteousness which is accepted with God, is the righteousness of Christ; and man can only be justified, or accounted righteous, by his faith (inspired by the Holy Ghost) in the righteousness offered through the death of Christ. For His departure presupposes the successful witness of His death; and, as we see Him no more on earth, we must see Him now by faith.

9. *many things.*—We may take the three subjects of the witness of the Spirit just spoken of, as the general heads of these many things which were to be made clear to the Apostles, His chosen witnesses to the world. He had much to say, doubtless, regarding the sacrifice of His death completed, His ascension, and present work of mediation; of the call of the Gentiles to the faith; of the foundation and government of His Church, and of the numerous questions which must wait on the decision of the Apostles. We need not suppose that, when Christ ascended to heaven, He left anything unsaid, which He wished to say to His disciples. We are not told what were the occupations of those forty days, which He spent upon earth after His resurrection; but the result of them was, that those, who now had no place for anything but the sorrow which had filled their hearts, returned from the mount of the ascension, where they had parted finally with their Lord, "with great joy"—so entirely had His com-

cannot bear them now. Howbeit when He, the Spirit
of truth, is come, He will guide you into all truth : for

munications to them removed the present burden of sorrow. Still
they could not see His work in all its bearings, or their duties with
regard to it, until the Holy Spirit made all clear to them.

10. *cannot bear them.*—The present burden of sorrow was so over-
powering, that it mastered them, and precluded all hope of their seeing
what lay beyond it.

11. *He, the Spirit*, etc.—(See **xxv.** *d.* 11.) The original for *" Spirit "*
is of the neuter gender ; that for the pronoun *" he "* is masculine—a
clearly intentional statement of the personality of the Holy Ghost,
against any supposition of His being merely a quality or attribute.
His designation, as the " Spirit of truth," is a grand and noble title,
which none could possess but God alone. He thus intervenes between
the disciples and the possibility of their misconception of Christ's
words, and the conveyance of erroneous impression to the world.
Men may err, and will err, on points the most vital ; but the plenary
inspiration of the Spirit of truth precludes the possibility of error on
the part of those so inspired. In Him alone, and in no man, or
council, has resided this infallibility. All good is the inspiration of
the Spirit of truth ; but this inspiration seems to have been the
personal distinction of the apostolic witnesses to the truth of Christ ;
and it did not give to them infallibility in all things, but regard only
to this special purpose.

12. *guide*, etc.—Gk. " show you the way into the whole truth."

13. *all truth.*—Gk. " all *the* truth," *i.e.* " the whole and perfect
truth." What Christ had declared to them had been truth ; but they
had had only a limited perception of it, and much that He would fain
disclose to them, they were not now fitted to receive. But the Spirit
of truth would fill in the details of every outline, and bring to their
remembrance every word of Christ, and inspire that spirit in them,
which could see the whole truth, in its perfect completion and unity.
This declaration is an important one, as it discountenances an error
of modern times (held, under various aspects, by various bodies of
Christians), that the truth, as shown by Christ, was not in itself complete, but that it admitted of further development and progression in
after ages. This is a dangerous error, because it claims for the intelligence of men, in after ages, an inspiration of the Spirit supplementary to that of the Apostles. Knowledge may, indeed, develop and
extend itself ; mankind may see, more clearly than in past ages, the
full bearing of what the Apostles delivered, and thus approach nearer
to the knowledge given to them, and which they did undoubtedly
possess. But this is not the possession of new truth, or any addition
to the truth, or a further development of the truth delivered ; it does
not, in a word, have reference to the development of truth itself, but

He shall not speak of Himself; but whatsoever He shall hear, *that* shall He speak: and He will shew you things to come. He shall glorify Me: for He shall

to the development of the power, in man, to receive and apply the truth already declared. If, therefore, we hear of development of truths (*i.e.* additions to the revelation of truth, as closed with the volume of inspiration), we may safely declare that the real designation of such should be development of error.

14. *of Himself.*—The revelation of the Spirit would be no new Gospel, different from that of God the Father, through the ministration of Christ; or even supplementary to it. He could not speak without communion with the Father and Christ, but in entire concert with them. What He hears now, and has from eternity heard, in the Divine counsels of the Holy Trinity, concerning the salvation of man, He will make known, and illumine with His inspiration in the Church of Christ. His communications would, therefore, be nothing new or original; but, as God the Father had willed the salvation of men, which Christ had effected, so would the Holy Spirit bring this purpose and work within the reach of man, by His sanctifying influence. Those who carry on the witness of the Spirit, in all ages of the Church, the ministers and stewards of Christ's mysteries, will ever best succeed in their mission, when they most remember that *they may not speak of themselves;* they must forget self, and forego self-assertion, if they would guide others into the perfect truth of Christ. (See 2 Cor. iv. 5.)

15. *He shall hear.*—Hear, in the councils of the Father and the Son with Himself. (See John viii. 28, xiv. 24.) He will thus unfold to man the purposes of the triune God, as an eye-witness, and personal hearer, and participator in their council.

16. *things to come.*—Gk. "*the* things to come." Not prophecy in general, but as it regards Christianity; the revelation of the faith of Christ, in its effect upon the future ages of the world, until the end of time. (See note 13.) This promise was most notably fulfilled in the instance of the Apostle who has recorded it. (See Rev. i. 1.)

17. *glorify Me.*—It is the special work of the Spirit to declare the glory of Christ (see 2 Cor. iii. 18); and the height of knowledge attainable by man, may be summed up as, "the light of the knowledge of the glory of God in the face of Jesus Christ." It had been the work of Christ to glorify the Father; it was now that of the Divine Spirit to declare that of Him, who had " sought not His own glory." And the lives of all Christian witnesses to His truth must illustrate the same glory, in the faithfulness of their lives' obedience to the example of Jesus Christ. Again, the witness of the Spirit is the standard of all human witnesses; as they must speak, not of themselves, but of the things of Christ, so must the object of their witness be to glorify Christ, not themselves. (See note 14.)

receive of Mine, and shall shew it unto you. All things that the Father hath are Mine : therefore said I, that He shall take of Mine, and shall shew *it* unto you.

A little while, and ye shall not see Me : and again, a

18. *Mine.*—Christ speaks of deep mysteries, when He says, "All things that the Father hath are Mine." The kingdom, the power, and the glory, all the attributes of God, and here, very especially, the truth, and doctrine, and work of redemption, are His likewise. These the Spirit should make manifest to the Apostles ; and, in so doing, "show them plainly of the Father" also. For He proceedeth from the Father and the Son ; and, in the light of His Divine inspiration, they should see Christ the King, in more than all the royalty that their hearts had conceived, and been disappointed not to realize; and a kingdom far more glorious and extensive than the kingdom of their father David, or than any realm of earth, extended far beyond the utmost bounds of empire yet attained by man.

19. *a little while.*—After these words our Lord returns to the subject of His departure. "He does this to accustom them to the mention of His departure, in order that they may bear it well when it does come ; for nothing so quiets the troubled mind, as the continued recurrence to the subject of its grief." (*Chrysostom.*) Like the great prophecy of our Lord (see xviii. 9), there appears to be here one meaning rising behind another, until the extreme range of distance is attained. (i.) The first and obvious interpretation, is that, in a few short hours, Christ would be removed from them by death, and then the grave would hide Him from them ; yet a little while more, and they would see Him come forth in the power of the resurrection ; and all this was preparatory to His going to the Father. But this is far from being all that the words convey, for (ii.) yet a little while, and He should be removed from this world altogether ; until, after what would seem to the Church triumphant, looking back upon it from the happiness of heaven, to have been but a little while, He would come again in glory, because He was now going to the Father, to be their Advocate and Mediator. To the disciples, who had known Him on earth, there would be (iii.) this special realization of His promise, that, though they had seen Him personally on earth, and He was now, for a short time, removed from them to go to the Father, He would come again, and receive them to Himself, in the hour when their witness to Him should cease, and God should give them rest, in death, from their labours. But there is yet (iv.) another sense, favoured by the use of different words in the original for " *see*," which is very important and true. In the first instance, the word implies beholding with the *natural* sight; in the second, seeing *spiritually :* A little while, and ye shall no more behold Me with the eye; and again, a little while, and, "the eyes of your understanding being enlightened," ye shall see Me with the eye

little while, and ye shall see Me, because I go to the Father. Then said *some* of His disciples among themselves, What is this that He saith unto us, A little while, and ye shall not see Me : and again, a little while, and ye shall see Me : and, Because I go to the Father ? They said therefore, What is this that He saith, A little while? we cannot tell what He saith. Now Jesus knew that they were desirous to ask Him, and said unto them, Do you enquire among yourselves of that I said, A little while, and ye shall not see Me : and again, a little while, and ye shall Me ? Verily, verily, I say unto you, That ye shall weep and lament, but the world shall rejoice :

of faith, spiritually present in the midst of you ; for now I go from earth to My Father, which is in heaven. Those who thus "know Christ now by faith, shall have the fruition of His glorious Godhead " in the kingdom of His Father, for that further reality shall reward the intelligence of faith. (*See Collect for the Epiphany.*)

20. *what is this.*—There is here, again, a distinction to be regarded in the Greek, in the words translated " saith." The first may be so rendered ; the second, more accurately, "is speaking of." "What is this that He saith, 'the little while?'" (the article defines the phrase). " We cannot tell what He is speaking of." Our Lord had already distinctly said He was going to the Father, and that they would see Him no more at present (John xiv. 28, xvi. 10) ; but, apparently, what perplexed them was the expression, " the little while," in connection with His departure. Whether this awakened old hopes, or excited new prospects, it is difficult to say ; but it involved an uncertainty, which they were most anxious should be defined to them.

21. *Jesus knew.*—He is always aware of the thoughts of the heart, and most attentive to the united desires of His people, wherever two or three are gathered together to express them ; it is enough that they are desirous of asking Him. A spirit of earnest inquiry after His meaning and will, is sure to gain His ear, and to be favourably regarded and answered.

22. *ye shall weep.*—The answer is not direct ; but when the interpretation should unfold itself, in the course of fulfilment, this reply would give far more comfort, than any direct explanation. And, like the declaration to which it is annexed as answer and consolation, it has various and extended meanings: Ye shall weep and wail, as those who mourn the dead ; the world shall triumph, as if victorious over Me, and over your hopes. Your condition shall be full of sorrow ; but from that very sorrow shall arise your rejoicing, when I rise from the dead, in the power of the resurrection, victorious over the grave,

and ye shall be sorrowful, but your sorrow shall be
turned into joy. A woman when she is in travail hath

and over the world. The fulfilment of this is evident. From the
moment when the disciples returned from the mount of the ascension,
with great joy, their attitude before the world was cheerful and hopeful,
"sorrowful, yet always rejoicing." The change of words in the Greek
is again most expressive. We have, in the A. V., "weep, lament, be
sorrowful;" the two former express, severally, the *tearful* sorrow, and
the loud *wailing*, of those who mourn in their bereavement; the last,
the continuous and *painful affliction* of the bereaved.

23. *shall be turned.*—It would not be a new happiness in the place
of that which was lost, another joy instead of their present sorrow;
but this very sorrow for the absence of their Lord, should be turned
into the joy of His presence.

24. *travail.*—(See Isa. liii. 11.) In this comparison there is again
the same extension of meaning. There is (i.) the expression of the
great truth, that, with regard to all suffering and self-denial in the
cause of Christ, "they that sow in tears shall reap in joy." But (ii.),
to the disciples especially, there seems to be, in the general consent of
writers, ancient and modern, the experience of that mystical agony
which preceded the birth of the new man, the first-born, and the
pledge of the resurrection; this the Apostolic Church of Christ
experienced before her Lord came forth from the grave, new-born into
the world, with the joy of victory. S. Paul (Gal. iv. 19) speaks under
the same form. Our Lord Himself gives this explanation of the
anguish of the Apostles, in saying that they shall so sorrow until they
see Himself again risen from the dead ; when the joy of His resurrection
shall be such, that none can take it from them. The Passion and
resurrection of Christ Himself, was the type and earnest of this travail
and birth. Besser points out that, during the Forty Days, all those
whom Jesus had once called "His mother" (Matt. xii. 49), because
they received Him in the hearing and believing His word, sorrowed
and mourned; and their anguish, like that of the travailing woman,
strove towards the joyful moment, when, in the resurrection, that Son
was given to them afresh, who is the joy of the whole earth. There is
(iii.) the further sense, that the Christ is typified by this woman (see
Rev. xii. 2), in pain and sorrow until her sons are delivered, heirs of
immortality; and the day of her great and eternal rejoicing will be
that of Christ's coming again to receive them. There may be (iv.)
a type of the trouble of the second, or spiritual birth, in every soul
which is "born again" into the kingdom of heaven, and the happiness
of seeing, in Christ, the Saviour, and, at the last, the glory of His
people. The constant use of this figure in Holy Scripture, as expressive
of spiritual birth, is very remarkable; a glance at the column of a
Concordance on the word "travail," gives a variety of illustrations,

sorrow, because her hour is come: but as soon as she is delivered of the child, she remembereth no more the anguish, for joy that a man is born into the world. And ye now therefore have sorrow: but I will see you again, and your heart shall rejoice, and your joy no man taketh from you.

And in that day ye shall ask Me nothing. Verily,

which are worthy of study. It is a wonderful instance of the mercy of God, which underlies all His judgments upon men, that the sentence which He pronounced upon Eve (Gen. iii. 16) thus affords type of the sufferings of the spiritual birth, which are followed by such untold joy; that every mother should thus see God's mercy to herself, in the fact that there is typified, in her instance, the resurrection and second advent of her Lord, the spiritual birth of the children of God, the trials and the glory of our mother Church. The use of the definite article in the Greek, which gives the right rendering, "*the* woman" (not indefinite, "*a* woman," as in the A. V.), is very expressive in this instance; it brings the whole race, every woman, into the terms of the comparison, rather than a mere solitary example. A remark of Dean Alford is very noticeable; this use of the article "is not only generic, but allusive to the frequent use and notoriety of the comparison. We often have it in the O. T." There is the same definite force, again, in "*the* child." "He saith not a boy, but a *man*—a tacit allusion to His own resurrection." (*Chrysostom*.)

25. *in that day*.—The day when the dispensation of the Holy Spirit shall have taken the place of the personal presence of Christ.

26. *ye shall ask*.—The original makes use of separate words here, which are expressive. The first, "Ye shall *ask* me nothing," implies making no inquiry, *by word of mouth*, from Christ personally, asking questions; the second, "Ye shall *ask* the Father," implies making requests known to God *by prayer*. Though Christ should be removed from them, and they, therefore, would no longer inquire at His mouth, and receive from Him oral instruction and direction; yet there should be full answer from God, to every prayer offered to Him in the Name of Christ. They should lose nothing, even in this respect, by His absence from them. "Whatever" they should ask—first, in Christ's cause, and according to His will, in obedience to His command; and then for their own work, success, and interests—all should be granted; provided only that it be that which Christ has asked, or would ask, the Father. Thus, our prayers must be prayers of His. "He who holds any notion concerning Christ, which should not be held of the only Son of God, does not ask in His Name. But he who thinks rightly of Him asks in His Name, and receives what he asks, if it be not against his eternal salvation. He receives when it is right he

verily, I say unto you, Whatsoever ye shall ask the
Father in My Name, He will give *it* you.   Hitherto have
ye asked nothing in My Name : ask, and ye shall receive,
that your joy may be full.

These things have I spoken unto you in proverbs : but
the time cometh, when I shall no more speak unto you
in proverbs, but I shall shew you plainly of the Father.
At that day ye shall ask the Father in My Name : and I
say not unto you, that I will pray the Father for you:

should receive; for some things are denied at present, in order to be
granted at a more suitable time.   Again, the words, 'He will give it
you,' only comprehend those benefits which properly appertain to the
persons who ask." (*Augustine.*) (See App. V.)

27. *in My Name.*—Henceforth the way of access to God should be in
the prevailing Name of Christ; who, first of those who wore the form
of man, had merited acceptance with God, and the right to plead, and
to prevail, in the behalf of mankind. All prayers, therefore, should be
offered " through Jesus Christ our Lord," according to His order ; and
urged by us, as sent to the Father to use His Name, in which all the
gifts, and graces, and riches of salvation, in this and the future life, are
centred.

28. *your joy.*—In the grant of their prayers, they should receive the
consciousness of the spiritual presence of Christ ; a deeper source of joy
than that of His personal presence, to answer questions such as they
had asked before, in the imperfection of their knowledge of Him.   As
yet, they had not prayed in Christ's cause, as they had not exercised
their apostolate; but henceforth their prayers, so offered, should gain
such speed, as should cause them the fulness of joy in their success.
This command, coupled with that reiterated formerly by our Lord, as to
perseverance in prayers, means, " Ask until ye receive."   The application is, primarily, to the Apostles, but also, generally, to all Christians.

29. *proverbs.*—In dark and figurative language, implying more than
the literal surface meaning; conveying, in fact, much mystery, by type
and analogy; opposed to " plainly," *i.e.* without veil or figure.   The
derivation of the original word for " plainly," implies that *every word*
has its clear and literal sense, and no more.

30. *the time.*—This expression, and "at that day," which follows,
both refer to the same period as that of note 25.

31. *I say not.*—Christ does not mean to say that He will at all leave
them to pray for themselves, without His aid ; as the very fact of their
approaching the Father in His Name, is the urging of that plea of
unity which He had spoken of. (See xxv. c. 10.) But rather He says,
I do not now say, as before, I will plead alone in your behalf, because you
shall have ready access to the Father yourselves in prayer; and you

for the Father Himself loveth you, because ye have loved Me, and have believed that I came out from God. I came forth from the Father, and am come into the world : again, I leave the world, and go to the Father.

His disciples said unto Him, Lo, now speakest Thou plainly, and speakest no proverb. Now are we sure that Thou knowest all things, and needest not that any man

will address One, who, for My sake, and for your devotion to Me, will receive and hear you graciously, when you plead My merits and Name.

32. *I came forth.*—The sentence is an epitome of our Lord's being. He came forth from the Father into the world, when, in the form of man, He lived and died for the world's salvation and redemption. He now ascended from the world to go to the Father, with whom henceforth "He liveth to make intercession for us." Yet He had never left the Father (John iii. 13), with whom He was one; He now withdraws his visible presence from the world, but yet leaves it never (Matt. xxviii. 20).

33. *His disciples said.*—Their words are extraordinary ; they show attachment and faith, but certainly an imperfect comprehension, and some excitement. They appear to have caught at His declaration, that they should not need to ask questions of Him personally (note 26), and that He would speak plainly, without figure, to them ; whereas He was referring to the time of the advent of the Spirit, and was now actually speaking to them, as before, in figure. S. Augustine says, "They understood not that they failed to understand Him." They were not conscious that they really had missed His meaning, and that He was speaking of a manifestation not yet made. But they are, apparently, also influenced by His knowledge of their thoughts and wish to inquire His meaning (note 21), and of His reply, without their having expressed their desire in words, and to have thought this a fulfilment of His promise, that they should not need to question Him when they required His guidance. It is, however, difficult closely to follow the drift of a remark, on their part, which was both founded on misapprehension, and expressed misapprehension ; but this is clear, that they spoke in sincerity and faith, and that they at once took the fact of Christ's answer to their thoughts, as a proof of His Divinity. They were sure that Christ came from God ; and, in their indistinct apprehension of His full meaning, seize upon that which they felt they can understand, and give credit for the rest.

34. *needest not.*—With others, who are teachers, it may be necessary that they should be interrogated ; that they may, by the drift of the questions asked them, ascertain the want of information on the part of those they are instructing, and how to put their instruction with success. But not so with Christ; His command of the thoughts of

should ask Thee: by this we know that Thou camest forth from God.

Jesus answered them, Do ye now believe? Behold, the hour cometh, yea, is now come, that ye shall be scattered, every man to his own, and shall leave Me alone: and yet I am not alone, because the Father is with Me. These things have I spoken unto you, that in Me ye might have peace. In the world ye shall have

the heart, and of its infirmities and ignorance, enabled Him to dispense with all means of probing the ignorance, and gauging the capabilities, of His servants. As the disciples confess, this surely is the attribute of a Teacher "come forth from God," Himself Divine.

35. *do ye now.*—Or, "ye do now believe." It is generally agreed that there is no interrogation here. Our Lord accepts their faith, which He sees to be sincere, though He knows it to be at present imperfect, and so soon to be shaken.

36. *now come.*—This was verified an hour or so later, within the compass of the same night.

37. *to his own.*—To his own home, and his own matters, which he had, in the first instance, left to follow Christ. The same phrase is used in John xix. 27 (see xxxi. 27), in a somewhat closer sense; again, in a more general sense, in John i. 2. When our Lord appeared to them, after His resurrection, He found seven of them, on one occasion, at their old calling of fishers upon the Sea of Tiberias.

38. *not alone.*—Not alone, because God's presence could never desert Him; not alone for the ministration of the angel world, though alone for all men. The truth is a practical one, capable of the widest application; for none whom the world abandons, to suffer and struggle, alone and discountenanced, in the cause of God, are ever deserted by God. His presence is ever with them, in their solitary maintenance of the path of duty; they are "compassed about with a great cloud of witnesses," with the sympathy thus of *martyrs* before them, and with the presence of angel friends; and there is with them also the love and the sympathy of Christ. "He was their Saviour. In all their affliction He was afflicted, and the angel of His presence saved them" (Isa. lxiii. 8, 9).

39. *these things.*—What has been said in the terms of this farewell discourse.

40. *peace.*—What all aspire to, what all efforts profess to aim at, what man's heart recognizes as a supreme blessing, but what the world cannot give. There may be a lull, or calm, amidst its troubles, but no more. But, if there be one sure hold that cannot fail, a man, possessing this, may defy the pressure of trouble; the vessel with a sure anchorage can ride out the storm. And, if there is the consciousness

tribulation : but be of good cheer ; I have overcome the world.

XXVI. *THE PRAYER OF CHRIST.*

S. John xvii.

These words spake Jesus, and lifted up His eyes to heaven, and said, Father, the hour is come ; glorify Thy

of the presence of Christ in the heart, the tribulation that must come may come, but Christ's servants will be of good cheer ; they, too, shall overcome, as certainly as their Lord overcame. The tribulations of the world are outside the soul ; the peace of Christ within. The former are of short-lived power ; the latter is eternal. Like their Lord, they overcome them, because "greater is He that is in them, than he that is in the world" (1 John iv. 4).

41. *ye shall have.*—Or, "ye have." The best MSS. read the present, rather than the future tense.

42. *the world.*—The world, with its temptations, its offers, its might in opposition. To all who are Christ's, the same contest is proposed ; by them the same victory must be won. For them, "this is the victory that overcometh the world, even our faith. Who is he that overcometh the world, but he that believeth that Jesus is the Son of God?" (1 John v. 4, 5).

1. *these words.*—The concluding discourses, generally, but not without a special reference to the last words in them ; for His example shows that, in the presence of tribulation, though with the assurance of victory, His people should lay the exigencies of that hour before God, in prayer.

2. *lifted up.*—This gesture seems to have impressed itself on the mind of S. John, who is not generally, as S. Mark, observant of gesture. He thus expresses his sense of the formal solemnity of the occasion, and of the fact that our Lord, for man's sake, prayed publicly, rather than, as often before, in retirement. What S. John read in our Lord's countenance, we read in the prayer itself, the pleading of one who had power with God to prevail.

3. *said.*—This prayer is one of the most wonderful things contained in human language ; its diction, like that of the Lord's Prayer, is remarkably simple and plain ; but it speaks of mysteries which cannot now be fathomed by man. It is divided into three principal parts ; in the first of which Christ prays for Himself, in His character of the Messiah ; in the second, He prays for the Apostles especially, in the singular difficulties of their work and position ; in the third, He extends His prayer to embrace all Christians to the end of time,

Son, that Thy Son may also glorify Thee : as Thou hast given Him power over all flesh, that He should give

believers through the witness of the Apostles. The force and earnestness of the prayer, and the evident assumption of merit and right, and the certainty of success which breathe in it, show us what Christ urges in prayer in our behalf; or, rather, we may argue from what this prayer, offered on earth before the glorification of Christ's humanity, is, what those prayers now offered by Him in heaven must be.

4. *Father.*—This address has been noticed by many writers. Our Lord would not associate men with Himself, by saying, "Our Father;" He would not, whilst pleading in human form for them, draw the line between Himself and them, by saying, "My Father." But the word no less claims the eternal Sonship which He has with the Father, and is therefore a distinct assertion of His proper Divinity.

5. *the hour.*—(See **xxiv.** *d.* 24.) This is the hour of final struggle with the powers of evil, when the promise made to Adam and Eve, and renewed so often since, should be fulfilled in the sacrifice and victory of Him who should bruise the serpent's head; the hour foreordained in the eternal councils of the Holy Trinity.

6. *glorify.*—*i.e.* make the glory manifest, which is Mine and Thine. "Glorify Me; I have glorified Thee:" these are strange expressions in a prayer, and possible only to Christ. The Father and the Son were both to be glorified in this hour, each by the other: *the Son*, by receiving that support and strength which His human nature required, that He might perform God's will unto the successful end, and be accredited by God as the appointed Saviour; *the Father*, by the accomplishment, through the Son, of His gracious purposes in the redemption of mankind, by the perfect obedience of the Son to the Father's will, and by the declaration to the world of His mercy. None but the Son could thus approach the Father without confession of unworthiness. Here Christ assumes an equality with the Father, whom He addresses; for what man, in addressing God, could propose a mutual glorification? The objection of the Arians here fails, "The Son desires glory from the Father, as being inferior in glory to the Father;" for the terms on which the Son approaches God, are those of an equal proposing an equality in glory.

7. *as Thou*, etc.—*i.e.* "according as." This explains the manner in which the Father is to be glorified by the Son. For now was the crisis in which man's salvation was to be won by Him, into whose hands God had committed the salvation of all mankind.

8. *that.*—*i.e.* "in order that;" universal salvation being the object of His mission.

9. *all flesh.*—The expression is a universal one; it may be illustrated in the words of S. Paul (1 Cor. **xv.** 22): "As in Adam all die, even so in Christ shall all be made alive." It does not, however,

eternal life to as many as Thou hast given Him. And this is life eternal, that they might know Thee the only true God, and Jesus Christ whom Thou hast sent. I

imply that all who are thus subjected to the power of Christ, receive the blessed fruits of His victory, any more than that all are subject to the last penalties of sin. Those who accept Christ's mercy are saved by Him; those who refuse it "come short of the glory of God;" nevertheless, they have been objects of His mercy, contemplated in the everlasting purposes of the Holy Trinity, and given over to Christ for redemption. "This power, which was given to Christ by the Father over all flesh, must be understood with reference to His human nature." (*Augustine.*)

10. *as many as.*—Gk. "everything which Thou hast given to Him." The neuter gives the sense of universality.

11. *this is.*—(See xxi. 14.) Not merely, "thus may be gained," or, "this knowledge leads to" eternal life; but in this it consists. And, as this knowledge is granted now upon earth, in its earlier and less perfect stages; so also is life eternal commenced here below, with the commencement of our knowledge of the true God and our Saviour. By our Lord's declaration here, the more we have of the knowledge of God, the "more abundantly" we have of the blessing of eternal life. Even in this life there is a great difference amongst men, in vital power and energy, and in the highest enjoyment of life. It seems that there will be this also hereafter. (See xxv. a. 3.)

12. *know Thee.*—Not only with the understanding, but with the heart; and so acknowledge this faith. The word, in this sense, is equivalent to *worship.*

13. *the only true God.*—The Arian and Socinian heresy has appealed to this passage, as proof that the Father alone is God, to the exclusion of the Godhead of the Son. The appeal is not justified by the truth; for, in fact, this passage is proof directly in opposition to such teaching. Christ is here speaking, as God's ambassador, of the result of His mission to earth, and of the knowledge which earth's inhabitants must have of the being of God, and of the mission of the Son. In such an aspect, He who sends is greater than He that is sent. To show, however, the absurdity of supposing any inferiority of Divine nature intended, we have (as a critic suggests) only to substitute the name of Abraham, Moses, or even the highest created spirit, in this passage for that of Christ, to see how impossible it would be to accept the statement. None but Christ, the Son of God, could stand on such a footing with the Father's Name. S. Augustine, and other early writers, thus turned the passage, so as to bring the sense into clearer prominence: "That they might know Thee, and Jesus Christ, whom Thou hast sent, as the true God." But the A. V. is correct, which thus manifests God, as He is revealed by

have glorified Thee on the earth : I have finished the work which Thou gavest Me to do.   And now, O Father, glorify Thou Me with Thine own Self with the glory which I had with Thee before the world was.

Christ, whom He sent to reveal Him, as the true God. The real emphasis is on the word " *true.*"   God alone is true ; none others who are objects of worship are so ; thus involving the acknowledgment that there is but one God.   And thus Jesus Christ is here put on the same level with this one true God, as, in all that has preceded, Christ has insisted on the unity of the Father and the Son.   S. John (1 John v. 20) repeats these words of our Lord, and, at the same time, expresses our unity with the Saviour, as our knowing "Him that is true," and being "in Him that is true, even in His Son Jesus Christ. This is the true God, and eternal life."   And then he gives caution against our believing otherwise : "Keep yourselves from idols."

14. *Jesus Christ,* etc.—There is considerable emphasis in this mention of Himself by name and title.   He is to be known by man as the *Saviour* (Jesus), and the Messiah *anointed* (Christ).   This must be read also with the preceding words ; mankind must acknowledge Jesus Christ as the only true Christ, whatever pretenders to that title might come into the world.   Thus, we acknowledge the Father the one true God ; and, in perfect unity and equal Divinity with Him, Jesus Christ, His Son, the one true Saviour, " very God of very God."

15. *sent.*—The Messiah, therefore, promised to the world, and sent into the world in accordance with that promise.

16. *I have glorified.*—Here our language wants the subtilty of the original, which, by the use of the *aorist* tense, expresses the present incompletion of the action which is in process of completion, and which is spoken of, in the anticipation and assurance of faith, as done. This sense is worthy of notice, as it shows that the Passion and death of our Lord, not yet finished, are here included as parts of the whole mission, or " work."

17. *with Thine own Self.*—Our Lord here prays the Father that, as He had sanctioned the taking of the manhood into God, He would now give glory to that humanity, by receiving it into heavenly places with God ; and sanction the union of it with the Divine nature, in that glory which Christ had from all eternity, as His own proper glory with the Father, before time began, " or ever He had formed the earth and the world ; " and, further, that the proper Deity of Christ, and not only the glory of His humanity, may be recognized, both in heaven and earth.   In this prayer, almost every word contains a doctrine.   For instance, in the words, " I *had* with Thee," Christ expresses what was His everlasting condition ; He *had* this glory as His own, as opposed to any heresy which might say He *received* it, as a creature would receive a gift.   Again, it was *with* God, as One with God, " in the

I have manifested Thy Name unto the men which Thou gavest Me out of the world: Thine they were, and Thou gavest them Me; and they have kept Thy word. Now they have known that all things whatsoever Thou

bosom of the Father;" not as a separate gift *from* God to Him, as from one superior to an inferior. Both these the original distinctly expresses. To notice each point in turn would require a separate work, and then only the apparent and surface truths of the profound mysteries of Divinity, contained in this prayer, could be touched on.

18. *Thy Name.*—The special name by which Christ manifested God to the world was, "the Father." This was a new revelation of Him altogether. He had been formerly manifested in awe, as the self-existent and eternal God; even in covenant, this was His Name. Christ has manifested Him in love, as the Father; and the proclamation of the Gospel is, "God is Love."

19. *Thou gavest.*—Our Lord had explained to the disciples this truth, that God only could draw men's hearts to Him; they must hear the voice, and receive the teaching, of the unseen God, before they could come to Christ (John vi. 37, 44–46).

20. *Thine they were.*—That they were so by creation is not enough; for so were "the world," out of whom they were given to Christ. They were, further, in covenant relation with God, as children of Abraham, and heirs of the promise; and they also manifested that disposition which God delights to see, a readiness to receive God's teaching, and to obey His voice, before they became "the sons of God through faith in Jesus Christ."

21. *Thy word.*—Not merely the Law which God had given to their fathers, though, no doubt, that is included, as being the chief way in which the children of Israel could show themselves to be God's children; but also that special calling of God, which brought them to Christ (John vi. 45), the decision and act of their own will, has been given in concurrence with the will of God. This is a noticeable characteristic, and it was often verified in our Lord's day. Those who were readiest to come to Him, were those who were sincere, devout, and humble in the practice of the ordinances of the Lord God of their fathers, whose will and delight was in the way of His commands. It is now the same. God places this honour upon the appointed means of Christian grace; He utters His voice through these. Christ calls *sinners* (meaning here those engaged in the ways of sin) to repentance by other and sterner means, because they refuse God's voice, calling to them in ordinary ways. He is truly the Saviour of sinners, "the Saviour of all men, *specially* of those that believe" (1 Tim. iv. 10), who hear and obey the voice of God, calling to them to come to Christ in the way of His appointing.

22. *now.*—This marks a further step in their salvation. Having

hast given Me are of Thee. For I have given them the words which Thou gavest Me ; and they have received *them*, and have known surely that I came out from Thee, and they have believed that Thou didst send Me. I pray for them : I pray not for the world, but for them

received the call, and obeyed it, they now have been privileged to receive from Christ the knowledge of God, as manifested in the Son ; namely, that all His miraculous works, and all the Divine words of His teaching, were of God.

23. *I have given.*—This was one aspect of Christ's work on earth, which He had now finished. He had delivered to them the words of eternal life. They, on their part, had received these ; they had recognized the Divinity of Christ's teaching, and understood that He was a Teacher come from God ; and they had, therefore, accepted His mission, and acknowledged Him as the true Messiah. "Faith cometh by hearing, and hearing by the word of God ; " they had embraced their faith by this means.

24. *known surely.*—Their own words, lately spoken, were, " Now are we sure . . . by this we believe that Thou camest forth from God." We cannot but connect these words of the disciples with this their faith, as acknowledged by Christ before the Father—a faith which Christ declared to be imperfect, and soon to give way to pressure of distress. And so we may fairly draw the conclusion that Christ is prompt to mark, and gracious in acknowledging, the faith of all His followers, though He knows it to be far less perfect than they think and intend it. He does not despise " the day of small things."

25. *I pray.*—The original word is expressive ; it implies the equality of Christ with Him to whom He makes this request. It is a word entirely different from that which He uses of human prayer. (See note 45 ; xxv. *b.* 2).

26. *not for the world.*—Gk. " I am not praying for the world." Not *now* for the world ; My present prayer is for those faithful ones, who have continued with Me in my temptations, and have believed on Me. Some writers have supported, upon these words, the notion that Christ does not pray for the unconverted, but only for the elect—a sadly distorted view of His mission, which certainly was to no restricted society, selected from the mass (no worse than they) doomed to perish ; and, as they say, mercifully, but it would be really with favour, called to the heavenly inheritance. The whole tenor of Christ's life and mission, as the Saviour of the world, is against any such restriction of this prayer. And, in this instance itself, the reason for His specially pleading now for the disciples, was that they might have the grace necessary for their special office, which was to go forth and evangelize the world in His behalf, " *that the world may know* that Thou hast sent Me "—a sufficient reason for specially praying for them. And, indirectly, this

which Thou hast given Me ; for they are Thine.   And all Mine are Thine, and Thine are Mine ; and I am glorified in them.   And now I am no more in the world, but these are in the world, and I come to Thee.   Holy Father,

special prayer for the Apostles was, therefore, a prayer in the true interest of the world.   Dean Alford proposes a simple rendering, idiomatically impossible of misconstruction, and literally correct : " I am praying for them ; I am not praying for the world."

27. *they are Thine.*—Now in a far more intimate association than that spoken of in note 20; and conveying the assurance that their being given specially to Christ, did not lessen either the Father's interest, or right, in them as His children ; for, being Christ's " brethren," they were now emphatically children of His Father.

28. *all Mine.*—Not all My disciples are Thy sons, as this rendering suggests; but, in a more general sense (including that one, of course), " all that is Mine is Thine."   The neuter plural is used, conveying the sense of universality.   (See note 10.)

29. *Thine are Mine.*—What is Christ's is obviously the Father's also.   And so might men, in proper humility, say, " All that is mine is Thine."   " All things come of Thee, and of Thine own have we given Thee " (1 Chron. xxix. 14), is man's apology for offering of his substance to God.   But none but He, who is " equal to the Father as touching His Godhead," could say, " All that is Thine is Mine ; " for that is a most distinct claim to all the attributes and works of God.

30. *in them.*—In their faith in Christ, as their Redeemer and Lord, He is glorified in His office of the Messiah ; the glory of the Saviour is illustrated in the lives of those whom He saves.   Carrying on the sense of the preceding words, on which these have an evident dependence, we conclude that, as far as is their portion, all that is Christ's is theirs—His example, His righteousness, His principles, the glory of the resurrection, the mansion which He has prepared, the kingdom which He has promised them.   He is also glorified when, in their lives and ministry, His truth and Gospel are illustrated, and His glory manifested to the world, now that He is no longer personally present therein.

31. *and now.*—Our Lord speaks here, as elsewhere in this prayer, by anticipation of the actual fact.   His work was ended ; and, with it, His concern, in the world, for those who had been with Him in that work.   His future relationship with them was in their spiritual life.

32. *but these.*—These His disciples, so dependent on Him for guidance and comfort, would remain, to meet alone the front of opposition which had presented itself against Him.

33. *Holy Father.*—It is thought that our Lord addresses God by this title, as He is bespeaking for them the protection of His holy keeping, that they may be kept holy in their nature ; that, " as He

keep through Thine own Name those whom Thou hast given Me, that they may be one, as We *are*. While I was with them in the world, I kept them in Thy Name :

that called them is holy," so might they be holy (1 Pet. i. 15, 16). The word "holy," as applied to God, is one which is most difficult to understand. It has been amply considered by many writers; but the impression left by their comments, with a comparison of the previous passages in which this attribute of God is mentioned, is that it is one of the deep things of God, which man cannot fathom. There appear to be involved in it the several ideas of mercy, and love, and purity ; and it is connected with awe, and worship, and praise on our part. It is an attribute in which God reveals Himself to man, and by which He is known, in the adoration of heaven, as the "Holy, holy, holy, Lord God Almighty." In uniting this attribute with the name of Father, Christ brings us near to God, in one of the most glorious attributes of His Divinity. His holiness speaks to us of love, rather than of the unapproachable majesty of God. Dean Alford says, "Holy, as applied to God, expresses that penetration of all His attributes by love, which He only who here uttered it, sees through, in its length, breadth, and height ; which angels (Isa. vi. 3 ; Rev. iv. 8) feel and express ; which men are privileged to utter, but can never worthily feel; but which devils cannot feel nor utter—they know His power and His justice only. But His holiness is especially employed in this work of *keeping*, now spoken of."

34. *through Thine.*—Or, "*in* Thine own Name," *i.e.* in the knowledge and faith of that Name which I have revealed to them. The best MSS., and most modern writers, read here, "keep them in Thine own Name, which Thou hast given Me," *i.e.* commissioned Me to reveal to them. The relative pronoun agrees, in number and case, with the word "*name*," not with "*them*;" it is not, therefore, "those which Thou hast given," but "Thy Name which Thou hast given." Some writers, who adopt this reading, render "Keep them in Thine own Name, in which Thou hast given them to Me;" but the former is preferable, and it is far the best supported.

35. *one, as We are.*—This is most suggestive; as united together, in the Divine word and faith of Christ, as Christ and God are in their nature. This was most important to those who must be *one* in their proclamation of the Gospel. For, as we ourselves may fall short of this aspiration in our practice, it should be a foremost aim of all Christians, as it is here a foremost petition of their Lord for them, that "all who confess God's Holy Name, may agree in the truth of His holy word, and live in unity and godly love ;" carrying on the same grand work, one in faith and in practice.

36. *I kept them.*—The *aorist* is here again used. (See note 16.) Christ here commends them to God, as being on equal terms of power with

those that Thou gavest Me have I kept, and none of
them is lost, but the son of perdition ; that the scripture might be fulfilled.   And now I come to Thee ; and
these things speak I in the world, that they may have
My joy fulfilled in themselves.   I have given them Thy
word ; and the world hath hated them, because they are

Him—a point so often manifest in this prayer, so often put forward for
the consolation of His people. I kept them whilst with them in the
world, with Thy power and authority, for " those whom the Son keeps,
those also the Father keeps ; " do Thou keep them now. The Greek
word here is not the same as that translated " *kept*," earlier in the
same verse, and it would be better to mark the difference by rendering
this second term " guarded," as the exact force implies.

37. *none of them is lost.*—This passage places them all on the same
original footing, of being called by God. One only is lost ; and he,
because he repudiated that call. He is lost, as the Scriptures foreshowed, and should have warned him ; and in spite of the earnest and
constant warnings of Christ. The fact that he was called, as were the
rest of the Apostles, is a strong proof that there is none who is doomed
of necessity, by God, to final reprobation ; that there is, on Christ's side,
no restriction of His universal offer of salvation. The fact is, that
Judas sinned in the face of greater opportunities, than have been given
to almost any other man ; and thus was his sin most terribly
aggravated. (See xxiv. c. 19.)

38. *son of perdition.*—A common Hebraism for one worthy of perdition. So " child of hell," " child of the devil," and others in the N. T. ;
" son of death " (2 Sam. xii. 5, marg.), " sons of Belial," etc., in the
O. T. It is the terrible distinction of Judas, that his sentence, as the
one lost, " the son of perdition," is recorded alone before the day of
doom. (See xxiv. *d.* 6.)

39. *that the scripture.*—See xxiv. c. 20, *d.* 5.

40. *those things.*—Our Lord now states the reason for His uttering
this sublime prayer in the presence of the disciples. He would have
their sorrow for His departure turned into joy ; and His last words
speak comfort to them in their despondency. How deep must have
been their comfort, to hear Him so solemnly dedicate them, and their
work, to the Father, and to know that none of them was lost, who had
elected to maintain His faith, though at the moment that cause seemed
to droop.

41. *My joy.*—See xxv. c. 17. See also " My peace " (xxv. *b.* 19).

42. *Thy word.*—I have put them in charge with the Gospel, the
ministry of the word of life, and its powers.

43. *hateth them.*—Because they are in commission of God's word,
and give the example of their life in accordance with it.

not of the world, even as I am not of the world. I pray
not that Thou shouldest take them out of the world,
but that Thou shouldest keep them from the evil. They
are not of the world, even as I am not of the world.

44. *not of the world.*—The possession of this trust, and their duty
of evangelizing the world, drew a line of entire separation between the
world, as it lay before them, and themselves. They were not of it, in
the Scripture sense of being conformed in mind to its maxims and
habits, but of the spiritual kingdom of Christ ; and before they and
the world could become one, the world must be subdued to the obedience of Christ's faith.

45. *I pray not.*—(See note 25.) The original word for *pray* expresses
a familiar and equal footing on the part of Christ, who thus addresses
God ; it is used in John xvi. 26, and elsewhere. Though knowing the
evil of the world, Christ would not pray that they should be taken out
of it, but that they should be preserved from the evil influence of its
usurper prince, and from the temptations and dangers of the worldliness
with which they came in contact. They had, like Himself, to witness
to the truth, and to win the crown of life. Their present duty was to
mix with the world, in its social and business life, and to go down
to the sinner, in his life of sin, with the offer of salvation. In all
innocent pleasure and gladness, the world's hours of rejoicing were to
be sanctified by their presence and doctrine. In all its sorrows, human
life was to be consoled; in all its nobler aspirations, turned heaven-
wards; in all things, purified and hallowed. No recluse's life was to
be theirs; their witness was not to be confined to the denunciation,
and bemoaning, of the world's sin and folly ; but they were to be,
passively, " the salt of the earth," keeping it from corruption. And,
" as a city set on a hill " that cannot hide the eminence of its position,
they were to be, actively, the light-bearers of Christ's truth, penetrating
and scattering the world's darkness, that all might gather towards the
light of Christ in them. They had too much to do for Christ, in the
midst of human society, for Him to pray for their removal from it ;
but He did implore that that wicked one might not touch them, so as
to prevail against them ; and that the wickedness of the world might
not contaminate, thwart, depress them.

46. *the evil.*—Gk. " the evil one," as in the Lord's Prayer. All
forms of evil are here personified in the author of evil. The two
clauses of this petition illustrate well those of the Lord's Prayer,
" Suffer us not to be led into temptation, but deliver us from the evil
one."

47. *they are not.*—Not a repetition of the former words, but dependent on the last sentence. They should not be taken out of the world,
for already they are not of it ; they are out of it, by the separation of
the true faith which they hold.

Sanctify them through Thy truth : Thy word is truth. As Thou hast sent Me into the world, even so have I also sent them into the world. And for their sakes I sanctify Myself, that they also might be sanctified through the truth.

48. *sanctify*, etc.—Gk. "sanctify them *in* Thy truth;" that being the means, or element, of their sanctification. The word has here a formal and technical sense; it is not merely that they are to be sanctified, as all believers are sanctified by the Holy Ghost, but also *consecrated*, or set apart for their office of apostleship. In this sense, the special purpose for which they were consecrated, was centred in the truth. "Separate them for the ministry of the word, and preaching." (*Chrysostom*.) Both senses refer to the influence of the Holy Spirit, who is "the Spirit of truth," and who should make manifest to them the living force of the words, the doctrine of truth, which Christ has spoken. And, therefore, though the agency of the Spirit is not directly mentioned, it is included in the terms here used. Whitby thus paraphrases the passage : "Consecrate them to the propagation of thy Gospel, with the inspiration of Thy truth."

49. *sent Me . . . sent them.*—As God sent Christ into the world as His Apostle (Heb. iii. 1), so was Christ sending them, as His own Apostles, to disseminate the gospel of truth.

50. *I sanctify Myself.*—(Heb. ii. 11.) The word *sanctify* has here a meaning not quite the same as in the former sentence. Christ could not be sanctified in the sense that believers are, of being made holy, for He was holy by nature from His birth ; but yet, during His whole life, He sanctified that nature by trial, and suffering, and work, voluntarily undertaken. In everything in which Christ would sanctify and ennoble humanity, He has left us the example and victory of His own experience. He grew in favour with God, as He rose, in His humanity, from being simply pious, to being victorious in the struggle against sin, and in His experiences of that contest, and in all good and noble work. His life was thus sanctified in a very different way from what it would have been as an inactive life of religious meditation in seclusion. He has, therefore, for our sakes, sanctified, in His Person, our common humanity. Nor could it be said, again, that Christ was consecrated to His Messiahship, in the same sense as an Apostle was consecrated to His mission ; though no other example could be set before a consecrated Apostle, in His mission, than that of Christ in His Messiahship. But the term has, in the judgment of many of the ancient writers, the special meaning here of self-devotion, as a sacrifice for the sins of the world ; and this our Lord undertook, in offering Himself as a victim, voluntarily, for the sins of the world, for our sakes. The result, to us, of this voluntary sanctification and self-sacrifice, was that His servants might be sanctified *in* the truth. They would be

Neither pray I for these alone, but for them also which shall believe on Me through their word; that they all may be one; as Thou, Father, *art* in Me, and I in Thee, that they also may be one in Us: that the world may

raised, in their spiritual nature, by the same good works after His example, and by prayer, and by the living word of His truth; and thus they could effectively promulgate the truth in Christ.

51. *neither pray I.*—This is the third division of the prayer. Our Lord now specially prays for those who should come to the knowledge of the faith, through the efforts of the apostolic witnesses; and thus for us all, to the very end of time. It was not the Apostles only, who were borne before the Father in this intercession of the Redeemer; we each of us have our share and mention here, as we each have our part in the great sacrifice of redemption. But it is noticeable that the prayer refers only to the living; Christ says not a word about those especially His care, and still "living unto Him," who have departed, in time past, in hope of His advent, or died in faith in His name. Had it been our Lord's will, that we should pray for the dead, we should not have found mention, in this prayer of His intercession, of the living only, and those to live. There is the same reticence on the part of the Apostles, with regard to this subject; it is one far too important to have been accidentally passed over, or omitted.

52. *their word.*—Their promulgation of the word of Christ, as aided by the Spirit of truth. To some they ministered it orally; to us all, by their inspired writings.

53. *may be one in Us.*—Or, "may in Us be one." The prayer was not merely for their unity amongst themselves, independently, or simply in the profession of the truth of Christ, though this is most emphatically included; but they were to be one in the Father and the Son. Thus, the unity of Christ's people, each with the other, is through the unity of each with their Lord, and with the Father—a far more catholic and living view of unity, than any unity in the faith they profess in common. They could not naturally be one *with* the Father, and with Christ; but their unity with each other would be perfected in their unity in the Father and the Son, through the Spirit. For unity amongst Christians can only be perfect when they are united to, and through, the Father, the Son, and the Holy Spirit; there is no true union except through the blessed Trinity. It is a deep mystery, this unity of Christ's Church in that of the holy Trinity, severally and unitedly engaged in effecting our redemption to eternal life. The same truth of unity in the love of God is taught in 1 John iv. 16.

54. *that the world.*—This is a further aspect of unity. It is vitally needful that there be unity between Christ and His members, for they could not else be living members in Him; but, also, their success in the world depends upon their being in unity amongst them-

believe that Thou hast sent Me.   And the glory which
Thou gavest Me I have given them; that they may be
one, even as We are one: I in them, and Thou in Me,

selves, holding the faith in unity of view and profession, and in unity
of practice and love. (See Eph. iv. 4, 6.)   Here we notice that our
Lord is praying to the Father in the interests of the unbelieving
world. (See note 26.) The remembrance of this truth is necessary on
the part of those who preach Christianity, even in a Christian country;
but a nearer parallel with the duties of the Apostles, may be found
in those of a missionary to the heathen. Those who have had the
opportunity of noticing the work of missions in foreign countries,
will know how desirable it is that there should be unity on the part of
those who serve Christ in this noble work. It is a sad loss of strength,
and it must also be at the price of much loss of the spirit of Christ,
when there are distinctions presented to the heathen, not only of rival
Churches, sects, denominations; but of considerable difference of method
and doctrine amongst those who are, nominally, members of the same
Church. The object of every missionary to the heathen, and of every
Christian also (for the life of every Christian in a heathen land has its
missionary value), should be to set forth the unity of Christ's Church.
If this spirit is not in them, it would be better to spend their energy
and devotion in Christ's work in their own land; where, alas! dissension, being habitual, is understood. For certainly the heathen
judge His servants according to our Lord's own rule: by their being
"one in Us, the world may believe that Thou hast sent Me." (See
App. XII.)

55. *the glory.*—That of unity partly, judging from the context of
the sentence; that, also, of the working of miracles in support of the
truth; that of being set in trust with the Gospel, and of winning men to
salvation by the Gospel of Christ—for "the ministration of righteousness exceeds in glory" that of the Law. And before them, also, was
all the glory in the future, which God had given to mankind with the
promise of Christ, of sitting at the right hand of God in His glory
everlasting. We must not, however, confine this altogether to the
Apostles; for, though the day of miracles is past with the necessity for
them, the glory of Christ's presence remains in His Church, and with all
its ministers, and with every member of it.   The wonders of the first
age of the Church were less than those which have accompanied the
progress of Christ's kingdom in the world. They were signs to un-
believers; what remains has a far more general and permanent glory.
We may even compare their splendour with that of the presence of the
Spirit, in the language of S. Paul with reference to the Law (2 Cor. iii.
11): "If that which is done away was glorious, much more that which
remaineth is glorious." See also the prospect which he places before
believers, in their present experience, and in the future consummation,
in 2 Cor. iii. 18.

that they may be made perfect in one ; and that the world may know that Thou hast sent Me, and hast loved them, as Thou hast loved Me.

Father, I will that they also, whom Thou hast given Me, be with Me where I am; that they may behold My glory, which Thou hast given Me: for Thou lovedst Me before the foundation of the world. O righteous Father, the world hath not known Thee : but I have known

56. *perfect in one.*—The unity of Christians is manifested to the world in love (see 1 John ii. 5, iv, 12, 16, 17); our keeping God's word is the proof that we are animated by love to God.

57. *the world may know.*—The world has always recognized the exhibition of Christian love, as the true characteristic of Christ; and as an evidence that those, in whom it is manifested, do possess the Spirit of Christ. It is a virtue which has always arrested the attention of the world, as being one not natural to itself.

58. *I will.*—This is Christ's testamentary desire for His people. He has now advanced from simple prayer, or, rather, the prayer of one who has a right to ask, to the expression of His desire and will. It is His dying will, in His people's behalf, that they should inherit His kingdom, and see the eternal glory of Christ, in His enjoyment of the Father's love.

59. *whom Thou hast given Me.*—Here is another use of that comprehensive *neuter*, in the singular number, already pointed out. (See notes 10, 28.) Literally, we should translate "Father, concerning *that which*" (neuter) "Thou hast given to Me, I will that where I am, they also (masculine) "may be with Me." The neuter word gathers the whole Church of Christ in its unity, as the gift of God to Christ; and then He expresses His will concerning them, each and all, the Church and its individual members.

60. *O righteous Father.*—This, like the term "Holy," (note 33), is a remarkable title, as addressed to God in this prayer. We cannot think, with some writers, that the Saviour simply hands over the world, which had not known Him, to the doom accorded by God's attribute of justice, as it refuses that of His mercy, which desired to intervene. It seems to be, rather, the utterance of His compassionate sorrow, that God's justice must take its course with those who have refused to accept His sanctification. He sees their inevitable fate, as one sees it who sacrificed Himself in vain to avert it. He sees two deaths paid for one misspent life : that which He gave; and that which the sinner, refusing Him, must pay. He acquiesces in the justice of the award ; but it is the one great sorrow of Christ, and, therefore, finds its expression in this great intercession.

61. *I have known Thee.*—Stier says, speaking of the necessity pointed

Thee, and these have known that Thou hast sent Me. And I have declared unto them Thy Name, and will declare *it :* that the love wherewith Thou hast loved Me may be in them, and I in them.

out here, that Christ should first sanctify Himself for the sake of those who believe in Him : "Let him that would take away from the offering for sin all reference to the Father's righteousness, that a vainly imagined love only might remain, humble his ignorance to hear this word of the Son Himself: Righteous Father, I know thee! and in Thy righteousness! that righteousness which spareth not Me!" Much less, therefore, will it spare the world, which refuses "to know Him, and the power of His Resurrection, and the fellowship of His sufferings," notwithstanding all His efforts and prayers, that it may recognize and believe in Him, and be saved.

62. *will declare it.*—With the effectual witness of the Holy Spirit, in a far more ample degree than has yet been done.

63. *I in them.*—The prayer closes with words which are the key-note of all Christ's intercession on behalf of His people, in the aid of their own prayers : "Extend Thy love to them, as to Me; hear them mercifully and graciously, for My sake; behold Me in them!" (See Eph. i. 6 : "He hath made us accepted in the Beloved.")

END OF VOL. 1.

LONDON:
PRINTED BY WILLIAM CLOWES AND SONS,
STAMFORD STREET AND CHARING CROSS.